THE CATHOLIC WOMAN'S DYING WISH

JOANNA WARRINGTON

All rights reserved

The moral right of the author has been asserted

Copyright © 2015 Joanna Warrington

ISBN: 1511936703

ISBN 13: 9781511936705

❀ Created with Vellum

THE CATHOLIC WOMAN'S DYING WISH

Disclaimer and background to the story

This story, spanning two books ('The Catholic Woman's Dying Wish and 'Every Family Has One') is a work of fiction. Names, characters, businesses, places, events, incidents and the human experiences are either the products of my imagination or are used in a fictitious manner. Any resemblance to actual persons, living or dead, or actual events is purely coincidental.

This book is about the search for Kathleen. It can be enjoyed on its' own but the ending leads into the next book 'Every Family Has One' which is about Kathleen's life. 'Every Family Has One' can also be read on its' own without first having read this book.

This story was inspired by my interest in the Magdalene Laundries: institutions that existed in Ireland until 1996: maintained by religious orders in the Roman Catholic Church these homes were run by nuns for women labeled as 'fallen' by their families or society. There has been a great deal of interest in these institutions over the past 15 years;

immortalized in films like The Magdalene Sisters and Philomena. Through my work as a funeral celebrant I had the privilege of meeting the family of a Magdalene survivor and some of my information about the laundries has come from this family and other witnesses. I would like to thank the families for helping me with this project and for their information about Liverpool. I would also like to thank Mr Culshaw; Liverpudlian born and bred, Liverpool Historian Ken Pye and the Liverpool Central Library.

'The Weeping Lady' Magdalene Laundry is a fictional institution and does not necessarily represent what happened within the laundries and convents across Ireland at this time. However, it may provide a glimpse into the life of the laundries that many may indeed recognise.

My heart goes out to all the women who passed through these institutions and their fight for justice, the search for missing relatives and the long-term consequences of their incarceration. Kathleen's life is fictional, but it follows an emotional pattern that many women might identify with.

The story was also inspired by recent and widespread media coverage of historical sex abuse cases by people in positions of power and authority and explores some of the emotional and physical consequences of child abuse through the character of Darius and Kathleen as well as touching on the recovery process.

Maria's death was based on the observations of my own mother's death in 2012.

The opinions and views expressed in the book are the opinions and views of the characters and not mine, the author or any living person.

This book contains adult scenes and strong language. 'Every Family Has One' contains a rape scene and drug use.

This book is not a replacement of my earlier, now

unavailable book 'The D Word' but several scenes in 'The D Word' have been used again in this new story. The characters are new characters, but they do bear some similarity in the way they behave, think and talk.

Please note that legal advice has been taken prior to publication of this book.

∽

Please visit my website which is a blog about all issues beginning with the letter D.

1

Maria
December 2008

I SHALL FIND my fallen daughter before I'm a long time dead...

GOD CAME to her as she slumbered - gently at first - his words on replay. Round and round, night after night, pricking her subliminal consciousness, eking and scratching as she tossed and turned. Sometimes Maria wished she could flick the eject button, but they came unannounced and uninvited, echoing a burning need within a heart that ached with pain and regret.

In her dreams, flames licked at her feet and hands. *You lied. You weren't there. You let her go. Why?*

She woke disorientated, muttering the words into the silence of the room. A dog was barking. A mouse scratched in the attic above. The radiators were making a gentle bubbling hum. Feeling clammy and with her nighty sticking to her body, she flapped the quilt.

She sat up, grabbed her walking stick which was propped against her bed and pulled her orange lifeline pendant from inside her nighty. Loathing the paraphernalia of illness and old age, Maria eased her feet into slippers. Turning the bedside light on she reached over and popped a blood pressure pill, then a water pill from blister packs she kept close to hand. Death coiled its grip around her as she remembered the heart surgeon's words ten years ago. *The surgery we carried out should give you an extra decade of life, Mrs O'Brien.*

She pulled open her bedside drawer and took out her rosary beads and a tatty black and white picture postcard of the Pope, postmarked County Kerry. This had been the only contact from Kathleen since the day she had sent her pregnant teenage daughter away to a Catholic institution run by nuns over in Ireland. Thirty-five years had passed.

Mum. On the 10th September 2009 at 3pm I'll be in the Sistine Chapel by Michelangelo's painting of the Last Judgement where I will atone for my sins.

September was nine-months away—time wasn't on her side; Maria's health was failing. There was no way she'd be able to travel to Rome to see her long-lost daughter, Kathleen. But more than anything in the world she longed to see Kathleen, to beg for her forgiveness for sending her away.

Maria made the sign of the cross and prayed.

'Hail Mary, full of grace. The Lord is with thee.
Blessed art thou amongst women,
and blessed is the fruit of thy womb, Jesus.
Holy Mary, Mother of God,
pray for us sinners,
now and at the hour of our death. Amen.'

Through her troubled thoughts she whispered into the moonlit bathed room...

. . .

I SHALL FIND my fallen daughter before I'm a long time dead.

∼

FINDING KATHLEEN WOULD NOT BE easy. She would need help. And so when the sun nudged above the Chilterns, daylight illuminating every corner of her flat, she pulled out her black leather handbag from the kitchen drawer and headed down to the newsagents to buy the Daily Mail. It was Saturday and she looked forward to reading Monica Porter's weekly newspaper column, *Missing and Found*. The stories were intriguing and featured the tales of people who were searching for long-lost friends and family members: childhood pals, wartime comrades and evacuees, old flames, former work colleagues. All of life was there. Sitting down each Saturday at around eleven with an iced bun and a milky cuppa, she'd smile at the light-hearted, poignant stories and cry at the emotional reunions after months, often years of searching. She often imagined her own emotional reunion and wondered what Kathleen looked like after all this time and where she was living. Kathleen must hate me, Maria thought, otherwise why hadn't she been in touch?

Back from the newsagent she spread the paper across the table to read the latest stories. She glanced out of the window to the smudgy green hills in the distance and found herself asking the same questions over and over. Had she been such a terrible mother that Kathleen couldn't face returning home? If they met would they get on? Or would she still be the argumentative teenager that Maria remembered? She hoped not.

Maria finished reading the column and taking a sheet of Basildon Bond she began to pen a letter to Monica detailing all the raw facts hoping that she would find her daughter. She gave the date that she sent Kathleen to 'The Weeping Lady' Magdalene Laundry in Southern Ireland in 1974. She assumed the nuns at the 'Weeping Lady' had arranged for her baby to be adopted.

Maria put the pen down, dabbing her eyes as she thought about the grandchild she had never met. What had become of it? And then, not for the first time she questioned her motives for sending Kathleen away. Would it really have been so difficult to allow Kathleen to stay, have the baby at home and help to bring it up? She sighed, rubbed her forehead and tried to wheel back in time, recapturing the emotions that had been her driving force: the terrible fear of shame, the sin of sex out of wedlock. And suddenly those emotions were as raw and intense as they had been the day she'd arranged for Kathleen to go. There had been no choice. She would have brought shame upon the family, upon the community and what would the priest have said? If she'd had her time again, she would, in all probability have made the same decisions. But hindsight was a wonderful thing.

Something inside her heart was changing. Maybe it was the influence of the new church she had started to attend. It focused on God's grace, His love, His forgiveness. She remembered something the minister had said in church:

Unless you forgive yourself, forgive the situation, realise the situation is over you cannot move forward. Maria no longer went to confession. She was filled with the love of God and He had forgiven her, forgiven Kathleen. Formal confession served no purpose. But despite coming to know a loving God in recent months there was still a strong part of her that couldn't shake off the power of sin and all that it meant.

She turned her attention back to the envelope, enclosing a copy of Kathleen's birth certificate and her national insurance card which had arrived in the post two years after she'd left. She had already contacted the Magdalene survivor's group to see if they could help but it would take time. Within the various institutions there had been a policy of secrecy. She had been informed that the penitent registers and convent annals remained closed despite many families asking for information. She was just one of thousands wanting answers. The last Magdalene Laundry in Ireland had closed in 1996 but from what she could gather there were very few records to account for almost a century of women who'd passed through their doors. She had contacted the Catholic Church as well for their help but with so many other families clamouring for help in tracing their loved ones she didn't hold out much hope.

Maria also needed her son Darius's help. She would wait until the New Year before tumbling her big ugly confession to him and beg him for help.

~

MARIA CHECKED her diary after breakfast. It was now the 10th of January the day Darius was returning from Canada. She woke early, nerves dancing in her stomach as she began to dread his visit and the conversation she needed to have. Without a diary entry she would have completely forgotten when he was away. He went on so many business trips. She couldn't keep up.

It was only five in the morning, but she prepared two teacups, a milk jug, a teapot and a plate of biscuits under a cellophane wrap and set it on her hostess trolley with a doily - ready for later when he'd call by. She had forgotten to ask what time that would be, so she sat next to the window for most of the day looking up and down the road until finally she saw his shiny black Mercedes pull up at 5pm.

~

DARIUS FIDGETED IN HIS CHAIR. He'd glanced at the clock on the mantelpiece four times during the past twenty minutes as they'd talked. Then he looked at his watch and checked his mobile three times. She knew he didn't want to be there. That was clear. Why bother visiting, she thought. She'd spent the day waiting and looking forward to him coming and he was now checking his mobile for the fourth time.

'What's it like out?' She asked glancing out of the window.

'Warm. What have you been doing lately, Mum?'

'I made some rock cakes on Tuesday.'

'Right.'

A brief silence followed.

'Done anything else?' He asked in a flat tone.

'I've filled in a form for a new disability badge.'

Maria looked out of the window again. Darius took a sip of tea.

'What's it like out?'

'Warm.'

'Seen anyone?' He asked.

'Only the postman.'

He gave a spectacular huff.

'Much happening in Eastenders lately, Mum? And Emmerdale?' He sighed again.

'Oh dear Mary Mother of God. The usual arguments. People having affairs, everyone sinning. The usual.' And then she remembered Kathleen.

He eased his bottom to the edge of the settee and shuffled to get up. The familiar creak of his old leather jacket and the jangle of money in his pockets as he put it back on made her heart tug. There wouldn't be any other visitors that week. Not until the plumber called.

'I suppose I'll have to get home. Unpack, put the washing machine on,' he said. Maria watched him adjust his jeans, pulling his belt tighter as he always did when he stood up.

Darius returned his cup to the kitchen, rinsed it and set it to dry on the draining board. She waited in the doorway wondering how to begin. It had been so long since they had talked about Kathleen. He'd ask *why now?* But she needed his help to find her. Blood pricked and thumped in her head. She leaned against the door frame for support, worried about how she was going to tell him she'd lied all these years and that Kathleen hadn't run away, she'd sent her away. Her fallen daughter. Suddenly she felt the huge weight of guilt at having lied to Darius for so long.

She followed him into the hall, her slippers squeaking on the lino.

'I'll just nip to the loo before I go,' he said.

'Shut the bathroom door while you're in there,' she reminded him.

When Darius returned to the hallway Maria raised her eyebrows, about to complain but she was sick of reminding him and dreaded the expletives that frequently tumbled from his mouth, like smoke from a chimney. She often joked to neighbours that his mouth was like the Mersey Tunnel. Why was it always so difficult for him to close the door while he was using the loo? But instead, she just shook her head. He reached for the door handle and touching his hand, she caught a *what now* look plastered across his face. He sighed.

'We need to talk about Kathleen,' she suddenly announced.

She watched the expression change on his face from boredom to a cloud of shock, to deep unease.

'Fuck. Have you heard from her? Where is she?' he asked, taken aback.

Maria beckoned him back into the lounge, made him sit down while she tumbled her confession and explained that she had sent Kathleen to a Magdalene Laundry in Ireland back in 1974 to have a baby and atone for her sins. It was the big ugly secret that she had kept locked away for thirty-five years.

'Why the fuck didn't you tell me she was pregnant? Whose baby was it? You told me she'd run away from home. Now I discover who've lied all these years. What sort of mother would lie to their own son?' He looked as if his world was crashing in.

Maria's mind went blank. For so many years she had told herself that Kathleen had died. Death was more final. Less painful somehow than knowing there was a daughter out there who didn't want to return home. Death meant she could avoid facing the pain, the agony of the truth. With death there was no looking back. It tied up loose ends, stopped her head drumming out questions and demanding answers. It prevented her dwelling on the difficult issues that maybe could have been solved between mother and daughter. It was the only way to cope with her disappearance. She had neatly placed Kathleen in a box, along with her husband Paddy - who had died in 1971, caught up in the Troubles on the Falls Road in Belfast while visiting his sister.

'Who took her there?' Darius asked.

'Father Joseph arranged it.' Maria said.

'The bloody priest. I wondered when he'd enter the discussion. That evil man who hovered over our lives like a big mean black crow. And I suppose you thought he was doing the right thing in suggesting a Magdalene Laundry? Have you ever stopped to ask yourself why he would offer to help? Have you?'

Maria looked away, feeling as if her life essence had drained away. She could sense him, inches away, his eyes pinning her with a cool, unwavering stare. Then he walked over to the window but didn't share what he was thinking.

'I wasn't one of the flock in that dreadful Protestant school,' Darius said. 'Have you any idea what that school was like for a Catholic lad? I had my bloody head rammed down the toilet in the first week. And you wonder why I never shut the toilet door. Bastards they were. No one messes with me. I've learned that much. Why do you think I got this spider tattooed onto my bloody neck? I remember Kathleen's birth. What the fuck was it all about? Up the duff in your forties. Jesus, Mary and Joseph, Mum. What were you both thinking of? We had no space in that house in Liverpool with the whole bloody family crammed in and the back room taken up with old crap like gas masks and home-made dandelion wine. Why did we still keep a stack of musty old gas masks? And if you hadn't invited my dreadful aunt and uncle and cousins to live with us then maybe, just maybe things might have worked out differently.'

'Dear Lord, they lost their homes in the war. Where were they supposed to live? Bootle was destroyed. Flattened to the ground so it was.' Maria wondered why she had agreed to move south, to Marlow to be near Darius.

They both looked at each other and there seemed to be a mutual understanding between them. They were carefully side-stepping around the real issue that sat heavy between them. Neither wanted to speculate. Neither wanted to pick at the pain but his name hovered on their tongues. *The priest.*

'I've got to go. I've only just flown back from Canada. My body's in a different time zone.'

'You've never got time. Always in a rush.'

'What do want me to do, Mum? It's all in the past,' he snapped.

'Find her for me Darius. Bring her home. Before it's too late,' she pleaded. 'You've got a computer. I'll pay to find her. I don't care what it takes.'

He hovered in front of her, his arm on her shoulder.

'Sometimes Mum we have to let people go.' He pinned her eyes, giving her time to think.

'How can a mother ever let her child go? I'll never be whole again until the missing piece is back.' Tears glittered in her eyes.

'But you've been like this since Dad died. Your world fell apart. I'll do what I can, but I think Kathleen was missing Dad.

They were very close. She spent so much time with him, wandering round the docks, walking by the river, up the allotment. You don't want to admit the truth, Mum. She was closer to him. You both rubbed each other up the wrong way. You would never have chosen each other as friends. It's too late to think you can come together and return to how it was because the how it was only exists in front of your rose-tinted glasses. It didn't exist in reality.' He'd hit home.

After he'd gone, Maria closed the door, wrapped her dressing gown tightly around her waist against the evening chill and the thoughts that disturbed her.

As she settled back into her comfy chair adjusting a cushion behind her, she reminded herself once more of her dying wish. *I will find my fallen daughter before I am a long time dead.*

∼

Darius

A COUPLE OF MILES AWAY, in a house that he referred to as his *shitty rental*, Darius was stirring from a bad dream. Several years had passed since he'd had a similar dream which had left him sweating, traumatised and calling in his sleep. The conversation with his mother about Kathleen had stirred the past and that past entered his dreams.

In his dream the hand was reaching for him. Now half-awake he could still see it; claw like and gnarled. He could feel it on his warm flesh, the crawling sensation of ants on skin, the cold tips making tracks towards his groin, finding the secret place. In his dream the sounds had seemed so real. The swish upon the flagstones ...His heart banged in his chest as he desperately tried to erase the image.

And then he turned towards the open window, the streaming light making patterns across the room, the gentle swish and flutter of the curtain in the breeze. The past had returned to his dreams through the sounds in the room. The curtains had to go. His dreams were merging into his present environment in a new and disturbing way.

2

DARIUS

January 2009

It had been a long day in the office. Darius had worked through a raging hunger but was now beyond eating. In the frantic week before the mag was 'put to bed' it was always like this. He hated returning to his rental in Marlow. He turned the key in the front door desperate for a fag and the second whiskey and soda of the day he knew he shouldn't have. He looked at the mail lying on the mat, his stomach knotting when he saw the familiar black ink on the cream envelope – another demand he was sure from his exwife's solicitor for half his pension or a request for a statement of earnings. *Fuck,* he thought. When would that bitch ever give up? I've worked my arse off for decades to build for retirement. For what? Lawyers at my heels like a pack of hounds. I'm on the verge of losing what I've spent a lifetime building. He began to climb the stairs, tore open the envelope, cast his eyes across the letter then tossed it over the bannister.

As he reached the fifth step he stopped. He remembered that he was going to pour himself a whiskey and soda. No longer wanting one, he rested his arm on the glossy handrail and looked up. It suddenly seemed a long way to the top. His legs felt like they would give way and his arm felt heavy against the handrail. His head swam. He sat down waiting for the feeling to pass. At 54 what did he expect? He was a burned-out wreck living his life in the speeding lane as if he were 25. Was this the strain of a hectic lifestyle working 24/7 worrying constantly about profit margins and balance sheets?

Thanks to the bitch - his ex - the dream of early retirement lay shattered. She'd squandered so much money leaving them broke and was now using greedy £400 an hour lawyers to settle the divorce. As he leant against the wall he wondered when his personal Iraqi conflict would draw to a close. They were about to lose the marital home and he'd be working forever to rebuild his life. He had to keep going but dreaded looking over the hills into the valley of old age and inevitable poverty.

It had been a cold day. The house was chilly. So why was he sweating? He inched to the seventh step, wiped the beads of sweat from his brow and rested against the icy wall hoping it would cool his back. Maybe he had flu. After a few moments he lowered himself onto his knees and as if moving through porridge he climbed the remaining stairs like a drunk, resting at the top before crawling into his bedroom. His legs felt heavier than ever.

Something wasn't right. Warning bells were ringing. He sat on the bed, his shirt clinging to his body and suddenly he saw the parody of his life in the lyrics of his favourite song by the Beatles: *'Yesterday all my troubles seemed so far away, now it looks as if they're here to stay.... suddenly I'm not the half man I used to be... there's a shadow hanging over me.'* He remembered his dad singing it to him by the dockside back in Liverpool.

And then he gripped the bedside table as waves of sour tasting nausea rose. With acid burning his throat, a projectile of flecked vomit spilt out. He was drained, had no energy to go to the bathroom to look for a cloth. Nursing his throbbing head, he needed to lie down but as he climbed onto the bed, resting his head on the pillow, a thought wormed into his mind. *Is this how I'm going to end my days?*

He'd read enough. He knew the signs. He'd watched his uncle go through this. Part of him wanted to dismiss the mounting anxiety, forget it and wake up in the morning refreshed.

But he wasn't going to take the chance. He reached for the landline mustering as much strength as his body would allow. As the publisher and editor of an international magazine on the doughnut industry everything depended on him. He had a business partner who wasn't pulling his weight, but ultimately Darius was the boss—*he* carried the can. The business couldn't run itself. He was Darius the doughnut businessman, the globe trotter who scoured the world with his two bags; containing his clothes and his laptop and all the other crap needed to ply his trade looking for stories about the world's insatiable desire for the calorie laden sugar bomb, forecasting the growth of this doughy treat, predicting new trends and nearly always travelling economy. It was a prosperous niche in a barmy world where journalism was fast disappearing in an ocean of press releases published verbatim by cut and paste hacks. He couldn't afford to be ill. He mustn't be ill he thought, as he pressed the digit nine three times and waited for the answer.

'Emergency. Which service do you require? Fire, ambulance or police?' 'Ambulance. I think I'm having a heart attack.'

Feeling woozy, he didn't move while he waited and dreaded the thought of passing out. The wait seemed long, though in reality not. It was a relief that the front door was still unlocked. He'd told them to come straight in and find him upstairs.

Not long after making the call, several pairs of feet pounded the stairs. Someone called. Another was talking to base. Reaching him in his bedroom, the ambulance crew ran through a series of questions. In no time at all they had diagnosed a mild heart attack explaining how the equipment - a twelve lead electrocardiogram worked. He heard the words ST elevation and myocardial infarction.

Blue streaks flashed across the lawn as they carried him into the ambulance on a stretcher and on the journey explained that a blood test at the hospital would detect the presence of specific types of proteins released into the blood from the damage in the heart due to the attack. Once confirmed that he had suffered a mild attack he'd be given an angiogram to find out the exact location and the seriousness of the blocks in the coronary artery. Darius wasn't taking it all in.

His mind was whirling, worrying mainly about his 30-year-old son, Sam. He couldn't leave him in the shit. How would he survive without his financial help? And back in the office there was no one else to write the articles and coordinate the team. And to a lesser extent he was concerned for his mum. Who would find Kathleen for her? Who would organise a care home when the time came? And he thought of his Uncle Jim all those years ago dying from a heart attack. Maybe he'd always known he'd suffer the same fate.

Darius woke the next morning in hospital plugged up to monitors and a cannula piercing his skin. As the nurse took his bloods, he looked around. Everyone else was much older. Some looked like living corpses waiting for their last breath. He shouldn't be here. He felt fine.

But he knew he couldn't take his health for granted any longer. Was this the wake-up call he needed? Was he going to carry on smoking? He didn't know. Maybe he'd try patches again. His body craved for the rush that tobacco gave. It was odd but for the first time in his life he actually felt lucky to be alive. He'd long ignored the warning indicators on the dashboard: raised blood pressure, high cholesterol.

Over the next few days as he rested in hospital the feeling of relief at having pulled through started to change. Once more he felt negative about his life.

The doctor came to discharge him, and Sam arrived to give him a lift home. He hadn't seen the lad in a while. Sam was always too busy, out partying. A lad of that age should be settled down with a nice wife and two kiddies by now, Darius mused.

Sam approached his bedside chuckling. 'Bloody hell Dad. You're not still wearing that dreadful wig? It looks like an explosion in a pubic hair factory.' Sam leaned down, flicking a tuft of his grey locks.

'Fuck off, Sam. If your mother hadn't taken a coat hanger to my head, I wouldn't need to wear it.'

'I like the curly bits at the side. They look like public hair. You want to look in the mirror Dad. You look like Donald Trump.' Sam was choking back laughter, glancing round to see if he had an audience.

'Samuel Pepys wore a wig, and no one laughed,' Darius replied.

'If it was a long wig I'd be tempted to get on your back to ride you like a horse,' Sam spluttered.

Darius looked disgusted.

The doctor came to discharge him, clipboard in hand.

'You've been lucky. This time. And you don't need a stent. I'm going to prescribe a spray in case you develop more chest pain,' the doctor explained.

'It widens the blood vessels to help the flow of blood and oxygen to the heart. I'm also going to prescribe beta blockers to lower your blood pressure and Warfarin to thin the blood. It's quite a cocktail I know. I'll book you in to see a dietician and some regular exercise will also help but for the moment I'd say just some gentle walks each day.'

'Dad thinks he can hammer his body like an old company car, but it's time he gave up the fags,' Sam joked to the doctor.

Darius felt mounting irritation. 'I only hear from you when I forget to pay your rent. Christ you're 30 and I'm still supporting you. Why the hell did I send you to boarding school only for you to choose hairdressing as a career? You've only been here five minutes and already you're having a go. This whole mess is down to your mother causing me stress with her lawyers, destroying everything, stalling the sale of Nettlebed and trying to steal half my pension. It's outrageous.'

Sam rubbed his stubbly chin. His mop of long dark curls looked like it hadn't been brushed or cut in a while. Great appearance, Darius tutted, for a man who was supposed to be a top stylist at one of London's premier fashion houses. Darius noticed how tired he was looking. And he thought he could smell a whiff of beer on his breath. There was something a bit tramp-like about him.

'Calm down, Dad. You'll have another heart attack at this rate. You bang on about the divorce every time we speak. I'm sick of it. Get over it. Your pension is an asset just like the house is.'

Darius looked at the pink sweater Sam was wearing. Jack Will's. Obviously too much money to waste.

'What's this?' Darius tugged at the sweater. 'You look like a fairy on a birthday cake.'

Sam shot him an icy warning, said nothing but looked directly at the doctor in a concerned but authoritative way. Suddenly Darius could see him in his role of helping customers and he felt a brief flush of pride for his son, which rapidly evaporated.

'He needs a proper regime? And can you give him some patches to stop the tobacco cravings?'

'Keep out of it, Sam. I'll ask the questions.'

'Yes we can.' The doctor answered. 'And I'll leave you with some leaflets.'

Darius looked around the sterile ward and over to the elderly patients lying opposite, then to the doctor.

'I don't need to read any bloody leaflets. I'm not a kid. And exercise? Do behave. Where would I find time for that? I'm working and travelling 24/7. Some of us have businesses to run.'

'Ditch the car and walk... sometimes.' The doctor ignored his rudeness and making an upside-down smile he shrugged. 'You don't want to be back in here. This can be managed very well but you need to do your bit too.'

'I'm car reliant.'

'Well, I'm sure with the help of the dietician and a few changes in what you eat, you could get your weight down to a healthier level.'

Darius sat up. 'Have you lived the life of a jet-setting businessman? Have you any idea? The time differences, lack of choice on the plane. What should I do? Pack sandwiches in cellophane like a schoolboy on a trip to the museum? Food the world over has become Americanised. God damn it, I have to pose for photos with a greasy, sugar jam-laden doughnut stuffed in my mouth. Doughnuts make me money. Everything's laden in fat and sugar. I can't do diets. I eat out regularly with clients, have late night drinks at fancy restaurants. I can't sit there with water. What would be the point in living? I know I'm on the road to a slow death.'

'The fast road if you're not careful. If you calm down a minute, maybe we can make a plan for you,' the doctor offered.

'A diet plan that would suit a retired person with nothing better to do.' Darius scoffed.

The only plan Darius had was a double whiskey and soda in The White Hart in Nettlebed.

'Dad. Man up for goodness sake. When I came in here yesterday you were taking it seriously.' In a patronising tone he added, 'as you should be.' Darius watched Sam. He thought how thin his face was and wondered if he'd lost weight. He looked gaunt. The lad was an extra worry he didn't need. 'What's happened in the past few hours? You're like a storm cloud. Why are you back to being complacent about your health?' Sam gave his arm a friendly nib.

Darius knew he'd been complacent about his health but never admitted that to anyone. It was his uncle's fault getting him into smoking. He could still smell the dreadful camphorated oil he had frequently used to clear his chaining smoking chest. But today, Darius felt differently. He needed to get out of hospital. He swiveled his feet to the ground focusing on today - the here and now - making mental lists of all the things that needed doing in the office. All he could think of was making money. He had to rebuild his life, post-divorce. He thought of his week ahead. For sure he'd go back to his old ways because he always did. He had no choice. Life went on, heart attack or no heart attack.

DARIUS AND SAM were quiet in the car on the way back to Marlow. The gulf between father and son felt wider than ever.

'You ok?' Darius asked as Sam filtered into the left lane. 'You don't look it.'

'Thanks Dad.' Sam reached for the radio and flicking it on, he turned up the volume.

'Well you *don't* look it. What's going on?' Darius persisted.

'I'm just tired. I'm not sleeping well.'

'You worry me. It's not as if hairdressing is a demanding job. If you'd gone into a proper profession...'

'You never miss a trick do you, Dad? And you're just thinking about the money you give me. It's not my fault they pay so poorly.' Sam rammed the stick into second.

'S'pose. You've seen what's just happened. My health is against me. I can't support you forever.'

'I went to Berlin last weekend to see a band.' Sam made a

quick switch of conversation.

'Berlin? You didn't tell me. I don't know anything that's going on in your life these days. Who with?'

'A new friend.'

'Girlfriend?'

'No. I don't do girlfriends. Unless they're platonic. You know that. His name's Rory but I don't think I'll be bringing him home to meet you. Not with the reception you're likely to give.'

Darius started laughing. 'Jesus Mary and Joseph what would Grandma's priest say to that?'

'What's your bloody problem?' Sam steamed.

Darius knew exactly what his problem was. It was a problem that wasn't going away. Often twice a night he woke in a sweat with visions swirling in his head as he remembered his dark past. And the more he reflected, unable to come to terms with certain things that had happened, the more he feared for his son. The fears were unfounded, he knew that.

Darius was quiet for a few moments. 'Who paid for the trip to Berlin? I don't pay you ten grand a year to go swanning round the world,' he asked as they approached Marlow.

'Money again. You're obsessed. Mum paid as it happens.'

'Your mother gave you money for a weekend away? Her latest statement of earnings said she'd earned nothing. Where's the money coming from? At the end of the day, it's my money. The hard-earned money she stole to fund those reckless Florida investments.'

'Just drop it. I've had enough. Can't you just be nice for a while. I'm sick of all your bitterness, remorse, regret.' His hands tightened around the steering wheel.

∼

A WEEK AFTER HIS DISCHARGE, Darius woke sweating from another nightmare. He could see Kathleen pinned against the wall in the vestry, the priest mauling her breasts. Then he was back there, in the cloakroom, and it was happening all over again. I'm a grown man, he thought. Why are the nightmares returning?

Then he lifted the sheet and looked down. There was no hard on. It was like watching the filament in a light bulb fizzing out. Were things now on the slide he wondered? Was this the beginning of the end? Was this what generally happened to men in their mid-fifties or was this the power of nightmares.

First to be screwed financially by your ex-wife and then screwed by your best friend down below. If his dick had been a cruise missile he'd consider decommissioning it. He sat up, then looked down again. In the good old days it was a missile; he'd ejaculate too quickly but now it was like flicking a switch waiting for something to happen, but the solenoid in his genitals was failing to respond. He wanted his best mate back, but the train had been cancelled. He tried accessing the coital memory folder. That usually worked. He scanned the folder of the '100 Great Fucks' of his past but all the best bits on the tape had been erased and in its place was the hand of the priest.

Maybe he had a *cyclical dick*. There was nothing worse than apparatus you couldn't be sure of. It was the unpredictability of it. If he met a woman how would he know how it would behave? There was no rhyme or reason. He wracked his brain but couldn't find one. 'It' and 'him' had become separate entities, two estranged friends no longer working to the same agenda. In short, his dick was behaving like a Morris 1100 in Basil Fawlty's life – the sketch where he ended up thrashing the car with a tree branch.

It wasn't going to perform to order like a street entertainer. It was like driving a car with soggy suspension or a faulty electrical circuit. Maybe it wasn't important for the moment, because there were no women currently in his life, or none he wanted to enter into a sexual liaison with.

3

DARIUS

February 2009
Darius slammed the boot lid with force, glanced at his watch as he approached the traffic lights. Just enough time to call in on his mother before heading towards Heathrow on another business trip. He was off to Bangkok. He loved the city. It was teeming with everything forbidden.

It was always a performance waiting for his mother to answer her door. As he waited, he hoped she wasn't going to mention Kathleen again. He'd been thinking a lot about Kathleen. He'd sat down at the computer the day after the discussion with his mother and began to make some tentative searches. Starting from everything he knew about her: the date and place of birth through to the schools she'd attended and the friends she'd played with. He went onto various sites and found her birth certificate on 'My Past' and worked from twenty years on to find out if she had married, but he couldn't find a marriage certificate. He had also typed her details into Friends Reunited and Facebook, as well as Twitter and ploughed through reams of Kathleen O'Briens, coming up with nothing. It was a popular name in Ireland and had taken him all afternoon to do these initial searches. At the back of his mind, he knew that with the right resources and the help of a private detective, he could probably find her quickly. But there was something holding him back. He felt uneasy about travelling back into the past. He knew that to carry old bricks into the present would be to build the same house that fell apart before. He had enough of his own problems to deal with. This was an added burden he didn't need. And yet his mother seemed determined to find Kathleen and eager to enlist his help.

She seemed to take longer than normal to answer the door and when she unlatched the inner door, looked flustered. He took her arm noticing that she was a little unsteady on her feet and guided her back to her comfy armchair where a mohair blanket rested on the arm.

'Darius you've got to find Kathleen. I need to know the truth. I'm not sure Monica Porter can help. She's inundated with letters. I need to know why Kathleen never returned home.'

'Steady on. I'm doing my best. I've been onto all the websites. I've paid quite a bit of money so far in joining some of the sites to access the material we're looking for.'

'And what have you come up with?'

'Nothing yet. Give me time.' Darius saw no need to rush. It wasn't his project. It was hers.

'I'll give you some money, but I don't want any private investigators onto this. God knows how that would look if Kathleen found some creepy ex-copper sitting outside her house, fishing into her bank account or pay slips. I don't like the methods those companies use. I don't imagine they're ethical. I want you to use good, old fashioned methods to find her. And if the search takes you abroad, I'll pay.'

'It won't come to that. Why should it? Anyway, I do have a business to run, Mum. Where am I going to find the time to go jet setting around the world in search of our Kathleen? You're not thinking in a practical way.'

'Ireland's not far. Go and visit the laundry, please? And take some photos of the place. Make enquiries in the village. Find out what happened to the girls after it closed, in 1990. I know that much. The survivors group told me.'

Darius sighed. He had enough on his plate. He wanted to tell her again that he didn't have the time, but he was pricked by a conscience telling him this was her dying wish and also by a nagging need to find out more about Kathleen and whether she had suffered at the hands of the priest. But turning to leave the flat, he didn't tell his mother any of this.

Tears were trickling down her ashen face. A melancholy dragged in the air as he left, and he sensed - through the thick atmosphere that lay between them -the importance for her in finding Kathleen.

Driving away, he thought about the burden his mother was becoming. About a year ago she had expressed an interest in a care home for former dockyard families in Liverpool. She knew people there and had seemed to like the idea. If she moved back up north, she wouldn't trouble him so much and settling into a fresh routine would meet new friends and forget about Kathleen.

4

DARIUS

February 2009
Darius woke the next day, dreaming of Kathleen. He tried to remember what she looked like, but his memories were fuggy, and he couldn't summon her image into his mind. Many years had passed.

There was no telling where she was or what she was doing. Darius shuddered as he thought of all the brothels he'd visited over the years. What if he'd been offered his own sister in a line-up?

Suddenly in his mind he was back in a brothel. The first time he'd visited a brothel it had all happened by accident. Cruising round North London he'd driven through an area of Finsbury Park not realising it was a redlight district. Those were the days of kerb-crawling. Through the driving rain he saw a woman waving at him to stop and being naive he thought she needed help. He'd wound down the window and she asked if he wanted to do business. Suddenly the penny dropped. In a flash he had one of those 'fuck it' moments and thought *hell why not?* They went to a cheap hotel and he discovered the term 'hot sheet hotel' and afterwards he felt as if he had emptied his bollocks into a toilet and couldn't wait to escape the shame. Yet at the same time the experience had given him a forbidden thrill.

The encounter with the prostitute at Finsbury Park all those years back had confirmed a question that had hung over his life ever since he was a ten-year-old choir boy. Was he gay? How did he know he wasn't gay? Until then he hadn't known for sure and even then, he needed to return to prostitutes to confirm his sexuality.

He shuddered now as he recalled the mixed emotions he'd felt all those years back, as a young choirboy in the Catholic Church. A burning sensation swept across his face. He recalled the fear and disgust, mixed with pleasure. How could he have felt pleasure for what had actually been abuse? As he'd emerged into adulthood he knew what had happened to him had been wrong but he now felt shame, guilt, anger and bitterness. How could that man - the priest -have fucked his emotions up in the way that he had and why was he still letting him control his life all these years later?

The brothels had served one purpose: throwing off the cloak of Catholicism that had smothered his whole upbringing.

He got out of bed, fired up the computer and began to research women who had died in childbirth at the Magdalene Laundries because he wondered whether Kathleen had died in the care of the nuns. He stumbled across a story about a mass grave of unidentified bodies in the woods near one of the laundries. Darius looked at the name of the laundry, relieved that it wasn't the 'Weeping Lady.'

He had also spoken to a lawyer who was investigating the possibility of claims for damages for Magdalene victims.

But Darius was mystified yet again about how he would break any ground in the search.

5
DARIUS

March 2009
Darius was on a business tour in India. Doughnuts were finding their way into the all-day snacking habits of the Indian consumer and were set to become the snack option of the Indian urban youth but the doughnut war was on with competition from vada pavs and kaati rolls.

'I'm not so bad for 56,' he told his reflection in the hotel mirror.

He'd recovered well from the heart attack. He took his cocktail of drugs each day and didn't give it too much thought. He took his wig off, gave it a shake and a flick - as if removing pesky nits - then hung it up on the back of the bathroom door to give it an airing. He examined the zigzag of scarring on his head. It reminded him of a flash of lightning. A Harry Potter scar but much bigger. He wondered about clipping the solitary bristly hair that stood up on the landscape of his bald head. It looked like a car aerial.

His chest was like bread dough, his belly descending to Australia and he had floppy man boobs, but he was a bloke so what did it matter? It was different for women. They were the flowers for bees to be pollinated: no attraction, no pollination.

The predictable repetition of vanilla bland hotel chains across the world had become his life and he loathed it all. Light switches were the most irritating things, never located in obvious places and when you turned them all off to get into bed there was always one left on and it took ages to find the switch. He never used the radio alarm. They were way too complicated, and the air con was always a piss off. The TVs were usually huge with 100 channels of shit. The beds were vast with a great collection of pillows but nobody to share it with.

It never took him long to trash a hotel room. He liked to behave like a rock star–– in other words a complete slob. Dumping his toilet bag and a mountain of medication in the bathroom he made a quick check of the suite: no floaters blocking the toilet or stray pubic hairs in the shower. Nothing *yet* to complain about.

He hated the tedium of business travel: the grubbiness, the coffee breath, the furry teeth, the mixed currency jangling in the pocket, the perspiration, the heavy luggage, the frisking at security. But he was always pleased to luxuriate in the hotel bath when he had arrived at his destination, filling it right to the top and rolling up a couple of towels to add as a buffer in case the water sloshed over the edge.

Wandering down to the ground floor he passed a statute of Lord Vishnu – and silently begged him not to put a curse on his sensitive bowel.

He pushed through the revolving doors into the oppressive heat of Mombai. Watched the taxis pulling in, he wiped beads of sweat from his forehead. Beyond the fine granite forecourt and brick pathway surrounding this five-star grandeur was no man's land - a dustbowl of red rock, in which rubbish and fine grit swirled in the light breeze. In the distance, set against the backdrop of derelict buildings and rapid building programmes, were scraggy tarpaulin tents dotting the landscape. He could see bare-footed children running around their parents, cooking on open fires and taking showers next to the roadside. Out of habit he felt in his pocket for a packet of fags, then remembered he was trying to quit.

It was the weekend. He hated weekends away. He pushed through the revolving doors back into the cool air-conditioned foyer. He swiped a sweet as he passed the bowl on the reception counter, flicking the wrapper onto the floor unashamedly in front of the smiling receptionist. The lift propelled him back to the solitary confinement of his hotel cell where the only pleasures in store was internet porn until the working week began again.

What was he supposed to do on weekends away? Aishwarya Patel, his Indian Mr. Know-all, owner of a new doughnut factory he had just visited hadn't the social skills or grace to provide entertainment of any kind, not even a doughnut line up at his house. And as for his business partner, Vulture Vinnie he was a dead loss. Darius often dreamt about buying Vinnie out, but with no collateral it didn't look likely. Vulture Vinnie was a drain on business resources. He claimed every business expense he possibly could and when they were away, he chose the most expensive restaurants and the fine dining options with a bottle of wine for the starter, a different wine for the main followed by a dessert wine, and then, just as they were getting up to leave, he would decide that he was still hungry and needed cheese and biscuits and a large port. The man was vulgar, vile, vociferous. Vehemently determined not to abandon his ways Darius had caught him many a time crouching over a toilet in the gents vomiting into the bowl after gorging on so much food. And when clients were entertaining them for the evening Vinnie would eat even more. Darius wondered how they had managed to retain their clients given his voracious ways. The man had every possible V word attached to his name. Victory Day would soon come with any luck, then he'd be out.

The corridor was quiet. Two maids chatted next to a laundry trolley. He'd visited the tourist attractions numerous times on previous trips. He didn't want to wander aimlessly round a market either, getting hassled by street traders.

Shutting himself in his hotel room, Darius soon forgot the poverty and squalor of the world outside, blissfully protected by the crispness of the white cotton sheets of his bed and the smell of fresh shampoo in the bathroom. Life outside seemed so cheap: a daily brush with death and chance, small children fending for themselves, crouching by the roadside at night, their eyes bright in the headlights of passing cars. There were beggars on every street corner and cripples too. Women with babies that seemed comatose and all the rest of sad humanity in the city where, in all probability his bank's call centre was located.

It was hard to believe looking out of his window that this country was being slowly transformed into a world superpower.

He flicked on his laptop, sat at the desk, still feeling bloated from breakfast. It was too early to be tempted by a mini bar break in of Pringles or Toblerone.

He got up. Went to the loo while the laptop booted. He wished at this point in the day that he was in Japan - sitting on a warm 'Toto' with all the high-tech advanced features of bottom washing and deodorisers.

He returned to the desk to check emails, wondering whose bare bottom had sat on the seat before his. Then he clicked the 'favourites' bar. The moans of Mick-The Lick's team of luscious happy ladies. He liked to watch a good orgy. He moved his hand into his trousers to cradle the warmth of his balls.

But it was useless. *Stupid intermittent unreliable dick. Mick-The-Lick never has this problem.* He looked down at the pathetic flaccid thing coiled between his legs. Seeing such huge black cocks on the screen made him feel a mixture of shame and inadequacy. If only he had a cock like a Michelangelo painting.

He had always been embarrassed and ashamed of its size, going way back to changing for PE at school or lining up at the urinals taking a sideways glance at all the other boys. Looking back the only one to appreciate his cock had been the priest. He shuddered to accept that was the fact of the matter. Over time Mr. Small Cock had become Mr. Super Unreliable Cock. If only they could invent a plug-in charger, a gadget to clamp to the balls to recharge the limpet.

'Who's master? You or me?' He asked his friend. 'How am I going to have another relationship?' He flicked it with his finger. It was a friend with issues.

As if to add insult to injury he could hear the deep moans of a couple having sex in the room next door: 'Humping Hilaries,' he always called shagging neighbours in hotels rooms. Jesus. This was all he needed. He turned up the sound of Mick-The-Lick's team.

The noise had subsided, both from next door and from the team – who were splayed out in all sorts of erotic positions on a heavily stained bed.

He leaned back in the chair returning to a fresh Google search. This time he logged into his usual dating site. There might be an intelligent woman: one with a mind and a body but with a fresh, wet pussy not a shriveled up dried old prune. He wanted the perfect combination of 'mind' and 'meat.' He could see a new name for a dating site using those two words.

In an ideal world that woman would be life partner material. There had to be a real connection. She'd be informed about current affairs, the economy and science to hold an interesting discussion. Darius doubted there were many women of that calibre out there. Most were dull, shallow, vain; only interested in their hair and clothes. That type of woman would drive him crazy. The only thing you could realistically do was fuck 'em and forget them.

He had discovered the possibilities of internet dating within days of leaving his ex- wife. But he knew that love wasn't going to solve all the shitty problems in his life.

Internet dating in the beginning had been exciting. It was one giant meat market within his living room - like bursting through a wormhole in the fabric of space into another universe.

Since his initial discovery of this whole new world, he usually had a couple of women that he chatted to on-line. Only a couple had actually materialised into dates. Stick insect Moira - with the dried-up fanny being one. And Sandra, the cellulite blob being the other. He'd seen all manner of human life hidden behind those passport style pictures: the desperately lonely, the desperately broke, the desperate for sex, the depressed, (like himself) the dumped, the divorced, the bereaved. The list went on. The saddest 'cases' he came across were women who were trapped in the most tragic of situations caring for very sick and elderly parents, the fun in their life over as they put duty first. And worst – women watching their partners decline in mental health – incarcerated within the walls of early onset dementia. Their relationships all but over they were crying out - not exactly for an escape route but a form of solace.

He uploaded a new profile and hoped that the woman he would find would help him in his search for Kathleen. Kill two birds with one stone, excuse the pun. It was a cheaper way of employing a private detective. Women were natural detectives, always checking up on their partners, poking round looking at bank statements and Facebook accounts and anything else that wasn't theirs.

Changing the username on his dating profile to *Magic*

Flying Trouser Press 99 Darius wrote his opening words. *Magic Flying Trouser Press seeks travel companion and lover.*

That was bound to arouse some interest, Darius thought. After all that's what most women were after – a free lunch and a free plane ticket. He'd long sussed the dating game. Into the dating site's search engine he began his fresh search for ladies within the age range 40 to 60 who liked travel.

Within minutes of fishing, a daily shoal of wrinkly old troats had plopped into his virtual net. Half he tossed overboard. Many lacked the imagination to write anything other than clichés. Others hadn't even bothered with that.

Most of the profiles contained somewhere the phrase *I'm looking for a soul mate to cuddle up to on the sofa with a bottle of wine and a DVD.* He wondered if Blockbusters and DFS were secret sponsors of the dating site. And what was a 'soul mate?' Some illusive airy-fairy term that women used.

Predictably they invariably said, *I'm looking for a man with a good sense of humour.* Darius always wanted to reply, *well find a comedian then.*

I also like to go to the pub, have meals out (Italian, Chinese, Indian) go to the cinema, go for a walk, cook a meal at home, go on holiday and I like shopping. These profiles were shopping lists. They might as well have added to the list *milk, butter, cheese.*

He was looking for just one single solitary sentence that would do more than make his intestines contract. He was looking for that elusive pique of interest.

And it was just when he was about to return to Mick-The-Lick that he saw her. He noticed her hair before he read her opening gambit. One side of her dainty frame stood in the shade of a Cypress tree in the graveyard of an ancient village church. The people milling in the distance told him this was a wedding. Light illuminated part of her dark hair, tones of red and ember, like a blanket of fallen autumn leaves, glossy and gleaming. It was freshly washed and styled in curled layers; blended well with the shimmery burnt orange she was wearing. This woman had class. Her warm shy half smile beckoned him in.

Her screen name was *Finding Nemo 620*. She described herself as the girl looking for an adventure. Finding Kathleen was going to be an adventure. Was she up for that, he wondered?

I'm looking for more than just a relationship. I want to go on an adventure with someone. Life is a mission and I'm on a mission. Call it Finding Nemo.

And then his eyes caught the words *travel, tennis* and *politics*. And best of all she said her favourite country was Ireland. That was the first place he intended to take his new woman because that was where the search for Kathleen would begin.

Maybe she was the rare gem he was searching for – someone with class and brains and someone to lead him to Kathleen.

He thought about a TV dating game show of years ago, called *Blind Date*. He asked the type of question the presenter, Cilla Black would have asked. But would she ping a return email?

6

FAYE

March 2009

Shayne's bloated lips were inches from Faye's, making her heart thud and her cheeks burn. His breath was upon her; raven eyes boring into her soul like an owl on a perch watching its prey. There was nowhere to escape. His frame filled her exit route, blocked out the light. She spied the straggly grey hair around the base of his neck. It badly needed a trim. When they had been together, she had been the lawnmower to his face and neck.

'Ave you left the Sharon?' He looked up the corridor. His jowls flapped as his head moved. Faye squirmed. What had possessed her to sleep with him all those years ago?

'Sharon? What the hell are you talking about?' But she knew what he meant.

'I can hear water dripping,' Shayne said.

'The *shower* is dripping. But it's not your flat. I'll be sorting it.' Over his shoulder she could see Chrissie watching Angelina Ballerina curled up on the settee pulling fluff from her blanket as if she were a white slave in a carding mill.

'Erm? Erm?' Shayne had forgotten the shower, peered at her through slitted eyes, pleading once more. She looked at her watch. She had a train to catch.

'I still like you, you know.' He put his finger on her cheek, traced a line. She pushed it away. 'You look nice today. Why don't we go to your bedroom for a while? Erm?' He continued to plead. 'You always used to like it.'

He tried to whisper but Shayne didn't know how to whisper or do anything quietly.

Faye moved further into the space between the front door and her computer desk toppling a wooden chair over with a jerky twist of her body. She wanted to grab his faded paint splattered t -shirt, coil it into a knot then slam him hard against the wall like swatting a fly. Every time he picked up or dropped off Chrissie, she was reminded of the sordid act that had taken place in the car park of a Little Chef on an arterial road in the back of his swimming pool blue Fiat Panda in 2002. She could still see the image of his hairy bottom pounding away on top of her, the front tyre bouncing in the pothole, the car knocking against the bins and the gormless expression on his square face. If only she could wipe the slate of the past. If she hadn't had the affair with Shayne, Trevor would still be alive and the twins would still have a father.

His face was now closer. He had egg on his chin - always had egg on his chin even when he hadn't eaten egg. Runny bright smears and clumps of yellow crusted into his stumble. Her stomach was doing somersaults.

'We've been over for months. Why don't you look for someone else?' Faye wondered what it would take for him to finally get the message. She wanted to tell him to just take Chrissie and go but she knew what he'd say. She could hear his baby tantrum in her head. She struggled to be assertive.

'You're so 'orrible to me. I don't deserve to be treated like this, Faye.' It was easier to go through the motions. Let him work through a tantrum.

'Stop it. We're over. I've always been clear about that.'

'You came round me first. Made the first move. I thought you were happily married. Are you ill?' He asked, matter of factly.

'Oh please. Because I don't want you, I must be ill! Shayne you're pathetic,' she screeched, feeling deeply insulted. 'You were a mistake. We all make mistakes.' She flung her arms up in despair. 'I should have made my marriage work. If I had, Trevor would still be alive. Because of our sordid little affair, he couldn't take it anymore,' she shouted.

'It was already over with Trevor when we started an affair.'

Faye had always known that having an affair had made things worse. 'We drove him to end his life. You should have respected the institution of marriage.'

'I didn't enter into it. And you can't blame me for what Trevor did. He must have been suffering from depression.'

'You were at our wedding. A witness in effect.' Faye turned her nose up at him, in disgust.

'You're saying you regret your daughter?' Shayne asked, his eyes scrunched into a smirk.

'Don't twist things around. If that's the case, I'd regret Tim and Meg too because marrying Trevor turned out to be a mistake.'

Faye remembered so clearly the turning point in her marriage to Trevor, the catalyst, the touch paper that sparked the affair - the day Trevor called on her mobile during prayers in a church service. Trevor hadn't cared. His needs had always come first. The ring tone had bounced across the cold walls of the church and up to the heights of the steeple. She had pushed her way hurriedly along the pews, her heels click clacking on the stone slabs squinting as she adjusted to natural daylight to see Trevor's face, a picture of thunder under the kissing gate.

'Hurry up, we'll be late. Get the kids from the crèche. Get into the fucking car. Now,' he'd screamed, his harsh words echoing across the yard and probably heard in the silence of the church by the whole congregation. She could still see his bright red face in her memory, desperate to get to his golf tournament, frantic they were going to be late to meet his friends, wound up that he'd been deprived of a shag that morning. Sex had been his daily tonic together with the wine and beer that had crept up in measures by the week. But when he'd started being nasty to her, she found it harder and harder to have intimate relations with him. And it hadn't taken long for her to feel repulsed by him.

Denied sex, at first Trevor had seen the funny side never imagining this would go on.

'One of these days I think I'll die from lack of sex,' he'd said.

But as his patience waned, a furious temper had taken over. 'You frigid whore. You have other holes I can ram it into.'

He'd exchanged the loving nickname, sweet angel for dozy bitch. There had been days of silence and childish moods when he'd escaped to the pub, returning hours later swaying on the doorstep. In bed he'd get out his dick, thrusting it into her face. 'Do you want to put this around your lips?'

She remembered the feeling of dread when his hard dick had rubbed against her back as she breast fed Meg and Tim at two in the morning, or his hands cupped around her breasts demanding a 'titty fondle' as she stood at the sink scrubbing at greasy pots and pans while the children ate their breakfast in the room next door. He'd had the sexual appetite of a twenty-year-old and had remained ferocious from the day they had met.

In the early days of her marriage to Trevor they had made love all night. It had been fun back then. But then the marriage changed. Night after night she would wake to the bed shaking as he tossed off under the covers hearing his final muffled whimper and then the tug of the sheet, an unspoken 'fuck off' to her rigid body lying there in the darkness. By then he'd long given up pulling her hand across, stretching her limp fingers around his shaft.

It was only after Trevor's suicide that everything had fallen into place. The huge debts he'd run up, his inability to talk to her about his financial problems, turning nasty and driving her ultimately into the arms of another man. If only they had been able to talk rather than him turning to anti-depressants behind her back. They could have shared the worry and maybe he wouldn't have jumped in front of the train.

'Where are they?' Shayne said. Faye's thoughts snapped back to the present.

'Steve's just picked them up. He was on time. He never comes in and lingers like you do.' Steve was Faye's brother who looked after Meg and Tim from time to time, to give Faye a break.

But the moment she said that she regretted it. The words were out.

'He's Mr. Perfect I suppose. If he wasn't your brother, I'd be suggesting you marry him.'

How dare he? Steve had been amazing: stepping in to pay maintenance, looking after the twins, doing all he could to fill the role the father they had lost. Without Steve she didn't know how she would have coped. She certainly couldn't rely on Shayne.

Shayne began to pull baby faces, flinging his arms around. Sometimes when he was like this, he'd kick something – anything, like the time he kicked his mobile across the street when it didn't work, or the time he jumped on his sat nav.

She waited. Looked around. Stared down at his dirty shoes and the laces that were always undone. Without warning he flung his foot into the skirting board, then yelped in pain and began faking tears.

'Oh for goodness sake Shayne. Grow up,' Faye shouted. She pushed him out of her way and called to Chrissie to get her shoes on. It was time they left.

'You always rush me. Like you're ashamed of me. We never get to talk these days.'

He was right. She was ashamed that she had scraped the bottom of the barrel and slept with him in the first place. He was the very last man on earth she would have looked at. But when her marriage had hit the rocks, he had been a mirage in a sea of trouble – a long-standing friend, a listening ear to her troubles, a shoulder to cry on.

But unfortunately, things had spun out of control. She had been under some sort of spell, temporarily detached from reality. Their torrid affair had spelt the death knell of her marriage to Trevor. Looking back now, she had no idea why she had entertained a relationship with a man who looked like Mr. Bean, acted like Mr. Bean and had the same ability to irritate as Mr. Bean.

'Shayne we're over. We've been over a very long time. In fact there never really was an us. You were in the wrong place at the wrong time. I'm sorry.'

Shayne had been the leapfrog relationship but about a year ago she had discarded him like a broken hoover. He'd served his purpose. And it was now high time she met someone she wanted to be with long term.

'There *is* nothing to say. I'm going out. I've got a train to catch.'

She locked her front door, feeling proud of her flat. She didn't own it, but it was home all the same.

Her marriage had hit troubled waters around the time Gordon Brown had introduced tax credits back in 1999, sold as a solution to poverty for hardworking families. All her other friends, whose marriages were up the creak too, were discussing tax credits in the playground, cafes and the toddler groups. They were coming to the same conclusion. There was no financial benefit to remaining in a bad marriage. These new tax credits made divorce possible. There was a positive excited feel to their chatter as they planned their freedom. Some might have left regardless of the costs, but tax credits certainly helped them take the plunge and gave them their confidence back.

Tax credits had given her a massive step up. After the marriage break-up and Trevor's suicide, Faye got a job in a factory, unable to get anything better and earned the same again in tax credits. Her friend Katie who lived around the corner helped out when she needed to work a night shift. She had more than enough to live on but would never be able to buy a property. No mortgage company would lend to her. Her earnings were too low and because of Trevor's debts there had been no equity left in the marital home.

She began the short walk to the station. She was meeting Darius in Brighton at noon, a two-hour journey away.

At first, she'd loved the freedom of life without a man, but there were times when she felt lonely. She didn't like being back on the shelf, gathering dust. The dream of finding love once more was out there.

One bored weekend Faye had loaded a picture and put up a profile. Internet dating felt like a giant candy store. But over time it was in fact like panning for gold – most of it turned out to be fool's gold.

The dating site was an art gallery of meaningless faces. Some reoccurred each day like the repetition of an advert for a pay day loan. There were toothless men with icy stares, balding men with facial scars, tattooed arms radiating danger. Sagging bellies and rippling man boobies in tight vests. There were builders and window cleaners, lorry drivers and carpet cleaners and football fanatics and bungee jumpers.

And then... just as she was about to give up, bored with the tedium of the searches, the meaningless emails back and forth that felt so like Groundhog Day, the virtual winks and smiles, the virtual champagne, chocolates and roses - Darius arrived in her inbox one Saturday afternoon. In all the months of online dating this was the first *long* email she had received.

He hadn't listed his food tastes as a tedious shopping list.

He wrote: 'Ducks do not have souls. Please don't tell me you are an animal rights protestor swinging your anti gavage placards outside my favourite store, Fortnum and Mason. You'll see a lot of cruelty in British farming. Foie Gras is no more the evil delicacy of despair than battery farming of hens. Every decent restaurant should have it on their menu.'

He didn't list the restaurants he liked. He wrote about the ones he didn't.

'You won't get me in a carvery. They're full of dribbling pensioners in wheelchairs and bloated chavs queuing for their weekly blow out–– as much as they can fill their gobs for a fiver. Carveries stink of old congealed gravy and brussel sprouts.'

And his opening question, very Cilla Black, although a little cheesy, had made her think about her outlook on life:

When you are handed a rose, what do you see? A stick covered in thorns, or a beautiful flower?

Her reply had been equally cheesy:

I would want to know the name of the rose because there are thousands and the origin of their names can be very interesting. I would also draw it close to my nose, inhale the aroma, close my eyes and think of a beautiful summer day, with bees buzzing and the clink of fine bone china teacups on a freshly mowed emerald lawn. The colour of the rose would be yellow or orange because red, while symbolising love is also the colour of blood and conflict. There has been too much conflict in my life.

When you look at a rose it's important not to ignore the thorns.

I've met many pricks and don't want to meet anymore. Will you be a thorn in my side or the sun that unfolds my petals?

From that first email they became drawn in to all sorts of discussions.

He looked a little like the gorgeous George Clooney. But he hadn't selected the clearest of pictures. He was sitting on a sandy beach in somewhere like Tenerife, squinting against the sun. It looked breathtaking, so healing that she was reminded of a poem by WH Auden. 'In the desert of the heart let the healing start. In the prison of his days, teach the free man to praise.' He was squinting against the evening light, friendly creases radiating gently around his eyes. His face was beautifully tanned and stubbly, his hair thick and wavy, a salt and pepper mix of different tones of grey. She liked the sexy way his green-rimmed trendy glasses rested on his head and her eye was drawn to a light sprinkling of hair revealed in the opening of his navy shirt.

They began to text and this became a daily pattern from the moment they woke:

'I'm from Liverpool originally but I live near Marlow. Tomorrow I'm taking a train to Dhaka in Bangladesh.'

'That's sounds like an incredible experience.'

'I won't get to see much. The visit is mainly a tour of a recently opened doughnut emporium.'

'I guess you could link the article you're writing to their way of life.'

'In a sense. Bangladesh is a rapidly changing country. The people have no collateral, but they have ability. In the west we're screwed by the banks more than we know it. I can't convey in text the chaos, dirt, the sheer numbers of people here. The way business works here is like a building society model. It's not like western lending. The economy is growing at 6% but it's not a capitalist model. They aren't relying on debt to do things. Once you can start to tax people you can start to develop a society. These people have cultural and educational aspiration. They aren't ashamed of their abject poverty.'

'I feel as if I'm there with you.'

Texts pinged from the moment she woke to last thing at night. She felt as if she'd been in India and Bangladesh with him during the past week.

One rainy evening, as she sat with the kids watching Coronation Street on her chinzy sofa the phone bleeped.

'We're taking a rickshaw.'

'Where to?'

'To eat. Where do you fancy?'

'Pizza.'

'We're in India, silly.'

'Curry?'

'What about spinach curried kebab? Vegetarian is amazing over here.'

'What am I drinking?'

'Tequila.'

'Nice. Only one ice. It has to be 50 degrees plus to have more than one lump. Actually you're in India. Maybe one ice.'

'Dire Straits is playing in the corner.'

And the following evening there were more texts.

'What dress size are you?'

'12. Why?'

'I'm choosing a long floaty dress for you in a bazaar.'

'How will you know what suits me?'

'Darling I just will.'

As she sat now on the train heading to meet him for the first time she continued to text. 'I'm sitting opposite two nuns with huge metal swaying crosses. One of them is on her mobile!'

'We'll talk about nuns later. I may need your help. If we get on.'

Faye joined the throng of people squeezing through the barriers at Brighton station, swarming down towards the town and the sea front and wondered what he'd meant by the comment about nuns.

She crossed the road at the clock tower, diving between taxis. She was less than a minute from the '3 for 2' stand in Waterstones where they had arranged to meet. Crumpled receipts danced around the entrance.

A bearded man with a dog and a blanket looked up at her as she went in. 'Big Issue?' he asked.

7

DARIUS

March 2009

Darius waited for Faye by the '3 for 2s.' He thumbed through a fat biography on the former prime minister that Faye had referred to in a conversation as *that evil woman*. At some point in the future, he imagined she would enjoy raising a glass at a *ding dong the witch is dead party*. But what the hell was he doing about to date a Blair Babe and single mother? Single mothers were firmly on his list of 'hello but no thank you' – another group to sneer down upon along with the job shirkers, drug addicts, benefit scroungers and more. And yet when he looked at the age group he was in who were likely to find him appealing, a high percentage would be single mums. He wondered if he had the courage to deal with the other angles of such a relationship if it developed.

With reservations mounting, Darius watched her come into the shop, pull her jacket zipper down to reveal a beautiful cleavage and trim figure. An inner voice chirruped '*three kids, two dads.*' He pretended he hadn't seen her. He picked up another book '*101 Things To Do with a Dead Body*' and waited for the Iraqi roadside device that was this sexy single mother of three kids, two dads - one dead and buried - to recognise and join him at the stand.

∽

Faye

They were laughing - engulfed in great gulping uncontrollable tidal waves sharing the silliness of the coffee table book he was browsing.

The book now returned to the table left them exposed and vulnerable, their buttress gone.

She found herself looking up into the pale blue eyes of a Winston Churchill lookalike with a thick doughy neck and a wavy mop of grey hair. There was something unnatural looking about his hair that she hadn't noticed in his photos. It looked like a rug had been glued onto this head. His face and neck looked like the devastation of a forest fire; a blunt or ineffective razor had left random hairs, like charred trees across a rugged landscape. Her eyes locked onto his wispy eyebrows. Strands were shooting out in all directions as if they had been caught in a tornado and he was much taller and broader than she'd imagined. She preferred shorter and trimmer men. The vision of George Clooney melted away. *Steve Irwin could go hunting for snakes in those eyebrows* she thought to herself. A helter skelter of disappointment spiraled from the top of her chest to the pit of her stomach but as they began to walk down West Street towards the sea, she laughed it off in the breeze.

They chatted on, buoyed by humour. The sparkling sea ahead and the chewing gummed pavement below and the pleasant tones of his voice were distractions from the reality beside her. By the time they'd reached the front she wondered how to reconcile her developing feelings for him in the virtual world with the crushing downer of him the man, in flesh, walking next to her.

They crossed the stream of traffic chatting over the thunder of motor bikes and the wail of police sirens diving to the safety of the green faded railings. Tatty posters advertising events long gone, fluttered in the breeze. She caught a glimpse of a small scar above his eye, making a mental note to tactfully ask at some point how he'd acquired it. She imagined a fight one evening in Liverpool, in his youth. His dating picture had been taken far enough away to hide the scar. Why had she imagined he would look like George flipping Clooney? The image of his dating profile picture; the image she had warmed to was fixed on the canvas of her mind.

The screech of a seagull overhead and its descending splat suddenly sent Darius into theatrical mode.

'Arrh, the seagull's had a dodgy ruby.' Soon they were laughing again. Darius wobbled his head like a weeble. The weight of her disappointment had started to lift, because humour counted for so much in relationships.

'Miss Faye, India is full of stinky poo. One day I take you there.' He bowed. And as they continued walking, he talked about his trip to India and the Indian worries about terrorism. He carried on. 'Taxi driver charge me seven rupees for visit to Rajastan Palace and market to buy fine lady a garment.' He could do a great Indian accent, but it was tinged with Scouse-- rather intriguing she thought.

'Teach me some Scouse.' She laughed, the breeze lifting her hair.

'You've got to get a key phrase in your head to get you started. Repeat after me... I wanna go on the rob, it's me gran's birthday and she's thirty.'

She watched his salivary mouth and rolling tongue as he repeated the sentence several times before she had a go.

'Ay. You sound like you're trying to be a ventriloquist so you do.' All this laughter-- the first date wall had come tumbling down.

Darius stopped walking and presented her with a brown parcel.

'I'm impressed. I've never had a present on a first date.' She said excitedly. She blushed as she unwrapped the parcel. A pink and blue dress escaped from the packaging. It seemed to go on and on, like a magician's trick tumbling from a top hat.

'Do you like it? Will it fit?' Darius looked concerned. She liked his concern.

'How big did you imagine I would be? Did you ask for tent size?' She held it up to her body laughing. 'If we ever find ourselves without clothes or in need of a parachute, we'll be ok.' She grinned.

'It would fit my ex. She's hideously large - an elephant!'

She stopped laughing, told him it wasn't fair that people got bigger as they grew older. She looked at him trying to work out who or what he reminded her of. Was it Bert from Sesame Street or a bloated pink jelly baby?

His body was a bendy metal coat hanger performing a very poor job of supporting his weighty clothing: jeans that were too wide, too long, too baggy, too bunched up. He was drowning in a weathered brown suede jacket, which reminded her of an antique sideboard in a bric-a-brac. She felt sorry for him. Her heart tugged slightly. She couldn't work out what she felt: a mixture of repulsion and intrigue.

A police helicopter hummed and a plane embroidered the blue sky with garlands of vapour as they headed for the pier - Brighton's magnet. Darius was telling her how he had spent two days of his Indian trip on the toilet. He described the heat and intensity of the place. Soon they were comparing notes on airport experiences across the world.

'I hate the fucking Disney experience of airports - endless queuing for security checks.'

She found his constant swearing amusing and disarming and she liked his open and honest opinions.

Her boots clattered along the planking out to sea, adding to the thud of fun fair music, different tunes and beats competing from every direction. They paused to lean over the railings, sticky with salt.

'It's like a British Ibiza down here.' She sensed his shadow over her face as he spoke, studying her, her eyes closed against the sun, breathing in wafts of nauseating grease, candy floss and sugared doughnuts.

'Brighton has everything. It's nice to come somewhere different.' She opened her eyes to the wavy outline of the cliffs in the distance, along the coastline towards Seaford.

'I used to come down here in the 80's for Tory conferences. It was either here or Blackpool. I miss the 70s and 80s. Those days were such fun,' he told her.

'I'm surprised you're a Tory, coming from Liverpool. All that history of radical socialism. Generations grafting as dockers, probably earning a halfpenny. I imagined you might have joined Militant Tendency.'

'I couldn't wait to escape all that. That's why I ended up coming south, to seek my fortune, so I did. And well I guess the Conservatives were the only party determined to crush terrorism, take a tough line. My dad died in the Troubles, in 1971,' he told her.

'Oh God. I'm sorry. He was a soldier?' Faye stopped to look at him with concern in her eyes.

'No, but he was caught up in the Troubles visiting my auntie on the Falls Road. I think they showed his picture on the news, but my mum wouldn't let me watch it. She never watched the news from that day on. His death changed everything. It was as if a dark cloud had passed across our house. All the fun and happiness seemed to melt away. He was a great bloke. Very different to my mum; relaxed, fun to be with but my mum lives her life around the Catholic Church; but not so much these days. She's started going to a free church near her flat and the experience has mellowed her but when we were growing up she was a cold, serious and God-fearing woman, guided by the priest on everything.

They were quiet for a time as they walked along. Sensing a change in the tone of his voice and manner when he talked about the priest's influence within their family, she felt uncomfortable and quickly switched the conversation to a lighter footing.

'Would you ever live beside the sea? It's lovely and vibrant here.'

'You can only go one way. It would be too far from my friends back in Liverpool. Not that I had many. I went to a Prod school because it was nearer than the Catholic. They gave me a rough time because I was different. Back then Liverpool was still divided on sectarian grounds, but the divide was breaking down. It was much worse before I was born. I felt excluded from their world. It's strange to think two churches could be so very different in their outlook but yet both follow the teachings of the same man.' He took out a pack of cigarettes and lit one. Smoke curled into the breeze. 'Where I'd really love to be, is back in the marital home in Nettlebed. The house has been on the market for months. The bitch, my ex still lives there but she's stalling the sale. I just want her out. She can live in the bloody gutter for all I care. She knows we'll come out with nothing.'

His thoughts were starting to rattle Faye's cage. She hated the lack of a social conscience that some Tories had.

'She'll have to sell at some point. You should get your lawyers onto it.'

'They're costing me a bloody fortune. We had to remortgage because she got into debt investing in property in Florida before the crash. I had no idea. She did all that behind my back.'

Faye couldn't imagine a scenario like it; not knowing what

the other person was up to. But then she was back to thinking about Trevor and his debts that she'd known nothing about and how the situation -compounded by her affair with Shayne led to him taking his life – an event she could not possibly have predicted.

'When I found out I went mental, but she transformed into a crazed animal. She ran upstairs in a rage, grabbed a metal coathanger from the wardrobe and attacked me. She was like a banshee. She seared me with the metal prong as if my head was a lump of pork. Fucking painful it was. Bitch. I've got several scars. That's why I have to wear a wig to cover the scars. I don't expect you noticed, it looks incredibly real doesn't it?' He stopped walking and looked down at her.

Faye turned towards the helter skelter with the faint hint of a smile. She didn't tell him she had known as soon she'd looked up at him. For a time, they looked towards Shoreham. She took a deep breath and boldly asked, 'how did you get the scar above your eye?'

'The bitch attacked me with a razor after I challenged the investments she'd made on some Florida properties.'

'She sounds dangerous.' Faye said.

He sucked on his ciggie then stubbed it on the railing. They watched its descent into the sea.

Seagulls hovered overhead in battle formation.

'Bloated seagulls. They seem to get bigger and fatter. See that one looking at us with its beady eyes. It's like a copper.'

'They're like MPs on the scrounge.' He eyed a gull pecking on a discarded wrapper.

The comparison made Faye smile. 'Pigs with snouts in the trough. That's what the papers said. I suppose you can't blame them. If there's a loophole people will abuse it. MPs don't earn enough, that's the problem.'

'None of us do anymore. The country's finished. It'll be irrelevant who wins the next election because there are no big visions anymore or great visionaries. It's just about managed decline,' he said.

'Lots of people still want to come to Britain so things can't be that bad. Look at London. It's booming.' Faye kicked a chip through a gap in the planking and fixed her gaze on the West Pier – a pile of little black matchsticks in the sea. 'The West Pier. Look, it's like the tangled wreck of our lives.'

'Maybe. Or it could symbolize the tangled wreck of the British economy. It's the remains of Northern Rock. No amount of cutbacks are going to raise our economy. The debt is the biggest issue facing this country,' he said.

Their arms were touching, their eyes transfixed on the steely sea. Faye caught a glimpse of his stub nose and his tight mouth. She thought of a cat's arse. She didn't want to imagine kissing him. Wiry black hairs shot from his nose in every direction, from the ridge at the top to the bulb at the bottom. It was as if he was cultivating a garden. She wanted to attack him with a pair of tweezers or a mini lawnmower. And then turning to glance at him as he talked, she noticed something small and black on his neck in the corner of her eye. Her heart missed a beat. She panicked. Her first thought was that an insect had landed. Then she saw what it was.

'Yikes. A tattoo.'

'Do you not like tattoos. I didn't ask?' Darius squinted against the sun.

'Not really. If I'm honest. I've always thought they're the mark of a chav.' This was, for Faye one of those Marmite issues and she was firmly in the tattoo NO camp. But in the next breath she back-pedaled with a nervy laugh, pushed her hair away from her face.'But I could make an exception for you.' Faye smiled, offering him the answer she knew he wanted to hear while all the time she weighed up the likelihood of a second date.

'It's the only one I've got, so it is. I had it done during my rebel days when I couldn't stand being a head teacher anymore. You can be who you want to be when you manage your own business. In fact, it's all par for the course. I set the pace. Everyone else follows.'

'That's incredibly presumptive. And why would you want to go through that pain though?' She wanted to know.

'Because it symbolises something much larger.' A venom had crept into his voice. 'It scares people, it's a warning.' He paused for effect, his finger on the black spider. 'Not to cross me.' His voice was suddenly spiked with evil. Her heart did a flip. He looked down at her through steely eyes, his tone sending a chill through her body.

'No one messes with the O'Briens. As George Bush said *you're either with us or against us*. If anyone dares to humiliate, they get kicked hard.' His tone was sharp, icy.

'Next you'll be telling me you've got a vicious Rottweiler at home.' She laughed.

'Fuck no. I hate dogs.'

Suddenly she remembered something her grandma had said years ago. *Choose a man who likes dogs. It shows they've got a warm heart and compassion.* In her head she marked another black cross against the possibility of a second date.

She felt the first small flutter of anxiety as his eyes impaled her momentarily, but standing in the warm sunshine, to the beat of cheerful music she waved it away.

They started to walk again and as they approached the helter skelter, 'Gerry and The Pacemakers' was pumping *Ferry on The Mersey*. Darius took her hand. Soon they were skipping to the tune, their arms swinging, singing at the top of their voices, laughing, first date barriers down.

'Reminds me of home, so it does.' Now out of breath he cleared his throat. 'Sadly I was a wee nipper when they made their debut at the Cavern in 1960. My dad was there though.'

They were quiet for a time as they walked along, hand in hand, at ease and then Darius let out a small laugh.

'What's funny?' Faye asked.

'I was just reminiscing about those days; the late 60s. My dad organised spaghetti nights, inviting everyone to our house even the bloody priest, and any passers-by in the street below. Everyone was encouraged to bring a musical instrument along to make the loudest clatter they could–– maybe a tambourine or even a wooden spoon and tin. The noise was deafening. The bugger used to bulk out the spaghetti with porridge to make it go further.'

'Oh funny. Sounds like the whole city was alive with music of different forms.'

'So it was. My auntie and her tuna can and wooden spoon. She made me laugh.'

When the laughter had subsided, floated out to sea, Darius changed the subject.

'What do you think to quantitative easing? What's your take on that?'

Faye was enjoying the topics of conversation. In her world she mingled with mothers who didn't talk much about current affairs.

'It's totally unique. A bold move on the part of Gordon Brown. That man will go down as one the country's greatest leaders,' she stated.

'Labour have ruined the economy with their massive spending projects,' he said.

'I couldn't have got divorced without Labour's great tax credit system,' she said.

'Arr so that's why I pay so much in corporation tax.' Darius nudged her teasingly. 'To support all you Karen Matthews out there.'

She remembered Karen Matthews–– the woman who'd recently been jailed for kidnapping her 9-year-old daughter in an attempt to make money by claiming a reward for her safe return.

'She was on loads of benefits. Six kids, six dads, I think. I'm better off than when I was married. Tax credits make a huge difference. I don't think the government's aware just how much they've contributed to the rising divorce rates. I left the marriage when house prices peaked, and interest rates were so low that I was able to pay off the small mortgage on my flat. I could never vote Tory. It's the nasty party.' She frowned.

'Women gain and men lose. I lost thousands. My divorce was a shipwreck. And I'm still trying to salvage the remaining treasures,' he said.

'I often ask myself when was that pivotal moment, when it all went wrong? Do you ask yourself that? It's a tough one to answer,' she asked.

Darius lit another ciggie and puffed hard before he spoke. The breeze lifted his hair and for a minute she wondered if it would take off.

'I can't possibly remember every day of my marriage but it's the bad bits that stick out as a series of blows. She did that, I did this, she wept, I laughed, she hit, I hit. When I look back, I see it as a series of scenes like in a movie. I can focus right in on the detail and in a second I'm back there. Sometimes it's as if I'm looking for a scene on a DVD and I'm winding back, forwarding, freezing the scene. I'm seeing it all on a split screen. They're cues to the memories each and every day—smells, songs, places. It eats me up. There's no escaping the past.'

'I read about a condition called hyperthymesia. Only a handful of people in the world have it but it's where someone has a highly superior autobiographical memory. Everything returns to them with intense clarity,' she said.

'That sounds awful. Sometimes I want to erase the past.' He shuddered.

THEY AMBLED past the crowds drinking in the seafront bars, the stalls selling hair braids and ethnic style dress, chatting about the mistakes of their past, sharing regrets, losses and dreams. Hope for a better future fizzed through every conversation and there were small suggestions of where they might go on future dates. And then the conversation turned to Kathleen.

'It was an awful time. It was the mid 70s and although the Catholic Church was beginning to lose its grip over the moral path as it were, it still had a massive influence in our lives. Not so much in Liverpool but certainly in Ireland. My mother lived her life by the church. The priest was God on earth. That's why I'm a firm atheist. I threw off the oppression. Especially after what happened...' His sentence trailed into the air.

'What happened?' Faye snapped. They stopped walking and she saw a deep sadness in his eyes and wondered what pain lay beneath them.

'It's a bit of a heavy and emotional story for a first date and on a lovely day by the sea. If we see each other again, you'll discover my demons,' he said.

'What happened to Kathleen?' she asked.

'She got pregnant. She was only 14 and the priest made arrangements for her to go to a Magdalene Laundry in Southern Ireland. Mum was so fucking pious and God fearing. I don't know what she imagined would happen. She was worried about the shame Kathleen would bring on the family if all the aunts and uncles and cousins found out. Times were different. Your experience of single motherhood is very different to the one Kathleen would have had, with no Government support and negative attitudes. Maybe I could have done something. Stopped them sending her away but I didn't know anything about it. Not until a few weeks ago. My mum wants me to find her. It's all a bit ridiculous after so many years. If she'd wanted to come home, she would have done. Part of me doesn't want to know the truth. Part of me is curious. I thought she had run away. That's what my mum had told me. But she lied to me. My wife lied to me too. What is it with some women that they can't just tell the truth?' He looked up at the sky. A pained look on his face.

He continued. 'We didn't hear anymore from Kathleen. I was doing well, rising up the career ladder in the grammar school. Now it turns out she was pregnant, and my mum has been dwelling on it for years and wants a sense of peace in knowing what happened to her. There is this big gaping void, so many questions and no answers and no body to help. I don't know if I can find her. When the girls entered those places, they gave them new names, a new identity and so many records went missing or were mysteriously destroyed. It's her dying wish to find Kathleen. I have to respect that. She's even given me some money to find her. But I'm going to fail because there are no leads. I've contacted the Irish Government, the Missing Person's Bureau and there may be a TV programme at some point over in Ireland. My mum wants me to go over to Ireland and just see the house where she stayed and pick up any leads in the process.'

'And will you?' Faye asked.

'Want to come?' He challenged her.

'We hardly know each other.' Faye smiled.

'I've got to show her that I'm doing something at least but there's no rush. Hey we should celebrate. Us? A happy new beginning? Do you fancy cocktails at the Grand Hotel?' Darius changed the tone of the conversation to a more cheery level.

∼

Darius

He waited for her to confirm the idea of a 'them.' She had

opened up to him about her life as a single mother and widow and the struggle to juggle work, kids and a social life. Part of him felt a tinge of sadness for it all and for the life that Kathleen would have led as a teenage mother in a different time and place.

He was beginning to think that maybe his ideas about single mothers were a little harsh. But whatever he thought of them as a group he knew he wanted to get to know this particular single mum. She was young and full of life and had an infectious energy about her.

The Grand Hotel, a reminder of a former age loomed above. He thought back to the Conservative Party Conference and the night in 1984. Prickles of fear skittered up his arms and across his back. He'd never forget the vision of Maggie, resolute yet exhausted, keeping her nerve, carrying on. He studied the white peeling facade as they crossed the busy road. It looked like Miss Haversham's wedding cake, the Charles Dickens character.

'It's seen better days,' Faye said as they waited to cross the second line of traffic. 'You've no idea what a treat this is. Single mothers on tax credits don't go to the Grand Hotel.'

She was striding up the steps - a socialist making a presence among the British establishment. 'We're fighting a ridiculous war in Afganistan to keep the streets of Britain safe – so the politicians tell us.'

But he was remembering when the IRA threatened daily life. Looking up at the building, he recalled the night of the bomb attack. He could see the debris, the falling chunks of concrete and plaster, the twisted balconies, could taste the dust.

'It's a new kind of terrorism now. Back then...' They ascended the Axminster carpeted steps. He looked around at the chandeliers and pianist playing and people enjoying afternoon tea. His voice trailed away. The sedate, sophisticated atmosphere reminded him of the Titanic and how everything could turn to tragedy in an instant.

'Ding dong the witch is dead,' she sang as they strode to the bar. 'It's a great shame they didn't get the old cow.'

She seemed to enjoy being the bull in the china shop, the little woman causing a stir. She reminded him of a Labour version of Anne Widdicombe. Newspapers rustled in front of a few pompous faces. The memory of wailing sirens, screaming and Kate Adie reporting filled Darius's head.

'What's your fancy then young lady?' He asked.

He ordered Kir Royales, took a swig of his and handed Faye hers.

'The plot to blow up this hotel was a complete disaster,' Darius said. 'It was on a long delay timer planted under a bath. Jesus Mary and Joseph, it was just as well. We would have lost our great leader. We nearly did.'

The barman curtly smiled and offered a dish of peanuts.

They sat and Darius removed his laptop from a green leather case to show her where he was visiting in Ireland.

'Cheers.' He clinked her glass. 'Can't quite believe I'm on a date with a Blair babe. The party that destroyed this country - leaving us in huge debt. He leaned over to touch a flower in a vase on a coffee table. 'Artificial flowers.. Hello to the age of austerity, Faye my dear.' He inched back into the velvet chair.

'But at what cost? The collapse of all our services.' Faye rose to the challenge. '*She* destroyed all sense of community,' she provoked.

'Thatcher? You're referring to the coal mines closures? They were uneconomical.'

'The policies of *your* government were pretty short sighted and despicable from 1981 onwards. Thatcher had no belief in science, supported the city elite. The types that come in here, pretty much.' Faye sniffed glancing around the room. 'Miners couldn't be turned into city bankers. These were big men, built like brick shithouses. The miners were on the scrap heap. Treated like old computers. And now we have whole communities with deep social problems created by *your* government.'

'You Luddite. What about evolution? Transformation? Economic change. Come on. I'm a businessman. I have to adapt all the time.' He was enjoying the challenge of conversational tennis.

'People need government to help them. There's a moral duty to help. You come from a working-class area. You must have seen grinding poverty when you were growing up. Didn't it prick your conscience?'

'You've got to be pragmatic in this life. It's dog eat dog. I do my bit by employing people, but if they don't pull their weight, they're out. Plain and simple.'

Faye

Faye sensed a harshness about him but drowned out the unnerving feeling that had crept over her with another sip of the delicious Kir Royale.

He carried on. 'Would we really have wanted to carry on sending people to work in complete darkness for hours on end? It was dirty and hazardous. It was about progress, development and that came through blue chip enterprise. The country is far wealthier now and especially since the unions were smashed once and for all.'

Darius leaned back in his armchair, huskily cleared his throat, resting his glasses on his head to read an email. He had an air of authority and charisma which lured her in. She took a sip of her drink and thought to herself yes, maybe I'll stick with this, for a while, see where it might lead. I might grow to like his looks. But an inner voice screamed from deep within *don't settle for someone you don't physically desire.*

8

DARIUS

April 2009
What a thrilling way to spend a Saturday afternoon, Darius thought to himself as he got out of the car.

He was with his mother. They had arrived at Curry's on Slough's industrial estate to help her chose a new toaster and matching kettle. Why she needed them when the ones she already had worked perfectly well, he really hadn't got the foggiest. He loathed these little trips and was quite grateful when he was away on business and had an excuse not to help his mum. Sitting in a queue at the roundabout on the approach to the big stores – Asda, Hobbycraft, MFI, Staples lining the route, was his idea of hell. But to his mother it was a Saturday afternoon treat.

He stood behind her in the shop catching up on all the news on the Telegraph on his IPhone, as she walked up and down. An hour had passed and still she couldn't decide between a Morphy Richards or a Kenwood, agonising over the colour scheme in her kitchen and the liquid capacity of each kettle, asking the staff about warranties and availability and bus routes to the shop in case she changed her mind and needed to come back.

Darius had had enough. He'd managed to maintain a carefully painted-on-smile but that was beginning to crack as impatience rose inside him, threatening to burst until he could hold back no longer.

'Mum, for fuck's sake. Do we have to spend all bloody Saturday looking at kettles? I've got better things to do with my time.'

She grabbed the table for support, wiping her brow, turning red and panicky, making a play of the fact that she wasn't well. But Darius saw through the drama. Old people were very clever at putting on an act.

'I can't think quickly. I need time. My brain doesn't work fast. Not since the stroke.'

'Well go to the doctor then.' He snapped unsympathetically.

She recoiled in shock. 'You've made me all muddled now. I need to sit down.'

Darius went to find a chair, irritation mounting.

'That's better. Now I wanted to ask you - how is the search for Kathleen going? Hurry up and find her.'

'I'm making enquiries.' Darius sniffed, looking at his watch wondering where the afternoon had gone.

'Are you? You never talk about these enquiries.' She looked as if she didn't believe him.

'Where would you like me to begin then?'

'Ireland of course. Near Killarney. That's where the Magdalene Laundry was.'

'I'll go as soon as I can. You know that the last laundry closed in 1996, Mum, but I might be able to find something out from the locals. That's what I'm hoping. It's just finding the time. It's very hard. Sinn Fein have been calling for a helpline. I've been in touch with an organisation for survivors of the laundries. But the problem is those places issued women with new names. Their identities were erased. We may find it's impossible to find her. Prepare yourself for that.'

She looked disappointed and shook her head. 'Oh dear. What are we going to do?'

'Nothing right at this moment here in Curry's.'

'Shall I have the blue kettle or the purple kettle and what about a matching toaster? And what if I change my mind? Oh dear.'

Darius sighed and rolled his eyes to the ceiling. 'Just hurry, Mum. I'm bursting for a wee.' Darius wondered at that point just how serious she was about finding Kathleen judging by how swiftly she switched the conversation back to kettles.

'You're making me all giddy. I think I'll leave it till next weekend.'

'Mum. Jesus, Mary and Joseph. I am not bringing you back next Saturday. I've just met a woman on the internet. I want to spend time with her.'

∼

'HAVE YOU GOT TIME FOR A RELATIONSHIP?' Faye asked over the phone, the day after their Brighton date.

'My life is like the M25 - fast and furious. I've no idea if we're a good match but I'm willing to find out. What about you?' he asked.

'I can't just dismiss you after one date and a thousand texts.'

'We've got a brain connection.'

'Feels like we've known each other for years. We've vomited our thoughts via text like shipping forecasts; every minutiae of our daily lives sent up into cyber space.'

'If you don't hear from me, assume I'm dead rather than not keen. I'll be flying on one of those 777's with the high probability of its fuel systems seizing up with ice.'

He could see a relationship developing and wondered where it might lead.

~

A FEW DATES later Darius suggested the Regal Picturehouse in Henley. The Mercedes snaked over the bridge and the inky waters of the Thames.

'I took my mum up here once for a picnic. She loved it sitting beside the Thames watching the boats and the ducks.' He suddenly felt a stab of guilt that he'd not found Kathleen yet.

He tried to stamp on his thoughts as they descended into the town but was consumed with tangled emotions playing in his head. Reaching the car park, he momentarily scrunched his eyes, gripping the steering wheel as emotions ran in circles round his head.

'You feel guilty, don't you?' Faye asked.

He sighed. Took the key from the ignition. 'Yeah, I do. I feel lots of things. Guilt. Sadness. Shame. But sending Kathleen away was her decision. The bloody priest was though. That black beetle that always loomed large in our lives. I think he was more responsible than she imagines, and she's been denying the writing on the wall for years. She can't ask herself the question. She can't work it out for herself. If my dad had been around when it all happened, I reckon things might have been different. And I think looking back Kathleen was missing our dad. She didn't get on with Mum. They were always arguing. There was a big clash between them. And the priest used that to his advantage. Bastard.'

'You seem to be coming to some conclusions. But don't assume. I can see that you're alluding to something he did... but you may not be right.' Faye didn't spell out the words.

∼

Faye

After the film they had a curry in a pub by the Thames. He tore a naan, took a swig of lager.

'Knat's piss.' He pulled a face in the direction of the waiter.

Faye savoured each mouthful of Korma. It was much creamier and nuttier than the 99p cartons of Korma or Masala Shayne used to serve up on a Friday evening on his messy dining room table, surrounded by washing hanging on racks to dry and piles of ordnance survey maps littering his filthy, threadbare carpet. Even the poppadum had the edge on the slightly chewy ones they sold on the end aisles of a value store.

He swapped his Cobra for a Kingfisher.

'So. This weekend. Is it your weekend with the kids? I can't keep up. Glad I'm not a single mother. Think I'd want to shoot myself.'

She sniggered. She found his comment both amusing and slightly insulting. 'They're with me. Sorry.' She wondered why she was apologising.

'You won't be able to compartmentalise your life forever.'

'It's convenient. For now.'

'I couldn't have handled all that single parent shit. All the tooing and froing.'

'Your own family is broken. Remember?' Faye said, watching him cram shards of broken poppadum into his mouth.

∼

Darius

He reached over and placed his hand over hers.

'You're a lovely earth mother.' Darius thought back to the previous week. An impromptu visit to Faye's flat with a gigantic chocolate egg wrapped in yellow ribbon to surprise her. Watching her spoon-feed a butternut squash mix from a pink plastic bowl into Chrissie's mouth that afternoon had stirred something in him. Was it a deep longing for the grandchild he knew he'd never have? He hadn't made a big deal of the visit, hadn't wanted it to be puffed up into some big important and awkward 'meet the family for the first time' occasion.

∼

Faye

Faye took a mouthful of korma. She remembered him visiting her flat bearing an early Easter egg: his faraway hooded eyes, hypnotic, rather like a dog communicating hunger to its owner following her round the kitchen. She couldn't work out what the look had meant.

'What are Sam's ambitions?'

'Fuck knows. He's wasting his life. Sometimes I'm ashamed to call him my son. I'd like to see him managing a team of hairdressers rather than cutting hair. If it wasn't for me, he'd be on his own. His mother is a waste of space and a liar.'

'What lies?'

'She let him down years back. She was meant to set aside some money for a world cruise. Jesus. You wouldn't believe it. I thought she'd booked it. She even let me pack. Sam and I went along with the whole thing. She let me book the taxi to the fucking airport. The taxi arrived and suddenly she's crying and out the big confession tumbles. She paid the deposit for the trip but couldn't afford to settle the remaining bill. Can you imagine the disappointment for Sam?'

Faye looked at the lump of naan on her plate.

They were quiet for several minutes as they ate, Faye digesting chicken and the horrors of his marriage.

'She also re-mortgaged the house behind my back to invest

in a Florida enterprise with her lover. Her lover was another dirty secret she kept to herself. The investments went tits up during the 2007 crash. That's why there's no equity in the house.'

'Blimey. You had no idea this was all going on?' Faye found it hard to grasp the idea of not being aware of what the other half was up to.

'When I found all the evidence for the Florida enterprise and confronted her all she did was flare up at me for weeks. And me? What do you imagine I was doing? Shitting bricks. The scale of the debts was so enormous. We'll be lucky if we come out with a few thou' when the house is finally sold.'

∼

AFTER THE CURRY and cinema Darius glided the car out of the car park.

'I'll show you the house. Nettlebed isn't far from here. It'll mean more if you see what I've lost. Silly ungrateful bitch treated me with utter contempt after everything that I gave her – the lifestyle, the beautiful home.'

They drove through the dark country lanes and soon they were in the village of Nettlebed, passing a pub called The White Hart where the windows were lit up and a gaggle of people were emerging. They turned left into Watlington Street. A few minutes later they parked the car in a pool of orange light.

'All the walks over the Chilterns used to keep my weight down. Now look at me. I'm a big fat blob,' he said, patting his belly and pulling a fag from a packet.

From his description she had expected grander housing but then she noticed a discreet driveway surrounded by tall foliage and straggly trees tucked in the corner a little way from the other houses.

They got out of the car and he led her a short way along a graveled drive until they reached a corner in full view of a primrose painted cottage which looked centuries old.

'Jesus. I haven't stopped paying the mortgage. And we're creeping about like a pair of burglars.'

'It's beautiful. I can't quite see the detail but is it wisteria and climbing roses around the windows? It reminds me a little of the TV historic drama 'Larkrise to Candleford.' Faye said.

'We had a local gardener twice a week. And someone to clean out the swimming pool and maintain the tennis court. It was too big to manage. I didn't have the time and she was basically too lazy. I found out she had given up paying all the workers. It was embarrassing. The man who cleaned the swimming pool was a nice guy, trying to earn a living like the rest of us. He became more than a cleaner. He was a friend and doing that to a friend is a real shitty thing to do.'

She was standing a little way off. He stepped onto the verge pushing a branch aside for a better view.

'Oh God,' he suddenly said. 'What's that little shit doing here? That's my son's brand new Corsa on the driveway. The car I've just bought him.'

'He's allowed to visit his mother.' Faye looked incredulous. 'He loves you both. Why would he take sides?' Faye started walking back to the car.

'I think she's away in Florida with her lover. Every now and again I have a peek at her Facebook. I saw a picture of the fucking geezer on the beach with her. Both of them grinning, both grossly overweight. That means Sam's staying in my house with that Rory guy he's seeing. Oh God, Faye. I can't take anymore.' His hands flew to his forehead as if the sky was crashing in around him.

'You need to accept who he is. He's happy, healthy. Those are the things that matter, not his sexuality.' Faye put a placatory hand on his arm.

'You're a sweet girl but you haven't a clue what I've been through.'

She prickled. He could be so condescending. She put her arms around him and kissed him. He needed to relax, was always so wound up. 'It's ok to be angry.'

'It's the idea of him doing... well you know. I can't erase the thought.'

'Well don't think about it then. You do have a choice.' She laughed, nudging his arm.

'How can I not?' he replied glumly.

They stopped talking and she let the question hang in the air as she looked again at the house, her eye tracing around the thatched roof and the neat red brick pathway leading to an archway of roses climbing around the front door. It looked such a peaceful place to live. If ever there was a place called heaven on earth this was it. A cherry blossom was in full bloom in the front garden and there were neat borders around the edges of the lawn.

It was as if Darius could read her thoughts. 'I created my own heaven here. And now Sam is destroying that. For so long my past and everything I went through when I was young - I won't tell you the gory details – it defined who I was. When I look back there are the ordinary memories, set in Kodak, sealed in albums and there are the trauma memories. The closed memories we all put in a box. For a long time, I couldn't see those memories. I knew they had happened, or was my mind playing tricks? I wasn't sure. It was a blur and there was no one to ask, because it was always the dirty secret. No one ever challenged the actions of the priest. Maybe I was unconsciously erasing it all. The past was the past. Except that it wasn't. It was affecting the present. Maybe it still does but it's become a part of who I am. I feel uneasy about Sam. Yes, I get defensive. I can't help it. What he's doing and what Rory is doing to him makes me angry.' He curled his hands into fists then pummelled his cheeks.

'Can't you get beyond that vision of the two of them in bed? Can't you just think about two people in a loving relationship?' she gently asked.

'No I fucking can't. Because it's not natural.' His voice was rising with the passion he felt.

'But it's natural for them. And that's what counts. Homosexuality has always existed. It's not going to go away. It's actually as natural as heterosexuality. It's just that many people don't look at it that way. They feel somehow threatened by it. She put her hand on his shoulder.

'I can see peace in this house. But there was a marriage breakdown here so it can't have been peaceful,' Faye said quietly.

'When we came here it was. Before we came here it existed in my mind as a safe mental place I could escape to. For years when I closed my eyes at night all I could see was the gnarled hand of the priest. I tried to sleep by creating a cottage and a meadow in my head. I added a swing, a stream to dabble my feet in, a place where I could talk to my past and in that meadow relief flowed out of me. But then it became real–– in the form of estate agent blurb. The meadow, the swing, the stream were real and exactly as I had imagined them to be. The tall grass, the wide expanse of blue sky, the buttercups, the daisies, the splash of Summer flowers. There were many days I spent just lying in that meadow, like a snow angel. The wider I stretched my legs and arms the freer I became, the stronger I became. I hadn't realised it was a healing journey.' Darius was pensive as he looked towards the house.

∼

DARIUS HELD her head with both hands, slipping his fingers through her hair, feeling its soft bounce for the first time as they stood in the beam of light streaming from the lamppost. Then he raised his lips and planted a simple kiss on her forehead and another on her nose. And soon they had found each other's lips. Her taste was sweet, her mouth deliciously moist, almost succulent.

Thoughts of Sam, the priest and the past momentarily melted away in a haze, the physical contact a relaxing aphrodisiac.

∼

Faye

Faye hadn't planned to kiss him. Was it pity or desire? As their lips met, he became a slobbering Labrador who had eaten the leftovers of his master's chicken vindaloo. His lips smacked clumsily against hers missing the target then edging round meeting once more. His tongue was a shy cave snake. He wasn't going to succumb to tongue hockey, even when her tongue courageously and boldly made encouraging gestures. Tiny ripples of confused pleasure travelled downwards. She slipped his jacket off, reaching up and began kissing his thickened neck all the time thinking that it was possibly the ugliest neck she'd ever kissed. And then she noticed *them* – a whole mass of huge unsightly black and brown moles like splashes of mud. She pulled away straightening his shirt, physically and dramatically recoiling.

'We better go. I need to get back for the babysitter.' She turned to the car.

∼

Darius

It was after midnight when Darius dialed Sam's number. This was about principles.

'I'm not going to stop seeing Rory. You need to get used to my sexuality. Back off Dad.'

'I wish you would give women a chance. You'd be so much happier being normal if you could only put your mind to it.'

'Get over it, Dad,' Sam shot.

When Darius came off the phone his head was in turmoil. He didn't like the thoughts he had swirling in the vortex of his mind as he remembered the bitter struggle with his own sexuality, during his teen years: the developing desire to hold a woman's breasts, his curiosity to explore a clitoris with his tongue, desires which merged and competed with the pleasant memory of blood coursing through his penis under the caress of the priest's hand. For a long time, when the abuse had ended, he longed for a hand to grip his penis but in his confused state he hadn't known whether it was a longing for a man's hand or a woman's hand. Blood pricked and thumped now in his head as he shuddered, revolted at how the memories of those sexual encounters in the vestry and toilets were still tinged with pleasure.

His son's homosexuality disturbed him in a deeply carnal and illogical way. Every time he thought about Sam in his new relationship with Rory all he could think about was the priest at the altar, many years before, pulling his trousers down. He had visions of his son in bed; images that wouldn't retreat.

Sometimes in his dreams Rory would appear with a mocking look on his face: a face that became an implement of torture. He'd never met Rory. he didn't want to meet him, and he certainly didn't want to acknowledge that this man made his son happy. What did Sam know about happiness? The more Darius dwelt, the more his troubled and blackened mind concluded that Sam had turned gay deliberately, as an act of pure vengeance, in defiance and as a reminder for all that he,

Darius had suffered years before. Deep down he knew this was illogical. But reason went out the window. He had told Faye how he felt but he now felt ashamed and exposed. If his thoughts were common knowledge to all, he would be condemned to the court of homophobia and in today's world that was not a pleasant place to be.

9
FAYE

April 2009

'Trevor used to grope me at the kitchen sink,' Faye teased.

'You're starting to turn me on. Naughty girl,' Darius said.

'But when I stopped wanting him, he bought a pink vibrator to use on himself.'

'Yuk. I don't feel so turned on now.' Darius sounded as if he'd just trodden in dog dirt.

She wasn't sure how they had ended up in Darius's bedroom naked. It was a tidy bedroom. She'd been expecting clothes to be strewn over a chair and socks to be dumped in the corner, dirty coffee cups on surfaces and screwed up balls of tissue littering the carpet. But the floor looked freshly hoovered and the surfaces clean. After the pit that Shayne had lived, in Faye was impressed.

The bathroom door creaked in the breeze. Dodgy hinges. An instant turn on, warming her below -the Pavlov Dog effect. She tried to ignore the door and its enticing creaks. Tonight ,she'd be getting the real thing. She'd ditched the huge knickers she called Rover and had donned a silky black pair of Ann

Summers, with red ribbon and matching bra. Just putting on this new set had made her feel alive again, a warm fizz shooting through her body.

There was something strangely horny and appealing about sleeping with a man who was much older, so much taller and basically unattractive. She felt like a prostitute and suddenly her mind had escaped into a brothel. She looked at the colony of mud splashed moles, the sagging belly, the sprouting nasal hair; his grey curls falling around his head and smelt the whiff of bad breath that never seemed to go away. She cast her eye down to his long wide legs – those of a shire horse.

Her head screamed. *What am I doing? How have I managed to press the 'disgust override' button to be standing here naked in front of him?* But her revulsion had become a curious turn on.

It had been a long time since she'd bedded a guy. Shayne had been the last. He had a seriously wide girth, a cock well hidden in a nasty baggy foreskin. Clumps of Gorgonzola clung in its folds. She shuddered at the memory and the pain of intercourse with such a well-endowed man.

Faye twirled her naked flesh as Darius lay on his bed gazing up at her, that faraway look in his eyes. He was wearing a tatty hearing aid beige towelling robe that had seen better days but at least covered his lower region. His belly, much bigger than she had imagined it would be, unclothed, protruding from the robe with not an ounce of shame. Faye wondered how it had grown so huge, for everywhere else he was slim.

She knew every guy loved her pert nipples, her small compact breasts and her peachy bottom. It was her saggy middle that let her down – the folds women called 'the mother's apron.' She held her breath pulling it in, but she could see Darius was looking at it. She suspected he longed for the smooth outline of a woman in her early thirties, whose body hadn't been wrecked by the childbirth of twins, stretched and pulled and twisted in all directions, leaving its marks and sags.

The Catholic Woman's Dying Wish

Sometimes she felt like she'd fulfilled her purpose, as far as men were concerned. She was too old for more kids, had 3 already and certainly wouldn't entertain more.

A gentle breeze fluttered the curtains and church bells rang in the distance.

'Get over here,' he thumped the bed.

Climbing onto the bed, she dreaded what she'd find under his robe. He'd had referred to it as the anaconda. Her friends had warned her – tall man, big dick. Penetration was going to be painful, *what am I doing?*

He looked so old. But he was old. Fourteen years older. In a strange and dirty way this was a turn on, and she started to feel warm below, sordid thoughts creeping into her head. She was the young mistress, he the grandfather, a strange fantasy. Leaning closer she saw how scraggy and turkey like his neck was and saw mottled liver spots across his hands. His blue eyes glittered and flickered over her nipples. Soon their bodies were entwined, his belly wobbling and distended against hers and his wiry chest hair tickling her nipples as they embraced in slobbery kissing.

She wondered where he kept the condoms. The way he had referred to it as an anaconda made her imagine it might be too big for a standard sized condom. When he failed to produce one, embarrassed she asked if he had any.

'I don't think I've got any. Not used one in years.' The way he said it he was turning the condom into a quaint antiquity - an ancient relic found under glass at the British Museum. He glanced towards his bedside drawer making no effort pull any drawers. 'You'll be okay. I'll explore you with my tongue.' He laughed.

Minutes later she was staring at the stained ceiling, charting rivers in the cracks, while his tongue made sloshing, unappealing noises down below, like a toddler slurping a bright red Slush Puppy drink. What was it with men? She'd not met a single man who could be creative with his tongue, who knew where to hit the jackpot. It wasn't about big gulping licks to an ice cream, it was about curving and flicking and twisting the tongue into the shape of a cigar. It was about an artist making careful actions with a paint brush.

The sooner it was over the better, but she had no intention of doing a 'When Harry Met Sally' full scale fake. She'd have to just lie there and wait for him to come up for air or his tongue to go numb and drop off. At least she was in control. If his technique had been good, she'd have been tempted to forget the condoms and whizz down to the chemist first thing Monday, to buy a £22 morning after pill – an expensive shag.

It seemed to go on forever. Most men got bored if they bothered at all. Most were desperate just to plunge in. Finally over, Faye knew she'd have to match the time otherwise it would look selfish. She hoped he wouldn't make her gag. Reluctantly she pulled his towelling robe off. His chest was the hairiest she'd ever seen. She had never made love to a man with a hairy chest, let alone one with grey hair. His belly looked almost comical when compared with his narrow hips and trunk legs and painfully thin arms. And then her eyes moved to the mass of grey hair around his groin. For a few seconds she thought about how different the hair was to the wiry, grey hair of his chest.

She couldn't see anything, tried to hide her alarm. Where was it? His dick? Should be hard, rod-like and reach his belly button. There was nothing - just a mass of hair. Like a wild pig foraging in the undergrowth for truffles--where was it? For one awful moment Faye wondered if he wasn't actually a man at all or whether it had been surgically removed and he hadn't told her. She stroked his belly, amused at the way it wobbled from side to side. Her hand moved towards the mass of soft hair. It was like delving into a bird's nest, not knowing what you might find, scared of damaging the delicate eggs. Faye fumbled through his bush, almost *afraid* of what she might find.

This was one of those mega disappointing moments, when your whole new relationship's future flashes before you. And the turning point came when she noticed it, coiled beneath the hair – something so small, so shrivelled, if she had been a Martian just arriving from space, she really wouldn't have had the foggiest idea what it was.

It felt and looked pretty much like a squelchy button mushroom – the type you find in tin cans drenched in brine. His balls were no bigger than tiny marbles wrapped in flesh. *It* wasn't moving and looked like it had been beaten to death. She looked at the button mushroom wondering what it would be like in her mouth. A tiny droplet trickled from its head and imagined a slippery fish in her mouth.

And then she thought of the 'Cock Trump' cards played at Ann Summers parties. Her mind scanned through the encyclopedia of cock types. This wasn't the Joystick or the Darth Vada. It wasn't even the Twinkie or the Witchetty Grub or even the Baby Carrot. This was the Weener – the card that lost you the game. In stamina, girth size and cleanliness this was a big loser way off the Richter Scale of cocks. For the first time in her adult life she could suddenly see the appeal of an Ann Summers' Rampant Rabbit; despite the £49 price tag.

What the hell was she supposed to do with it?

10

DARIUS
APRIL 2009

Darius wanted to spend time getting to know Faye and so the invite to stay over for the weekend was a natural progression of their relationship. But was he drained? He'd returned from a business trip to Vancouver the day before to a messy house. Faye had mentioned she liked a decent cup of coffee so he'd dashed over to Henley to pick up the very best in De Longhi bean to cup professional style coffee machines. At £1200 it wasn't the most expensive kitchen gadget he'd ever bought, but it looked great on the work top and the smell wafting up the stairs first thing in the morning was bound to put her in the right mood for some hard thrusting. But that of course would very much depend upon his little friend down below.

Things had been so different a few years back when the hydraulics worked. If only he could return to those virulent days when his cock performed to order. The work trips away, free to behave as he'd wanted sauntering into a brothel, making his choice from a selection of women and twenty minutes later pulling his trousers back on, feeling slightly ashamed and dirty but returning to the hotel bar to chat up a stray lass over a drink or two, ending up in bed together. Sex had been so easy. But now? He couldn't work out when and why things had changed. Maybe this was his punishment for his appalling marital behaviour. But he still had hope that 'normal service' would resume. Faye was young and pretty but if things weren't any better, he'd call in the 'engineers' to see what they could offer.

Faye's eyes and body begged – leaning over the bed her pert erect nipples hovering over him, her swollen distended belly drooping towards her bushy mound. Her pubic mound was like a helicopter pad. He studied her bush. She was a trim not a shave all type, but the trim was haphazard. He slipped his hand inside his robe pretending to massage the anaconda. He reached for her red angry nipples, flicking one and taking the other in his mouth.

'Have you got some condoms?'

His fingers were now inside her feeling the wetness, thick and clear, like fresh egg white from a broken shell; forming great peaks, baked as delicious meringues. He wanted, in that moment, to push her down, climb inside her and come for England.

Condoms. What the fuck? Putting a condom on a limp dick was like trying to put up a tent in the pouring rain. It was on the tip of his tongue to say you didn't worry about condoms last time you did it, you dirty slut. Look what you produced that time? He held off, slightly irritated that she was happy to shag Mr. Neanderthal Man Shayne without a condom but not him.

'The anaconda would like to explore inside but that's ok there are other things we can do.' He licked his lips suggestively and flicked his tongue, his fingers rubbing her bloated vaginal lips. She'd soften. With a fanny that moist and a tongue that could weave magic how could she resist the anaconda? She was bound to succumb. If it mattered that much, she'd be on the pill. She'd have whisked herself down to the doctor days ago. Why were women so unprepared?

He spread her legs and began to explore with his tongue. She lay motionless, her body rigid, no sign of enjoyment came. It tasted good – sweet. There were none of the unpleasant odours he'd encountered with the ex. That had been as rank as Billingsgate Market. It was no wonder that he'd strayed. He hadn't enjoyed dipping his wick in, let alone his tongue. But this was good.

And then she reached up and untied his robe. She looked desperate for it. Perhaps he'd been wrong. Maybe his tongue had fired her. He looked down wishing beyond all hope that he could be as stiff as a piece of Brighton rock. It was not to be. His cock lay curled and lifeless. He might as well be exposing himself in the centre of Oxford Street's Marks and Spencer on a Saturday afternoon for the embarrassment he felt.

At that moment it felt like he was sitting down to a plate of the most delicious food in the best restaurant in town with raging hunger like there was no tomorrow but then picking up the knife and fork, moving them towards his mouth but realising at the last moment that he had no mouth.

This was unbearable. He couldn't tell her what it was like: the pain that thumped through his head, never going away and always the same problem - the first encounter with someone new – a fear that took hold. She had taken the lead. Touched him without warning. And in those seconds her hand became *his* hand. *The priest's hand.* Back on his groin. The gnarled, creeping hand with the cold tips. It wasn't her fault. If he had explained, she would have felt awkward and so would he. His past and what had happened was the biggest killer of any sexual encounter. Next time he would have to be quicker. Take the lead. Take her hand and guide it down. It would get easier––he was certain of that. He hoped she was going to stay quiet and not pick up on the issues he faced. He didn't need therapy. She was gently moving her hand around, down to the balls, fondling his shriveled penis - which refused to pay any attention whatsoever. At that point he wished he had a baseball bat because he would have wacked it, if it was detached from his body like a wounded animal in the road that you needed to put out of its misery.

She stopped. She had full marks for trying. She said nothing. Nothing that would make him feel any smaller than he already felt. But part of him felt irritated that she had ignored the issue that lay between them, that prevented them from making love. He imagined her working on a corpse. Would she silently work away hoping it would stiffen?

And then from nowhere he started to laugh, a laughter which rose from his belly.

'Stand up, stand up for Jesus,' he sang, coughing and spluttering between verses. 'This cock is well and truly beyond its sell by date. I'm old, I'm knackered.'

11

FAYE

May 2009

DARIUS HAD PERSUADED Faye to go to Ireland with him to visit the Magdalene Laundry where Kathleen had lived in the 70s. It was their first weekend away together. Hardly glamorous but having never been to Ireland, she was excited. She had always imagined Ireland to be a dark and poor country where it rained endlessly and everyone lived on potatoes and pottage. The plane moved across the dark blue of the North Sea green fields and the occasional farm dotted the landscape under a mantle of cloud crawling across the sky. Leaving the plane, the wind and drizzle slapped her face.

∼

AFTER DRIVING for miles down windy country lanes, flanked by dry stone walls and the occasional farmhouse, they came to a long driveway fronted by two property developer's boards. They got out of the car breathing in the country air and for a few moments stood admiring the shimmering emerald landscape which they imagined was bleak and foreboding in the depths of winter. White and grey billowy clouds scudded across the sky, the light on the land changing the shades of green across every valley and every hill. Birdsong from a nearby copse penetrated the silence.

'What an incredible achievement these stone walls are. Must be centuries old.'

Darius looked up at the sky feeling the first drop of rain. 'It would have been impossible for Kathleen to leave. The women were prisoners out here with nowhere to escape to. The land stretches for miles. She wouldn't have survived. And no money either. The cows look well fed and happy. It's a wilderness out here and with only a few farms in sight they would have tracked her down.'

'What are you saying?' She frowned at him.

'My guess is that she stayed a few years, maybe even until it closed down in the 90s. Even if she left of her own free will, where on earth would she go? You can't just walk into a job?'

'She could have ended up in a brothel in Dublin. I'm sure many did,' she said.

'But when it finally closed maybe she was transferred to a convent. I've rung every convent in the entire country Faye. You forget that. I spent two days making phone calls.'

They stood looking at the view for several minutes against the bite of the icy breeze. In the distance Faye could see sheep.

'Look. A black sheep. Not often you see one.'

'I think it's an omen. My mum always said Kathleen was the black sheep of the family. Everyone has one. I wonder who your black sheep will be. Time will tell. There's always a faller. At some point.'

They crossed the road and began the walk up the long

avenue and although the boards at the entrance indicated the property developers had purchased the house, there was no evidence of any building work going on. Tall conifers lined the route, and a dense wood flanked the road on one side. They began to sing a song they'd learned from listening to *You Tube*. It was by Patrick Dwyer and was about the Magdalenes.

'I'm not a fallen woman,
I only fell from hunger
I never fell from grace
It's a national disgrace
The state never protected me...'

As THEY SANG, crows began to rise from the conifers whirling like charred paper from a bonfire, adding to the eerie atmosphere around them.

To one side there was a row of oaks, their trunks set deep as ancient teeth along the high bank, vast, elephantine and grotesque.

Several straggly yews led the way as the road swept round and then they glimpsed their first view of the remains of the house – 'The Weeping Lady' – which had clearly suffered a devastating fire. It was a vast and impressive red brick and sandstone Italianate style house, fronted by sandstone canted bays through each floor, and along the flat roofing were imposing statutes of Jesus holding a lamb and the Virgin Mary.

They stopped and took in the view with the haunting cry of crows behind them, which sounded almost like the cry of babies and Faye commented that the building looked like an exclusive public school.

'Fucking nuns. Evil bitches they were. Back in Liverpool when I was growing up the nuns were harsh and aggressive. They were worse than the priests. Every child made sure they didn't get into trouble with a nun. I think they saw taking the veil as some romantic act. It was about giving their hearts, their minds and their souls to Christ and maybe that felt romantic,' Darius mused. 'But somewhere along the way they changed. But why?'

'The girls were incarcerated behind these walls.' Faye was studying the building as they continued walking. 'But the nuns were incarcerated too. They were groomed by the church, trained and were part of some sort of conspiracy. They were taught to shed blood the way Christ had done. To beat human failings from someone to make them purer. It became symbolic. It's a dangerous doctrine if you take it to the extreme. Shedding blood, doing penance made them holier, drew them closer to God. Maybe that's what they were hoping to achieve in bringing pregnant girls here.'

'You mean Jesus suffered so everyone else had to suffer. Those poor girls.'

'Something like that,' Darius replied.

'And what about the priests? What was their part in the Church?' She asked turning to face him.

Darius shuddered. Suddenly he could see the priest's reptilian eyes in his mind. He stopped walking, couldn't focus.

'He was God's representative on earth. His body was sanctified so I guess whatever he did, wasn't treated as sin. That's why I could never tell my mum what had happened to me. She wouldn't have believed. It was blasphemy to accuse the priest of any wrong doing. The entire religious structure was based on lies and deception. They were all living in a hypocritical cloak of righteousness. Everyone set up as spies to report on sin. You couldn't trust anyone. The church was great at brainwashing techniques. Where the fuck does it say in the Scriptures that you have to confess your sins to a man? And my guess is....'

'What are you saying Darius?'

'I think the priest raped Kathleen. I think that's why she

never came home. Why would she want to risk facing her abuser? Look in her mother's eyes and lie to her?'

'You don't know. You might never know the truth.'

'Believe me, don't you think I know that? Why do you think as an adult I've never come forward to name and shame that bastard? Because I'd be up against the power of the Church hierarchy.' He walked ahead.

∼

THEY WALKED in silence for a time, letting the air between them clear.

'I don't know what I'm hoping to find inside the wreck. I feel like an investigator boarding the sunken Titanic. I haven't come to salvage silver chalices or look for any relics,' Darius said, breaking the silence.

'What *have* we come for?' she asked.

'I don't know Faye. Maybe just to see where she lived. I could take some pictures, but I think it would make Mum feel even sadder. It's a wreck, overgrown, ready for demolition.'

'So why hasn't it been demolished yet?'

'House prices over here have taken quite a tumbling. The property crash across Ireland has been one of the most severe ever experienced by a modern economy. I'm guessing property developers bought with a view to demolishing and building new homes, but their project has been suspended. I'm not sure we'll find anything inside, but we can look.'

'Is it safe to go inside?'

'Probably not, but we've come this far.'

By now they were standing at the bottom of a series of broken steps. Mature weeds had forced their way between the cracks in the paving and black bryony laced its way down the steps like ribbons at a festival. Aquilegia in full bloom displaying purple flowers competed with bindweed twisting and choking and covering every plant in sight in one dramatic weed carnival.

Clearly the garden had been left in this state of neglect for many years but the sense of doom and oppression that had always existed, Faye could see. The house was fighting to live on.

'Despite the fire you can see it was never a happy house. Who knows what evil happened within these walls. It gives me the creeps. The bars on the windows... were they to stop the girls escaping?' Faye asked.

'Possibly. What is a happy house? I wouldn't say my home was a happy one. It was full of lies and secrets and suppressed emotions. We lived under the veil of the Catholic Church. Everyone trying to do the right thing by the priest.'

'People make a home. Despite everything, I think Kathleen probably had friends here, as well as enemies. Friendship might not have been encouraged. It may have been stamped on, but you don't need words or hugs to make a friendship. Simply sharing the struggle, day to day, was enough to create a lasting bond. In their hearts they will never forget that friendship. They will never forget what they went through *together*. They were sisters in a struggle for basic humanity.' Faye was pulling at weeds as she spoke, tearing leaves into shreds.

'What a wonderful tree.' Darius had stopped and was curling a tooth pointed leaf in his hand. 'A strawberry tree. Shame we've come at this time of year. It's beautiful in the autumn.'

'My friend Katie used to talk about strawberry trees. She said they grew only in certain parts of Ireland. I think she used to come over here on holiday or something. She might even have lived here. I'm not sure. I think it was her that said they get their name from the Roman Pliny The Elder. 'Unedo.' It means eat only once. Whether he meant eat it only once because it's a luxury and to be savoured or he only ate it once because it was tasteless. The berries taste of figs not strawberries. Weird.'

'You talk a lot about Katie. She must be a good friend.'

'Yeah. She's the one who looks after Tim when I do night shifts. She never talks much about her past. I just pick up bits and pieces but she knows a lot about Ireland and the plants here.'

'I don't like the idea of you working nights.'

Ignoring the DO NOT ENTER, TRESPASSERS KEEP OUT signage they picked their way through bramble and broken bricks to a porch way and blackened front door. A broken brass bell lay on the ground. Glancing down at the door knocker they expected it to be locked but to their surprise nothing barred their entry.

'I can imagine our Kathleen peering into that knocker to check her makeup. She was quite vain.'

'It's too rusty to use as a mirror.'

'Back then I'm sure it gleamed.'

Inside a large entrance hall, the air was dank and musty. Flaking, bubbled magnolia paintwork - like the bark of a silver birch - clumps of black mould, sooty smears and graffiti adorned the walls on either side of a long corridor leading to a staircase. The staircase had escaped the ravage of fire. Neither of them spoke, consumed by their own mental images of long ago when the silence would have been broken only by the swish of the nun's habit and the clack of rosary beads.

They stopped at the foot of the staircase and looked up.

'It might collapse if we go up.'

'We've come this far.' Darius reminded Faye. 'One at a time.'

Darius began the ascent, slowly, two steps at a time, pausing for creaks, waiting until he felt it was safe to continue, with Faye following when he'd reached the top.

They arrived in a large empty room at the far end of a corridor. The window panes were broken, their wooden frames in splintered pieces on the window ledge. Across the floor lay charred debris, an old bath and sink and parts of a broken metal bed frame.

'Look at the wallpaper.' Faye gasped, walking over to pull a piece of orange and brown geometric design from the wall. This reminds me of my childhood. Hideous. It's 1970s. It was possibly freshly decorated around the time she arrived.'

'So maybe it looked welcoming. Is that what you're saying? I don't fucking think so.' Darius snorted.

'I'm just trying to hold onto any positives,' Faye said looking wounded.

They walked around the room, reading the graffiti, examining the charred remains that littered the floor in the hope that the debris contained clues–– clues about the life that Kathleen had led and where she might now be. Faye was at one end of the room. She picked up a window frame lying on the floor and Darius was rooted to the doorway, hesitant to enter the room.

Dust and ash swirled as Faye moved the frame and then she gasped. Froze to the spot.

'Shit.' She called over. Her heart was suddenly thumping.

Darius stepped over the debris, joining her at the end of the room to look at what she'd found.

Faye was holding a small handmade stuffed toy that looked like a gingerbread man. Although its filthy fabric was still intact it was a design she recognised and had seen before. Its eyes were made from black buttons and its mouth from pink felt.

'Oh fuck.' Darius put his hands to his face, his heart thudding in his chest.

They both stared at each other.

'That belongs to Kathleen. She made it when she was about ten. She loved sewing.' Darius smiled, tears forming in his pale eyes.

'I thought their belongings were taken when they got here.

They were given new clothes, new names. But then maybe things had changed by the mid 70s.' Faye was turning the toy over as if hoping to find a signature.

'It's made me go cold to think that something of hers has remained here all this time. It could be a lead.'

'Yes, it could be a lead because I'll tell you this Darius. I've seen this toy before. Tim has one exactly the same.' She stared at him.

'Maybe it's a standard pattern, standard fabric,' he said dismissively.

'No. You're not listening to me.' She put her hand on his shoulder. Her face was burning, tears pricking.

'I'm telling you that Tim has one that's identical. The same person made it. I know that with absolute certainty. The stitching is exactly the same. The way the felt mouth has been cut. It bears the mark of the same craftswoman. I'm absolutely convinced. What if I know Kathleen? What if I've met her?' Faye was spooked by the thought.

'Who gave the toy to Tim?' Darius didn't look so convinced.

'I don't know. When he was born he was given lots of cuddly toys. It could have been anyone and maybe someone bought it from a handmade craft shop.'

'Does he still have the toy?' The wheels inside Darius' head were whirling.

'I've not seen it around in ages. I'm always taking stuff to the charity shop. I could have got rid of it long ago. Or it may be in the loft.' Faye's eyes misted over as she lapsed into thought. She would search the house, top to bottom on her return. She had to find it. This was a mystery that needed solving.

Tucking the soft toy into her pocket they headed back downstairs - glancing into rooms along the corridor - searching for a main office containing, they hoped, a filing cabinet.

'In here,' Darius called. 'Looks like the office and bloody hell we could be in luck. There's an old metal filing cabinet.'

By the time Faye reached the room, Darius was yanking at the filing cabinet.

'It won't fucking open.'

'Maybe we could carry it away. Go to a hardware job and buy some tools to smash it.'

'Do you have a brain?'

Faye shrugged. 'Just an idea.'

Darius gave one final hard tug and the drawer came free, sending him crashing backward onto the filthy floor. Faye rushed over to help him up. He dusted himself down then peered inside the drawer.

'Fantastic. This is exactly what we're looking for,' he said, picking up a dirty ledger, but when he opened it, the fine pages fell away from the spine, swirling in all directions like a flock of seagulls. Faye hurried to gather them up.

'Hopeless,' she said.

Darius turned to the window, looking defeated. They didn't say anything for a time.

'The writing was illegible, slanted. Even if it was intact, I don't think we would have been able to read it,' Faye said breaking the silence.

'That's it then. Where the hell do we go from here?' Darius kicked is foot against the filing cabinet, feeling the frustration and futility of the search.

The silence around them was suddenly broken by shouting.

'I know you're in there. Come out. It's not safe.' A door creaked.

'Shit. We could get into trouble for ignoring the signs.'

A gnarled hand appeared around the edge of the door and then an old man's weathered face came into view. They immediately stood up, joining him at the door to explain everything and apologise for trespassing.

Out in the open, Darius brushed his clothes and Faye smiled apologetically at the man who said he used to be a gardener at the property before the house was sold off. He pointed to a nearby cottage where he'd lived for many years with his wife, taking it upon himself to watch over the derelict house until demolition work began and the place was properly secured from trespassers.

'What happened to the women when the place was sold off? Where did they go?' Faye asked him.

'There weren't many living here by the time it closed in 1990. Some were lucky. They went home. I think that was rare though. Some went to live in convents across Ireland.' He was leaning now against his fork.

'I've already contacted the convents. But if she used her new name that's why I can't find any trace of her.' Darius said turning to Faye.

'A few escaped. That I do know. Many of the laundries had high walls and tall hedging but not this one. I think the nuns took the attitude that where would they go and of course they didn't have any money. This place is surrounded by miles of countryside,' Faye said, looking towards the hills in the distance. 'It's miles away from Dublin or any town for that matter.'

'Vehicles coming into and out of the laundry.' The man explained that there had been rumours about women leaving in vans.

'Logically that would make sense,' Darius said.

'They inspected every van before it left. Doubtful, but who knows,' The man added.

'What about down in the village?' Faye asked.

'If you can call it a village. There's only a pub and a post office, a couple of houses. I think a few women may have worked at the pub after the house closed,' he told them, pointing in the direction of the village.

'That's our next port of call then, my sweet,' Darius said, his eyebrows raised to Faye.

The Catholic Woman's Dying Wish

THE GREEN SHAMROCK in the nearby village of Tontinp was a beamed, low ceilinged pub that looked several centuries old and stood at a crossroads a short way along the single track, heading to the west of *The Weeping Lady*. After the house, the pleasant smell of potato and leek broth, the tang of ale and the chatter of locals was a welcome respite from the emotional hit of what they had just been through. Darius ordered drinks and asked for the menu. As he waited to be served at the bar, the old barman frowned and asked where they were from.

'We don't get many travellers in these parts, but lately we've had a few property developers in here from the big house up the road. But that's all on hold for the moment.'

'Do you know much about the laundry? I'm trying to track down my sister who was sent there in the mid 70s. We've come over from England. It's my mother's dying wish to find her.'

'Oh Lord. All the way from England. It was a closed community. We didn't have much to do with them except that...'

'Yes?'

'Oii don't want to give you hope but...'

'Go on,' Darius coaxed.

'Years ago, several of the women escaped and oii hid them in the attic for a couple of days.'

'Really? What did they look like?'

'Oh, now you're asking. Oii can't remember that, but oi helped them escape to Wales to work for a friend of mine who runs a hotel near Conwy. Oii thought they'd be safe over there. Over time the nuns lost their hold over their girls. Oii helped quite a few get jobs at my friend's hotel in North Wales. They were cheap labour you see.'

'Do you remember exactly when this was? And anything at all about the women?'

The barman thought for several minutes while Darius took

a sip of his drink and glanced over at Faye who was scanning the menu. The barman served other customers then returned to Darius with a grave look on his face.

'If my memory serves me correctly it was the winter of 1975 or even early 1976. Two of the women oii think had recently had babies. One baby had died in childbirth and the other was adopted by Americans. The babies were born out of wedlock. You're aware of that?'

'This hotel in Wales. What's the name? Does it still exist?' Darius asked.

12

DARIUS

May 2009

For Darius the whole relationship with Faye hinged on his unreliable cock and the sexual hang-ups that never went away. He'd call in the engineers, fight the problem with chemical warfare. Then he'd take her away on a romantic weekend to the Brodwin Hall Hotel in North Wales where some women had allegedly ended up working following their escape from the laundry. He didn't imagine for one moment that Kathleen would still be working there after all these years, but they might be able to pick up some leads. Somebody was bound to know something. He looked at the website of the hotel and was amazed to see what a stunning property it was. It looked like a converted castle but had been considerably extended and the new section looked Victorian, rather like an old workhouse complete with Florentine towers. The scenery looked stunning.

He'd ply Faye with chilled champagne from a bucket and they'd swallow lemon drenched oysters. He'd book a room with a four- poster bed and a massive sunken bath. He'd feed her with good food, good company and quality spunk and maybe catch a glimpse of Liverpool playing on the Saturday afternoon if Faye allowed him to. It sounded like a Tory party initiative. It felt as if they had so much to see and do to make up for lost time and all the wasted years spent in lousy marriages.

He emailed his bucket list of places he wanted to visit with her.

Subject: My Bucket List:

1. Dubai. Huge potential there to expand the doughnut industry.
2. Vancouver. Doughnut capital of the world.
3. Australia. Few of my cousins live there.
4. Belfast to pay tribute to my dad.
5. Liverpool to show you my old haunts.
6. Weekend in Marrakesh. You'll hate the toilets though. You end up shitting everywhere.
7. Japan. You'll love the toilets – the famous arse washing, blow drying Toto.
8. Manchester Science Museum – real sewers that smell.
9. Butlins just for the hell of it.

AND SHE EMAILED her bucket list.

Subject: My Bucket List:

1. New England in the Fall.
2. Memphis to see Elvis' Gracelands. (Tacky I know)
3. A cruise to Alaska. (Did you like baked Alaska as a kid btw?)
4. India.
5. Macchu Pichu. (My aunt went there).
6. Dubai. (Croydon in the sun?)
7. Belfast. (To see the graffiti on the side of houses in the Falls' area).
8. A hotel castle in North Wales.

9. Anywhere on a cruise as long as we don't play bingo and enter knobbly knee contests.

10. Not Butlins or Pontins or Centre Parc.

They'd work through those lists. They had all the time in the world.

What he needed, Darius mused was a Fison's Gro bag for his limp cock. But joking aside he decided that something needed to be done. He went to see a doctor in a private clinic in Slough. Having had a heart attack he suspected that Viagra interacted in a deadly way with some heart medicines and he was told he couldn't have a testosterone jab with the medication he was on. This was all very frustrating. A simple jab in the bottom; a slow release hormone - a bit like Depo Provera for dumb girls who couldn't remember to take the pill – would have been simpler, less messy. He was all too aware that erectile dysfunction was often a symptom of cardiovascular disease; the 'canary in the trousers' but in his case the problems were also linked to the sexual abuse of his youth.

He wasn't going to discuss all this with the doctor though. He couldn't bear the idea of discussing -with a grown man or anyone else for that matter - what had happened to him as a young boy. That would have been the ultimate in humiliation. Sitting in the waiting room he made up his mind to ask for Alprostadil penile injections – but not the suppositories because they were placed into the tip of the penis; a truly nasty thought. He shuddered at the thought of using a needle to inject into his penis but he'd heard it was a very fine one. Building his nerves while waiting, flicking through copies of Home and Garden magazine, part of him wondered whether if it was all worth this effort. For the first time in his life sex seemed too much trouble. But when he thought of Faye's beautiful slender body, the curves, the smoothness of her soft skin he knew he wanted to devour her.

He left the surgery - having listened to the doctor's reassurances - and hoped the magic cure he'd been prescribed would transform him from an old git into an Adonis. He was looking forward to the return of the early morning hard on. In a couple of weeks he'd be a new man. His head was now full of visions of Faye's naked body, her wetness and her pert nipples. They'd hug and kiss and share a brain connection, sparking each other off with new thoughts, ideas.

He knew his problems were complicated and stemmed from the heart attack but his head was also filled with visions from the past. It hadn't put Faye off. For years he had tried to erase those jagged memories by bedding as many women as he could. Prostitutes had helped purge his soul and confirm his sexuality. There had been so many women - all used as toilets; money handed over, receptacles to wank into, then flies up and away; the scuttle of shame. But just at the point he thought he might cum with Faye, the memories of his choir boy days - that he'd tried so hard to suppress for so long, with the help of prostitutes and porn– were returning as he dug into Kathleen's past; wondering what had happened to her.

He knew there were no guarantees. And deep down he knew he couldn't reverse the body's decline. It had begun. This wasn't like exchanging a clapped out car for a sports car.

13

FAYE

May 2009

The chauffeur-driven Mercedes meandered its way down a palatial drive, took a final corner, sweeping past a cluster of tall emerald evergreens. A graceful mist swirled lightly between the trees like a veil hanging in anticipation and reminding her all at once of love; how it crept up slowly and ensnarled. And then she saw it. The grade 1 listed house–– currently owned by the National Trust it was used as a hotel. It had magnificent views over Pydew mountain and the medieval castle at Conwy and deep blue lakes. The internet had described it as a 'lost Eden': one of the finest most imposing baronial mansions in Wales - a mix of castle and mansion and the grandest hotel in Wales. Faye's eyes traced the outline of towers and turrets, porticos and crow stepped gables. It was framed by heath-clad, snow-capped mountains, grand and majestic - like an oil painting in a gallery. It had possibly been built as a watch tower for Conwy Castle the hotel's website informed.

'You've transported me to the world of celebrities. We always went on a Sun newspaper £10 deal to Pontins or Butlins when I was with Shayne. The kids sardined along the back seat of his Fiat Panda. I can remember the wafer-thin mattresses and plug in wall heaters and queues at the food court. Traipsing round carousels in pouring rain with overweight parents, dressed in tracksuits, garnished in tattoos screaming at their children who always seemed to be called Chelsea or Ryan. Swayne's such a twat... one of his hobbies is bidding on ebay for Butlin's badges.' She rubbed his arm. He reached over and kissed her ear.

'There'll be many more weekends like this. Champagne, fine food, stiff cock.'

And then Darius noticed Faye's eyes descending into a misty sadness.

'What's the matter?' he asked.

'Let's just remember what brought us here. Kathleen didn't feel like a celebrity. She was here to work; a fallen woman, cut adrift by her family with nowhere else to go. Knowing her plight I feel guilty that we'll enjoy the weekend here. We're privileged. Blessed I suppose. She came here to serve others and maybe worked long hours for a pittance, who knows? To think that all the time I was leading a normal childhood, reading Jackie Magazine, dancing to The Police and YMCA and watching Dallas and Upstairs and Downstairs while she was scraping a living in the kitchen here, maybe working 12 hour days.'

'Get the visions of Butlins and Pontins out of your head and enjoy the treat,' he said cheerily.

'Aside from thinking constantly about Kathleen I can't stop thinking about something my brother Steve said when I asked him to have the kids this weekend. It was quite upsetting.'

'What did he say?' Darius looked in alarm.

'Off for a dirty weekend with your new lover? When are you planning the next little bastard?'

'The man's a cunt.' Darius spat. 'Relax. We don't get weekends like this very often.'

They waited for the chauffeur to take their bags to the concierge. Darius kissed her ear and ran his hand through her hair, sweeping her into an embrace.

'Love you.'

'Love you too.' She studied his face. He wasn't good looking but had an alluring charisma and a sense of power and authority that appealed to her   the charisma of distinguished men like John Humphreys and Robert Redford.

A four-poster bed with cream sheets in a sumptuous antique-filled room awaited as they climbed the stairs which looked down upon a row of welly boots for the guests to wander around the vast estate.

'My feral mum.' Darius leaned over her shoulder.

She gasped. 'The size of this bathroom. It's bigger than my lounge.

'I don't do down-market. Are you interested in something else that's getting rather big?' Darius said in a soothing voice.

'Wow. Look at these soft white towels neatly folded like delicate sandwiches at a funeral.' Faye ignored him.

She held one to her cheek feeling its softness. He slipped his hands into her bra, cupping her breasts.

Still ignoring him, she said, 'Molton Brown shampoo bottles. Wow! They're really expensive. Nice gold taps. And the bath. Crikey.' His hands were still firmly clamped.

'We could sit in it together, accommodating all our middle-aged wobbly bits.'

She looked at them both in the mirror. His hands were working round her nipples. His eyes were faraway, hypnotic. A fizz of excitement shot up and down her body. Within minutes she burned with desire for him. Something was different this time.

Soon he was thrusting inside her. But all she could feel was his crushing weight on top of her pressing against her ribs, her swollen stomach and the taste of burning acid rising like fire in her throat, his clammy skin sticking to hers, wiry chest hair tickling. She couldn't feel the friction of him moving up and down, that tight sensation of pulling and the tip penetrating nerve endings. Waves of disappointment crashed around her. She was too old in the tooth to fake. When it was real, it was raw and feral. She became a Pentecostal church goer speaking in tongues. When it was disappointing, she told herself it was just the icing on the cake. This was hard work for him. She had to be patient, give it time.

~

THE FOLLOWING morning they ate a huge feast for breakfast of thick creamy porridge with a knob of butter on top, fresh slithers of salmon and poached eggs with flecks of pepper and coffee...served by a wild looking Scotsman in a kilt and a lady who looked like she belonged to the Adams family. Faye was feeling blissfully happy.

After making love for a second time, they sipped coffee in the morning room, where newspapers were spread across a large oak coffee table and where she posed in a rather ornate gilt chair resembling the throne of a queen for a photograph. The photo would be the Welsh collection. And in the months to come there would be the Florence collection, the Paris collection, the Salzburg collection, the Istanbul collection.

They descended the tiered lawn to rare box hedges filled with sweet-scented herbs, a rockery and several lily pad ponds.

'Look this way,' Darius called from a short way off, breaking her daydreams with the snap of his Nikon. He neatly framed her head with its tumbling curls, under the rain hat she was never without and her pastel pink mac contrasting against the dark mountains.

'I feel like Princess Di and Prince Charles in the Highlands posing for their engagements photos. Where's ya kilt?' Faye chuckled.

He carried on clicking as she walked towards the wood skirting the hotel grounds. A squint in the sun. A backdrop of beautiful bright pink rhododendrons. A view of her bottom bending to pick bluebells. A close up smile as she peered round a twisted knotted branch in the dim light.

'Take your hood off. I want to see that beautiful Shetland Pony hair that I fell in love with,' he called pursing his lips into a kiss from afar.

'That's perfect. Look at this one. Your hair looks luxuriant – the light has captured it so well. Can you see the tones? This camera is sharp.' He was scrolling back looking at the pictures.

They walked on, crunching leaves curled like tobacco under foot and into a darkened area, where the trees hid the light and moss and lichen lined the route. They began to kiss against the rugged bark of a tree, his fingers gently touching her face and reaching into her top to caress her nipples.

'Remind me again why you love me,' she whispered as slivers of passion stirred.

'You're bright and sparky and I fell in love with your springer spaniel hair.'

'Looking after kids all day has given me a bit of a mushy brain.'

'I've found your re-set button.' It was beginning to drizzle as they came to the end of the wood, through a clearing into a secret walled garden. A blanket of bluebells spread before them. 'Bluebells grow in ancient woods.' He bent to pick one. They tiptoed to a broken greenhouse on the far side of the four walled garden. 'There has to be the perfect combination of sun and rain for so many bluebells to grow. They can quickly spread, as they have here, but it's getting the right combination.'

He bent down and took a tiny drooping head of the dainty violet flower in his fingers. And then he took her hands and started to sing the great Liverpool anthem 'You'll never walk alone,' and soon they were out of breath skipping around a pond, nearly losing their balance.

Walk on, walk on, with hope in your heart. As she sang they looked at the harlequin of colour around them and she felt hope in her heart.

They wandered into the greenhouse tiptoeing around the broken glass and pots.

'If only I'd met you 30 years ago.' He looked sad. 'But then with our age gap I would have been labelled a child molester. Oh God, I hate all child molesters. I wish I could herd them all up and wipe them out.'

'There's a reason why people abuse children. I don't think you'll ever be rid of the demons you're carrying until you understand their mindset.'

'What is there to understand about child abuse? You're not condoning it I hope?' Darius was shocked.

'Of course not. But there are reasons why people behave as they do. You have to crawl inside their psyche, hard though it is. Many have been abused themselves. It's often a perpetual cycle that's carried on generation after generation but not always. Sometimes it's about power and corruption, the need to control because maybe that person has no control over all the fundamentals in their life. We spend so much time fearing abusers, working out how to punish them but do we spend enough time working out how we can help them?'

'I don't want to have to think about that evil man and any wrongdoing committed against him. All I know is that you've come at the end of my life and maybe you've come for a reason, to help me make sense of the past, maybe to help me find Kathleen. But what you see is a crumbly old 56-year-old, battered, beaten, broken. I won't let you go now I've found you. I promise.' He pulled on her jacket, drawing her into a kiss. 'We connect at brain level totally. And we can be silly together. You're my equal. I know you care about me,' he added.

The air was still and silent. She sensed he was about to say something more but then he frowned slightly, turned into the drizzle.

Faye wondered how their life would have been if they had met first time round. She often dreamt of the security of a long marriage. In her perfect little dream they would have stayed together. There wouldn't have been any rifts, just blissful contentment. The hum of Radio Four and the smell of toast each morning. A house with a view over a village, a river or the sea, mortgage paid off and no debts, a pension pot for retirement. By now they might even be looking to buy a second property and their son and daughter (because they would have been blessed with one of each, of course) would be at university while they tinkered round the house fixing things and improving the garden and travelling the world: city breaks, cruises, relatives in far off places. The dream she had of what might have been made her suddenly feel sad.

She marvelled at couples who'd lasted the course. 'What is the secret glue that holds some couples together? What really is happy-ever-after? Do you know? I'm damned if I do. Maybe there are moments of happiness. I think you have to experience periods of unhappiness to understand happiness. At this moment in time I'm happy. I wish I could hold onto the moment and bottle it. How corny is that?'

'I don't know what I think, Faye. I know the couples you're on about though that stay together till the bitter end. You see them in the local papers, hugging, beaming up towards the camera from their built to last Parker Knoll settees. Those are the respectable marriages.'

'Love honour and obey and all that crap. An impossible

mission, rather like flying to the moon must have seemed before Neil Armstrong proved otherwise.'

'My dad was only 49 when he was killed in Northern Ireland.'

'I'm so sorry.' The words lingered in the air and Faye felt a chill rush down her spine. She couldn't imagine what it would have been like for him.

'Mum doted on him. When he died she went to pieces. She cried into his unwashed pajamas for months and wouldn't leave the house. It was the end of her world and so sad to watch. I'd ask how she was coping but always got the aggressive reply, how do you think I'm coping? But I know how she coped. That bloody priest came visiting every evening, probably taking advantage of her situation. Who knows? But always rattling his money tin, wanting coffers for the repair of the church roof appeal. She hardly encouraged sympathy. The longer you're with someone and the closer you are the worse the bereavement and loss is.' He seemed far away. 'Fuck. You've got me thinking of my poor mum again. I hope we can pick up a lead on Kathleen. We'll make some enquiries after dinner.'

'Doting couples. I'm quite envious. Maybe we are turning into a doting couple. Couples in bubble-wrap world, unaware that one day the bubble will pop.'

Darius was listening, walking slightly ahead. She carried on. 'I often see big groups of girls in Slough at night, like a group of wild animals hunting in a pack, on hen weekends, drinking to oblivion, tarted up with matching pink fluffy bunny ears, fish nets and flashing sashes saying Chloe's hen night. You see them sucking huge willy lollies. Maybe I'm just a prude. It's as if marriage is one big joke - an excuse for a party. What are they thinking? See how it goes? A handbag is for life, but a husband...'

She wondered if those women knew that the L plate would be needed each day for the rest of their marriage... to steer their way around differences of opinion, reversing down ditches of despair at three in the morning or driving in the fast lane to wedded bliss via the junction of compromise, through the tunnel of communication and reconciliation.

'If only ACAS could arbitrate every time there was a dispute over which TV channel to watch. I suppose it's called Marriage Guidance, or Relate. They didn't do much for me.' She laughed.

∽

AFTER DINNER the guests were invited into a side room where an old man was playing songs on a piano.

Faye watched his gnarled fingers tapping on the keys. The skin of his crepe hands were as thin as an onion layer and covered in liver spots, reminding her of an old banana in a fruit bowl. His brown eyes looked sad and faraway, yet at the same time intelligent, daring you not to even think about treating him like an old person.

'He plays so beautifully. I wonder if he's been playing here for years. Maybe we can ask him about Kathleen afterwards,' Faye suggested.

'Maybe he's only been playing here since he retired from some big multi-national company. He looks like he's got a talented head on him. For most, retirement is a period of catastrophic boredom with only one ending – death. But this guy is filling it wisely, until the doctor appears to shove a tube up his nose.' Darius chuckled.

'Maybe he spends the rest of his time pottering about in those greenhouses outside, killing insects, pouring lemon barley water for guests in the summer.' Faye laughed back, rubbing Darius's back.

'He looks part of the furniture here. He's probably here to stay until his arthritic fingers are bent double with pain and his whole face turns into one giant liver spot.'

They fell about laughing and Faye, not seeing a lady just behind her, knocked into her, sending her glass of red wine to the pale carpet. In the moments that followed several waiters rushed over to attend to the carpet and the empty glass and in the calamity Darius and Faye nearly forgot to sidle over to the pianist who had stopped playing when the glass had fallen. They wove carefully between the guests, edging away from wine glasses poised at arm's length and offered their hands to the old man at the piano stall who beamed up at them.

'What fine music.' Darius began with flattery showing an interest in the pieces the man had skillfully played until eventually asking whether he had worked in the hotel for long.

The man tilted his head and laughed. Nasal hair danced in his nostrils as he billowed and then he took out a neatly ironed white hanky, unfolded it and blew his nose loudly. Darius thought how thin and willowy he looked and guessed his age to be the mid 80s, maybe older.

Darius, feeling intimidated by the laughter waited for him to finish before asking why he'd found his simple question amusing.

'I own the hotel. I've lived here all my life. That's what's amusing. I don't run the place any more. My son does. This hotel has been in my family for decades.'

Darius sketched a gesture across to Faye. She stepped

forward as the old man explained that many guests had come through the front door over the years.

Darius explained the situation. 'But what about young girls from Ireland? You have a friend who runs a pub called The Green Shamrock? We met him the other week and he directed us here. The girls came to work here. This was the mid 70s. You must remember.' He was desperate to be able to take something back from the weekend to satisfy his mother.

'So many girls have worked here over the years. I'll need more to go on than that.'

'You do know The Green Shamrock?'

'Indeed I do. I only remember one young lass he sent over but there may have been several girls. It's such a long time ago now.'

'What do you remember? Please think.' He persisted.

'I'll tell you what. It's been a long evening. Let me mull things over, speak to the staff in the kitchen. Come and find me in the morning.'

~

AFTER BREAKFAST they loaded the car with their bags, then returned to speak to the owner of the hotel.

He was sitting in the morning room taking coffee. His thoughts looked as if they were lost in the purple mountains that laced the surrounds of the hotel and they gently touched him on the shoulder and sat down. Smiling, he held out a coffee pot and pointed to two waiting cups. Darius felt his heart thud in his chest. So much was hinging on this conversation. Apart from the postcard directing them to Rome in September this was the only lead they had.

'I've had a conversation with the staff some of whom have been here since the mid 70s.' He handed the picture of Kathleen, in her early teens back to Darius. 'Pretty girl.' He smiled.

'Yes. She is. Was.'

The old man put his finger to his lip in thought.

'You're in luck and it *is* a stroke of luck after all this time. The head chef remembers her. They kept in touch for a couple of years. The last he heard was that she was singing in a bar in a hotel in Dubai.' He pushed a piece of paper across the table containing the name of the hotel in Dubai and Darius stared at it.

'The Burj Khalifa?'

'Oh my God Darius can we go there? Faye asked. 'The tallest building in the world. There's probably a cocktail bar at the top.'

'I've been looking at her picture for some time. I don't want to send you down a path that will lead to a dead end and waste your time, but I think if you're determined to find her then maybe you will in Dubai.' The man turned to gaze out of the window, his misty eyes far away. 'She had a beautiful voice and used to sing to the guests outside on a summer's evening by the lake. I think I remember her standing just down there at the foot of the steps wearing a red dress. Did your sister have a beautiful voice? Did she sing? Does it sound like it could be her?' He stood up and pointed outside.

'She loved singing. Yes. And she had a beautiful voice. She was in the church choir, but Mum hated her singing around the house. Mum used to say that she had the devil in her and had fallen from grace,' Darius told him.

'She must have come a long way over the years. She would have sang pleasant songs here. Frank Sinatra tunes, that sort of thing. I guess you've tried the missing person's bureau and support groups that are out there? Going to Dubai could be a needle in a haystack scenario but maybe worth a thought?'

∼

THEY TOOK a train from North Wales to Liverpool, Darius's home city. He wanted to show her all the popular touristy sites and the road where he grew up in. The train ambled through rugged and windswept landscape, breathtaking scenery through Snowdonia's craggy peaks and Anglesey's stunning shoreline. He felt a cold chill pass through his body as the train screeched and scraped to a halt at Rhyl, like nails on a chalkboard and immediately the fear had returned. He peered out at the platform, light rain forming patterns down the grimy windows. He stared at the posters advertising a local show and the fun-fair but his eye was drawn to another poster - written by the British Transport Police – 'Help fight the rising number of sexual and violent crimes at this station.' He shuddered as he remembered what had happened in Rhyl years ago—church holidays run by the priest. But underneath those dark and feathery memories sat a mantel of happier memories skittering into view: walking along the sea wall to the Black Cat amusement arcade, the swing boats, the Mad Mouse and the Caterpillar at the fun fair and Horlicks at Sidoli's Cafe.

~

FROM THEIR HOTEL in the city centre they took a taxi out to The Baltic Fleet; the only pub to brew on its own premises. They stepped out of the taxi into a blasting wind hurtling down the Dock Road. Faye looked up at the Victorian pub. Standing alone in the midst of a time warp battle, one side looking out to the docks and the other to a building site which appeared to have been neglected due to lack of funds, she imagined. She thought it a strange looking pub, rather like a wedge of cheese, standing detached from everything else like a tram left at the wayside, it had a look about it that told the city that it would always be there despite all the change happening around it.
 What it may grow to, in time I know not.

The Catholic Woman's Dying Wish

They were the words of Daniel Defoe, talking of Liverpool. She read them on the bespoke wallpaper in the hotel, thinking of them now as she looked at her surroundings. But a part of her also wondered what she and Darius would grow to be. She smiled, feeling happy with the way things were going.

Escaping from the salty wind - rather like escaping from the deck of a ship - into the unkempt, smelly interior of the pub she felt like a passenger on a steamer crossing the icy North Atlantic and took in the noisy unpretentious surroundings: the wooden floor, endless maritime memorabilia adorning the walls.

'Bevvie?' Darius asked at the bar and she realised, despite his origins that this was the first time he'd used that expression. 'Don't worry they don't drug you and sell you into slavery anymore,' he laughed, catching her confused expression. 'My Dad used to bring Kathleen and me to this pub. I half wondered if I might see someone I used to know.' He looked around and with a shake of his head turned back to Faye.

'There are two secret passageways in this pub. One leading to the red-light district in Cornhill. Now you don't get that in Wetherspoons so you don't.' He laughed. 'My dad used to make up stories of prostitutes coming down the passageway. This is where I had my first pint of ale and my first desire to go with a prostitute although it wasn't until much later, and in London that I sampled the pleasures.' He picked his glass up, raised it into the air as if toasting the pub or his past in the brothels.

Darius

They listened to the music, chatted, drank ale. Darius stole a few moments to reminisce about his dad and his stories and he thought about the time when the warehouses and transit sheds lay empty, the cranes falling silent, the dockside infrastructure slowly dismantled and allowed to decay. And then he remembered all the reasons why he'd left the city and the teaching profession. It was 1981, thousands were out of work; a combination of unhappy circumstances and skepticism about the future had led to the city erupting in flames -the Toxteth riots - and that event had been his cue to flee, seeking his future in a different profession down south.

Faye

'This old Scouse is a risk-taker. Wanna be my bird? Marry me you daft cow,' he said against the din of the music. He had been in a dreamy state for several minutes and Faye had left him to his thoughts as she began to piece together a picture in her head about their childhood.

'What?' She pretended the music was too loud while she digested the question.

'You heard. Another bevvie like?' He said, getting up to refill his Wapping Ale as the ship's bell tinkled that it was last orders. 'Do the Desperate Scouse Wives bit, be me bird, Faye.' Faye watched him go to the bar, pulling the back of his trousers up as he went and she was too stunned to think. This was one big surprise.

'Well? What do you think?' He asked sitting back beside her.

'I know we've had a fantastic weekend but that was just three days. We've only known each other for eight weeks.'

'We could have a great future together. We don't have to rush into it, but life's short. You know that.' He looked at her with those soppy blue eyes.

Faye sat up, taking control. 'I thought you said you didn't want to do the wifey bit again.' She grabbed an advert for the next sea shanty night, started curling it into a cigar. 'You said something along the lines that you'd always thought the wife thing was like one of those old-style power tools which you could turn from drill into circular saw sander. But those tools were useless.'

Suddenly the tension was gone. They were laughing and

kissing and several drinkers at the bar had turned to look. He took her face in his hands, kissed her forehead.

'You're life partner material Faye. I've told you that before. Wanna spend the rest of your life with me? I don't think you'll bin bag me.' His accent had returned, the effect of coming back to his home city. All trace of his years in the south had disappeared, the barriers were down. She was seeing him in a new light with an accent that was fast, funny and friendly.

'Think about it?' He shouted over *roll the rigging up*.

'The kids hardly know you.' Faye looked doubtful, pushed her finished plate of stew to one side.

'I've bought one kid up.' He looked defeated.

Faye's brain was a jigsaw of competing voices. She didn't know the way forward. She liked being on her own but part of her wanted to be looked after. Maybe he was her lifeboat rescue. But he was more than that. As clichéd as it sounded, he made her laugh. He kept her entertained.

'I don't know those kids but I'm a big enough and generous enough human being to care about them. And they are the closest thing to the person I love.'

'Life's short!' She put her pint of ale down, froth around her lips, leaned over and kissed his frothy lips. 'Yes, I'll marry you, you big Churchill lookalike.'

His face lit up and his blue eyes glittered. She had made him a happy man.

The singers were still chanting *roll the rigging up*.

'I'd like to roll your rigging up later.' He laughed in a deep Scouse accent. 'We're off to Dubai soon and I shall buy you the biggest most expensive ring.'

For a few moments the music around them lost its clarity, distorted like a muffled Dalek as they sat on the wooden bench gooey eyed and grinning. She was getting married. Again. And this time - she told herself it was going to be different. She loved this funny Scouser, this was her second stab at happiness, and she was going to make it work.

Darius

It had been a wonderful weekend, but Darius's heart sank as they pulled up at her flat.

Shayne was sitting in the window seat, waving to them, all comfy, drinking a mug of tea, reading to Chrissie, as if he owned and lived in the place.

'What the fuck?' Darius was fuming. His face pumped with blood.

'He still has a key. What can I do? He'll go mental on me if I change his little routine.'

'Ask for it back. What the hell are you doing Faye? It's time to move on, especially if we're going to get married,' he shouted.

14

FAYE

May 2009

'What the hell are you doing Shayne? You snide creepy little man.' Faye spat into the mouthpiece of her landline.

'I'm only thinking of my daughter,' Shayne whined.

'Ringing my friends to ask them what they think of Darius. How dare you!'

'And I'm worried about you going out with him. I still love you Faye.'

'When are you ever going to move on?' Faye was fuming. He had no right to ask her friends what they thought of Darius. It was an invasion of privacy.

'I don't care about *you*. I'm thinking of *my* daughter. If you don't want to be with me, then that's your loss. I don't want my daughter living with a man that's constantly swearing.'

'Oh piss off.' Faye slammed the phone back on its cradle, slumped onto the settee. It was useless. She would always be shackled to the past, to Shayne and nothing would ever change that. He would always be there in the background making life difficult, jealous of any new partner she had. Faye was the one and only woman he'd ever love. She knew he'd never look for another, was only interested in her.

∼

FAYE WAS CHECKING emails and noticed one from Shayne. She scanned through the contents. Fear coursed through her. When was Shayne ever going to move on and leave her in peace?

'Why should you have custody of Chrissie? Why can't it be me? You're only interested in having a good time these days going on all your holidays.' His email asked.

She phoned Darius and through tears told him what Shayne had asked. 'Stop worrying Faye.' He said wearily.

'What if he fights for custody?' Faye's worries were mounting.

'Calm down and listen to me. He'd never get custody. Check it out with any solicitor Faye. You're safe. It's ok. No court would agree to it. Trust me. That ignorant bastard needs a visit from me. I'll sort him out.'

But Faye wasn't so sure. Her family felt more vulnerable than ever.

Darius

Darius decided he would confront Shayne. He'd visit him one evening. He needed to put his stamp on the situation but he would keep it quiet from Faye. Faye was too weak to change any of the routines and ways of doing things. Shayne needed to face up to the fact that his relationship with Faye was never going to be restored. He didn't feel comfortable as things were.

He emailed Shayne and invited him out for a friendly drink to break the ice and reassure him that he wasn't a nonce and could be trusted to look after his kid. He'd put it off long enough.

But Shayne ignored the email. This only left Darius more determined that they would meet, even if it meant he had to confront the little shit on his doorstep.

15

DARIUS

July 2009
Darius squeezed his Mercedes into a cramped space and looked around. The neighbourhood was pretty much as Faye had described it: a non-descript, bland 1930s North London suburb, like any other around the London perimeter. George Orwell had called them horizontal slammers in *'Coming Up For Air.'* Darius imagined Shayne describing it proudly as leafy - on account of trees lining the pavement - probably believing he'd finally 'arrived.'

Number six had a broken fence, unkempt garden and soggy mattress sitting on the cracked pathway. Weeds were thriving through the cracks.

'Deluded cunt thinks one day Faye will come to her senses and get back with him. He has no idea about women.' Darius seethed under his breath and gave the mattress a kick.

'Piece of shit, forcing me to drive all this way. No social grace to answer an email.' He snorted loudly then spat across the lawn, sending a trail of mucous flying through the air as he headed for the door.

Reaching the door, he wondered why Faye would have slept with a piece of garbage, procreating with a low life.

One hand was curled into a fist, the other pressed the doorbell. He noticed the peeling, faded red paintwork of the wooden front door – which looked like flaking blood on an old crusty wound. He kept his finger firmly on the button waiting for the bastard to answer. What sort of a prat would paint their front door red? He glanced at the rubbish in the front garden, scoffing at the irony that this grubby little house was probably worth much more than his beautiful marital home in Nettlebed.

Then he remembered why he'd driven all this way. He was only doing what weak willed Trevor - the twin's dad - should have done years back after he'd discovered his wife's sordid little affair. But he'd taken the easy way out, ending his life mangled under a train. The door flung open. Shayne's hulk of a body filled the frame. Christ almighty. The man had gloopy egg trickling down his chin. Faye had swapped a high-flying accountant for this piece of trash.

He took it all in. The rubbish in the hallway - yogurt lids, beer tops, coins, nails, clothing, piles of junk mail and free local newspapers were strewn across the threadbare hall carpet. It looked as if he had thrown the contents of a bin bag across the floor. It was a squat. Faye had shagged this Neanderthal, had a baby with him, conceived in a swimming pool blue Fiat Panda in a Little Chef car park. He resisted the urge to swipe him one, keeping his cool––for now.

All at once he felt pity for Trevor losing his home because of the actions of this man. She must have taken leave of her senses, maybe had a nervous breakdown even. He couldn't understand why Trevor had meekly stood by and let it all happen.

The door slammed in Darius's face. No words were spoken.

He flipped the letterbox and screamed. 'I'm not going

anywhere, Shayne. Open the door before I have to break it down.'

He waited. The door opened again, more cautiously this time with the chain on. Then the chain came off. Shayne had shrunk in size. Darius thought he was about to start crying. His lip quivered and his eyes were scrunched up as if in bright sunlight. He muttered something about calling a solicitor or the police. In that moment Darius had an overwhelming desire to thump him.

'What do you want?' Shayne asked, except that it didn't come out like that. The words rolled into one, in an East London, whiny toddler drawl. 'Whadayou wan'' was how it sounded. His tone was flat, monotone, hardly someone with fight.

Darius remembered the biggest reason why Faye had dumped him. 'I couldn't stand the way he spoke, among other things,' she'd said. She did a good impression of how he asked mothers the age of their babies. *Harrod is 'e? What had possessed her? Why had she wrecked her marriage for this?*

'We either go to the pub for a man-to-man chat or we stand out here in view of your neighbours and sort this out. I'm not going anywhere. You ignore my emails. You slam the phone down. I've been trying to get in touch with you for weeks. For starters we'll have the key back.'

'My kid lives there,' he whined grabbing a tatty grey anorak from the bannister and slamming the door behind him. 'And I might need access.'

'Sorry?' Darius said loudly, looking up at the coward.

His voice had begun to grate on Darius as they headed for the pub. He'd only met the man once before, but once had been enough for him to get an impression. Shayne scuttled along with his shoe laces undone, head tilted to one side, constantly pulling his trousers back up to his waist because he obviously couldn't be bothered to wear a belt. All of these traits made Darius bristle with contempt.

Shayne ran slightly behind Darius, like a child trying to keep up. While he ran, he took the key off a ring and handed it to Darius, apologising in a servile manner. He continued to scuttle along behind talking randomly about anything that came into his head.

'That house over there, well they're having an extension. I don't see the point in extensions,' and 'the old Woolworths is going to be a carpet shop. We've got loads of carpet shops. We could do with a Halfords and Kennedy's Butchers is closing soon. It's been there for years. Such a lovely shop,' and then when Darius said nothing, he asked 'how long did it take you to get here?' except that it came out as, ''ow long did it take ya ta get 'ere.'

Darius stopped. He felt a sensation on his skin as if he were falling through feathers. He put his hands in his pockets and looked up at Shayne. Faye was right. The top of his head did look like the hair of a black pig.

'I thought I was having a déjà vu moment when you said that. You sound like a priest I knew years ago. Many times I just wanted to whack him one. He always said how long did it take you in the same irritating way except that he may have been referring to something entirely different. Jesus, I can see why Faye left you. Do you really care? You saw my car parked outside. Look, this is all trivia, Shayne. I don't give a damn about Woolworths pick n mix or sausages or any other damn shop for that matter. I didn't drive all this way to discuss your shopping parade.'

'Where did he live?' Shayne asked, innocently.

'What?' Darius snarled.

'The priest?' Shayne asked innocently.

'Fuck off. Which way is this pub?' Darius was very wound up now. Not only did this man sound like Father Joseph but his dark and reptilian eyes bore a striking similarity. He felt a chill creep down his body. These were the eyes of a child abuser.

They carried on walking at a faster pace this time.

'The pub is going to be refurbished soon.' Shayne commented as they pushed through the swing doors.

'Do you ever shut up talking such fucking drivel?' Darius asked as he passed Shayne a pint then took a bar stall.

'If you carry on insulting me, I'll just go back home.'

'We've got things to sort out.' Darius placed his beer on a mat. The froth sloshed over the rim.

'How do you mean? You're not making threats, I hope? All I want is for my daughter to be safe. I don't care about Faye. It's her loss she didn't stay with me.'

'And she is perfectly safe. What do you take me for? I'm not a nonce.' Darius took a sip, wiped his sweaty brow with the back of his hand.

'I hope you don't swear in front of my daughter.'

'Look I've raised my own kid pretty successfully.' Although Darius wasn't quite so convinced inside. 'If you'd given me a chance rather than snidely asking about me behind my back to Faye's friends and worse than that, telling your daughter she can come and live with you if she doesn't like me, you would see that I'm a decent human being.'

Shayne scrunched his eyes again. His smile was fake.

'I'm warning you, Shayne, that's all. Just back off and let us live our lives. Get used to the idea. Faye's not getting back with you. Ever.'

'And what about my daughter? Does she have a say?'

His voice sounded feminine, high pitched. He raised his eyebrows, looked triumphant.

'Maybe she would prefer to live with me. Did she have a say when you thrashed her the other week?' Shayne smirked, licking the foamy froth moustache away.

Darius froze. The words hung in the air like a dirty cobweb.

'Listen to yourself. I tapped her on the hand. What would you do if she were about to run into the road? Let her? Do you think Faye would still be with me if I was a child beater? Are you that stupid? Do you think I go around hitting kids all day? And no, she doesn't have a say. She's 6 years old and Faye is her mother. You can stop planting ideas in Chrissie's head.'

Darius noticed how hard Shayne found it to establish eye contact. Maybe he felt intimidated. Darius liked the thought, was determined to meet his raven eyes.

'Will you look at me when I'm speaking?' Darius demanded. Shayne briefly looked up then quickly glanced away, a child in front of a headmaster with the threat of the cane looming for some awful misdemeanor and muttered something about the number of colourful drinks on display behind the bar.

'I haven't done nothing.' Shayne mumbled.

'Anything. Learn to speak properly.' Darius shook his head, swore under his breath. This guy was seriously thick. 'All I'm going to say to you is this. I'll say it once and I expect you never to forget it.' Darius took a deep breath, trying to remain calm.

'If you cause any trouble and I mean telling Chrissie that if she doesn't like me, she can come and live up here in your shit hole or talking to Faye's friends behind her back about me I shall make sure we put a distance of 600 miles between you and us. Have I made that quite clear? My business can go anywhere. We can even move to America. I think Faye would be up for that.' Darius put on his best evil look.

Darius's voice rose, an air of triumph entering his tone. He sat up on his stall using his height to peer down at Shayne.

'We certainly don't need your pathetic 300 a month in maintenance. I can make that sort of money in an hour.'

'I pay more than the CSA guidelines. I don't want my kid to go without.'

'She won't have a great lifestyle on that shit money if that's what you're thinking.' Darius smirked.

'Are you rich or something?' Shayne asked in a childish way, his voice squeaky.

'Shayne, look, I was shredded by my ex. You have absolutely no idea about real life and the damage that divorce does financially not to mention in every other way too. You're living in Noddy Land. You didn't have the guts to commit to Faye. When you could have sold that shit hole you call home you chose not to, even when she was carrying your baby. You owed her big time after wrecking their marriage and driving Trevor to jump in front of a train. I'm working my bollocks off to rebuild my life and let's not forget we're living through the worst recession in living memory.'

'Well you are entitled to half the house,' Shayne replied weakly.

'Shayne. You don't get it do you?' Darius leaned in towards him. He had an overwhelming desire to punch his lights out. The ignorance of the man was astounding. 'Do you know anything about debts the size of mountains and legal fees that run into thousands? You've not been married and by all accounts you never will. You whinge about the pathetic amount you loaned Faye to help her pay the rental deposit on that dreadful little flat to put a roof over *your* kid's head. You should have done the decent thing and given the money to her.'

Shayne said nothing. Darius couldn't believe it. Why did this man never rise to the bait? He was like a cowardly boxer hunched in the corner of the fighting ring, nursing a nosebleed. He had no backbone and skin the thickness of a Rhino. He was dismissive, evasive, weak, and non-confrontational on every front.

∼

DARIUS FELT BETTER for having driven to Shayne's, in the same way he felt better after bollocking one of the staff in his office. Had he achieved what he'd set out to achieve? He wasn't sure, but he had Faye's key and a good feeling he'd put him in his place and established a few ground rules. There was a semblance of control back in the relationship. This man wouldn't be messing with him. Faye didn't have the guts to confront him over the key and the things he'd said to her friends. He didn't understand why she hadn't, why she was so timid.

Was the pathway now clear to move ahead with Faye? Or were there more problems ahead?

16

FAYE

September 2009
Faye was looking at the postcard from Kathleen sent many years ago. Maria had given it to her to take with them on their journey to the Sistine Chapel to find Kathleen. She read the words on the card again:
Mum. On the 10th September 2009 at 3pm I'll be in the Sistine Chapel by Michelangelo's painting of the Last Judgement where I will atone for my sins.

THE BOAT ROSE and dipped and slapped the deep sapphire waves like a belly flop, froth jetting and foaming from the sides like the parting of the Red Sea. The sun was low in the Autumn sky flickering between the ornate buildings and statues. A fine pink haze smudged the horizon. It was an artist's, filmmaker's and photographer's paradise and over the next day it would be their paradise.

'We're not really in Venice,' Darius shouted above the slap of the waves. 'We're Somali pirates on the high sea.' A variety of boats navigated around each other in a precarious nautical M25 of confusion.

'Feels like we're in a Bond movie,' Faye shouted back, salty spray hitting her face and wind in her hair.

'See that cruise liner over there? That's the floating council estate.' Darius laughed.

Faye was staring at the sea and the buildings ahead. 'The sea never sleeps. It's alive as if it has a beating heart. It's like looking down on upon a liquid mountain range one minute then when it's still it becomes a shining pathway of clingfilm across a foily sea. The sea has the energy of a child rising from darkness and the rush of water to a plughole. The foamy waves are like a shy child's playful smile one minute then foaming Persil the next. Just look at it all. I think this has to be heaven on earth.'

Darius, sitting behind her wrapped his arms around her waist and kissed her neck. 'And we still have a beating heart. I feel so relaxed with you.'

'So do I. Love you.'

Faye had persuaded Darius to take her to Venice before going on to Rome. She was looking forward to wandering round the labyrinth of alleys and squares. She wasn't looking forward to Rome, having heard that the drivers were among the most aggressive in the world and the pick pockets second to none. She imagined them kissing on a gondola under an arch, licking an ice cream together in the shadows of the magnificent public buildings, sipping strong coffee in St. Mark's Square and eating dinner in their hotel overlooking the sandy beaches. It seemed like heaven.

'I might as well use the money my mum gave me. The Kathleen budget I call it.' Darius laughed.

'You'll inherit though as well.'

'You shouldn't plan for inheritance. Anything can happen but I sold the house in Liverpool at a good time. It was the early

80s and developers were carving up the dock area for regeneration. I persuaded her to plough the money into unit trusts. They've done pretty well. When the inheritance comes - not that I'm willing her to die - it should solve my housing problem. Fuck knows, I've lost enough money through divorce.'

~

FAYE CLOSED her eyes against the swarming Chinese and Jap's - snap happy with their cameras pointing in every direction – and enjoyed the gentle movement of the gondola. Darius leaned over to kiss her lips.

'I was just thinking. Why don't fannies smile?' Darius laughed.

'The weird thoughts that go through your head.' Faye smiled.

'Fannies have limp smiles.' The reflection from the yellow sandstone buildings was flickering in his eyes.

'Take a lick of this ice cream. It's delicious.' As she handed him the pistachio ice cream, a dollop plopped onto the red velvet cushion they were sitting on.

'I'd rather put a dollop onto your tits and fanny and lick it off.'

'You've had a heart attack. Remember.'

'Stop spoiling the fun.' He pouted his lips, feigned tears.

'In between admiring our punter in his striped top and that fabulous bottom of his I was thinking about Kathleen. I don't understand why she didn't come home after she'd had the baby.' He was quiet for a few moments. A melancholy dragged in the air, rising and mingling with the sweet aroma of garlic and basil around every corner.

She watched his eyes wheel back in time. 'Deep down my mum knows the answer. I think she's been in denial for years. She wasn't very maternal. It was as if Kathleen was an inconvenience to her. Especially after my Dad died. She was wrapped up in her own grief. Kathleen was only eleven when Dad died. Fuck she'd just started secondary school. She had a lot of change and she was extremely close to Dad. We didn't see much of him because he was away working, but when he did come home he made quality time for us. I can see her sitting on the front seat jigging to the Beatles tunes on day trips to Lytham St Annes. She was about 5 or 6. The Pier at Lytham was really long stretching over the sand and they'd run along hand in hand.' Darius paused, closed his eyes as if to capture the moment.

He continued. 'That's the problem. They were very close. Three years after he died, Kathleen was pregnant. The one person she would have turned to wasn't there for her. Dad would never have sent her away. Mum was the pious one. I think Dad just went along with the rituals, but he didn't embrace Catholicism like Mum did. He looked at life differently. He wouldn't have given a damn what the neighbours thought about his pregnant daughter. I think Mum's head was still in the 1950s. And she turned to the priest for help. The same priest who put his filthy hands down my trousers and probably all the other choirboy's trousers.'

'Why didn't you say something? You were an adult by then. You could have reported him.' Faye frowned at him.

Darius waved the thought away. 'Partly shame. Partly guilt.'

'Why the hell would you feel guilty?' Faye looked stunned.

'I do blame myself. I know it's irrational. And I wanted to protect Mum in her bubble world. Losing the man she loved was bad enough. The priest - despite his faults - was there for her. It's hard for you to understand because you're not a Catholic but believers put great faith in the priest. They still do. He was God on earth. She wanted to believe he had all the answers. Without him she would have gone to pieces and maybe I felt a tinge of guilt. My career was just taking off, I had my life to lead. I didn't want the burden of my mother and her grief. And I'd lost my dad. The one person who'd supported me. I wasn't close to my mum. Not back then. Time has changed things, a little.'

∼

Rome

They were standing in the middle of the St. Peter's Square. Tourists clustered in groups; school trips, coach trips, cruise outings, Saga tours. People everywhere. How on earth were they going to find Kathleen in a sea of faces, old and young, black and white? Suddenly Darius felt the weight of the task ahead, cursing himself for the needle in a haystack approach he was taking to the search.

'I know in my head that she's gone, and I've made that adjustment but all the time my mother doesn't give up, I can't. It's her dying wish. I can't let her down.'

They joined a long queue to enter the Sistine Chapel thinking it would go down quickly. Waiting, they caught snippets of information from nearby tour guides addressing groups of tourists. 'Rome is the eternal city built on seven hills, all roads leading into the city... St. Peter's is the largest church in the world; 44 altars, 800 pillars and everything about St. Peter's Square is monumental.' Another guide was explaining the meaning of transubstantiation.

'I don't feel like a tourist, do you?' Faye asked.

'Most definitely not and I'm certainly not here as a pilgrim. I'm ashamed to call myself a Catholic. I gave up being one of God's children a very long time ago. Trans bloody substantiation. I can't wait to get out of here. The place is giving me the creeps. I remember the first time that evil priest told me, as a young boy that the bread and the wine were really changed into the body and blood of Christ. Even then I knew he was talking crap.' Darius spat, aware that his contempt was starting to gather an audience of listening ears. 'And we're all going to hell and I tell you what... I shall enjoy the warm fires.' He smirked. 'Bless me father for I have sinned.' Darius started laughing and couldn't stop.

'I wonder if Kathleen still believes.' Faye said.

'Joking aren't you? Not after what they would have put her through.'

'Don't be surprised if she is a devout Catholic.' Faye said.

He shook his head and looked disgusted.

'You'll love her whatever. She's your sister. And when your mum goes, she's your family.'

'But too many years have passed. I'm not sure I'll want to get to know her. I'm only doing this for Mum. I couldn't care less about her.'

'I think you care more than you're prepared to admit. And I think religion has got in the way. You're forgetting there's a person behind the religion. A young girl that's probably crying out to be loved.'

The queue grew longer, weaving around the square but soon they were inside the chapel.

They found the painting of the Last Judgement and waited on a nearby pew. Faye immediately noticed a change in Darius as swift as a storm cloud. He slumped low into the pew, began tapping his feet, a habit unknown to Faye and wrapped his arms around his chest, then began rubbing his legs up and down. He couldn't stop fidgeting.

'All the religions want 100% market share. They're as greedy as the business world. They can't fucking accept that people like to window shop. They like to dip in and dip out, test the water. They want the pick n mix. A lemon sherbet then a strawberry bon bon and what's wrong with that? But no, the Catholic Church has devised a clever way of keeping their customers loyal and it's called sin. That big-loaded word that loomed over my entire childhood. I'll tell you where I'm going to take the sins of the world to Faye. I'm going to take them to hell, fire and damnation. I'm going to spread shit over these walls then I'll plan a car bomb up your fanny.' Faye quickly saw through the mask of humour. He was still jiggling his legs.

'Charming. And while you're planning all that don't take your eyes off the people looking at the Last Judgement. It's nearly 3 o' clock. She'll be here any minute if she's coming,' she reminded him.

She couldn't bear to watch his legs jiggling any longer. She put a hand on his leg to stop him but the humour kept rolling. It was his way of coping.

'There should be an OfGod, the official regulator of religions with a phone number to call to complain about having to pray five times a day or put in a compensation claim when you choke on the communion wafer or develop an allergy to communion wine. And if the religion isn't big enough, they tell you, sorry mate, you're just a cult, we only deal with the big five. Bit like supermarkets these religions are.' He began to laugh, snorting like a horse let loose in a field.

'Stop fidgeting, Darius.'

'It's the smell of incense. And the choral music. Ave Maria. It's a haunting piece. Did you know it's the Hail Mary in Latin? Mum likes Perry Como's version. I remember her playing it every time the priest visited. The priest. In my head I'm still his hostage. A cold fear has slithered up my body. My head is screaming *get me out of here.*'

Faye frowned at him. He was now looking up to the ceiling, his hands clasped as if in prayer, silent tears escaping down his face. She wondered if his faith was still there, hidden in the essence of his soul. Deception had caused his faith to stray, but the past was where the past had to stay, she thought to herself.

Faye was enjoying the peace the music brought, but had her

eyes on the people moving up and down the aisles. Without warning she gave Darius a hard nudge.

'Look.'

'What?'

'That woman. Is that her do you think?' Faye was looking at a woman with long dark curly hair. She'd seen lots of pictures of Maria when she was a younger woman and there was a definite striking resemblance.

They looked at each other, their faces frozen, reminiscent of two startled deer caught in the headlights. They shuffled along the pew. With Darius shaking Faye walked ahead to the woman who had been looking at the painting, now heading for the altar to pray. They waited. Darius looked at Faye, hope glittering in his eyes. She smiled encouragement and when the woman went to stand up, Faye nodded in the woman's direction.

'Excuse me.' Faye touched the woman's shoulder tentatively. As the woman turned to look at them, it was a heart thudding, nail biting moment.

'Posso aiutarla?'

'Oh. I'm so sorry to disturb you. We were looking for someone. Do you speak English?'

The woman frowned, looked agitated. 'Qual e il problema?'

'She doesn't speak a word of English Darius. It can't be her.'

'Kathleen?' He pinned the woman with a stare, unable to let go just yet. He knew he wouldn't instantly recognise her. Thirty years was a very long time.

'Nessuna persona sbagliata.'

'It's not her Darius. Give up. I don't understand what the hell she's saying.'

ADJUSTING to the bright light outside in the square, watching the crowds still pouring in from all directions, stalls selling ice creams and souvenirs they stopped to take stock.

'Complete waste of time. I shall kill my sodding mother for sending us over here.' He pulled out a tissue from his pocket and wiped his brow. 'I need to sit down in the sun for a while. I feel sick and giddy. The incense. The music. The visions.'

Faye stood next to him as he sat on a wall, eyes closed looking into the sun as if to warm every fibre of terror in his body.

'Try thinking about it from her point of view. She was pinning all her hope on one postcard with a puzzling message. Maybe Kathleen didn't write that postcard. Have you both considered that? The nuns might have written it. Maybe some kind of sick joke. Maybe she died in their care and they wrote that to throw the scent off course.'

'Of course she wrote it.' Darius shouted. 'She wrote it to get her own back for being sent away. I still maintain what I've said all along. She was a dirty little slut. Shouldn't have got herself up the duff in the first place. She made her bed...'

'That's not fair. You've no idea who got her pregnant. Maybe she was raped. Have you considered that idea? You can't condemn her without the facts.'

'The way she used to dress she was asking for trouble. She was as much to blame as the bloke, if not more. My sister was a little slut and it's about time we all admitted it.' He waved her away, marching ahead, over the cobbles.

Faye was upset now, but she could see that her words were slowly sinking in. He looked up to the sky then threw his arms up in mock defeat, slamming them on his hips.

'Oh God. If that woman had been Kathleen... in a splinter of time everything could have locked into place. But if she had been, I'm not sure I was ready. I'm terrified of meeting her, Faye. I can't explain why but I'm terrified. I don't want to open up the past, but equally I don't know where we go from here. It feels like I've tried everything. The Missing Persons' Bureau, various helplines, we've followed leads. Apart from the Jeremy Kyle style show over in Dublin – and I can't remember the fucking presenter's name - but he is planning one for next year; there's not much more I can do.'

She pulled him into an embrace, rubbed her hand up and down his sweaty back and for a few moments they clung to each other, two ships cast adrift at sea.

∼

THE FOLLOWING morning Darius woke with a bad back. Stress manifested itself in either back pain or headaches.

'Rub my back darling.'

She sidled up to him and gently began to rub his back.

'I dreamt about the priest again. Those dreams are coming with such frequency now.'

'It's because we're raking up the past. All the reminders. You need to let go of the anger you feel. It's gone. You were just a child.' She kneeded his neck, trying to ease the stress. I'm here now. We have a future. Life goes on. You can't stay locked in the past.'

'But my mum is locking me to the past. Some people are best left in the past. Kathleen. I don't want to think about her anymore.' He mumbled into the pillow.

'Sadly, your mum won't be around forever. She's just trying to come to terms with her regrets. She wants to die with peace in her heart knowing she tried, at least to make amends for her mistakes. I feel sorry for her, I really do.'

'Don't take your hand away. I need your hand. On my back. In marriage.' He simpered.

They lay in silence for several moments. Faye gently flicked her fingers up and down his back.

'I could patent a new product and call it The Hand and get Morphy Richards to sell it. The Hand by Morphy Richards. Imagine that? I could keep it on the bedside table and summon the disembodied hand each morning. I could call out *hand give me a wank. Hand stroke me. Hand scratch my arse.* It could have different settings and future models could mind read. Can you nip in Dyas and buy me The Hand for Christmas?'

'You are funny. That's why I love you.' She planted kisses on his back.

'Of course it could all go horribly wrong and develop a virus or it could join forces with the Al Qaeda hand network and kill you in the night, strangle you, cut your head off.' Darius shuddered.

'Active mind this morning I see.' She flapped the sheets feeling hot after turning the air con off.

'I can see the box for the hand. It's black and green. It has a sealed plastic bag and limited instructions and uses Everhand batteries that don't need recharging. There's a finger bandage if needed. But it could all get out of hand with the invasion of alien hands that take over peoples' homes. People could get deeply attached to the hand. The hand is vermin, like rabbits. You could have hands with long nails for scratching, wanking or a soft hand that knows exactly how to grip your cock or an oriental hand or a little hand that wipes your arse. But of course that hand gets filthy. It looks disgusting.

Oh God I can see it so clearly; its fingernails encrusted in shit. I'm making myself ill thinking about it. I've forgotten the toilet hand is only for the toilet and now its gone off to do other chores. But that poor overworked hand; it's got to massage you, get your coffee and it attacks you because it's so overworked, so you get your hammer from the toolbox and you smash it. That fucking bastard hand. And now it's lazy and mangled and broken. Some hands become feral, others are homeless. They are like bugs walking the streets, poking you, jabbing you, doing unpleasant things, pulling your hair, knocking things over. Britain leads the way in The Hand. My mind is a fucking creative sewer I can't shut it up. The hand is crawling all over me.' He slumped back on to the pillow, stared at the ceiling then covered his eyes with his hands.

'Shush. Let go of the nightmares. Blow them away.' She whispered. 'Say fuck you priest. He can't harm you anymore. You were a child. An innocent child.' She whispered in a soothing voice.

'I think I'll lie here and have a good fart. That always makes me feel better.' He turned on his back and forced one out.

'Lovely. We're in romantic Italy and all you can do in bed is fart.'

'I'm a failing engine Faye. You could have a fartometer to measure farts.'

'Oh good Lord.'

'It could record each type of fart, categorise each one and publish it in the journal of farts. You could have Britain's Got Fart Talent, you could have the Fart Discovery Channel or a film Seven Farts For Seven Brothers.'

'Jeez..' She laughed.

'You can never have conversations like this with a tart in Bangkok. In and out within 20 minutes, flies up and away.' He laughed.

'Bloody hell Darius.'

'You need test strips to measure the intensity of the colour of farts.'

'They're colourless in case you hadn't noticed. Am I going to get a shag this morning or are we going to waste all day in bed?' She lifted the covers, reaching down.

Darius pulled the duvet and looked down. 'I could flick the switch, but nothing would happen.' He slammed his hand on his head.

17

FAYE

December 2009
She wasn't sure she'd like Dubai. She imagined it was Croydon in the sun, a bunch of towel heads with money. But recently Piers Morgan had done a travelogue on Dubai and it looked amazing.

Dubai was more glitzy, glamorous and space age than she'd imagined. An upmarket London Docklands: an Arab theme park, Disney for adults, a fantasy world created in the desert with oil money. At the airport security the booths looked like they were manned by Opec members.

'What's the price of oil today?' Darius asked.

As they drove to the hotel the taxi driver, pointed out the landmarks. 'Meester Darius where you from, England?'

'Yes. And our Queen by the way is just a little old lady who reads the 'Mail on Sunday' but if she came here, she would like your horses, your kings and your polo. And if I came to live here, I wouldn't miss England. I'd save half a million in five years in tax. They should sell Dubai on the basis of no politics, no tax. If I was a Jew it would be Jewbi!'

'If you moved here it would be goodbye. I can't move away.' Faye said, still mesmerized by the view from the window.

'Would you miss England's green and pleasant land? All the priests and the kiddy fiddlers? I wouldn't miss the old ladies in Eastbourne and priests sticking willies up little boy's arses. Burn the cathedrals, torch the lot. Eliminate religion. Kill the Labour Bastards. Where did you say you are from?'

'Manila, Meester Darius. Phillipines Sir. I been five years now.'

Faye was in awe; wasn't listening to Darius's rant. The skyline looked like a futuristic space scene, the tallest building sitting next to a crescent moon bright in a red, purple sky. She thought she'd arrived on Mars and imagined seeing people travelling in bubble cars in the sky.

'England's over mate. Well and truly over. The banks are screwed and I'm sick of paying more into the system and getting less out.'

'Come on Darius you get a lot out of the system. All that heart medication and treatment. You can't keep saying Britain's over. We're still the sixth largest manufacturer in the world and the third largest in Europe, I think. Our aerospace industry is the second largest national aerospace industry in the world and pharmaceuticals make an important contribution. Just because we don't see headline grabbing inventions constantly on our screens doesn't mean we aren't productive and inventive – hello, you have a Dyson, don't you? And what about satellite technology?'

'And this is why we're together, my feisty spirit. We love to argue and debate.'

'I can't do dull, bland pipe and slipper men that agree with me on everything and don't have opinions.' She nuzzled in, feeling the warm winter sun on her face through the glass.

'I hate all the PC shit out there.'

'Meester Darius, look this way sir you see area to left? They build Universal Studios. And Meester Darius and madam too we have new airport is being built. Going to be biggest in world.'

'You drive fast. I like speed.' Darius smiled, clutching his red satchel. 'I'd love to drive out here.'

'Speed limit 160 kph. Police allow to go over by twenty, sir.'

'Un-bel-iev-able. I'm moving over here Faye. I've never liked the ridiculous restrictions in the UK.'

As they approached the hotel, Faye spotted a row of Ferraris and up market motors parked up.

'So much wealth. In the UK you go shopping and think can I afford it? All these beautiful cars and nowhere to piss off to apart from the desert,' Darius laughed.

'Wow. Maybe Kathleen has found a rich man and settled down here with a family by now. She's probably glittering in gold, dripping in diamonds.' Faye said.

'And soon you will be my darling. The first thing on the agenda is a visit to the dazzling gold souk where I'm going to buy you a beautiful diamond ring. And I barter the price down. Something they don't do on the British high street.' Darius said.

'Last of the romantics.' Faye tutted.

'Then I must visit the doughnut emporium over in Al Qusais to film their director and his team so that I can write a piece about his new enterprise. Dubai's best little fritters are filled with cream and plum jam. The director describes them as a scone sent from heaven. Then there's their new baked not fried doughnut––a bit bready and not as sweet but not heart attack inducing.' Darius said.

'You go to desert while here? See camels?' The driver asked looking in the mirror.

'That would be fantastic. Apparently, you can go to a bedouin village and watch belly dancing and watch the stars twinkling in the sky. I love views. Can we have a cocktail floors up in the Burj Khalif and look down on all the man made islands and waterfalls?' Faye asked.

'We're gunna do it all, princess. Only the best for you my love,' Darius leaned over and kissed her tenderly. The kiss lingered and as they withdrew their tongues she felt almost giddy with excitement and anticipation - a child in a candy store. His cotton checked shirt was undone and wisps of grey hair poked out. His green glasses were sitting on top of his head, IPhone in one hand. Looking at him now, he was her George Clooney.

'They say camel milk is natural Viagra Meester Darius.'

'We won't be needing that,' Darius laughed.

'There is no fat in camel milk. You can't make cheese from it. It very salty you may like to try.'

∼

SITTING on the hotel veranda the following morning eating breakfast, drinking a lime and chilli smoothie overlooking the most perfect beach, Faye felt that she had 'arrived.' Feeling this, convinced Faye that Kathleen was here. Why would anyone want to leave here? She asked herself. This was paradise on earth.

Ravens sat on pillars squawking and screeching, waiting for crumbs. Stray kittens moved between table legs.

The beach was the most perfect beach Faye had ever seen, soft white sand and a low winter sun. It felt like being on a beach right in the middle of London Docklands, an Armani creation, for tall metallic buildings with amazing curves and angles. Some were lit up in different colours which changed periodically. Some buildings dazzled and glittered in the sun, lined the shore, reaching to the sky. Helicopters flew overhead.

'It's an upmarket Benidorm Faye. Those helicopters are on an Arab suicide mission.'

'It's nothing like Benidorm. I've been there. Perfect white beach yeah but full of trash and the call of bingo and cheering of football matches everywhere you go. Ghastly place.' Faye said looking around at the metal buildings gleaming in the sun and the soft white sand.

'Out here there are no beggars, no impoverished elderly, no drunks, no rubbish, no drinking and singing in the streets. The sheiks just think, what do these people need? Nice houses, jobs.'

A smiling, relaxed Indian topped up Darius's coffee and they chatted about Sri Lanka and Tamil Tigers. He took a sip of coffee and looked at the man. 'I called you about my phone bill last week, why are you still here?'

'You're outrageous,' Faye smiled into the sun. 'Darius,' she said after a few minutes gazing into the sun. 'I don't reckon you're doing everything you could be doing to find Kathleen.'

'Fuck off. And what do you know about looking for a missing person?' Darius slammed his IPhone onto the table.

'Don't get cross. Have you used the General Register Office to check if she got married? Electoral registers? Mind you that would be hard. Have you tried any of the websites for tracing a missing person?'

'Do you think I'm stupid?'

'I didn't say that. We don't seem to be approaching this correctly. All we're doing is floating round the world enjoying ourselves, on the back of your mum's generous pay out.'

'Yeah well. Don't complain.'

Faye felt a sense of unease. Something didn't feel right. Every time they hit a brick-wall she could see relief wash across his face and knew that deep down he didn't want to find Kathleen, maybe fearing the truth of what had happened to her.

~

It was late in the evening. Lithuanian women in long black dresses had guided them to the lift. Faye's face was now pressed against the window of the toilet cubicle on the 120th floor of the Burj Khalif, looking down upon a lego board of exceptionally tall buildings. Every ten minutes a spectacular illuminated water fountain display jumped high into the air, weaving round into the most magnificent display of shapes she had ever seen. She felt as if she was looking down from a porthole in a plane. Far below there were twinkling lights in the trees surrounding the Burj Khalif but they were a smudge of light in the distance below. It was possible to make out the motorway and the brown landscape and swimming pools that looked like fishponds. It was a sight that she would never forget, leaving an indelible imprint in the data bank of her memories. Days of awe were too brief, too sketchy but a page in her book of life that would define the stories she told.

Darius ordered cocktails and they discussed the names of the cocktails on the menu list, swirling the cherries on sticks round their glasses, playing with the parasols, fingering the sugared edge of the glasses.

'How about a new name for a cocktail called a Marlow Mayhem. It was mayhem after my fucking divorce.' Darius said flicking the small umbrella onto the glass table.

'And one for Slough?'

'I'd just call it Slug. You could have a High Wycombe Wank or a Harlow Harlot. Or a Borehamwood Whore.'

'Yes the possibilities are endless. But any sign of Kathleen. Have you asked to speak to the manager yet?'

'I did. While you were in the toilet for half an hour powdering your nose.'

'I do not powder my nose. I was looking at the most amazing view over a fountain display. Go and see. It's stunning. So, Kathleen?' She jerked her head in the direction of the toilets.

'Nar. Nothing.'

'Wha'? We've come all this way for...?'

'Nothing?'

'Precisely.'

'Oh. Well in one sense I'm not complaining. I'm having a fantastic time and you've visited a client, so it's not been a waste. What did the manager say?'

'He said there's such a high turnover of singers here. Her face didn't look familiar. He's asking the other staff though. I've given him my business card in case.'

Faye looked at the woman singing next to the piano in the corner of the room.

'It's too high up to see much of the view,' Darius said.

'If you go to the loo you'll see more.'

'I was just wondering why the singer is wearing red.' He frowned.

'Ah?' Faye frowned. 'Appropriate given the song. My first ever slow dance was to Chris de Burgh's Lady in Red.'

'Kathleen served the life sentence for the crime she committed––pregnancy out of wedlock. For years we ate the shit the church fed to us. Eventually the system beat us down to a pulp. It reminds me of the Michael Douglas film 'Falling Down.' He has an unpleasant divorce and one day in a traffic jam he abandons his car and has a series of encounters leading to him psychotically and violently lashing out against everyone. He walks round a restaurant asking everyone where's your self-respect? Where's your dignity? How can you eat this shit? That's how I feel towards the church. How could my mother eat that shit for years?'

'Sending Kathleen away wasn't exactly a crime. It's just that your mum couldn't cope. She did what she thought was the right thing.'

'Kathleen hasn't forgiven her though. Otherwise, she would have been in touch.' Darius looked glum.

'We don't know. Maybe she found it easier to make a new life after the baby was born. And as for your mum...well she was a struggling widow. She didn't know what else to do. And she was probably worried about what the neighbours would think, how they would judge her. Your mother's God fearing.'

'Bloody hell they're no better out here. Same God, different brand.'

The manager drifted over towards the end of the evening as they were about to settle the bill. 'I'm sorry sir but nobody has any information about your sister.' They watched him walk back towards the bar. Darius sighed. Faye spun a beer mat on the table.

'So what now?' Faye asked and again she saw the look of relief in his eyes.

18

FAYE

February 2010
It was early morning. Darius was busy setting up a stand at the conference centre on the waterfront in Belfast. He planned to touch base with several important clients over the next couple of days before spending the final day in the city with Faye, maybe visiting the Titanic exhibition or strolling round St. George's market.

Faye paid for her ticket for the city tour and clambered to the top of the red bus to get the best view. Taking her seat to admire the grandeur of the Portland stoned City Hall, she had no idea that she was soon to see something very unexpected and odd, that would make her blood run hot and cold.

Half an hour into the tour she was looking onto the Falls area. Her overriding thought was that the two communities – Catholic and Protestant – needed to instigate change. They were caught in a quagmire that only they could get themselves out of. She knew that fundamentally the Troubles had never really been about religion but about identity. The Catholics saw themselves as Irish, the Protestants, members of the UK. The hostilities that had existed between the two communities had improved considerably and life was now more peaceful following the Good Friday Agreement, but she was fascinated by the continuance of the graffiti political walls, the corrugated sheeting and barbed wire still separating one community from another and couldn't help but wonder whether still more change was needed.

Under an oppressive cloud of grey, the bus trundled up a hill past a boarded-up pub and shuttered shops. She noticed a big painting of Bobby Sands the hunger striker on the side of a building and other works of graffiti painted by powerless groups and individuals using whatever means they could to instigate change and make things better because the politicians had failed them. A few moments later they were in Lanark Way and she was looking out across a vast no man's land–- a fly tipping free for all of rotting mattresses, swathes of all kinds of rubbish from tyres to clothing. Tatty carrier bags and t-shirts flying at half-mast on barbed wire, a lonesome shoe swinging from a telegraph wire. More paintings on the side of buildings. She had seen wastelands like it before: across countries like India and Egypt. Scenes which were markers of poverty and deprivation. From the ashes, the phoenix of prosperity needed to rise, but the region had suffered and it was going to take time, investment and regeneration to pull this backwater out of recession.

Victorian terraced housing circuited around the open spaces and in the background the foothills served as a reminder of the beauty and tranquility of this country, a contrast to the political struggles that had endured for so long.

The bus trundled closer to the red brick terraces, the neat row of chimneys and white doors seemed to go on to infinity.

And then she saw it.

On the end wall of the terrace. Bright and clear and so easily recognisable and incredibly well painted – in fact a perfect replica. The tour guide was babbling on, a potted history of the Troubles, but inside she was fighting the mounting trouble that she was about to unleash when she returned to tell Darius what she had seen.

∽

It was the early evening when they both returned to the Falls Road, having been dropped off by a taxi in the light drizzle.

The mural loomed before them, a splash of colour on red brick, brightening the drabness of the dilapidated area all around. It was a tribute to a man lost - in the wrong place at the wrong time - not even fighting for either cause, not even politically-charged; an innocent man like so many others. But without the intention of being a political symbol ...it was. There was no doubting that. Like all the other murals it was an expression of the complex struggles that had divided two communities.

Daddy. Paddy. Died here in the Troubles. 1971. Read the caption.

'Fuck.' Was all Darius could think to say. 'Jesus, Mary and Joseph.'

'Exactly,' Faye said, her eyes glancing over the carefully painted picture of the same cloth gingerbread toy they had found at The Weeping Lady. It was about 20 feet in size extending half-way up the wall.

'She's been here alright. This is where my auntie used to live, before she died. I never visited her. My mum and I didn't have much to do with her. Kathleen must have stayed here, after the laundry, at some point. Why the hell didn't my aunt call my mum to let her know that Kathleen was safe? What a bitch.'

But Faye knew why, and Darius probably did too. She didn't want to be found. She had a new life. Kathleen had wanted to move on in her life and forget the past. But a part of Faye thought that sometimes people didn't know they wanted to be found until they were found, and until they had experienced that grand Gatwick style reunion.

'I'm tired of chasing her, trying to fix the past for my mum. The past is the past for a reason because that's exactly where it's supposed to stay,' Darius said. 'It's time to move on in our lives,' he added, taking Faye's hand and guiding her back to the waiting taxi.

She stopped, her eyes soft and caring as she looked into his. 'The problem is when someone has regrets, they live in the past. She just wants peace, to tie up the loose ends.' Faye touched his face in comfort.

Faye bent her head to get into the car determined to make a fresh search of the cloth toy as soon as she got home. She had an unsettled feeling about finding the toy. Something was disturbing her. At the back of her mind, she asked herself a question.

Do I know Kathleen? Is she one of my friends? But it was a ridiculous thought and she quickly brushed it away, but the truth was, until she found the cloth toy in her own house, she didn't know for certain they matched each other and without that match she couldn't begin to ask questions.

19

FAYE

March 2010
Faye was watching the glint of her new diamond solitaire in the afternoon sun.

Ducks were bobbing on the fast current of the Thames, like toys in a draining bath. Faye loved to watch the ebb and flow of the river and the variety of boats passing by. In places it was tidal. It was a relaxing way to spend a Sunday afternoon. They watched the cars stream across Marlow's suspension bridge; a prototype of a much larger bridge across the river Danube in Budapest and imagined climbing to the heights of All Saints steeple. And they thought about which tearoom to pig out in.

'It's a wonderful feeling to be a couple again. There's a future to look forward to. Ever since divorce I couldn't see any future. Having this beautiful ring on my finger sort of makes things feel perfect. I've got a good feeling about this. We're older, wiser. It'll work second time around. Don't you think?' She smiled confidence in his direction, squinting against the light. She pulled at a blade of grass and put it between her teeth.

'You're my two-legged Prozac, Faye. We're two desert creatures going into hybernation. It feels like the shit could be behind us.'

'We could burrow a den somewhere.'

'I'm going to call the solicitor in the morning.' He paused. 'Two guesses what I'm thinking?'

'I've no idea. We haven't developed telepathy yet. What are you thinking? Will I like it?' Her eyes were fixed on a cluster of daffodils nodding in the breeze.

'We could marry soon.'

Her face turned to clay. 'Why the rush? Give me a chance to tell the kids.'

'They'll love the idea, you see. They'll get to live in a big house and have plenty of money spent on them.'

Faye said nothing. She looked away, watching a terrier scamp up the bank in the tall grass. Darius nudged her.

'Just think we could go on a luxury honeymoon to the Far East. Sit on the beach for a week and have endless sex. What d'you reckon?'

Darius

From Faye's expression he knew she was processing this forbidden fruit, an idea hard to resist.

He braced himself. He knew that what he was about to say would go down like a lead balloon, but it was something that needed to be discussed.

'I'm thinking beyond the dress, the venue, the honeymoon. We need to discuss pre-nuptials with the solicitor.' He looked away, one hand on his head, worried his wig would take off in the breeze.

'You certainly know how to demolish romance in one massive hit.' She tutted. He wanted to reach out to stroke her hair. It was luxuriant and the colour of burnt ember in the sunlight. But he knew she would brush his hand away with the shock of his thoughts.

'I'm not taking the risk of being fleeced twice over. Faye

we're not 20. We need a pre-nuptial agreement.' He wriggled on the grass.

He was Darius O'Brien and wasn't prepared to play the Vegas style divorce game a second time around without an agreement. He knew the hard facts, women could be cows, hoovering up the pennies and the pounds.

'But they aren't legally binding. They're pretty pointless,' she said.

'One day they might be legal, then they'll carry weight. I've got my business to protect and a future inheritance from my mother and you're basically poor. And I'm not supporting your kids if we split up. They're nothing to do with me.' He laughed into the breeze it if he'd made a joke, but he knew the words were harsh and untactful.

Darius saw a change sweep her face – a child whose toy had been removed. He could read the horror mapped out on her face.

'You don't trust me? Just because I don't have money, you assume I'm going to treat you like a piggy back and run off with yours.' Her voice had risen. Her eyes were glittering with tears. He'd flicked the right button for an argument and immediately regretted the conversation, but it was an issue that was bothering him. It needed discussing.

'I don't trust anyone. Not after being shafted.' And he pointed to the spider tattoo; a gentle reminder not to cross him.

'If I didn't trust you ,I wouldn't be marrying you. Maybe you should question whether marriage is really what you want.' She was placing the tanks on the lawn and he didn't know how to retreat.

'I'm not marrying without one. It's as simple as that. You're being niave. The courts could make decisions otherwise.' He defended his idea but made no attempt to placate her feelings.

'Everything has to be about the courts with you. What

about what *we* decide?' Her face looked like a saggy cushion as she stared in disbelief across the water.

'What if I have another heart attack and need carers? They might award me more of the money. It's all about need. You don't know the first thing about how the courts work.' He knew his tone was patronising and that she would react, but his point was a valid one.

'And I don't want to know. Two people should be able to work things out without the cost of a solicitor.' The strength had suddenly gone from her voice and he knew he was winning her over.

'This is real life, not Lego Land, Faye. I stand to lose. My business could be worth a million plus. I'll be paying the mortgage. You earn peanuts. Let's face the facts. You're not bringing any money to the marriage and won't be putting anything into it. Financially we aren't an equal match.'

Faye

She looked down at the diamond ring and in her mind it had transformed into a rock of salt on her finger for the sting on her face. Then her face melted and she began to twirl the diamond. How could he be so cruel, she wondered. She wanted to get up and walk away and never see him again. But something stopped her. She wasn't sure what. Maybe it was love or maybe she had become so embroiled in the search for Kathleen.

'That's a horrible thing to say. I can't help being on the minimum wage. And it wasn't my fault that Trevor got us into debt and killed himself. You're right, I don't have anything to bring to this marriage. Maybe I'm a waste of time. Why don't you find someone else–– a rich woman? All you Tories are the same. Cruel bastards.' Her voice was starting to crack, her eyes watering over as she tried to retain her composure. She didn't want to crumple.

And then he turned and grabbed her in an embrace,

planting kisses on her head, telling her he loved her. Rich or poor he still wanted to marry her.

∼

A FORTNIGHT LATER, having argued and discussed the details of a pre-nuptial agreement they drove to Slough and sat with his solicitor to discuss the formulation of a pre-nuptial. It felt as if the honeymoon period of their engagement was over. His mind was made up. No pre-nuptial, no wedding. It was her choice.

They came out of the meeting both feeling mentally exhausted. Maybe now that they had formulated an outline plan, he would stop talking about the financial inequality within their relationship.

On the way home he kept reminding her about why he needed a pre-nuptial. It was as if he felt a tinge of guilt seeing her upset.

'Things are different second time around. The first time two people marry they don't have money to worry about. They can throw caution to the wind. I can't afford to.' Darius looked at her, could see sadness and disappointment in her face and hurt in the tart way she responded when the word pre-nuptial was mentioned. But after a diet of deceit, deception, lies, debt and huge loss, he had to be resolute. His head had the last say, not his heart. The future was founded on firm pillars of trust and honesty, enshrined in a formal document, not taken for granted in a haze of romantic platitudes.

Darius

There was another issue playing on his mind as they drove back from the solicitors. He had a strong sense that Shayne would create problems for him. The path wasn't going to be smooth. It would be much easier to put thousands of miles between them. In his head he was starting to make plans to move to North Wales or Ireland. How was he ever going to win the kids over otherwise? They need consistency. It would be confusing for them growing up being told so many different things. Faye didn't need their maintenance. He earned enough to support them all. Chrissie would soon forget Shayne and the twins had never really known a father. All this rubbish about Steve being a step-in father to replace Trevor was farcical in his eyes. Neither men added any value to their lives.

But he would bide his time on that one. Maybe wait until after they married before muting the idea.

20

FAYE

April 2010
Sit down, turn the TV off. I need to talk to you about something important.

The words stuck in her throat like scratchy toast. She looked round the lounge as if searching for a manual that would explain how to break delicate news to kids. This was the most difficult speech of her life and she had put it off for long enough, only wearing the ring in Darius's company. Her heart thudded. She felt like a naughty teenager. She strutted the room bracing herself.

'We're trying to watch Scooby Doo. What's up, Mother?' Meg looked up. Faye wondered why she called her mother, not mummy. She could see Steve referring to her as 'your mother.'

Faye began strutting again, her heart now in her throat. Big announcements were so cheesy, cringey, corny.

'I can't do this, I can't do this, I can't do this.'

'What are you muttering?' Meg huffed.

What happened next was crass. Immature. Farcical. She took her hand from her pocket and flashed the ring at each in turn. Her face burned. She waited for the big response. Tim strained to see the TV. Meg gasped and gave several 'oh my Gods' in quick succession.

Chrissie put her blanket down. 'Can I try it on?' She looked at the other two.

'What do you think?' She waited for their approval. It didn't come. What an idiot I am, she thought. *Maybe I'm turning my life into a middle-aged fairytale.*

Meg began to laugh, deep and mocking from the pit of her belly. On and on. The kid had morphed into the adult and Faye the blushing child. They were Eddie and Saffy in Ab' Fab.

'It won't last.' Meg mopped tears of laughter with her sleeve.

'Thanks for the vote of confidence. Am I that crap at relationships? Second thoughts don't answer that.'

'What do *you* think Tim? You like Darius don't you? And Chrissie? He's nice to you. He reads bedtime stories. He's been staying over for a while now.' Questions drummed across.

'He read me one story about a bear and then he stopped when his mobile rang.' Chrissie momentarily unplugged her thumb from her mouth. But then it was back in and her gaze fixed once more to Scooby Doo.

'We don't like him.' Meg made the big and bold announcement. Faye's sky fell in. She didn't know what to say. She tried to push the words underwater holding them there, but they were out and staining the room and future.

She sucked in air.

'You know... one day you're all going to grow up and leave home and what about me? You want me to be all alone?' Faye's voice started to crack.

'He'll probably die before that. He's old, Mother.' Humiliation burned inside. Faye wanted to walk over and slap Meg across the face. Maybe she'd taken it for granted the kids would be ok with the news. She had to win this. It was her future. She was the adult. They were the kids. She'd also taken it for granted that Darius would fit in around her kids, but she was about to find out how wrong she had been.

~

FAYE WAS on her way to Dorset. It was half-term.

'Look, Faye, don't bother taking them all the way to Dorset if you're going to complain. They're your own flesh and blood. You're supposed to enjoy their company.'

They weren't the reassuring words she had expected from Darius. She wanted him to tell her she was a brilliant mum. She was in the toilet crying at the service station having negotiated foreign lorries on the M27, trying to listen to news about the corrupt elections in Afganistan, above three kids yelling at each other in the back of the car. A week in a cottage now seemed like a terrible mistake.

~

SHE CALLED him when they arrived. 'I'm at my wit's end Darius. Wish we'd not come to Dorset. Chrissie's been kicking off in a retail outlet because I refused to buy a pair of Dora the Explorer shoes and Meg has been moaning all day about an orthodontist appointment in several week's time. And Tim has been asking when we're going home. Chrissie's crying lasted a couple of hours. She cried herself to sleep.'

Faye's heart thudded. She wanted him to listen and become the reassuring step- parent - backing her up, encouraging and offering support. His response wasn't the sweet honey she craved.

'Why the hell didn't you smack her?' He shot. 'The kid needs a big wallop and you're not prepared to do it. If you start smacking the kid, she'll soon learn. Do it my way.'

Faye's heart sank. His words echoed around her head

muddying her thoughts. Smacking was wrong. Every adult knew that.

His methods worked, he told her and hers didn't. Then he revealed his real motive, catching her in her tracks.

'Unless you toughen up and get a grip, they'll get the better of you and ultimately that's going to impact on me.'

The rug of independence and freedom that single motherhood had brought was suddenly yanked from under her feet. At the same time, she clung to the dream that the castle of coupledom might bring.

By the time Darius arrived in Dorset for the weekend, Faye felt utterly deflated. Despite his negative comments over the phone, she imagined having his adult company for the weekend would help.

The kids had been saying they wanted a holiday abroad. Why couldn't they ever be grateful?

She was sick of reminding them she had no money and why couldn't they just enjoy it? They complained that National Trust properties were boring and for old people. And sealife centres were for school trips.

'Why did we have to come here? What was the point?' Meg kept asking and Tim said he would rather just sit in the apartment and watch telly than play slot machines in an arcade. And because Tim didn't want to do anything, neither did Chrissie.

A quarrel broke out early in the evening about where to eat. Darius had only just settled himself in, taking off his tie, sitting down to watch the football news.

'We're starving. Can we go to the Queen's Head over the road?' The kids were asking.

'It's a dive,' Darius glanced across the road from the window. 'We'll find somewhere nice and cosy with ambience.' They drove for miles in the dark. Found nothing. Ended up back at the Queen's Head.

'I told you we should have gone here in the first place. You wouldn't listen.' Meg had a *told you so* look on her face.

'Oh, you know everything.' Darius sounded tired and wound up. Faye wished he would laugh at the situation. They took a table at the back of the pub.

'Obviously you haven't learned any manners living on that council estate. Get down child.' Darius snapped. Chrissie was standing on the leather bench.

'And for Christ sake learn how to use a hanky. We don't want to eat our meals watching you behave like an animal. Do you not teach these kids anything ,Faye?' Darius shouted at Tim, catching him wiping slug trails with his sleeve.

'Well, this is really awkward.' Meg piped up, rolling out the words as if it were a song.

Faye felt crushed from all directions. Whatever she said ,she wasn't going to be able to change the atmosphere that had settled around the table. All she could do was paint a whitewash across the scene with polite gestures and a pleasant neutrality and hope that things would improve while at the same time quietly seething.

~

Darius

'The kids heard us having sex last week.' Faye dropped the bombshell.

'Fuck.' Darius was speechless. He turned the car engine off. It was getting late. It was a couple of weeks after the Dorset break. They had just returned to Faye's flat after a mid-week meal at an Indian.

'I'm sick of this pack-a-bag-and-go lifestyle, all these mid-week treks to yours. I don't want those kids to see me as the man who just comes to shag their mum.' Darius shuddered. The thought made him feel sick.

'We know it was you, Mummy. It was definitely your voice, Meg kept saying.' Faye told him as she opened the car door. 'Tim of course went bright red. I was so embarrassed.'

'We can't carry on like this.' Darius was in despair. 'We need to start looking for somewhere to live. We need a big house. Some space,' he snapped, taking the keys from the ignition.

'You still hardly know them and some of your attitudes are a bit Victorian. Did you read that step-parenting book I recommended?'

'Fuck off, Faye. I'm an old dog. Old dogs don't learn new tricks.'

'When we live together, you're going to have to fit in with how things are. You can't wade in and try to change everything. Kids are sensitive. They like consistency. And mine have had too much change in their lives,' she said protectively.

'I can only be me. And change is good for kids.' He felt defeated, looked it too.

'I wish you could be the fun person I know, not the serious you who visits on a Wednesday, delivering a weekly Reith Lecture. Quantitative easing, liquidity crisis and complicated theories about science and physics float right over their heads. Sometimes I wonder what you're trying to achieve by talking *at* them. It's pompous.'

'The weekend in Dorset didn't go well did it? What did they say to you? Anything?' he asked.

'It's like I say, you need to get to know them. Go easy on them. Be patient. Try and win Meg over first. She's the one who's not so keen on an *us*.'

'It's not complicated to work out the basic psychology of a child. They're all pretty selfish creatures. They'll be asking what's in this for me? Let's face it kids only care about themselves. They're only interested in what they want. And when they've worked out exactly what I can give them – a bigger house, holidays, computers, fantastic Christmas presents, everything will slot into place. This isn't rocket science, Faye. That's why our Kathleen didn't return. Mum had nothing to offer her. Not even love.'

'Kids need love more than they need money.'

'I need to sell them the package,' Darius said, his eyes lighting up.

'And how are you going to do that may I ask?'

'I have an idea. You'll like it. You told me the other day what Meg's big dream is.' His eyes were glittering with the idea he had.

∼

Faye

'It probably won't last. He's old and squitty, but I don't care, Mother. Keep him. I'm in New York and I'm living my dream,' Meg shrieked, spinning round the room on the 28th floor, like a ballerina, then crashing on to the emperor size bed.

'He's got hair sprouting out of his nose, and oh my God really bad breath, and he's so tall, but I really don't mind anymore. I don't want any more holidays in boring England,' she yelped, sweeping her arms and legs, making snow angels on the white sheet. 'I can't believe it. I've been on a Virgin flight, in a yellow taxi and this massive room all to myself with amazing views over skyscrapers. It's cool. Darius's cool,' she yelled.

Faye stood in the doorway to Meg's hotel room, instructing her not to open the mini bar and not to use her mobile. But she'd jumped from the bed, too busy looking out of the window and wasn't listening.

'It's like the whole universe is concentrated right here. I want to call everyone I know. But what would I tell them? That it is all so crazily amazing and so very different to anything I've ever seen before. I can't wait to tell Tim we're on

44th Avenue. How cool is that? I feel like I'm inside a film set.'

She went into the bathroom flicked on the light, picked up the shampoo, the bath gel, read the gold writing on the side of the bottles then arranged the collection back on its tray. 'Funny size bath. Bit old and this shower curtain feels damp. I don't think I want a bath and the shower looks too scary and complicated. I may not bother washing... You can go now, Mother.' Meg was fumbling for her phone, inspecting the massive TV. She began to take shots of the TV from every angle. 'It makes more sense to turn it on and take photos of each channel, but God I bet there are so many channels I wouldn't know where to begin. You two can go out for the evening. I don't mind staying in. I'm not hungry. This room is way too cool to leave. I'll just plump up the pillows and watch TV all night. I don't care what I watch. I'll watch rubbish adverts because it's all so weird and amazing. God, Mother why can't we move here? Just imagine what it would be like. No more charity shops or Primark or 99p stores. I could buy handbags and shoes in Macys and Bloomingdale and feel all glamorous.' She grabbed Faye's arm. 'Pleeeeeeeese can we move here? How difficult would that be?' Meg pleaded, her eyes like saucers and Faye tutted.

The following day Darius took them to Macys to buy new dresses and a trip to the top of the Empire State, after a huge breakfast of pancakes and syrup in a cafe Meg thought was 'so cool' because it was called the Red Rock 99.

'The UK is finished. Soon it will look like an Eastern Bloc country. You have dreams. This is where you should be. Where we all should be. There's no future in Britain for you. University funding has suffered, scientific research has been starved of cash for years now. There's no investment in manufacturing. The country's shit. Every time I come here, I realise that.' Darius ranted on.

Faye looked at his plate of sausages, stack of pancakes,

cream and syrup. It felt as if a syrup of despair was settling in her stomach, never mind his arteries. The cumulative effect on his arteries and the inevitable consequences not only for him but her as well seemed of no concern to him. She looked from the plate to his face, gave him a schoolmistress *you don't care* look, but he didn't pick up on it.

It was scary Faye thought, how easily a child could be won round with a bit of attention and money. The kid was overwhelmed. Darius acted the perfect gentleman, complementing her on her beautiful figure as she tried on different outfits in Macys, telling her what a stunner she was. She felt proud that she had met someone who could fulfill the dreams her children had. Money was no object. A part of her felt guilt leading her down a pathway, fooling her own kid just as he was fooling her regarding his heart condition. Maybe Meg would see what they were both colluding in.

21

FAYE
JULY 2010

'I'm your escalator to foreign travel.' Darius yawned, bunching his jacket under his head.

He was sprawled on a park bench in Salzburg in Austria overlooking a river and castle. They were in Austria visiting a patisserie machinery factory.

'You certainly are. I'm a really lucky girl.'

'Being away is like living in a bubble. I can forget work and all our exes.' 'Everything is somehow placed on a shelf to deal with later.' Darius yawned.

Cyclists, joggers and walkers were passing by along the path that skirted the river. The whole of humankind seemed to have passed by.

Darius fell asleep sprawled across the bench, head resting on his rolled-up jacket. The sun was sinking in the late afternoon sun. Faye was enjoying the flecks of sunlight through the maple leaves, the skeleton of veins revealed in each leaf and the sound of the fast river tumbling over boulders below. Cyclists crunched over gravel. A man with huge boobs and a swaying cross panted by. A blind couple felt their way with white sticks.

Faye couldn't remember when she had last sat for so long. Doing nothing. Just looking.

He gave a loud snuffle, woke. 'Urg.'

'Good post-orgasmic sleep?' She asked him. He pulled himself up, squinting.

'Yeah. This is the life, Faye. You'll be alright with me.' He sniffed.

'You made a huge deposit earlier judging by the grunts.' She stretched her arms, thinking about the wonderful sex they'd had that morning.

'Did any of my little swimmers reach the target?'

'What after five hours of swimming or spinning or dancing or however they travel – economy on easy jet or rocket to the moon? I should hope not. Pregnant over 40 that wouldn't be much fun.'

'Hopefully they've flown by Concorde. I'd love to see your belly swell. I'll never be a grand dad.. When the kids go to Steve and Shayne I always think of it being like a train arriving at Crewe and separating into two. David Cameron is right. Society is broken.'

'They're good dads on the whole. Some aren't. I could have a lot more baggage you know.'

'You might do. The future's an open book. Let's imagine Meg gets pregnant at sixteen and Tim gets killed in Afganistan.'

'Thank you. Nice of you to imagine the worst. While you were asleep, I watched people walking along this path. It's a bit like watching the M1 on a particularly heavy day. Every man, woman and kid is on some sort of mission. It's a microcosm of life.'

'I'm expecting Arnold Schwarzenegger to appear. Give me your boots. Your bicycle.'

'Too many Hollywood babes jogging by. I need to lose weight.'

'You're fine as you are.' Darius leant back, closing his eyes against the sun. 'The sun is setting in the sky Teletubbies say goodbye. And look. Now they've all shat themselves.' He laughed.

'Two women in burkhas over there. Imagine putting them in a time machine, zooming back to 1940. Wasn't long ago.' Faye thought about the Nazis marching across Austria.

Faye looked down at him, still partially slumped. 'You look like a homeless guy curled up next to me on your park bench by the way. Look the begging bowl is empty.'

'Not a dime. Lousy day's work. Either that or the ex has stopped off at our M1 service station to pinch it all.'

'You going to delve into the bin then for fish and chips?' she laughed.

'Yeah, I'm a wreck I know.' Darius stretched, sat up. 'Was that a hornet buzzing round just then? It probably thought your high visibility panties were a giant sunflower; thought it could pollenate inside your knickers.'

'What's wrong with my knickers? I bought them especially for you. Chrissie said I needed to be careful not to do a wet fart in them because it would spray through the meshing like liquid through a sieve. You should have seen the knickers I used to wear.'

'I need a shower. Water over my belly. Escape to the bathroom to fart after that huge lunch. If you feel like breaking wind Faye you have permission from the higher forces, the powers that be, but I want to feel you do it on my hand.'

'God, why would I do that?'

'Dunno. While I was asleep, I dreamt of making love, then I heard the cough of a child. It's the dirtiest thing to hear the cough of a kid when you're having an orgasm. Oh God my mind is one big sewer. A crazy generation game never stops in my head.' He sighed. 'That was a Saturn five of a shag this morning.'

'You've lost me.' Faye was confused.

'Enough force to escape gravity. I experienced the pull of six times the force of gravity. It was a magnificent orgasm. Best one in a long time. My bollocks felt like the firing shed of a steam train. My techy in the office is into trains. Stupid prick. But he's too busy re arranging and maintaining all the track set up in his garden to notice his wife's coal shed.'

'How sad for his wife.'

'After such good sex, it's like being stoned. A slight depression descends. My mind is a rolling film during sex of all the disasters that have happened in my life.'

'Well, I must say I've never had a triple orgasm before. Nobody has ever given me more than one orgasm in a row. It feels greedy but nice.' Faye was still in awe that a small cock could give that much pleasure.

'I'm an experimentalist and ready to publish a paper on this one. Better before sex, better after? I'm willing to do it a hundred times to give it statistical significance.'

'I will present you with an award.'

'Arh, I'll be claiming the Platinum Tongue Award in the Hall of Fame for fanny licking. The first orgasm was the missed train out of St Pancras. The second was the slow train down to Brighton. The third was the fast from Euston to Manchester calling at Crewe on route.'

'Imagine a ring tone with the sound of your orgasm?' Faye suddenly suggested. She didn't want to think anymore, about trains because thinking about trains made her recall that fateful day. She could remember the visit from the police officers that changed the twins' lives. The day they'd lost their father. *If only I hadn't had an affair*, she chastised silently in her head for the umpteenth time. *He might be alive today and maybe it would have worked.*

'And the phone starts ringing in the packed foyer of Victoria as you wait for the 5.33 to Southampton, train dividing at Horsham.' Darius persisted with the train theme.

'I would go bright red,' she said.

'Imagine toilet pan mats with faces of MPs on them. I would piss on all the ones guilty in the expenses scandal.'

'Or toilet bowls and seats with members of the Royal Family. And maybe Catholic priests and kiddy fiddlers.' Faye was smiling, her eyes fixed on the tumbling river below as they bantered.

'LIFE'S PRETTY GOOD RIGHT NOW.' She felt truly happy. A feeling she hadn't felt in a long time.

22

FAYE

August 2010

Faye remembered vividly the first Summer in her flat – the moment it felt like home. She had just hung Chrissie's paintings on the washing line. Paint dripped onto the rich emerald lawn, casting long shadows, the paper curling and flapping in the gentle breeze. The kids had friends round. The girls were making puddings and biscuits in the sand pit. The boys were dressed for battle, rushing at each other with swords. Cradling a cup of tea, she studied the exterior - the bricks, the double-glazed windows, the Laura Ashley curtaining and thought to herself – although I'm only renting this is all mine. And it felt good. She had Tony Blair to thank. From that moment on she looked forward to coming home to the flat she'd made their home. She even started to like the estate. The faces of the locals: drunks sitting on the wall outside the pub, the mentally ill who frequented the cafe, the overweight mothers lugging their Iceland shopping off the bus, the kids messing around on the waste land opposite. It was familiar and comforting.

But it was now the Summer of 2010. Politicians were talking about the fair society; David Cameron the new prime minister was working out how to fix 'Broken Britain' and its massive debt problem. As she turned the corner into her road, she could see the blob of red that was the To Let board pinned to the fence in her front garden. The past weeks had been a whirlwind.

'Are you lot sure about all this? You've not said much about Darius.' Faye had asked the kids several times, checking, re checking how they felt. It disturbed her that they didn't seem to have strong opinions. She almost expected them to violently disapprove and fight to protect the status quo.

'Don't back out now, Mother. We want a big house. Somewhere that isn't on a council estate.' Meg dictated.

'But what about living with Darius? You haven't said anything about moving in with him?'

Meg didn't seem bothered. It was as if Faye had asked if she wanted pizza for tea.

'He's alright, I suppose. As long as he takes me to New York again or gets me an IPhone, I don't really care.'

'For God sake. That's not what it's all about. He's not an open wallet.'

'Can we go to Disney? That would be so cool. Please.' Meg begged, as if the word please could turn a demand into reality. Tim just shrugged. Was it possible, Faye wondered for a kid not to have any opinion at all? But in her heart, she knew he had opinions but somewhere over time they'd been lost. She noticed how withdrawn and insular he'd become, little by little since the death of his dad and she didn't know quite what to do about it.

∼

AFTER MUCH DISCUSSION Darius had decided it was better they lived together in a rented house, and if things went well they could then buy somewhere together. Part of her felt let down by him: first the pre-nuptial plans and now pulling out of a commitment to buy somewhere together but she knew that he was just being cautious, in view of everything that had happened and deep down she didn't blame him. Maybe renting was for the best, for now, but rising house prices worried her. Hopefully it wouldn't be long before they decided to buy.

Faye wasn't hungry. She felt overwhelmed. They were in a restaurant and she was picking at the pizza like a small bird. Darius hacked away at his pizza - a butcher with a cleaver; the intensity of conversation in his cramped solicitor's Slough office had given him a raging appetite and thirst for a large whiskey and soda. This was their next visit to the solicitors to discuss a pre-nuptial.

'This whole pre-nuptial stuff doesn't seem clear. So much legal jargon. They aren't law yet so it's probably a waste of time. I don't know what to think Darius. What will it say?'

'You're not good with detail. From your point of view any money you inherit is yours. I can't touch it if we divorce. Same with me. When I inherit from my mum it's mine. You can't try and claim any of it for yourself, or the assets from my business.' Darius called the waitress over, asked for another whiskey. It niggled Faye that drinking and driving never worried him.

'Bottom line, I'm not their father. I'm not supporting them if we divorce. They're not my responsibility.'

'Nobody asked you to.' There was a strained silence. Faye pushed the crusts around the plate. Darius poured some fizzy water. Her hands were shaking, and she thought she might start crying.

'You can see things from my point of you.' His voice was stern.

'Sounds like you're starting to see my kids as a burden –

baggage we've picked up by accident at Terminal Three. This whole pre-nuptial thing isn't very romantic. I never had all of this with Trevor. It's like you don't trust me. History isn't going to repeat itself. You have to get the past out of your head.'

'You don't know what you'll be like. You've got three kids to support. People will do anything for their kids, fighting till they've won.'

'I'm losing tax credits getting together with you. I hope you appreciate that,' she snapped, irritation written across her face.

'Can't you think bigger, beyond a life of scrounging from the government?' He snapped back.

'You're just a bloody Tory. Everyone is a leach to you,' she said.

'I'm going to be picking up the tab, supporting your kids. University is the biggest expense. You've conveniently forgotten that.' Darius dabbed his mouth with a napkin.

'We're a team, aren't we? Helping each other. That's how Trevor and I looked at it. I've never asked you to help through university. I wouldn't dream of it. They'll have to support themselves, and take out loans. If I was on my own, they wouldn't have help.'

Faye had been curling the napkin. Now she was tying it into a knot of fury.

'I think in all of this you're overlooking a very important issue. You're not looking at things from every angle, are you?' She spoke like a detective, the words *important issue* rising to a lilt.

'What are you suggesting?'

'Kathleen. You're forgetting her.'

Darius looked startled. As if he'd been slapped.

'Well.' Faye pulled an upturned smile, shrugged. 'What if your mother's changed her will so that Kathleen inherits and not you.'

'Do you know what? I think at times you're an evil bitch.'

It was Faye's turn now to adopt the slapped-around-the face look.

'She's hinted things to me,' Faye said.

'What things?' Darius spat.

'That she needs to compensate Kathleen for the wrongs of the past. Whatever that means.'

Darius pursed his lips. His face hardened. He tapped the side of his glass.

'It's irrelevant. We haven't found her. And we're not likely to.' And under his breath he added *not now if that is the case*, but Faye didn't hear him.

∼

Darius

Darius had told Faye that it was better they rented a house for a while, just to be cautious in case things didn't work out. But he didn't want to tell her the real reason he was worried about buying another house. He was terrified about taking on a mortgage again, having lost everything. It was a gamble he didn't know he could take. Interest rates had been very low for a long time but what if they went up and continued to go up? They couldn't remain low forever. And what if he had another heart attack? She couldn't pay the mortgage. She was earning peanuts.

The country's economic problems, he believed went back to that lunatic Bin Laden - that hairy man hiding in a cave somewhere. He had a lot to answer to. Alan Greenspan, fearing more attacks, thought America would stop spending and investing; created the QE concept; a massive paper injection of money into the system; interest rates were driven down to encourage spending and restore faith which had led to a nesting instinct; Americans suddenly placing higher value on their homes. Low interest rates had served as the catalyst to accelerate the housing market. Banks were lending freely to anyone; the country had gone on a debt binge. And now he - Darius - needed a mortgage at just the wrong moment in time.

He could remember very clearly the start of the financial crisis and the broken property dream. He was in Florida on business in 2007. In 2006 his wife had bought property in Florida - remortgaging their Nettlebed house to pay for her ludicrous venture and he'd known nothing about it.

He had known things were going to be pretty bad. He was watching TV and thought it was a real cash machine stopping moment. The papers were full of the housing downturn. The whole lending system seemed so wrong, so unsustainable. Everything was falling apart. Things were really getting bad in 2006/2007. The reality of the housing market was that people who shouldn't have been lent to were defaulting. It was obvious it was going to happen in the UK. After all, America sneezes Europe catches the cold, Darius told colleagues. Duff mortgages had been sold in the UK too. His marriage break up hadn't come at a more worse time, because on top of the mortgage debt his wife had caused it wasn't going to sell for anywhere near what it was worth.

∽

'WHAT DOES everyone think to Windrush Close? Or would you prefer to rent Acordia Crescent? Both are awful. Two wrecks to choose from. Two grand a month down the drain to line some bastard landlord's pocket. And if we don't choose either, there aren't any more rentals to look at because they're being snapped up in this crazy rental market.'

The morning's rental viewings had been disheartening. They all sat in the KFC eating a bucket of chicken pieces.

Renting was the best option, but what a waste of money renting was going to be. Money down the drain.

The kids were discussing crazy ideas as they ate. Hide and seek in the gardens of Acordia Crescent and creating a spooky film set in the dilapidated barns of the overgrown garden of Willow Place which was in the back of beyond. Their minds were running away into a fantasy existence.

'You lot aren't paying for it all. It's an adventure for you.'

'Let them have fun Darius,' Faye snapped, tossing her chips aside and wiping salt from her hands.

Faye

'The best properties are snapped up so quickly. It's a heated market.' Faye liked this latest rental. She stood in the hallway and knew it was the one.

Winston Place was perfect. It had the edge on everything they'd seen. It was a 5 minute walk from the school and close to the station. Faye had never wanted to switch the kid's schools even though the kids liked the idea. Darius was quite capable of driving the 40 minutes to his office. It was no big deal. Ok he wanted to be closer but getting together had to involve compromise. She had kids. They came first. Any man entering her life had to recognise and acknowledge that.

He was impressed. The garden backed onto open fields reminding him of his marital home and the views over the Chiltern Hills and the happy memories he carried, of lying in long grass staring at the sky. He liked the little wood burner in the sitting room, the open fireplace in the kitchen and the oak flooring. He could see his furniture in each room. It was a spacious house and even had a study at the back overlooking the garden that he could turn into an office from home.

'It will be lovely in the winter, warm and cosy with the open fire,' he said.

When the kids saw it, they couldn't contain their excitement, playing hide and seek within minutes and planning who was going to sleep where and what new furniture they needed. Faye knew it was the right decision. Darius was happy, she was happy and more importantly the kids were happy. She felt a sense of calm. Maybe it had all been worth it after all.

Life was now on the up. But would a bigger home be enough to make them happy?

23

FAYE

August 2010

'You want to be an architect?' Sam smiled at Meg over the table. Faye watched the two of them chatting, sizing each other up. Meg was twiddling with the chopsticks, nervously. She wondered if Sam found her attractive then quickly remembered his sexuality. She studied his features. Why was it, she thought that gay men were so stunningly attractive. What a waste she said to herself. She was glad they were chatting so well. It couldn't be easy for either of them meeting for the first time. Yet the atmosphere around the table was so tense that Faye was aware of every sniff, every cough, every clink of glasses in the Chinese restaurant - on edge in expectation that something would go wrong.

Darius said very little to Tim and Chrissie. He looked over, tutted, shook his head in disapproval as they folded and unfolded a napkin between them trying out different shapes - uninterested in getting to know their future stepbrother.

'There's been a lot of programmes lately about the construction of famous buildings. And going to New York with my mum and your dad really inspired me. New York is amazing.'

'I'm going to make a wonderful stepfather aren't I, Sam? The kid loved New York.' Darius laughed.

The waitress took the order.

'We'll have Dim Sum and your finest chicken soup. And seaweed and duck and pancakes. No expense spared this evening. This is the start of our future together. Are we really moving in together in two weeks, Faye? It's all happened so quick.' Darius placed the order then took Faye's hand smiling.

'Dad likes to flash his money, Meg. You'll soon learn that.' Meg giggled and Darius was quick to reply.

'I needed plenty of it bringing you up and having to prop you up in a crap profession that pays so poorly. Hopefully you'll get into hairdressing management at some point and earn better money.'

A swift change came over Sam. It was as if a key had been inserted into his back and wound. He had been asking Meg questions, had listened to her career ideas. He had shown a brief interest in Tim and Chrissie. But now his conversation became erratic. His voice speeded up, the volume cranked up. He became a runaway train that wasn't going to stop for any passengers.

'I had a phone call from my old boss at Tantridge Salon and he wanted to have dinner with me...' Sam rambled on. Tim and Chrissie showed no interest. They were talking and laughing to each other and pointing to a fat man puffing his way up the road against the strong gale.

Darius and Meg didn't interrupt.

'Last week I went out for a drink in London and I got chatting with a guy who runs one of the most prestigious salons in the country and he offered me a job with management potential. He was really impressed by everything I said.'

There was strain behind Darius's smile, Faye noticed. As if a hundred balls were being thrown at him at once. His face said *I'm not sure I believe all this codswallop.* Faye was surprised he didn't interrupt, allowing Sam to ramble on and dominate the stage, only interested in himself.

And then the biggest bombshell of all hit.

'And I was shopping in Tesco and who should I bump into but Kathleen, your sister. It was so strange. I've always wondered what she was like. Now I know. She said she's been avoiding you all these years. She hates you Dad. That's what she said. She's pleased I'm in hairdressing and wants me to do her hair sometime...' Sam's words were racing ahead and Darius felt like a startled jockey on a winning horse at Ascot. He couldn't digest the words, the speed, the context. Sam's whole world seemed to be spinning out of control.

Darius had heard enough. He needed to take control. Put a stop to the nonsense Sam was spouting. Reality had kicked in. Bringing a tight fist down he slammed the table with a heavy thud. Cutlery tinkled. A glass toppled. Red wine splashed and bled through the fibres of the crisp linen making an obscure pattern among the shards of prawn crackers and curls of noddles. A waiter rushed over with a cloth.

'Stop talking fucking bollocks.' He slammed his fist again. Violence flared in his eyes. A feeling of panic coiled its way around the table.

People stopped eating. Heads were turning. It was as if somebody had zapped a remote control to freeze frame a movie scene.

∼

ON THE WAY HOME, Faye asked Darius what he thought. Faye had only met Sam a couple of times before. At first, she'd liked Sam, but now she found him arrogant and self centred. He gave the impression he was better than everyone else. He had treated Tim and Chrissie as if they were wallpaper covering; had made little attempt to talk to them. Faye had found this hurtful but excused him. Possibly he'd been gripped by nerves. Maybe he had very little experience of children. A stepfamily was a lot to take on.

'What was all that stuff about Kathleen? He didn't really meet her? Surely?'

'Of course not. It was all bollocks. I'm worried, Faye. He was making no sense in that restaurant. I'm worried he's taking drugs. Maybe cocaine. It seemed as if he was on a high.'

'Maybe he hasn't been sleeping very well or working too many shifts. If it's drugs, he'll deny it,' Faye said.

He sighed. 'I don't know Faye. I've got enough work issues of my own at the moment.'

'Well... that will never change.' Her words trailed into a forest of silence and then she had a thought.

'Maybe he's just coming into his own. This could be the new son you're just discovering. A man who's becoming more confident. I expect working in a hair salon he's getting used to chatting to customers all day long.'

'Rubbish Faye. You know it. This is different. I know my own son. I think he's on drugs.'

'Don't be ridiculous,' Faye snapped.

Darius

'This place is a bit greasy.' Darius put his fork down. Eating at the Yankee Diner was like being on a business trip in the States. He wiped his mouth.

'We could have stayed in that Vietnamese restaurant.' Sam said from across the table.

Nah. I didn't fancy eating Agent Orange soup.'

'Fuck off, Dad. That's a sick joke.'

'I think I'll be delivering a napalm bomb in the toilet after this nasty burger.'

'Don't be disgusting.'

'Or we could have had a sushi over the road. A Fukashima soup or the iodine platter.'

Sam stifled a snigger, used to his dad's tasteless jokes, hating them one minute, laughing the next.

They were eating in Covent Garden. It was the weekend after the Chinese meal. Bill Haley was rocking around the clock. A waitress in a crisp white pinny tapped her feet as she leant against the counter waiting for a strawberry shake to be passed across.

'You were weird last week, mate,' Darius said casually, trying carefully to tiptoe into the area he wanted to discuss.

'Is that what her kids said?'

'They don't have opinions,' Darius said in a withered voice.

'They were ok.' Sam smiled. 'Chrissie was a cutie. I talked to Tim about computer games. And Meg's a sweet girl. Bright.'

'But then you took over. What were you saying about Kathleen? You've never met her.'

'Is that what I said?'

'Yes, you fucking did. Sam... what are you on? You're taking something. I know you are.'

Sam seemed to have forgotten everything he had talked about in the Chinese restaurant.

'I was probably a bit drunk. I don't remember what I was saying.' He was dismissive.

Sam carved into his burger. 'I'm going on a trip to Brugges with Mum.' Darius stopped cutting, dropped his knife. This was some confession.

'You didn't tell me that. I'm the last to know everything. And how is your bitch of a mother financing this trip? And you? The money I give your landlord every month for rent is obviously way too much.'

'Stop referring to her as the bitch. She's my mother. How do you think that makes me feel? I don't think it's any of your business how Mum is paying for the trip. And so what if I'm taking the odd line of cocaine? What's it to do with you?'

'Now that's where you're completely wrong.' Darius felt a hot coal of anger burn in his chest. 'That bitch, did you just say cocaine? Oh Sam. For fuck's sake. Stay away from that gear. It's affecting you. Any idiot can see how it's changing you. You're not the same person anymore. I'm not supporting you if you're spending money on drugs.'

'She's your ex-wife and my mother. And it's my choice what I do with my life,' Sam jabbed back.

'I repeat...*that* bitch, you call your mother, stole thousands from me. Your memory is pretty crap these days, Sam. She should pay her debts first. How do you think she's paying? Out of my hard-earned money.' His voice was rising but he maintained a tone that gave him control.

'I don't care, Dad. The divorce is over. It's time you moved on.'

'You may sneer, brush it all aside. It's your future she's ruined. Are you too stupid to see that? No son of mine goes on holiday with a woman who bled his father dry and walked off with a rich Yank. You should disown her. It's the only way she will see sense and drop the pension claim.'

'Your divorce settlement has nothing to do with me. If you've been told by the courts to pay up, that's what you should do. They'll freeze your bank account if you don't.' Sam picked his burger up.

This kind of non-committal attitude stirred something deep inside. Darius's problems were Sam's problems too.

'Now that's where you're acting like a complete selfish cunt.' Heads were turning. He could no longer hear the music. Fries tilted on forks, glasses poised to lips, everybody freeze-framed like when a video in a machine gets stuck.

'Dad, stop being irrational. She's allowed a holiday.'

It was Darius's turn to boot where it hurt. 'You have no regard for my feelings or what I went through,' he spat. 'You expect to come to mine, sit around watching sport on my Sky package, let me take you out for meals. You know what? It's no wonder you failed your GCSEs if you can't even reach the correct conclusion about your mother.'

Sam scraped his chair back. A waitress glanced across ready to take the plate. Darius saw Sam's wounded look but was unmoved.

'I'm not going to let you treat me like this. My friends keep telling me I deserve better. When you've got something civil to say, call me.' Sam was curt, but calm. He pushed the chair, tucking it under the table. A knife clattered to the floor. 'The way you're going Dad you'll have another heart attack.'

'You don't just get up and walk out of a restaurant,' Darius hissed.

If this prick of a son couldn't be transparent about money it was high time to cut the cord. Why should he carry on supporting his son? If he had chosen a proper career, he'd be earning decent money by now. He could have been an accountant or a teacher. Anger bubbled and boiled and rose to the surface. Darius reached for his glass. Without giving time to think how ridiculous he was, he flicked the dregs of the sickly chocolate shake at his son's face. It felt good.

~

Darius was driving to Heathrow when he took the call, a week after the meal with his son.

A pleasant summer breeze thrashed his shirt like a sail at sea, wind smacking from all directions. He loved his soft top. It was a good sturdy car, safe but could handle speed.

His phone was vibrating in his shirt pocket. He didn't want

to stop, loose time. The check-in queues were always horrendous, particularly when flying to the States. He headed for the long-stay car park circuiting round, finally edging into a space zapping the car into neutral.

It was Sam. He wasn't making much sense. Darius couldn't decipher what he was really saying and the thunder of a plane taking off didn't help. The minute Darius asked any questions or tried to clarify, Sam would talk over him. Something wasn't right.

'Slow down Sam, for God's sake. I can't understand what you're saying mate. Deep breaths. Start again. You've locked yourself out of the salon?'

'Yes. The neighbour tried to help me get back in.' Sam rambled on. Darius was confused.

'I'm heading back to London now - got to get back. I don't feel safe at work. People are talking about me and whispering. They're planning something,' Sam said.

'Safe? What? You have your car keys then?'

'Yes, obviously.'

'Not *obviously* Sam. I thought they'd be on the same key fob as your house keys, that's all.'

'I stopped at Mc Donald's in Slough, but I didn't feel safe in there, so I continued driving and stopped at a massive Toys R Us. Dad, do you know what I saw in there?'

'Cut to the chase Sam. I'm about to catch a plane. What's this all about? You're rambling on about nothing. What have you been taking?'

'I saw a beautiful doll and a child's hairdressing set. Like the one you refused to buy me when I was six. I remember what you told me. *Boys don't play with dolls.* You bought me a Liverpool football team tracksuit instead even though I hate football. You've always tried to get me into football. The doll is on the back shelf of the Corsa, Dad.'

And then as swift as a storm cloud Sam tone changed.

'But what the hell? What would you understand? It's a fucking doll. And do you know what I'm going to do with that doll? I'm going to imagine it's you, Dad and stick pins all over its face. It's a boy doll. I'm going to stick pins up it's back side because that's what you'd like, Dad isn't it? You can't accept who I am. What I am. Can you?'

'xcuse me? Darius felt the slap of sarcasm and wondered what would come next.

'You're a cunt, Dad.'

'What?' Darius snapped. There was a pause while he tried to digest this latest gristle and lift his case from the car. The conversation was slipping into a dark and dangerous place he didn't want to go.

'Well fuck you,' he spat and ended the call.

He dragged his bags to the terminal. Was Sam losing the plot he wondered? Was he taking drugs? He felt so detached from his son. He couldn't work him out any longer. His moods had become unpredictable - sometimes sulky and evasive, sometimes manic.

Darius moved through the tedium of security and slumped into a chair at the gate to await the boarding announcement. He had twenty minutes to check emails and watch the slaggy cabin crew from dreadful northern towns tripping along the conveyor belt in heels so thin they might snap off at any moment ready to be rammed up their pert arses. His eyes shot away. The male cabin crew followed on, their hands and arms flapping all over the place as they chatted and laughed in their shrill voices. They were pretty boys looking forward to a short stop-over in Alicante or Malaga or some other God awful place with the prospect of picking up a tan and a Gary or a Robbie on the beach for a quick shafting before the return flight back to the UK.

His phone was vibrating again but it was Faye this time. He filled her in on the brief call with Sam, but she was already up to speed on what was happening. 'Jesus. I'm on my way to the States and the little shit calls to tell me he's locked himself out of the hair salon. What am I supposed to do, Faye?'

'Can I do anything?'

'Not really. He's a grown man. He's out of our control. If he's taking drugs, what the hell can I do?'

On the plane, Darius closed his eyes and dreamt of Sam, the young boy. He was running along the beach. Then they were digging an enormous and elaborate sandcastle. He saw images of toddler Sam sitting on bear's bench at the bottom of the garden. But each image was slowly erased by the dark shadow of his ex, spilling over the picture, turning it to grey mush. She seemed to drown out the happiness, the laughter. He wished he could airbrush her out of their past, his existence. She was a poison seeping through everything that had gone wrong.

∽

DARIUS WAS in the hotel bed, fighting the waking, each problem hitting him like missiles. The financial wreckage of his marriage, his mother's dying wish, his health and now Sam.

He thought again about the fallout from his divorce. He'd tried to make things work with his wife. But in truth he should never have married her. On their wedding day he'd woken with a feeling of dread. How ironic it now seemed. Losing a grand for an aborted wedding was nothing compared to the thousands she had swallowed, gambling it away on the Florida investments.

Sam was the marital sticking plaster, for a time. Darius had adored the kid. They had built a model railway in the garden when he was five and spent hours playing with it. And when he was seven, they'd started doing Air Fix kits in the shed.

His ex couldn't have coped alone as a single parent. When

she'd suggested Sam go to a private school, he'd thought it was one of her better ideas. Most of the state schools in Henley and Marlow were mediocre, massive comprehensives that churned people out like toilet rolls on a factory conveyor. He wanted him to have the best chances. But the lad hadn't found GCSE's easy and wasn't academic enough for A levels. Darius wiped away the knowing disappointment. Darius had been understanding but it was looking likely that he'd always be on a low wage and never be able to buy a property and stand on his own two feet. Darius was beginning to feel a level of despair. He'd forked out enough money. He was paying Sam rent. His pocket was a bottomless pit. It was all getting a bit beyond the call of duty. The kid wasn't young anymore. It was time he supported himself. *I'm an old engine* he'd told Sam. *I can't support you for much longer.*

∼

THE AIR HAD that musty cloying smell all rentals had. Darius began tearing open boxes resigned to his transient existence - his belongings were a travelling circus. He was sick of moving house.

With his sleeve he dusted a framed picture of Sam eating macaroni cheese splattered all over his smiling face, like pus. He tried to recapture the memory of Sam laughing and waving a plastic spoon, a cheeky glint in his eyes, but all he could see was the young man he'd metamorphosed into – moody and arrogant. Flecks of sunlight spilt onto his wispy dark locks, filling the scene with radiance and earthy heaven. Was the past just an illusion?

There was a level of disassociation that made him wonder whether this faintly familiar stranger was really his own flesh and blood. In the first few weeks of Sam's life he had also felt like this - but those were feelings of joy and love; touching and looking at perfection, a tiny miracle, wondering *is this little thing really mine?* He loved to feel the warmth of the small bundle lying on his chest. But now he looked at his son and felt an intense loathing.

This wasn't the boy he used to laugh and joke with. Or take to the beach to collect shells. Days of bliss now jagged shards of memory. He remembered with such clarity how he'd felt when Sam was just two, when he'd longed for the end of his working day so he could scoop the toddler into his arms and plant furious kisses around his neck. Then he'd chase him on all fours around the room, hiding behind the settee, jumping out, falling apart on the carpet laughing, teasing and tickling. They created the idea of the 'Domite' a fictitious animal who loved kissing and licking ears and would end up in a heap on the floor, both with soggy ears. He remembered the times he'd cuddled Sam in the late Summer sun, stroking his mop of dark curls.

'This will always be our special bench and our very own garden corner.' He'd smile down at Sam, whose bare legs dangled over the struts of the bench, pausing between pages of their favourite story about a rat in a shop. Darius remembered looking up from the book and over towards the meadow undulating away to the Chilterns. He never wanted his son to be scared of a single thing.

But now Sam was just the young man he took out for a meal now and again. He was part of a past Sam didn't understand or remember very well.

The relationship was sliding downhill, but he wasn't stopping to think about how strange Sam's behaviour was becoming.

Faye

Faye stood in the doorway with mugs of tea watching

Darius and Tim chatting to each other, reading the Ikea instructions for the new desk they had bought the day before and were now building, making mistakes with different pieces and laughing. It was late August. They had been living together for a week.

In that moment she knew moving in with Darius had been the right thing. Tim needed a male role model in his life. Fortnightly visits to his dad weren't enough. Something had been missing.

Darius looked up. Took the mug.

'The gingerbread teddy bear we found at the laundry. Did you find Tim's one when you were packing?' Darius asked.

'I'd forgotten about that. I did search the house thoroughly when we got back from Ireland. No. There was no sign of it. I must have taken it to a charity shop years ago.' But what Faye didn't know at that point was that the gingerbread man would turn up and unexpectedly, but not for another few years and under sad circumstances.

'That's a shame.' Darius looked sad.

24

DARIUS

October 2010

'God damn it Faye,' Darius snapped. They were in the kitchen.

'It's what teenagers do. You've forgotten,' Faye replied.

'It doesn't have to be like this.'

'I shouldn't have left them with you. You said it would be ok. I only went away for a few days.' Faye dropped her bag on the kitchen floor.

'While you were in Cornwall with Chrissie and your cousin, I was having the week from hell. Meg and Tim stayed in their rooms all week. They hardly spoke to me. I feel invisible.'

'You're winding me up?' Faye searched his face.

'Jesus. They live under my roof. I pay the bills. I deserve some bloody respect. Not this.'

'It's just the way they are.'

'Bollocks. It's deliberate.'

'You take everything personally.'

'What sort of imbeciles are you bringing up?'

'Steady on. That's a bit harsh.'

If he'd had his way, he would have confronted Meg and

Tim. They remained in their cells, doors firmly closed, as usual, while she tried to placate him by flicking the kettle hoping his feelings would dissolve in a peace keeping cup of tea.

∽

DARIUS SAT at his office desk, his mind drifting. An uneaten sandwich lay on a pile of papers, lettuce escaping. He felt sure women were programmed differently. Sometimes when he talked to Faye it was like watching something made of mud attempt to think.

Many arguments centred in the kitchen and were to do with food or cooking. Women didn't understand the science behind cooking. They understood the pretty colours on top of cupcakes and the art of napkin folding. The kitchen was no different to a science laboratory. Cooking was experimental science. To be able to cook and get it right you had to understand the physical processes - how to control temperature to avoid a soufflé collapsing and how to tenderize meat. But Faye didn't listen. She had a childlike frustration with anything scientific. She was like a Spanish dog – couldn't be changed. Getting worked up over heavy saucepans was like a scenario of a toddler throwing toys out of a playpen. He knew to step back, not to interfere at that point. She didn't see that practically anything technical was possible. It was hard to reason with her. Her voice took on a whine when she was frustrated and that became particularly apparent with technical equipment: hoovers, computers, telephones and dishwashers.

At the beginning of their relationship, he'd admired her frugality more than anything else about her. She had an incredible ability to save money. She'd managed to live on so little as a single mother. This was refreshing after the way his ex had lived. He'd swapped a spender for a saver. But as time went by, he wasn't sure he could live with either. It drove him mad to open an empty fridge.

Ever since Darius was a young boy growing up in poverty living mainly on offal – liver, hearts, kidneys, brawn and cowheel soup and pig's belly and pickled herrings, he was determined the fridge would always be full. His grandparents hadn't been able to shake off the ridiculous war mentality of using up every scrape, cutting off the edges of mouldy cheese and squeezing tea bags out for the fifth cup. He remembered the horrible Catholic tradition of fishcakes on Fridays.

᜼

'What am I paying you a grand a month for?' Darius asked Faye. He'd been thinking about money. 'When I set up that standing order, you were expected to spend a minimum of 200 a week on food. What are you doing with it? I'm earning 150k a year for what? To live on olives and Petit Filous yogurts? We're going to have to start shopping together.' He needed control back in his life. This was ridiculous.

He suspected she was scrimping, up to her old tricks and eccentricities as a poverty-stricken single mother. At the flat they had all shared an inch of grimy bath water and clothes were only bought from charity shops and boot fairs. Her measures were so extreme she had even made toothpaste from baking soda, salt and peppermint oil, to save up to pay the mortgage off. Darius couldn't understand this whole culture of extreme cost cutting. What was it all about? He hoped never to be in that situation himself. If things ever got that bad, he'd buy a rope and tie it to a very tall sturdy oak tree and hope the end came swiftly.

Faye

Faye was proud of herself. Food needn't cost the earth or leave you broke she told Darius. The words 'value' or 'basic' or 'economy' and 'budget' glowed on her radar, jumping into the trolley knocking a few pennies, a few quid off the final bill. Swiftly moving up and down aisles she had the regimentation of a Korean army corporal and the organization of the Gestapo. Lists were essential, crossing out items, moving onwards, never lingering or lurking in the chocolate aisle. A bottle of budget whiskey - a once-a -year-treat and the occasional stash of clotted cream rice pudding, hidden at the back of the fridge.

Faye loathed waste, which was so hard when you had kids. 'Waste not want not' was her mantra. It was better to buy in small quantities than buy a fridge full of stuff and end up throwing half of it out. As a young child her grandma had made her recite a poem every time she felt the urge to waste:

I shall not throw on the floor the stuff I cannot eat cause many hungry little ones would think it quite a treat. Tis wistful waste make woeful want and I will live to say how I wish I had that little crumb I once had thrown away.

She was used to an empty fridge but unlike Darius she hadn't rebelled against her childhood. She had been swept along with the values of thrift, frequently telling her kids *I'm not asking you to like it I'm asking you to eat it.* Cooking for kids was a futile exercise. She dreaded the plates cast aside because the meal was 'gus gus' but when it was 'lish lish' there was never enough. The poor blighters were always fishing for a fill up of biscuits soon after dinner, much to the annoyance of Faye.

Darius

He didn't like shopping, but it was important to have a say in what ended up on his plate. He imagined a smart fridge that ordered food directly or a 3d printer that synthesized food, cooked it and recovered materials from human waste. 'This will come one day' he told himself. The Samsung Gastro 3. He could see it. At least this way you could by-pass the downtrodden cashier in her fifties, nursing a prolapsed womb; a robot that asked the same thing, over and over 'want a bag for life dear?' He looked at the old bag behind the till and gave the same answer each time. 'I had a bag for life. Thank God I've divorced her.'

Faye had a wallet full of loyalty cards but he hated the concept of loyalty cards. They were designed to cleverly - or not so cleverly extract a customer's personal details and compile their shopping preferences. Saving up piddly amounts on loyalty cards was a complete waste of time and money off vouchers that spewed out of tills. Only the proles with their shortsighted mentality were conned by the farce of vouchers. Karl Marx could write a whole pamphlet on the subjugation of the proles by way of supermarket. *I don't do loyalty* he would tell the cashier. He enjoyed the shock on their faces. *I do infidelity, so if you have a card that clocks up infidelity points I would be more than happy to take one.*

But the biggest arguments – the ones that rocked the foundations of their relationship were toilet related. It had become a running argument every time he left the toilet door open when he was having a wee.

'Can you shut the door when you're in the loo. The kids might walk by.' She always screamed at him. Most of the time he went up to the bedroom to use the ensuite, locking the bedroom door behind him. But even locking that door was deeply nerve racking. She didn't understand and what was the use of explaining.

But the first of big arguments came a few weeks after moving in. Darius heard a blood curdling scream from the cloakroom. 'What's wrong?' He scrapped the chair across the wooden floor, flipped the lid down on his Mac. 'What the fuck have you done? We've only been here three weeks. Jesus. I'm flying to Japan at four in the morning and I need to finish this article,' he screamed.

Faye was watching water gush from the cistern like a liquid tornado. The toilet had come alive. It looked like a porcelain monster.

'Get the Yellow Pages. Quick.' Her feet were fixed to the ground, but it unnerved him the way she was blocking the door. She knew he hated to be penned into a toilet. His heart began to race.

She carried on screaming. 'The flush was too slow. I thought I'd just tweak the ballcock and this happened.' Her face was flushed. The toilet wasn't. She leaned over, peered into the cistern as if it were a mysterious cavern. The cistern, Darius thought should be a no-go area with a clearly displayed warning sign for women.

'You fiddle with this, you mess with that. Get the Yellow Pages, now. You stupid fucking woman,' he screamed, inches from her face, feeling like a Nazi general. 'Move it.' He went to look for the valve to stop the water. He slammed cupboard doors, cursing, frantically searching. Then he ran into the street looking for a manhole cover, came back to the cloakroom grabbing the Yellow Pages. Faye was still fixed to the spot, now hysterical.

'You're nothing but a cancer. A useless bitch,' he screamed.

Darius called a plumber and within half an hour was answering the door to a plumber and his tool kit––in all probability a toilet enthusiast for whom bogs were his bread and butter. By now the cloakroom looked like a documentary on the Niagara Falls.

'Get out of his way. Your life is like toilet paper – long and useless,' Darius shouted. Already he could see the bill. This toilet geek would be raking it in, in call out fees to fix broken, blocked and buggered toilets, probably loving the fact that most people grabbed the phone not a plunger.

That night he dreamt about life without a toilet - shitting in the garden behind the shed, admiring a steaming pile, coiled like a snake in a pit. Good manure for the roses and sprinkling of his wee - death to ivy and mint creeping up fences, strangling plants - more economical than half the stuff sold in garden centres. Who was going to spot his cock at the bottom of the garden, except under a bright moon?

In the morning he felt just as angry about what she'd done. 'You women are good at bleaching, scrubbing and wiping toilets. Fantastic at erasing the dribbles, the awkward, caked on skid marks but haven't the foggiest when it comes to the basic mechanics.'

Darius told Sam what had happened, over lunch, three weeks later. Sam laughed.

'I just want to weep.'

'See the funny side,' Sam urged him.

'Fuck off. That mini Noah's Ark flood cost me £400.'

'You got to admit it is funny.' Sam belly-laughed.

'I had a 4am flight to Japan the following morning. Her kids had been particularly obnoxious that evening.'

'Give them a break. Her kids are ok.'

'They were unsociable, doing their usual routine after dinner. I can still see the blank look of Chrissie standing in the doorway. That kid is weird. I can sympathise with Ian Brady.'

'That's a terrible thing to say, Dad.'

'Might have known I wouldn't get your vote of support.'

Darius looked in despair, fixed his eyes on the view over the street performers on the cobbled square of Covent Garden. 'Bloody women. She suddenly decides she's going to fiddle with the ballcock to improve the water flow.'

'It's not a big deal, Dad.' He was stifling a grin, half watching a pigeon strutting along a nearby wall.

'Why do women tamper with stuff they don't understand?'

'What happened next?' For a moment Sam looked as if he

was starting to take the conversation seriously. He rubbed the stumble on his chin.

'I've never seen so much water. It was like a gigantic tidal wave crashing through the cloakroom, destroying everything in its wake.'

'Exaggeration? Or trying to sound amusing?'

'Hardly. She was hysterical. She wasn't going to call someone out. I took her upstairs to calm her down. She'd transformed into a wailing banshee by this stage. The only thing I could do was slap her, hard across the face. It was like yanking out the lead from a socket. She needed a new Sim card inserted. She was screaming in my face, inches away. I could feel the spital. The wild look in her eyes. I had to do something to stop her.'

'Bloody hell. What next?' Sam seemed only interested in the theatrics.

'She slapped me back. My glasses flew off, skidded across the floor. I don't know what would have happened next if I hadn't left the room.'

'And then something else happened a week later, you said?'

'Her brother had just arrived to look after the kids for a week while we went on a business trip to Istanbul. It was the kid's toilet this time. I'm forever telling them not to put so much loo paper down in. They never listen. And Faye defends them every time. Keeps saying it's a slow flush and not the kid's fault. I put a banana down the toilet, flushed it to show them it works perfectly well. But her snotty nosed kid uses far too much paper to wipe his nose. He hasn't learned to blow his nose properly yet. I've tried to teach him. Hopeless.'

'It got blocked?'

'We couldn't leave it for her brother Steve to sort out. I was cooking. Faye can't cook a decent meal. If I left the cooking to her on a Sunday it would be pizza. I flung her the Yellow Pages, told her just to call someone out. But she wouldn't. She started screaming again. In the end she made a phone call. Half-way through the call she threw the phone at me. It hit me on the side of the head. My first thought...there's a screw lose somewhere.'

'Did it get sorted?'

'She used a plunger. Should have done that in the first place.'

'You're not having much luck on the toilet front then?'

'All the toilets are unclean. The en suite stinks of rotting cabbage or decomposing rats. I get the blame for the smell. She thinks it's my turds blocking the pipes.'

'You need to get the agency onto the problems.'

'And every time her ex, Shayne-the-wanker drops his kid back, he lingers in the hall trying to amuse Faye with infantile jokes. His latest joke, by sheer coincidence is *what's the worst thing you can buy in a charity shop? A toilet roll.*' Darius scoffed, eyes to the ceiling.

Faye

Faye was enjoying Istanbul, winding her way through the bowels of the Grand Bazaar, a rabbit warren of stalls, looking at carpets and trinkets and colourful sparkly garments.

Sipping tea, enjoying the flirtations of the stall traders she thought back over the night the toilet had flooded. She couldn't shake off the image of Darius shouting, 'you useless fucking woman, haven't you got any common sense? Are you that dense?' The words played mental tennis in her head. Trevor had always called her dense. Darius was doing the same.

She accepted another apple tea and watched the throng of people moving around the bazaar. It was a shame he couldn't laugh about things that went wrong. They'd both end up having heart attacks at this rate.

'I just wanted to show you I could sort a problem,' she'd told him.

'Are you an expert suddenly on toilets? Why tackle something you don't understand? It's the most stupid thing you've ever done.' He'd spat the words, anger filling his face every time the events were recalled. All she wanted was for him to hug her and tell her it was ok – it was only a God damn toilet.

When Darius was in a rage, he became Trevor and his words rang in her ears, feasting on reason, staining her, labeling her forever stupid, forever useless. Her hysteria had very nearly gushed over into something uncontrollable. She had never lashed out and hit another human being in her life. She felt ashamed to have lost control. But out of the fug she vaguely remembered him shouting that she was a mental case, a piece of useless shit. *You're as much use as a cancer.* She was certain he'd said that and couldn't quite believe it.

When they returned from Istanbul the drama was repeated when the kid's toilet blocked again.

'Your kids are animals. I'm going to make you lot pay the plumber's bill. You'll soon learn not to block it again,' he shouted.

'What did you do to it? Feed it a whole toilet roll, like an irresponsible visitor at the zoo? Jesus did you not read the DO NOT FEED sign clearly pinned to the wall? What animal precisely were you thinking of creating out of the brown papier mache mess?' Darius peered into the bowl poking at the brown paper sludge with the plunger, holding his nose. 'A brown bog monster?' he suggested, looking over at a glum lifeless Tim standing at the door, who just shrugged. 'Something mythical that will come to life?' he added.

In the end Faye unblocked the damn toilet claiming the certificate The Queen of Bogs. Shit had splattered her face. She was hot, sweaty, annoyed. The words *well done* didn't enter his head. She desperately wanted to hear those words. All he could talk about in the weeks that followed was the telephone she had thrown - allegedly at him after she had scoured the yellow pages, made some calls to plumbers. She had thrown it in a moment of pure animal anger and frustration. How dare he treat her like an idiot telesales girl. He could treat the people in his office how he liked. He could interrupt their phone calls, but he wasn't going to do that to her.

'How much do you charge? How soon could you come?'

But he'd kept shouting in the background as he carried on cooking. *Cut. Cut the call. Move on. Next call. End the call.* She had been livid. She hadn't heard their answers. All she had heard was Darius screaming for her to end the call. *They're time wasters. When are you going to realise? Dozy bitch.* In a flash Faye had ended the call, spun round and in one stupendous, glorious moment of fury hurled the phone across the room, watching it bounce, then crack across the hard floor.

Her first thought was that he'd apologise. But he hadn't.

'You should be locked up and the key thrown away,' he'd shouted. She'd felt like a helpless prisoner facing a firing squad. This was a powerless place. She'd been reduced to a childlike state.

25

DARIUS
NOVEMBER 2010

'Oh dear Mary Mother of God let me sit as far away from that woman as possible.'

The coach was inching out into the road, leaving the Amman Hotel to begin the day's excursion.

'Mother, why the fuck did we come to Jordan?'

Darius had initially thought it was a good idea to go away for a week with his mother. He had needed the break from Faye after the recent toilet arguments but going away with his mother wasn't ideal.

It had been his mother's suggestion; a suggestion that surprised him because he thought her days of travelling were over and didn't imagine she would have the energy, but she had worked everything out very competently, all considering.

'If it was a holy shrine you wanted to see we could have visited the holy wells of Cornwall and feasted on a heart attack clotted cream tea and I think there's a stream in Toxteth called the Jordan. Bloody hell we didn't have to come all this way to see the Jordan.

All you've done all week is complain. You don't like their tea. I did warn you about the mint tea and the cardamom tea.

They don't sell PG Tips out here or Yorkshire Tea.' He huffed, looked out the window watching street traders selling garments.

'Well dear you can take the English out of England, but you can't take the Englishness out of the English. And right now, I'm craving a decent cup of tea.' Maria adjusted her Mrs. Thatcher style handbag on her lap, unclipped the top to search for a stray tea bag.

Darius ignored her. Taking his mother on a Christian tour had been her choice not his. An impulsive decision arranged only a few weeks back and another of her dying wishes, he suspected.

'You've not stopped moaning about the tea since we arrived. And all this cadging tea bags from the other travellers is getting embarrassing, Mum. The coach's tea stock is dwindling thanks to you. We'll be on ration soon.'

'It's the hotel's fault. I checked to make sure they had tea and coffee making facilities. I went back in the travel agents twice to clarify the matter. They assured me there would be.'

'But they only provide a kettle. As you keep reminding me, Mum.'

'Why provide a kettle but no tea? It makes no sense at all.'

'Then you complained about the heat. This is the desert. You knew it was going to be hot. And now you're worried about that woman.' Darius pointed across the aisle of the coach to one of the other passengers on their tour.

'*That* woman might have a bug and you know I've got a delicate stomach. I sat on the toilet for the entire week when we went to Egypt.'

'*That* woman is probably pregnant. Look at her. All loved up to her husband, so she is.' He pointed.

'She said she was throwing up all night. She's ill and she's going to pass it round the entire coach. You mark my word, I'll be the first to catch it. I'm O positive and you know we're more prone to bugs than other blood groups. I keep reminding you. You see. Pass me the hand gel. I touched the handrail that she just touched. Did you pack the Imodium?'

'You might get the squits with all the lentil soup they keep serving up, but not from *that* woman, so for now just shut up and enjoy the view.'

'The view? I didn't imagine the Arabs would be such dirty people. Rubbish everywhere you look. All I keep seeing are bin bags dumped on wasteland, thorny bushes and cypress trees adorned in carrier bags fluttering in the breeze and piles of filthy nappies dumped by the roadside. Do these women have no shame?'

'Clearly not, Mum.'

The coach was now ten minutes into its 45 minute journey to the holy site of Bethany, where Jesus was cleansed by the waters of the River Jordan. Darius tried to block his mother's voice from his head as he watched the scenery outside the coach roll by like a film reel. There were donkeys on waste ground, heads of cows dangling from racks outside shops, a truck laden with bananas, boys playing games in the gutters.

The tour guide picked up the microphone as he'd done each day of their seven- day tour of Jordan.

'I wonder what he's going to say this morning.' Darius yawned. 'I preferred the old days when church services were all in Latin. I didn't understand a bloody word.'

'Let us pray that the finger of God will be upon those who are feeling unwell. Lord, thank you for this beautiful day and bless Assad for driving us. May we be led by God's wisdom and by the very presence of God. God's spirit lives within you. We are God's temple in this bus as the people of Israel were God's people in the tabernacle.' Passion and joy radiated from the leader's face.

Darius put two fingers into his mouth, pretending to vomit. 'If he mentions the finger of God once more, I think I'll ram his finger up his arse.' Darius surreptitiously stuck a finger up from behind the seat.

'Darius shush. You need to repent. This is supposed to be a holy trip. The Lord is trying to open your eyes to His Majesty and turn your heart around. If you'd only take that leap of faith, you'd see how much He loves and cares for you.'

'Mother you either have the God chip or you don't. It's like a circuit board. You're either wired up to receive the message or you're not. And I'm not.'

With one almighty swoop Maria brought her handbag crashing across his head.

'Fuck. Mother. Jeez what's in that bag of yours? I'm not wired up, alright?'

The tour guide had picked up the microphone again. 'Lord let us walk with you and speak to us in your own special way as you did through the donkey...'

'I'll be speaking in my language soon and it consists of two words. Fuck off.'

'Darius. Please. You're spoiling the experience. I need to close my eyes so that I can feel God's presence, feel his hand upon me, guiding me to our dear Kathleen.'

'We're not going to find Kathleen out here. I'll tell you that much. We might find her working in a brothel in Dublin but not here.'

He closed his eyes and suddenly he was back in the first knocking shop he'd ever visited. It had been like eating from the Mc Donald's of sex–– quick and cheerful. He tried to visualise the line-up. Girls with ridiculous names like Amber and Tia and Cindy. What if his sister had been in the line-up? He shuddered to think that actually - given the right brothel - that might have happened. He could see his first time. The girl, under 18 for sure but he hadn't cared. He'd tried to be as gentle as he could. In those days he'd come in buckets, then she'd cleaned him up with wet wipes: the full Mc Donald's style experience when the crew member rushes over to clean the table before you've had a chance to get up. Back then, when he was young, the fire of orgasm had been like the lash of a flame across a steak.

'I know that. We didn't come here to look for Kathleen.' His mother broke his thoughts. 'We came here to immerse ourselves and receive the Holy Spirit in the River Jordan and in doing so we'll be led by His spirit to her. I have all the faith in Him that He will guide us to her.'

'You're not getting me in a dirty polluted river. I'm not prepared to make a fool of myself. How are you going to get down the muddy banks at your age with a walking stick? It's ridiculous. You'll lose your balance.'

'I'll get two big men to carry me in and plunge me down. I need to be cleansed and saved by the holy waters.'

Darius shook his head. He wished his mother would stop feeling guilty for sending Kathleen away. No amount of holy water could wash away the shame, the guilt and the grief that she now felt or the destructive concept of sin she had learned through her faith, had carried for so many years, governing everything she did— a concept that had grown like a cancer, spreading to all parts of her life.

He closed his eyes against the sun beaming through the window and wished that he could grab the concept, squeeze it hard and toss it overboard. And he wished he could finally tell her about the priest abusing him, destroying his faith in the church, making a mockery of God. But it would have been useless. She was blinded by her faith, smothered by its rituals, its dogma and nothing would ever change.

He'd tried to find Kathleen. He recognised that decisions were made back in 1974 and nothing could change the course of history, for history would go on and every group of people were a part of their era and the morals that fitted that era. But now, to his mother one person missing in her world seemed like the depopulation of the whole world. Maybe people were only placed in your life for a short time and some were never meant to stay. His mother, despite her failings was, he realised a strong and brave woman to have coped with her losses for so long. He could see the strain of loss in her face.

'The trouble with religion,' Darius said as they clambered down the steps of the coach and into an overpriced factory shop selling hand painted plates and other tat, 'is that people can't accept that death means death so they have to create a whole theory about what happens after death.

Life after death, the soul, rebirth, reincarnation, the pearly gates, great rewards in a place called heaven, life with God. They can't accept that's it, no more. Fineto. People like stories. They like fantasy. It's part of our psych. Father Christmas, the Tooth Fairy. It's all nonsense, but comforting stuff when you're a kid. But as an adult, it's one big deception. I keep thinking there's going to be a big cataclysmic event that's going to happen, then I realise it's all in my head.'

'Look dear. What a beautiful statute of Mary Magdalene. Shall I get it? It would look nice on the mantelpiece.' Maria looked at Darius for his opinion. His arms flew in the air in despair and he went to look for a beer.

~

'THIS IS the great wilderness referred to in the Bible where Moses and his people wandered for 40 years. They grumbled about the manna God had provided for them, just as we have grumbled about the mint tea and falafels at every mealtime,' the tour guide said. Laughter rippled across the coach.

Darius looked at the rugged landscape around him: the mauve and grey mountains, the pink dusty sky and the herds of scraggy goats and donkeys braying. In the distance the call to prayer had begun. And as he looked around him - the beauty, the peace and the majesty of it all – instead of feeling the presence of God, he felt a sense of reality greater than he'd ever felt. Despite the peace of this landscape, religion had brought war, strife, inequality, hardship and so much unhappiness. Watching his mother smile as she looked around her, he knew that coming to Jordan had given her peace, but all he felt was the cold hard reality of this beautiful place. Religion was a construct, a myth that millions had falsely bought into. The Israelites had considered themselves to be a special people. Maybe that was why Hitler had hated them. What right did they have to call themselves chosen? It had created division for centuries to follow. Maybe they'd wanted to take over the world.

There was no way any group of people would have survived in this wilderness. Maybe there were juniper berries and olives but that wouldn't be sufficient in order to live and cover so much land walking from one end of the country to the other.

Darius had even tried reading the Koran but that had made even less sense than the Bible had. Every other chapter was twaddle, consisting of some stories taken from the Bible and with the sole purpose, he believed of creating an Arab race to take over the world. He wished he could convince his mother to look at the hard facts of science, disputing the existence of a God.

They stood outside the coach and looked at the vast wilderness. The tour guide said a prayer and then addressed the group.

'God breathes life into dry bones. He breathed life into this arid desert for His people to survive. Without God we are just dry dust. We start as dust and end as dust.'

'More work for James Dyson then. He'll need a very powerful hoover,' Darius muttered.

'Now over there is the cave where John-the-Baptist was imprisoned,' the tour guide explained. He went on to tell the story of the serving of John-the-Baptist's head on a silver platter.

'I can think of a few heads I'd like to see roll on a plate,' Darius huffed. 'How do we know that was the exact cave? There must be caves all over this region just like this one.'

'Well yes. I take your point. But it's this cave we have come to focus on in history,' the guide said.

'Jeez. It's all bollocks,' he muttered, kicking the dusty ground.

∼

DARIUS SHOWERED the mud and salt from his body. They were now staying at a luxury hotel that led down through a beautiful garden to the waters of the Dead Sea. Under the cool water he looked at the people in the still waters. They looked like rocks, contorted into strange positions floating on the salty water. His body felt energised, fresh and clean. He towelled himself down, still watching the people in the calm waters and the salt in clumps on the rocks beside the shore, before joining his mother at a table where she was sipping mint tea. There was something special about this place. He couldn't put his finger on what it was, only that he knew he felt calmer, more relaxed than he'd felt in a long time.

'This is what I imagine heaven to be like. I feel like I'm floating. My body feels at peace here.' Maria closed her eyes against the white hazy sun.

The scene around them was still and muted. The pale grey, whitish sea merged into the watery sky as one.

'I know what you mean. There's something very peaceful about this place. Maybe it's because it's the lowest point on earth. Hard to believe that in around 70 years it will dry up. That's the lifetime of a person,' he said, sitting down.

'Lowest point on earth yet the closest to heaven,' she reminded him.

'It's almost as if God has brought me here. I can't go in the sea, but God wants to speak to me. I know he does. It's as if my body's floating. I can't feel it. This is what is meant by being at peace.' She looked happier than he'd ever seen her.

Darius raised his eyes to the sky but quelled his response allowing her to enjoy her moment.

'And what does He want to say to you?' Darius felt uncomfortable with the question, but she believed, and he'd go along with it.

'He's forgiven me. For sending Kathleen away. He may not be able to bring her back, but I have His forgiveness. He's also sent a message to Kathleen to tell her I love her. The Lord is good. He's here on the still calm waters watching over us.'

Maria

IT WAS A WEEK AFTER JORDON. Maria was in her lounge looking at the photos she'd had printed at Boots.

She was glad she'd been to Jordan and received the holy water. Possibly it was the last holiday she would have. But there was still one important thing she needed to do which formed part of her dying wish. She got up and went to put her coat on, before checking her hair in the mantel mirror. She made the sign of the cross and said a prayer. She hoped she was doing the right thing. It was something she had thought about for a long time. It hadn't been an easy decision. She snapped her bag shut and headed for the bus, arriving at Bunn and Fausett Solicitors a short while later.

'There you are.' The young solicitor passed the new document across the table with a pen ready to sign.

'Sign here please.' The solicitor tapped her fingernail on the section marked with a pencil cross and then leaned back. Her pen hovered over the X. She hoped that what she was doing wouldn't cause strife. She just wanted to make things right. This was compensation for the pains of the past. And it was what God wanted her to do for God always answered prayer.

26

FAYE

December 2010

FAYE HAD LONG CONSIDERED her friend Katie's house at 53 Garish Avenue her second home for it was always warm and cosy, tidy and clean - rather like a show home. There was never any mess. No menus from the Chinese takeaway or adverts for the local cab firm littering the porch, no muddy shoes lining the hallway, no paperwork on the kitchen work top waiting to be dealt with. Throughout the childhood of Katie's son Ed - who was the same age as the twins - there were never any toys lying around, waiting to be tripped over. Everything was organised, stowed away in beautiful pine chests and built-in cupboards. Table lamps added soft lighting to each corner of every room. There were fine wooden cabinets with inlaid tortoiseshell finishes, bought from the local auction, dusted and polished several times a week.

Faye wanted a distraction from the recent arguments at

home that had left a tense atmosphere hanging over their relationship. Darius had never met any of her friends. It was about time he did. She had a good feeling about today. Katie always rose to the occasion of entertaining and she knew they'd get on well.

They turned into the neat brick driveway, Faye commented to Darius about how Katie took great pride in her home and garden. She'd built a new patio, cleared the bottom of the garden and the wood beyond, designing a woodland retreat with a shed where she could practice singing, playing the guitar and making cuddly toys.

Faye knew of no other friend that changed her carpets and furniture so frequently. Last year a beautiful cornflower blue carpet was fitted across the whole house and the furniture, ornaments and curtaining replaced to create a sea theme throughout, which Katie said brought the peace and tranquility of the seaside into her home. And then to Faye's complete surprise within months it had been replaced, at huge expense with a pale sage carpet and the furniture re -painted in a parakeet green. Each room was finished with a display of curtaining in silks and cottons, hanging from French pleats or goblet design. Even the walls were splashed with pictures which acted as matching accessories, of various country scenes in a full array of greens - emerald, crocodile, shamrock and seaweed offering - Katie said, a mental escape into the hills and the dales. Faye couldn't understand this obsession with her home and the need to change everything with such frequency. It seemed bizarre but at the same time she loved her for it. She found it amusing and often went to auctions with Katie.

Faye had been right. Katie and Darius found an instant connection. When she opened the door, they smiled politely at each other, both hesitating momentarily with frowns on both their faces and a look of bewilderment ,but this melted away when Darius handed her a bottle of red wine to accompany the lamb they would be eating and a bunch of her favourite flowers: white lilies, complementary to all colour scheme. Their size - Katie always said - made a statement.

Katie had spent a great deal of time preparing the table. The silver cutlery looked polished, the napkins folded into birds of paradise sitting on side plates and beside each knife sat a dainty lime green organza bag containing sugared almonds, tied in matching ribbon, matching the colour scheme of the room to perfection. Darius laughed that it looked like a wedding breakfast and Katie beamed at the complement.

A huge steaming leg of lamb was carved and served, and the conversation flowed with ease. It was as if they had known each other for years, but this didn't surprise Faye for Katie always got on with everyone. She was bubbly, gregarious, punctuating every conversation with an entertaining story having everybody in stitches.

Secretly she harboured a mild jealousy, wishing she could be as popular and in demand. But Faye held her jealousy at bay, aware of the destructive effects of the poison tipped claws of jealousy.

'So where do you come from originally Katie?' Darius asked. 'Have you always lived in Marlow?'

Faye noticed the hesitation, as she glanced away to her husband, as if planning a suitable answer, then she dabbed the corners of her mouth daintily with her napkin before answering.

'We've been here a long time. But I like to think of yesterday as history, tomorrow as a mystery and today a gift of God - which is why we call it the present. Isn't that right, darling?' She began laughing, raised her glass, beckoning a toast. 'More wine anyone?'

Her answer to the question had been enigmatic and Faye knew Darius would feel the same.

'We live our lives forward don't we darling, not backward.' Katie added looking at her husband.

'Oh definitely. The past is never where you think you left it.'

A silence descended and settled around the table for a few moments and then her husband Mike smiled and thumped his stomach.

'That lamb was delicious. It's sitting happily at the bottom of my belly.'

'Thank you. It certainly was,' Darius and Faye said together.

'Tell you what I do with carcasses and bones and the fatty skin, all the horrible leftovers...' Faye said.

'Fucking hell you don't want to know, Katie,' Darius interrupted, laughing. 'Without Faye there would be no fox population.'

'But they need feeding. Just because you hate animals and won't let me have a dog.' Faye defended her actions.

'Ah?' Katie frowned.

'I wait till it's late, then I put the carcasses and all the jelly stuff in the middle of the road. Next morning it's all gone. Much better than having it rotting in your kitchen bin attracting flies.' Faye wrinkled her nose and flapped a hand in front of her face.

Katie looked shocked. Faye expected her to laugh but instead she said nothing, her hand quivering around the edges of her glass and Faye noticed a tremour begin to play around her mouth.

'You ok darling.' Her husband took her hand as if sensing she was about to faint.

'The sound of foxes mating at night upsets her. She wakes up crying, sometimes in a cold sweat,' Mike explained.

'Don't. They'll think I'm daft.' Katie waved his comment away. 'They remind me of something – babies crying - I'd rather forget that's all.' Katie's eyes were wet and far away and Faye noticed a sadness that she'd seen many times but didn't know what lay behind it and wondered why the sound of babies crying would be so upsetting.

'Well on a lighter note, tell Darius the story of when you stayed at your friend's house. The way you tell that story, it's hilarious,' Faye said quickly changing the subject.

Katie cleared her throat, the anxiety draining away as she began to tell the story that entertained every dinner guest.

'It's a horrible story, Darius. It'll put you off your dessert.' Katie sniggered.

'Don't worry, he's got plenty of scatological stories of his own Katie, believe you me.'

'I'll tell you my filthy story first. That'll put you at ease.' Darius began. 'I was walking in the woods once and Christ I needed a dump really badly. I couldn't wait any longer, so I went right there in the woods hoping and praying nobody was going to come. Afterwards I looked back. A Jack Russell was racing towards the huge turd that I had deposited amongst the leaves and ate it all up. I chuckled to myself. Then he ran back to his owner jumped into her arms and licked the owner's face.'

Everybody fell about laughing. Tears rolled down Katie's eyes.

'That's fantastic. God what a horrible story.' Katie said struggling to compose herself after all the laughter.

'I've always wanted to design a can of liquid nitrogen to spray on dog turds so that owner's can spray the turd, pick it up in a solid frozen state to take home in their pockets. Frozen Sara Lee dog turds!' Darius laughed.

'What a marvellous idea.' Mike laughed.

'Now my story,' Katie said rubbing her hands in anticipation of a welcoming audience. 'I was staying at a friend's house years ago and they had a toilet next to the kitchen. It was an old cottage in Ireland. The plumbing was a bit archaic. I did this enormous turd but couldn't flush it away. It wasn't going to disappear.'

'Excellent,' Darius commented looking satisfied.

'I tiptoed into the kitchen to find something to break it up, but couldn't find anything in a rush, so I grabbed a pair of Marigolds sitting on the worktop and sneaked back into the loo. There was a small window high up and I fished the turd out of the loo and lobbed it out of the window. The next minute I heard screaming. My friend's mum was putting the washing out on the line. I hadn't realised. The turd hit her head and she fell over.' Katie was spluttering into her dinner.

Everybody laughed, the noise rising in octaves until their bellies ached.

'You've got the same humour as me Katie. I'll give you that. God knows where you got it from.' Darius laughed.

But he didn't know, in that moment how ironic his comment was.

~

'How's your friend Katie? That was fun the other week.' Darius was remembering the meal at Katie's house.

'I don't know. I can't work her out at all sometimes. I've known her since the twins were babies but she's up and down. One minute she's fun and bubbly and we'll go out, trawl the charity shops, have lunch out, tea out and it's great but then whole weeks will go by and she doesn't reply to texts and phone calls and I'll see her dropping Ed at school wearing big dark sunglasses -even in the winter - and she's crying and she blanks me out as if she doesn't know me. Last week I saw her in town and bloody hell I ran over to say hello and she stared right through me as if she didn't know me. Then later on she saw me and crossed the road quickly to avoid me. I haven't done anything wrong. She does it to everyone. But nobody knows why.'

'What a weird woman.' Darius looked confused.

'I can't help feeling there is something that happened in her past or maybe she's suffering from delayed post-natal depression. She told me that after Ed was born she stayed in bed for weeks refusing to see a doctor, turning health visitors away, just crying and crying. But she's not taking anything for it. Not that I know of anyway.'

'She's not necessarily going to tell you if she is,' he said.

'There have been lots of strange things that have happened over the years. When Ed was little and he got a small rash on his shoulder, she went mental. I told her it was only chicken pox, but she wouldn't have it. We had to drive all the way to the John Radcliffe. She was in such a state, crying the whole journey.'

'Sounds like a paranoid mother to me.'

'I'm glad you met her. She was on good form. Witty, fun. Apart from the stuff to do with foxes.' A sliver of concern niggled inside Faye as she recalled the fear in Katie's eyes when foxes were mentioned.

'Yeah. That was odd.' He gave an amused shrug.

'Didn't make much sense. Something to do with the past. She never talks about the past but then most of my friends don't. They're all quite wrapped up in their children focusing on what they're doing.'

'Mushy mummy brains.'

'I'm very casual with my kids. Tim walks home from school, but Katie would never in a million years let Ed walk home and it's odd, but she doesn't let him go to friend's houses for tea either. Never has done. She's protective of that kid.'

'Seemed like a nice kid though. Didn't come across that he's tied to his mother's apron strings,' Darius said.

27

DARIUS

December 2010

'How are you Tim? How was school?' Darius asked Tim over dinner. It wasn't a difficult question so why did he always get a shrug and a dumb whispered answer?

'About average.' Tim gave a cowering shrug.

'Does nobody have anything to say? Darius looked round the table at everyone. Nobody spoke. It felt like he'd moved in with a cardboard cut-out family. He watched Tim put his glass down, an inch from the mat.

'Put your glass on the mat Tim,' Chrissie screeched.

'Oh for goodness sake, the pair of you. Every mealtime it's the same.' Faye sounded tired. Chrissie picked the glass up. Put it back on the mat. Tim picked the glass up. Took a sip. Subtly placed it on the table, an inch from the mat.

'Put it on the mat, Tim,' Chrissie shrieked louder, then

yelped as Tim gave her a hard kick under the table. Where was he supposed to begin? This was kindergarten territory.

'Pack it in both of you,' he barked. The kids looked at each other in surprise.

'Can I go upstairs now?' Tim asked.

'I need my blanket,' Chrissie whispered. Darius looked at her. He could see her future stretched ahead and it didn't look great–– an adult tossed onto the pile of society's wasters.

'No. You can both sit there and finish your dinner and engage in some conversation for a change. I'm not putting up with silence,' Darius barked. It was time for change.

Darius looked at Meg. It wouldn't be long before she was applying for university, but the kid was basically ignorant about life. There was so much he could help her with: science and maths, history and current affairs. The world was an open door waiting to be entered. But she wasn't switched on. He saw a daily obsession with mindless You Tube crap such as 'Charlie Bit My Finger Off.' And dumb teen-speak such as *is pizza a vegetable because apparently the American Government say it is?* or the suggestion that the breakfast cereal *Cheerios is so up itself.*

Tim shrugged again, looked terrified and in a timid whisper, like the dying breath of an engine asked, 'Did you know we are all related to tuna fish?'

'Well at least that's a start. Where did that idea come from?'

'I think its Darwinian.'

'Now we're getting somewhere. And do you know what is behind the theory?'

Tim shrugged. 'We've all evolved.'

Faye

Twenty minutes later Darius finally finished explaining the Darwinian theory. Everybody looked like they were dropping off. He'd pitched his 'speech' at a much older audience. Faye watched as the kids looked at the door longing to escape, scraping their chairs back - planning their surreptitious exit.

The following evening, Darius asked Meg if she had anything interesting to say.

'Did you know that if you took all the space around an atom away the world could fit into an apple?' Meg was eying the apple she was eating.

Darius seized on this crumb. 'That's an interesting theory.' He began a long rambling lecture related to physics, went on for another twenty minutes.

In bed later on, Darius told Faye how the conversations were leaving him totally drained.

'I'm not surprised. You do all the talking. Your voice becomes a monotone. A bit like Melvyn Bragg on Radio Four *'In Our Time.'* You're heavy going.'

'They've nothing to say. One cowers and has been drained of all life form. One screeches or stays silent and the other starts a conversation then has nothing to add.'

'You barely give them a chance. They come out with interesting thoughts about apples or tuna fish or black holes and then *you* do all the talking.'

'I have to make a linguistic adjustment listening to them.'

'Is it so hard to be normal?' Faye was starting to rant. 'It's as if you're trying to fill three cups with ever more complicated concepts using words and ideas that go straight over their heads. It's no wonder they inch slowly to the door to escape.'

'Well fuck you. I'm tired of watching them step towards the kitchen door, fiddle with the knob as they nod and smile sweetly and politely, pretending to be interested in what I'm saying.'

'Jeez Darius. They don't have PHDs. Are you doing it deliberately to put them off you?'

'They'll never accept me. You're happy with their baby talk. I'm not prepared to sit through a meal listening to a bunch of imbeciles.'

'Can't you be more entertaining, light-hearted. They're easy-going kids. They aren't into drugs or staying out late. They'll never swear at you or be rude. Any bloke would be delighted to have step kids like mine.' Faye got into bed, started to take her make up off with cotton wool and baby cream.

'I sometimes wish they would swear. At least it would be a reaction.' His voice had little energy.

'When we're alone you're fun. Why be different with them?'

'Really?' Darius felt lost. He squeezed his face, kneading his chin as if it were a piece of dough. He let out a great sigh, then looked straight at her. He loved this woman, but for the first time in his adult life he didn't have a plan or a solution. Where was this going?

After a short silence, as they both took stock he said, 'Come here. You going to give this old Scouse a kiss?'

Darius

Darius loathed the way his work colleagues tried to give him tips on how to fit in with his new step-family. He didn't do fitting in. If people couldn't fit in with him then it was fuck off time.

'Why don't you have a Saturday night in with a takeaway curry and watch the X Factor together. Teenagers love it,' his office techy suggested.

He hated the X Factor. He called it mass-produced, poor quality, manufactured entertainment for the scum. One evening he suggested a DVD, but nobody could agree on the genre. In the end they sloped off to their rooms as soon as dinner was finished.

'You need to have a word with them – tell them how I feel. I can't go on like this.' Darius poured himself a cup of tea, sat down at the kitchen pine table.

Faye looked incredulous. 'Have a word with them? Tell them what exactly?' Her face looked pained. 'That they've got to transform into different kids? Sorry. They are as they are. Maybe I'm to blame for making them like that, or maybe that's what the big D word divorce does. Don't take it so personally. They're just shy. They feel awkward around you. Is that so surprising?'

It was a 'him and them' set up. He didn't belong anywhere. This family were a collection of dysfunctional individuals who had lost the art of communication and couldn't connect with one another in any meaningful way.

'They shut down a bit more with each passing day, like union members working to rule. I can't stand it. I've tried to engage. When I come home at night, surprise surprise they're always in their rooms, obediently coming down when called for dinner. Then we have Tim cowering - too afraid to speak - mumbling when spoken to, sniffing and wiping his nose on his sleeve. And Meg's face is always stiff. And a blanket permanently attached to Chrissie's face as if it were an umbilical cord. I keep asking myself, what am I doing here?'

Breakfast time was the worst time of the day. They sauntered into the kitchen in silence. He was invisible. What sort of parent dragged their kid up to be so unsociable? Each morning he made a point of trying to get them to engage. Christ, these kids would learn some manners if it was going to kill him.

Darius poured coffee. The kids had gone back upstairs to get their school bags ready.

'How can this be right?' He stood tall now, arms in the air doing the strut of despair. Then he turned to face Faye hoping for a direct answer. 'I shouldn't be here if that's the way they feel.' He waited, wondering how she might turn things around.

'You're here for me,' she pleaded. Me.

'It's not that simple. You come as one package. God knows, everyone keeps reminding me.'

'If you love me you should want to work with me, not against me. Accept they're teenagers. Maybe you've forgotten what Sam was like. I'm sure he wasn't so God damn perfect.'

'He would have made some effort. They make no effort.

They're all scowling mutes.'

'That's not true and you know it. They try their best. You have to gently encourage kids to talk. It's about boosting their confidence then they'll want to talk more.'

'Oh Christ. I'm too old and long in the tooth for all this.'

Darius could feel that heavy leaden weight falling to the pit of his stomach again and the prickling of a creeping headache like an insect across his forehead.

'This is way too complicated. I can't do it.' He raised his hands in the air, as if disarming himself. 'I brought one kid up. Now look at him. He's a mess. I'm in way over my head Faye.'

His arm fell to his sides, his head now hung low as if in shame. She hissed. Pointed a finger at him. 'You're going to lose that son of yours criticising him all the time. You can't change him. People need encouragement. They need their egos boosting in order to do better or gain in esteem. No wonder gay people have to go on marches to assert who they are. With Dads like you who refuse to be proud.'

'Christ. You do talk bollocks sometimes.'

Darius hurled the 'b' word from his mouth as if spitting out a piece of nasty gristle. Faye shot him her animal wounded look. Her upper lip had started to quiver, and she was standing away from him fiddling with the kitchen drawer. He couldn't work out whether she would turn on the water works or fly into a rage. He searched for a compromise, a tempered olive branch. He had an idea. It might not work but he was willing to try.

But just as he was about to put his suggestion to her, Meg burst through the door, her voice shrill and jittery. 'We can hear what you're saying about us you know.' Her tone was laced with sarcasm, her face a deep beetroot.

Darius's eyes widened. 'This is good. A kid that can speak.' It was like beckoning a spider from a crack.

Meg gripped the brass doorknob, turning it round as she spoke. Nerves, Darius thought. The knob rattled in her hand.

'Oh my God,' Meg shouted. Then she burped and laughed. 'You're a prick. We don't want a serious conversation with you, Darius.' Meg's pitch was rising, her voice wobbly. Her eyes were filling with tears.

He didn't know what to think. Maybe the barriers were coming down. Maybe this was progress. His head started to thump.

'Stop rattling that doorknob,' Darius barked.

'You're a prick. We don't care about your intellectual crap.' Meg continued to rattle the knob. Her skin looked mottled. 'We don't want to have heavy conversations every time we come through the door. We just want to go to our rooms and chill.'

The door squeaked and Tim pushed through. His face was beetroot too and his hands were in his pockets.

'And what do you think, Tim? Got anything to add to your sister's outburst?'

'No.' He shrugged.

'I just had an idea before your sister burst in. Why don't we try having family breakfasts at the weekends instead of everyone wandering down when they feel like it,' Darius said.

'Cooked?' Tim's face lit up.

'Now where you go wrong Faye...'

'More put-downs? Wondered when that was coming'. Faye swiveled round to face him, the wounded look returned to her face.

'You let them wander into the kitchen to help themselves, do what the hell they like. Start acting like their mother. Serve them breakfast. A decent breakfast. Not wood shavings you find in a pencil sharpener.'

Faye bristled. 'They're not babies any more. I do enough for them. Cooking, washing, cleaning, ferrying them around all over the place. Life is rushed. I don't expect your own family was perfect. I mean look at the way your mother sent a poor defenceless child away.'

'Don't bring Kathleen into this. You should make them help out.'

'We *are* here you know and listening. Stop being horrible to Mummy. She did very well before she met you.' Meg's voice was wobbly again.

'It would be a massive operation if I stood there serving toast on top of making packed lunches and getting Chrissie to do her spelling tests. We could try family cooked breakfast at the weekends though. See how that goes. What does everyone think?' Faye looked from Darius to Meg to Tim.

For Darius, happiness had always been dispensed through food. It was the key to any rift. There was something very basic and carnal about the power of food. And bizarrely some of his happiest childhood memories were of the fry-ups the priest used to buy him either before or after the abuse in the toilet at Rhyl. They were the best fry-ups he'd ever eaten. He would eat the breakfasts very slowly to prolong the meal, in the hope that time ran out and they'd need to get back to the main group and so eating slowly - much to the annoyance of his ex-wife - had been a habit he had carried with him from those days.

∽

Darius

To begin with the cooked breakfasts were fun. He liked a busy kitchen. The atmosphere seemed to change with everybody thrown into the kitchen, doing something together - cracking eggs, sizzling bacon, turning sausages in the pan.

'Pass over a piece of that horrible white bread that tastes like Kleenex.' He laughed, feeling relaxed for the first time.

The family breakfasts offered a small glimmer of hope but there was still a long way to go. The truth was, he felt completely lost. Would things get better or were they destined to fail?

28

DARIUS

December 2010

A MILKY SKY promised the first snow of the season. Forecasters warned of a bitter winter. A few flakes swirled giddily in the darkness. Darius was crouched by the hearth having arranged a stack of dry logs. The kindling caught fire immediately and he watched the flames leap and dance, blue edged and hypnotic. The curtain less room with its stark magnolia walls and oak panelling beneath his shoeless feet was instantly transformed by the vibrancy of colour. The magnolia softened into peach, the richness of the oak deepened and Darius's mood mellowed with it. Even the frozen smiling faces in the motley collection of family photographs on the shelf seemed warmer, more welcoming. It was early evening, a Sunday in December. Meg and Tim had just returned from Steve's. They never spoke about their weekends away. Steve returned them at bang on six. It was as if he set his watch to Greenwich meantime. Even if the car pulled up five minutes early the engine would run till six, the kids emerging onto the doorstep just as the hall clock chimed.

'Constipated arsehole,' Darius muttered to himself on hearing the doorbell. He gave a hard and pointless stab at the grate with the iron poker sending ash spinning, then another stab when he heard their feet pounding up the creaking stairs, as they retreated to their rooms without a hello.

At around seven, the doorbell rang again. It was like a stream of postal deliveries. A sudden gust of chill air blasted through the open door and crept into the lounge.

'Shut the door will you,' Darius called out. He gave a hard, determined jab at the fire, the vision of Shayne in the flames. He still lingered at drop off and clearly hadn't given up hope of Faye getting back with him. Sparks splattered up, fell again, like small fireworks.

'She's 'ad a bath. She's all clean. She's 'ad a bath this morning because the 'ot water goes off at ten. I've got a bit of a problem with the heating at the moment. The thing's gone wrong.' His monotone, East London drawl was like a cheap broken tin saucepan tapping against Darius's head. He was a Mr. Bean version of Trigger in 'Only Fools.'

'Tell him you don't sodding care,' Darius muttered as he listened to Shayne and Faye in the hallway. His whole body started to tense. He jabbed and twisted the poker into the oak flooring.

'I've washed 'er uniform. The tights are nearly dry. Feel 'em. Do they feel dry to you? They've been drying in the bathroom. I don't like to dry things indoors but they don't dry outside in the winter. Chrissie, take those clothes off. They live at Daddy's house.'

'Do we always have to have this dreadful ritual of stripping her off on my doorstep? It's humiliating for the poor kid and cold.' Darius listened, willing Faye to be more assertive.

'It doesn't matter where they live, Shayne. They're my clothes.'

Chrissie's small voice was the voice of reason. Darius smiled. He liked the way the kid called the sperm donor by his first name.

Faye sounded too calm, patient. He'd tell her that later. What was making her so God damn subservient to Shayne? Why couldn't she ever tell him to fuck off? He was just a useless lump that walked the earth.

He's taking the piss. He obviously still has strong feelings for you but you're not blunt enough. You let him linger. Be tough. Tell him to fuck off, he'd told her several times.

He hated the way Shayne ignored Faye's wishes - insisting on stripping the little girl off in the hallway and taking the clothes he had bought at Primark for her to wear at his house.

'We've been doing the Tables. She knows the sevens now. Go on Chrissie, tell mummy the sevens.'

There was a brief silence. Darius jabbed at the bricks surrounding the hearth. Sparks flew.

Shayne made a dramatic sigh. Most people sighed quietly. But Shayne didn't do quiet. A sneeze, a whisper, a cough were the noises of a beast in the wilderness. Darius put down the poker and covered his ear with his small hands, pleading silently for the torture to end.

'Go on Chrissie.' Shayne was almost whimpering. 'Do it for Daddy. Daddy's waiting. Ohhhhhh'. There was strain in his voice.

Darius thought that he sounded like a toddler in a play park whining for the return of his trike. It took all the restraint he could muster not to burst through to the hall and throttle him.

'She can do it. Honest. We've been learning all weekend. And she done a rhyme. Go on tell mummy.'

Darius picked the poker up again, grinding his teeth as he drowned out Shayne's poor grammar.

' I believe you.' Faye sounded frustrated but clearly didn't have the strength to make him go.

'Oh.' Shayne's voice descended with a thud. 'Stop knocking her. She can do the rhyme really well. Gooooooo onnnnn Chrissie.' His voice droned.

'First William, the Norman, then Willie, his son, Henry, Stephen, Henry, Richard and John, Henry and Edward, one, two and three, And again after Richard, three Henrys we see.

Two Edwards and Richard, if rightly I guess - Two Henrys, sixth Edward, Queen Mary, Queen Bess. Then Jaimie the Scotsman, then Charles, whom they slew, But receive after Cromwell another Charles (Two). James Second the Stuart ascended the throne. Then William and Mary, together, came on. Queen Anne, Georges four, fourth William all passed. Then came Victoria and long did she last.'

Darius contemplated sending his massive turd of Soviet typhoon class, by text picture to Shayne's phone. But Shayne had a crappy little Nokia. The picture would be a brown blur. It wouldn't show the wonderful banana shape and its amazing tones of brown gliding down the porcelain.

'For God's sake. Why do you keep teaching her everything by rote? She needs to gain an understanding of things. It's an autistic way of learning,' Faye was telling him.

'Oh Faye.' Shayne droned each word, as if they were painful sores. 'You always knock me, put me down'.

'I'm telling you. Accept it.' Faye snapped.

'And you're so wonderful I suppose, you and Rat.'

'His name's Darius. Don't call him Rat.'

Darius couldn't bear it any longer. He wasn't going to put up with the nickname of Rat. He'd show him. He swept towards the door, flinging it open, a gust a cold air rushing through.

'Out. Get out of my house now. And don't ask to use the

toilet either. You can piss ya pants for all I care.' And with that Darius swept him away, a broom to filthy debris, with Faye stammering and cowering behind the door telling him not to be so cruel and Chrissie shivering in her knickers and vest.

Faye

Darius was rubbing his forehead, huffing as he sat at the table waiting for dinner to be served. Faye handed out plates of lasagne to everyone.

'I fucking hate the tedious paraphernalia of handovers. There's no reason he has to stand talking in the hallway for so long,' Darius spat.

Meg waved her knife in his direction. She was gaining in confidence, learning to confront him. 'You shouldn't swear in front of little kids. Like, you knew Mummy like had kids when you met her.'

'Why do teenagers always litter sentences with the word like? You won't get through a job interview speaking like that.'

'Yeah yeah yeah' Tim sang in a jovial way masking a defiance he hadn't the courage to express. Tim knew his tone was sarcastic, but it was also funny the way he said it. He was never offensive. He was a meek sort of boy.

'We could move to Wales. House prices are cheaper there. A small mortgage wouldn't be a problem,' Darius suggested.

'It's cold and wet up there. We don't know anyone.' Faye sat down picked up her fork.

'We could even emigrate to New Zealand. The New Zealand government are encouraging business owners to relocate. My business can move anywhere. It's a much nicer way of life over there.'

'Yes pleeeeeeeeese. Oh yes please. Yes please.' Meg clasped her hands together pleading. She rested her head on Faye's shoulders pouting her lips with a soppy dog look in her eyes.

'That would be sooooooo amazing. Yes pleeeeeeeese.'

My daddy could come too,' Chrissie yelped.

'What do you think, Tim?' Darius asked. Tim flushed. He was gripping his knife and fork in his hands as if in battle, but his face was expressionless as if someone had asked him which ice cream he would prefer – strawberry or chocolate.

'Don't mind.' He shrugged, looking embarrassed.

'Christ. Do you ever have an opinion? You've seen the Hobbit. The scenery is spectacular.' Darius certainly knew the right way to tug at the children's strings.

'Oh yeah,' was all Tim could think of saying.

'Jesus. What do you talk to your Uncle Steve about? Do you say nothing to him either?' Darius said to Tim, who shrugged his shoulders again and looked increasingly awkward. Faye wondered what he was thinking and felt a rush of love and desperate need to protect her son. She sensed his vulnerability. She got up, put an arm around him. He flinched away.

'They just play on the X Box. They don't talk.' Meg said.

'I could never take them away from Shayne and Steve. You know that.' Faye was firm.

'That imbecile father. He's a nothing. And Steve is just playing at fatherhood because he can't have his own kids.' He spat the words across the table.

'You're always saying how fed up you are with Marlow and its attachment to your marriage and the pain of the past but when it comes to it, you're intransigent to the idea of change. You can't see any further than getting the kids through school. The schools are run of the mill, churning uninspired kids off a production line.'

Shock filled Faye's face. What was she doing allowing him to speak about Shayne and Steve in that way?

'Why would the kids miss them?' He carried on his tireless catechism.

'I'm not going to listen to this.'

'Go back to Shayne then. I bet you miss his big cock.' Darius scraped his chair back across the wooden floor, huffing as he retreated to the lounge.

Suddenly Faye had a moment of clarity and felt her heart harden. Her head was beginning to take control. She didn't know what she felt: anger or calm resignation. But she could see her plan B: she would find a new flat to rent. But part of her hankered for Darius to change. She didn't want to give in. The relationship had been good at the start. Surely it was possible to return to the good times? Maybe there was still time to salvage the wreck it had become.

She got up, followed him to the lounge, hovering in the doorway.

'If we move away, Shayne might stop paying maintenance,' she told him.

He laughed. 'He pays a pittance. That's not support.' He sneered.

'He pays CSA guidelines,' Faye said, defending Shayne.

'Fucking CSA. Decent fathers pay more than the guidelines.'

But Faye couldn't and wouldn't separate father and child. It was a precious bond not a flimsy spider's web. She had always done everything in her power to ensure that Chrissie saw as much of Shayne as she could. Her life was on hold, rooted to Buckinghamshire. At times she desperately wanted to move away, to start afresh, put the past behind her. But change was the one thing she was resolute about. Stability meant everything.

∽

CHRISSIE WAS STANDING on a chair hanging red baubles on the Welsh dresser. She had just finished her breakfast. Anything to avoid learning spellings. In the corner of the kitchen John

Humphrey's voice crackled on the radio as he reported the arrest of Julian Assange, founder of Wiki Leaks. An icy breeze buffeted the doors to the conservatory, a chill creeping to every corner of the room.

Faye shivered. 'Sit down Chrissie. We need to learn these spellings.'

The child was still mixing up Ds with Bs and 'was' and 'saw.' She hadn't shared her concerns with Darius. What was the point?

'Have you got any flash cards?' Darius had been listening to the Assange interview, eating his muesli standing up at the counter.

'Why?'

'You had some Dorling and Kindersley cards. Bring them here.' She opened a drawer, handed him the cards. He began to hold up each card patiently, calmly asking Chrissie to read the simple words on the cards. He tapped the cards on the counters, put them back in their box.

'Dyslexia. I'd lay a bet on it.'

'You reckon?' She looked at him incredulous and for the first time in a while felt warmth and hope.

'Get a psychologist's report. I'll pay. The school won't do anything. Budgets have been cut.'

'But what difference will it make? The school won't do anything.'

'It will. Trust me. I love you. They'll offer support, maybe one to one help with phonics.'

He took her hands, smiling sympathy and understanding. And in that moment, she could see why she was with him. Shayne hadn't picked up that there was a problem. He lived in a bubble of Victorian rote learning; methods he believed in. He couldn't comprehend concepts and ideas that hadn't been generated from his own mind or own narrow world and experience. She dreaded attending parent meetings with Shayne.

He was always focused on waiting for the teacher to finish talking so that he could proudly announce all the Times Tables he had taught Chrissie. It was as if he wanted Brownie points himself.

∼

It was three weeks after the chat about dyslexia. Faye had taken Chrissie for tests. They were in the kitchen making tea.

'You were right. Dyslexia. We were there all morning. And the school want a copy of the report. I think they will take it seriously.' Faye beamed at Darius and knew his experience as a teacher would come in handy.

'I'm so pleased. There's so much you can do to help her. I know a shop in London with learning games to support children with special needs.' The caring Darius was back. She felt a tug of love.

'Wow. Thank you.' She put her arms round him. They were together on this. Small stirrings of hope flitted in her stomach. Change was in the air.

It was a Saturday morning in the middle of December. Darius and Faye were in bed nakedly entwined, bathed in the smells and stickiness of sex. Darius had been singing the Eton rowing song 'pull, pull, shag, shag' to gain momentum and keep going as he pushed and shafted, plundering the murky river waters. 'Come on boys keep going. Push push, shag, shag. Who's wearing the semen-stained jersey? Team Darius, keep going boys, my perfectly healthy spermatozoa.' His humour reaffirmed why they were together.

'Christ.' Darius nuzzled her neck, the bristles of his chin an emory board making her giggle.

'If I'd met you when I was a lot younger, I would have used you like a urinal.'

'Charming.'

'That was a jolly well-timed shag my little cock.' Darius pulled at his dick, as if it were a loose bell cord.

'Maybe we'll have more later,' she suggested.

'We'll have to see. My cock is like a Morris Minor gearbox – the one exclusive.'

'When I lived in Watford, pussies used to walk along the wall outside my bedroom window. I'd lie there and watch them trotting up and down.' Darius sniggered.

'Is this a Mrs Slowcombe moment? We are talking cats not vaginas?'

Darius laughed huskily in her ear. 'I named those pussy cats after all the women I knew. Once I leant out of the window and poured water on one. It went crazy, behaving like a cartoon cat.'

'Shush. What was that noise?' They fell silent.

Faye grabbed her glasses, looked at the clock beside the bed. 7am and the peace was already disturbed by Chrissie pounding on Tim's door, her frustration notching up with each ignored bang.

'You should have put a cooking bag over the retard's head when you put her to bed last night. Sometimes I wonder whether the kid has dementia.'

Faye prised herself from his body, the stickiness of sex coated across their bodies like wallpaper paste. 'What? How bloody vile. I don't understand you. One minute you're helping to pay for an educational assessment, showing concern. Now this? What the hell's wrong with you?' She sat up. His words were like a hard cold slap back to reality. It was like stepping out of a warm cabin into a biting storm. She stared at her reflection in the wardrobe mirror. Who was she? What was she doing here? One step forward, two steps back.

'You had a kid with a retard what do you expect?'

His words hovered, then froze in the air between them, but still they didn't pierce her. She wanted to feel anger - the correct and natural reaction, like burning fingers on a kettle. All she felt was a slithering revulsion. 'Poor little girl. It's hard not having anyone to play with.'

It was strange hearing herself speak. What she really wanted to say didn't come out. She was disconnected from her tangible self.

She still hankered for the old Darius. The one she'd fallen in love with. The man who'd promised to be a good stepfather to her children. Why was he so inconsistent?

The pounding continued. 'Tim's probably reading Harry Potter.'

'The kid's always reading Harry Pothead.'

'I sometimes wish I could wheel back in time but with a different father. Be nice to have a father now. To help out.' Faye started to create an image in her head of the perfect hands - on father.

'You should go back to Wanker Shayne.'

Faye turned to face him. She was sick of him suggesting that. Needles of frustration coursed through her body. He knew the buttons to press. 'What a ridiculous suggestion. I finished with him.'

'So you say.'

Faye felt dirty, punished for the sordid act of sex with Shayne. She refused to rise to this last absurd comment.

'I would have thought her screaming every morning is a reminder of your sordid mistake. You're a moron, Faye. Like Kathleen. I wonder what became of her little bastard. And don't ever leave me on my own with Chrissie by the way. I'm likely to kill her.'

Faye couldn't process his words quick enough. Was he being serious? She wrestled with the duvet, pulling it away. Why didn't his nasty words make her react? Maybe she didn't want to react because to react might have pushed away the Darius she hankered for.

'He was the mistake. Not Chrissie. It's not the same. At least I had another kid. You were too pathetic to bring another child into the world.'

'Fuck off.' His words were spat across the bed.

She felt his now cold semen escaping down her legs. She waited for the next missive, wondering what had really happened in his family long ago.

'You can't deal with her. You should go and see to her. Stop imagining a fictitious father out there. We're all failed fathers. Failed offspring. Failed siblings. That's life. Go in there before I have to strangle her myself.'

Faye unravelled the sheet, put her feet on the bare, cold floorboards. 'Call yourself intelligent. I don't think so.'

'*You* didn't have much intelligence to go with the moron in the first place.' Darius spat.

Glancing in the mirror, she caught his eyes. Her heart flitted. His eyes were misty pools of sadness. His face had turned a shade of grey. This had nothing to do with Chrissie and everything to do with him. She didn't understand the confusion of his past but suddenly in that moment she understood that it was impacting on the present, in everything he did and said. While she felt a deep loathing for the way he was behaving, the vile things he was saying, directed at her and her children she now felt empathy for what he had carried for so many years. But the pain and the torture were now so deeply ingrained in his fabric, how could she possibly change him? It didn't seem within her power.

Darius

Chrissie's pounding of the bedroom door grew louder in his head until it filled every space. Her screeching. Her demanding. His stomach was tightening, head pounding, waves of nausea rippling in his throat. He was back there. The small girl at the door, beckoning to come in, rattling the handle, frightened she'd wet herself. He could hear the priest telling her to go away, find another toilet. And he could smell the woody scent that filled the cloakroom. The pine toilet cleaner. He could hear the tear of toilet paper. See the priest dabbing the tip of his penis, his face burning, spent, exhausted. When would these memories leave him? His head screamed.

29

DARIUS

December 2010

Darius sat on the windy station platform waiting for the train to take him to work. He stared at chewing gum on the platform, watching feet as they passed by.

He could see the future; a burden to Faye for the rest of her life if he suffered another heart attack or worse, a stroke. She was young. She had her own responsibilities. He felt more alone than he had ever felt. She was too new in his life to fully accept these challenges ahead. They didn't have the special bonding glue, the lifetime of shared history to make it work under trying circumstances. But he loved her. He cared for her more deeply than he had ever cared for another woman. He had known that for a long time. But life with Faye was no bed of roses; more a bed of Leylandii. How on earth were they going to make it work? He hadn't the foggiest and neither did she. And both of them had long stopped talking about marriage.

Darius shook his head and stared at the posters opposite. Marriage. What on earth had he been thinking? The subject had dropped off the radar, but he couldn't remember when that had happened. It all seemed irrelevant now, a fairytale dream that wasn't going to happen.

∽

IT WAS the Saturday before Christmas. Faye had booked tickets for the kids to go ice-skating at Hyde Park and Tesco vouchers for Pizza Express. It seemed obvious to Darius that they would drive into London.

'I never drive into Central London. That's ridiculous. Who wants to sit in endless traffic, drive round and round looking for a parking space? It's horrendously busy at this time of year,' she moaned.

'A bus? You are joking?' There was no way he was going to take a bus. Bile rose to his throat as he contemplated the horror of a bus journey.

'Yes. We can take the bus. It makes sense. The bus stop is outside the house. If you don't use public transport it will disappear. All we have to do is glide on, sit back and enjoy the view and not have to worry about parking or getting stressed in a traffic queue. And it will be a treat for the kids.'

'A treat? Fucking listen to yourself.'

She put her hat and gloves on, and they all trudged out of the door. He expected her to change her mind once she reached the bus stop and worked out how ludicrous the idea was. But the bus had arrived, and they all clambered up the steps. He stood on the pavement protesting and pleading with her. 'You bitch. You're doing this to wind me up. How dare you humiliate me.' He called up, put one foot on the bus, one hand on the rail. He couldn't do it. He closed his eyes willing himself to take the next step, but he was back there, on a church trip, the children screeching, laughing and fooling around.

'This is strictly a one off. I'm not fucking doing it again.' He called to her as he handed his money over. And turning to find a seat, all eyes upon him, mocking and looking him up and down. It was as if they knew. As if they were put there for a purpose – figures of torture. The painful memories were back. And then as he made his way down the aisle he stopped, froze, his heart banging in his chest as he caught a glimpse of a black figure to his right. He couldn't look but he could smell those familiar bus smells and the wheels were now in motion, the sound doing a death dance in his troubled mind.

It was all coming back: the weekend in Rhyl when he was ten years old. He could see the priest at the front of the bus and his snake-like eyes flickering over his bare legs. He could see his friends sardined along the back in their shorts and caps and the girls giggling at the front with buckets and spades.

Faye patted the seat next to her, smiled up at him. And then – in his head - the greasy smell of fish and chips mingled with the scent of fear filled his nostrils as he glanced over at the man in black sitting in the opposite row.

'I quite like going on the bus. It's nice to be free of the constraints of the car. No parking nightmares. No extortionate charges in the NCP. And you can chat to strangers it's so sociable. I love to watch the world go by. It's great,' Faye said cheerfully. But he didn't feel cheerful as memories collided into each other.

'You're doing this deliberately, aren't you? I didn't have you down as such a cow,' he snapped.

The memories were now returning like a collage on a pin board. Sand in sandwiches, the children dipping their toes in the water, the barbecue, the nighttime Bible readings. But mingled in with those blissful moments were darker moments crouching in the recesses of his mind. He could see the beds in the dormitory, remembered being fascinated that they could fold up into the wall during the daytime and the priest telling them all that Benjamin Franklin had invented the idea. But he could feel his arm being tugged at nighttime, the dark cloak of the priest kneeling before him dragging him out to the toilets. And then he could see donkeys on the beach, the long line of waiting children all eager to have a ride. Then the snake-like eyes of the priest telling him he couldn't have a donkey ride– he was going to spend time alone with the priest. And he knew what that meant.

'I'm not. Why would I do that? You're acting like a madman Darius. It's just a bus. Plenty of people get buses every day,' she said breezily, pulling his mind back to the present.

He didn't like her cheery attitude. Inside he was crying and asking himself *why were these memories returning*? What was driving him to look at the recesses of his mind? It was as if he was reaching into his mind for answers but there were no answers. And then he thought about Kathleen. Had she gone on a bus to Rhyl with the priest and the Sunday School? Did he deny her a donkey ride too? And then the ultimate question wormed its way back into his mind–– a question that had been there ever since his mother had announced her dying wish. Had the priest raped her, or had he only been interested in young boys? Would he ever find out the truth? The question would circumvent around his mind until Kathleen was found. And that was if, deep down he wanted her found. He wasn't sure he did.

'It would be nice to be a suicide bomber on a bus, or a train. If I could only pull the cord of my rucksack and that would be the end of all of us - great way to end my miserable little existence,' he said snapping out of his thoughts, but all the time his eyes pinned to the figure in black sitting at the front.

'I despise the way so many people rely on the state for transport. They're uncomfortable, they rattle along, stink and in the summer sweat drips off you because the driver can't turn the heating off. They're slow. Trundling all over the countryside. We're going to take a taxi home. That's the end of it.'

'You're going to waste money on a taxi?'

Darius enjoyed the shock descending on her face. 'Buses are the biggest gas guzzlers on the road. They burn diesel at a rate of a gallon every 3 miles. Cars are more efficient. If we stay together you better get used to driving me around.' He carried on, trying to make sure she was under no illusions and the measure was clear. No more buses his head screamed.

'You're lucky we aren't on a bus in India with poultry and cockroaches and near death experiences at every corner.' She laughed, sniffed and turned to look out of the window.

∼

IT WAS MONDAY MORNING AGAIN. Darius hated the start of the working week. As he alighted the train all he could see around him were society's failures, rejects, misfits and odd balls gathered together. They were the kids he'd loathed in the church. The ones he'd felt were turning a blind eye to what the priest had been doing.

The train was filled with people who could no longer drive, people who had no confidence to drive, too old to drive, too mental to drive. People on crutches, fat women in tight pink leggings chewing gum, bent over old ladies, paraplegics in wheelchairs. White trash of all shapes and sizes. The toothless, hooped earrings, tattoos, peroxide hair, screechy kids. Kids in flimsy buggies, Primark clothing. He wanted to line them all up, shoot them one by one, then turn the gun on himself. In a sea of faces they jumped out at him, poking and prodding and filling his head space. They became etched in his mind, a herd of elephants stamping and crashing in his brain. He was one of them. Sinking into a quagmire, a melting pit of despair. He couldn't climb out. He hadn't the strength. Too much time had passed. The years had rolled by and the priest had become a part of his existence-- an appendage that he carried around, unable to sever. And in truth he didn't want to be rescued. Rescued by whom? A bleeding-heart liberal, pedigree dog face, overbred, very nice-but-dim counsellor or clergyman or a court. He could see the local headlines. *56-year-old man accuses elderly priest of abuse.* It was farcical.

He was staring up from the bottom of the well of self-pity and despair.

~

AS THE FIRST GREAT WESTERN made its way towards Slough he imagined he was on a journey to hell. He was in Cormac McCarthy's *'The Road.'* This was his own personal catastrophe: Burger King coke cartons at his feet, sweet wrappers littering the seats, chewing gum stuck to the floor - sickly sweet smells of bodies and perfume in mortal combat. His world was burned to cinders. The trees were bare, the landscape bleak, dark and foreboding. Rain whipped and lashed at the windows.

The train clattered, rattled, glided and jolted. The passengers were zombies staring ahead and out. Moron faces going nowhere. Outside a dark mass of fields stretched to eternity. Corrugated roofing of warehouses, rows and rows of drab little houses, crammed in, boxes of glass tacked on the back. Divorcees mortgaged until death swallowed them, stuck in an apocalyptic nightmare. Everybody in post-industrial, post Northern Rock meltdown. There was no wealth in these little boxes lined up by the track. They were piles of debt just getting bigger and bigger while people carried on spending what they weren't earning. Darius looked at the houses and thought how like a tin of sardines life was. Everybody struggling to escape, searching for that sardine tin key.

The train journey was his test of endurance. Resting back, closing his eyes he wished that he could just switch himself off like an electrical device. Inside his head he was writing a suicide note. He imagined himself lying on the tracks below and the triumphant face of the priest looking down, his finger pointing up to heaven.

He wondered if this daily daydream to end it all would ever be any more than a daydream.

30

DARIUS

December 2010
He woke to a racing heart. Was he having another heart attack? He felt clammy and wondered where he was. And then he recognised the room: the cracked artex ceiling, the mirrors, the sheep in the field outside, the white washed floor boarding. Reality hit. It felt as if his recent life had been one long swim through sewerage with no exit pipe. For a time, he lay on his back, his great belly escaping either side of his torso. He turned to watch Faye sleeping, then felt her warm buttocks and her slippery crack. She reminded him of a toilet on display on a raised platform in John Lewis: clean and safe.

'The RAF are coming to bomb the target to smithereens. I want to leave you with a dollop of something to remember me by,' he whispered in her ear. She turned, nestled into the thick mass of grey hair, complaining that it tickled.

'I'm the spunk meister. My father's the fishmonger and I'm the whore monger. Can I go for a dip?'

'You stink of BO. I'd rather be in bed with a Glastonbury toilet.'

Darius rested one arm on his head. 'You've got the nose of a bloodhound. I should have bought you some Everglade from Poundstretcher for Christmas. You can go round spraying everything you don't like the smell of.' He huffed. 'I just want to die. Is that so difficult? I feel totally disconnected from you lot. I'm a walking disaster. Even human comfort and physical contact these days does nothing.' He took his hand away from her pubic mound.

She put her hand to his limp dick, a sleepy animal in a grey nest, hibernating in a perpetual winter.

'We're a train wreckage, Faye.'

She carried on touching around his saggy genitalia until he pushed her hand away and took her firm nipples in his hands.

'Are your tits going to give me the comfort I need? Your body's a playground. I wish life was a playground. Which part of your playground do I explore first? Your body's a clean toilet for me to trash.'

He moved down, teasing a nipple with his tongue, flicking then gently, pulling with his teeth. 'I'm waiting to find the braille on your skin to guide me. I wonder what fanny juice tastes like after death.'

Darius loved to watch her thrashing her head from side to side like a wild animal in Africa, when he went down on her. She looked possessed when she came: a look which calmed to a faraway, drugged mist in her eyes, stillness and exhaustion transforming her face to airbrushed porcelain.

He loved to lick. These days it was only thing he was good at. She was whispering *put it up me now, up me*. It was like a Punjabi script. But he couldn't. He wanted to. He loved it when her fanny vacuumed him. He wanted to feel his body rising and being torn open and that pleasurable exhaustion that followed. But it was no good. There would be another hydraulic failure. When it worked, he knew it was like Mr. Kipling sex... exceedingly good. But times like that were rare.

'It's asleep. I'm happy just for your fanny juice to decompose on my face. It's still lovely. I remember the first time I ever went down on you. Then I filled the car at the Shell Garage on my way home. I walked in to pay, smelling of you all over my face. Some people jump up and shower off the dirty deed. I don't. But these days I'm just old British fuel.'

∼

DARIUS HAD HATED Christmas as a child. Being a part of a Catholic family was a painful and ritualistic experience; dragged out of bed for midnight mass and his parents too poor to buy a turkey. At school there had been too much Jesus: hymns and carols and dressing up in ridiculous costumes to perform on a stage as a shepherd or a lamb. He hadn't really understood what it was all about, just the feeling that it was all complete twaddle. Most of all he hated the way the faith was heavily centred around sin and dogmatic holiness. Being part of what he called 'the evil empire' meant control over how people were supposed to behave and there were so many rigid practices. As soon as he was old enough, he'd rebelled against the traditions. It was all bollocks.

After Sam was born, he aimed for a bigger and fuller tree than the previous year with more and brighter decorations that sparkled and glittered. It was liberating and modern. He felt naughty, slightly guilty. He loved the feeling of defiance and extravagance that Christmas gave him.

But this year was slightly different. Darius wasn't in the festive cheer. He was dreading the usual routine of her kids escaping to their rooms, not being a part of the occasion and his son making a short perfunctory appearance.

∼

It was Christmas Eve. They were languishing in bed and it was getting late. Darius had enjoyed his post coital orange. The sweet fragrance filled the air. The curled peel had been tossed onto the floor and the pips poked their bare bottoms in bed. The dregs of a Baileys lay sticky at the bottom of wine glasses.

'Well tomorrow night we won't be having sex because turkey farts put me right off sex.' Darius started to sing, his face a weasel.

'My outer lips are pulsating. I should be masturbating... since there's nothing else to do, let us screw, let us screw, let us screw.' He struggled up into a sitting position, his belly wobbly with the laughter and unwrapped his fifth or sixth liquor.

'God, look at all the liquor wrappers.' Faye pulled the duvet off gasping at the mess.

He was examining the tray of liquors, wondering which one to eat next. 'This tray is a bit like the bar on the Titanic. I wouldn't have dressed in a penquin suit to play music on the decks. I would have asked the sea to take me. I feel like the Captain, drowning in style.'

'And I bet the ladies wouldn't have waved the cake trolley away if they had known,' she added.

'Christ. This bed is full of semen stains, grey curly pubes, crumbs, wrappers, old farts, tissues, debris, rubbish. It's like Tower Hamlets. And what a trash town this is. Maybe I'll take Mum and go back to Liverpool. Either way I'm soon out of here.'

'You didn't tell me. Your moods are constantly up and down like a yo-yo. I can't keep up.'

'You won't come with me. I know that much. You won't put 600 miles between the kids and that semen donor. There's no reason why you should saddle yourself with a defective product like me–– a man with a failing heart. Your kids don't want me here either. I can't put up with any more stifling and unbearable silences around the table. Christ, I'm not looking forward to tomorrow.'

And with that he pulled the duvet over his head sending liquor wrappers spinning, the tray tossing to the floor.

∼

THE KITCHEN WAS FILLED with the smell of cooking, the windows were misty with condensation and Darius and Sam were busy singing songs. For a short time they were friends again as they prepared the Christmas dinner together. Meg and Tim were in their rooms on computers and Darius's mother, who had to be persuaded to come, was reading stories to Chrissie in the lounge.

Darius poured himself a third glass of red wine then began to waltz across the kitchen with Sam singing to Bing Crosby, 'Oh my partner's just got a stiffy and my fanny's all a whiffy, and since there's no place to go this Christmas, let it snow let it snow let it snow. My cock is all a throbbing, the fire looks delightful.' Soon the pair fell apart laughing.

He sat down to Christmas lunch. He glanced round the table at the motley collection of people celebrating the day with him. What a pantomime it was. When he'd put his profile on a dating site, all that time back, he'd never imagined sitting down to turkey and sprouts in such an incongruous setting with a dysfunctional bunch of people. His son was inches away but at times felt a million miles away. The singing and the dancing in the kitchen were fleeting acts of father son bonding. The people gathered around the table were a cut-and-paste family, constructed from a cheap Christmas cracker. He wondered what things would have been like if they had found Kathleen. Would she have spent Christmas with them? Maybe she had a family of her own. He imagined a big family gathering and for the first time in a while felt reenergised to continue the search on into the new year. Maybe the new year would bring new hope of finding her.'

Darius raised a glass. 'Well.' He waited for everyone to pick up their glasses. 'Here's to our motley family. Here we are. Three years on from hurricane divorce and the United Nations is still bringing us Christmas dinner in a soup kitchen. I had hoped to move from the tent to a house in those three years, but I've landed in with this travelling circus. Three white rabbits who disappear when placed in a glove.'

He looked over at those three white rabbits––the kids. Their faces were in limbo land, balanced between uncertainty and confusion. His mother was the only one laughing, not really understanding what he was saying.

'And that fat bloated robin in the middle of the table is living on the fat of past credit. It should be a thin scrawny robin, a Cameron Clegg austerity robin.' Darius chuckled.

They began to eat. They were strangers around a table with fractured lives and broken pasts. He chatted with Sam about the people who used to be in their lives. And Faye chatted to his mother. The kids quietly bickered.

'I'm sorry I forgot the stuffing. We're having an Alzheimer's Christmas this year. The Brussels and parsnips are a bit hard, the turkey's a bit too dry because the oven here is crap. Still, later on we'll have turkey and cranberry sandwiches, and they'll look like I've murdered your three kids between two slices of bread... which of course, I'm sure I will if we're all still together next Christmas.' Darius laughed loudly, raising his glass again and gulping a mouthful wondered why Santa hadn't thrown a few hand grenades down the chimney overnight.

Darius's mother was laughing too, tears forming in her eyes. It had been a long time since he'd seen his mother laugh. These days she was so fixated on finding Kathleen.

'Were you warm enough last night by the way, Maria? We kept the heating on all night for you,' Faye asked his mother. 'I hope you didn't sleep in the gammon sandwich you bought with you?'

'It was plenty warm enough thank you dear. I've had to give up on hot water bottles. They just keep leaking.'

'You're probably incontinent and don't yet realise it.' Darius laughed.

Darius enjoyed the shocked look from Meg and Faye. He watched the spray of fine brown gloop hit the clean red tablecloth and the fat bloated robin through the spluttered laughter of his son and the blank expression of his mother who seemed to be going slightly batty.

'All the folk where I live seem to be using pads these days. I hope I won't be next. They all seem to be dying.' Maria smiled sadly.

'Put enough old folk in one place, they do tend to die. Watch the gravy, Sam. Use a napkin,' Darius ordered. 'Gravy is culinary hell. They serve it at all the nasty carvery chains. It's basically hot viscous engine oil draining from a sump. Anyone thought of it like that?' Darius looked round the table.

'The gravy's a bit too thin,' Maria complained.

Darius thought *here we go again*. She's going to start her complaining.

'It's fresh sludge piped through to your table from the local sewer farm. It's an amazing process to process raw sewer. You're basically taking out all the solid matter.'

His mother had her next mouthful poised in mid-air, fork hovering at her lips, uncertain whether to continue its journey.

He was enjoying her hesitation. 'There's a glutinous warm sweet Christmas pudding to follow with delectable nuts and stickiness. I love the feeling of being pissed and the best defecation ever at the end of Christmas day. It's really quite something.'

His mother put down the fork. Her laughter had turned to a blank look. She clearly didn't quite know how to respond in front of people she didn't know very well. Meg and Faye were exchanging looks of embarrassed disgust.

'I don't think I can eat any more. The turkey is much too dry, and these Brussels are soggy. Don't throw it away though. It might taste better tomorrow. I can wrap it up in tin foil and take it home with me,' Maria said.

'Can I have more skin? I like the crispy skin,' Chrissie asked pointing with a greasy finger.

Darius placed some skin on her plate. 'There you are, enjoy that bit of crispy foreskin.' He gave a wide smile at her but inside he was imagining the priest's foreskin toasting on a bonfire.

'What is the other meat on my plate?' Chrissie asked innocently.

'You've got the turkey's thigh. The rest of the turkey's in a wheelchair. It had its legs blown off in Afganistan.'

'Dad. Shut up will you. Just shut up.' Sam had turned angry. 'There are men out there my age fighting. So just shut it. They're coming back in body bags or they're screwed up mentally and end up on the streets.'

A while later Faye asked Meg, 'you're very quiet.'

'Your lot are always silent.' Darius responded. 'We have to insert a sim card for conversation, but the USB is fucked.'

Meg shrugged. 'I was quiet because of that comment about the turkey skin. And the weirdo comment about the gravy.'

Darius gave a big sigh. 'That was a successful lunch. And you won't have to put up with me much longer, Meg.' Sarcasm dripped from his mouth like gravy.

'Anyone for a Poundstretcher cracker? That would liven you all up.' He said.

'I'll have a cracker.' It was the first thing Tim had said all meal.

'You are crackers.' Darius reached out a hand and ruffled Tim's hair.

Sam left soon after lunch. Darius stoked the fire in the sitting room as they all watched, 'The Sound of Music.' This was the very first evening they had all sat in the room together, squeezed in on his velvet settees and he had a very strong feeling it was going to be the last. He didn't have a plan for 2011 but he felt sure it didn't involve Faye and her dysfunctional kids. He loved her and wished they had met years ago, when they had no health challenges or baggage or painful history and a real chance of making a go of it. Quite where his bags and boxes would land next he didn't know.

He took solace in the box of Quality Street sitting on the coffee table. 'Anyone for an inequality street? Delve deep into the tin who'll find the Poundstretcher, the homeless, MPs on the fiddle, Fred Goodwin drawing his massive pension.'

Darius sloshed back a swig of tea, took a large bite of mince pie. He'd always considered Quality Street to be an essential element of Christmas.

∼

BOXING DAY for Darius was possibly the worst he had ever experienced. They took his mother to her favourite destination – the industrial estate in Slough.

'Can we have a good look round the DFS before you drop me home?' she asked, clutching the foil wrapped turkey in case she got hungry while out and a carrier containing her gifts – soap, talc and a pair of fluffy bed socks.

'I haven't been here in a long time.' His mother said looking cheerful as she got out of the car. 'Would be nice to look for a corner cabinet to hold all my ornaments. I've been trying to find one.'

'What ornaments? A load of shit picked up from cathedral gift shops? Jesus, Mary and Joseph,' Darius scoffed.

'Is this the furniture shop that has fresh warm cookies and

coffee? What a lovely treat. I hope they've got a cosy settee we can all sit on. Not being able to drive anymore has made me really appreciate these little trips out,' she asked.

They placed their polystyrene cups on a coffee table called Nathan.

'This has to be the worst place to take someone on Boxing Day -someone that doesn't have a house to buy furniture for. You just enjoy taking the piss out of me, Mum. You've spent the last two years sending me all over the world looking for our Kathleen knowing that I would never find her, and this is how I have to spend Christmas. In the bloody DFS. It's all one big humiliation exercise, Mum.' And it was on the tip of his tongue to finally tell her about the evil priest, Father Joseph.

'Stop it, Darius. Your mother likes coming here. She doesn't get out much. It's a treat. It's either this or we take her to mass, and you know how much you love that. Not.'

Darius was fuming. He made his way to the exit, pacing up and down until they had finished their coffees and fill of chocolate chip cookies. What a Christmas it had been.

Would the New Year be any better he wondered?

31

FAYE

January 2011

Darius looked sad, deflated.

'I'll put the kettle on.' Faye took a couple of mugs from the cupboard. She heard him huffing.

Then he flicked the TV on. He was a bastard – but one she couldn't help loving and feeling sorry for.

He was a capable man but there was something needy about him. His moods seemed to oscillate between increasing high and lows and he refused to climb out of the pit of despair. Each passing day he sunk lower into that pit. She wanted to drag him out but didn't know how. He didn't seem to understand his own emotions, so how could she?

During the past months her emotions had lurched from anger to love, from shock to tears in a misty no man's land, which felt surreal at times. Sometimes when he was nasty she didn't feel anger and could only see his failings as a human being. He was just a weak and vulnerable man, bitter with life and everyone.

'You're back early. What's up?' Faye asked as Darius slumped into his leather settee. His face looked ashen.

'I don't like my son any more. He's a c u next Tuesday.'

Faye knew he didn't mean it. Despite his bravado, he was angry with himself, not really with anyone else. She handed him a mug.

'We had another row.'

'Not again. What about?'

'Fuck knows.'

'You must have said something. Was it about his sexuality again? He's not going to change. That's who he is, and quite honestly you're repeating the dogma of your own childhood in stopping him being who he wants to be. You need to break free from the past.'

'I think I called him scum.'

'That wouldn't help. It's time you respected him. It's time you met his boyfriend Rory too.'

She sat down. She still loved him but over the past weeks had pulled away little by little watching his moods slide, unable to help, telling herself to put her own future first and above all the kids first.

'You've put him through so much. It's unfair. You've tried to destroy him like the priest tried to destroy you. Which is why you're suffering from depression.'

Darius sighed. 'I can't take much more. I'll end up having another heart attack. It feels like a weight is descending. I'm completely overwhelmed. And the nightmares are coming more frequently. All I see is the priest's face. I just want him to leave my head. It all happened years ago, so why the fuck am I having nightmares now?'

'You need therapy. Just because you're older doesn't mean it goes away.' She said, rubbing his shoulder.

Darius

Darius had given up sitting down to breakfast. He stood instead at the worktop holding his bowl of muesli, watching everyone else.

The family breakfasts had broken down. Nobody came down at the same time and everyone served themselves, selfishly taking the last of the milk or the last slice of bread arguing over crockery or which chair they sat on. There was a perfunctory 'morning' from each child, to acknowledge his presence - the baseline of civility. He was biding his time, considering all options.

Tim came down carrying a flask and said morning in an extra loud voice, then told Faye that the flask containing the soup he had made on Friday, at school had pinged open and ruined all his books in his school bag.

'Some bugs don't need oxygen to grow. Christ. You don't teach your kids anything. You shouldn't be left alone with them.'

'Left alone?' Faye swiveled to glare at him. He didn't like the glare. Even she had turned sulky in the mornings.

'I would have thought you would teach them about basic food hygiene.'

'He forgot to take it out of his bag. It's what kids do. Your problem?' Faye snapped.

Darius felt huge despair. Chrissie came into the kitchen with plaited hair, complaining about a wobbly tooth. 'Not going to say good morning? Have you got dementia this morning?'

'She's got toothache. Give her a break, Darius,' Faye snapped.

'What's in my lunch box?' Chrissie asked picking the lunch bag up and pulling at the zip.

'Don't open it. It's all wrapped in foil. Leave it please.' Faye said. Chrissie opened the zip further and started to unwrap the foil.

'Leave it.' Faye pulled it away, zipped it. Then Chrissie picked up Faye's car keys from the table and asked why she didn't have a picture key ring.

'Just put them down, hurry up and finish your cereal then we can do some spellings.'

Darius was watching from behind the worktop. Thankfully he would be leaving for work before the dreaded spelling test began. He couldn't bear listening to the repetition of the same words over and over, words that she had been learning for months now.

It was hard to stand by and watch while all this went on.

'You horrible child. Why don't you just do as you're told? Why are you always doing what you're not supposed to be doing?' Darius looked at Chrissie with loathing. His eyes locked with the child's in a mind confrontation, replacing a thousand words. The cold hard stare was back. The one that riled him, ensnarled his emotions. The stare she saved just for him. Goddam it. What was wrong with the kid? And why did she keep reminding him of the girl in Rhyl?

'I was always told on parenting courses to concentrate on the positive things kids do, not the negative. If you praise the good things, children will do more good things,' Faye told him smugly.

He turned away. Chrissie's stare had been replaced by a glint of triumph he didn't want to see. Faye was talking bollocks again but what was the point?

'That's where you're wrong. That kid doesn't improve,' he said, avoiding looking at Chrissie this time.

'She's trying very hard actually.' Faye shot him a warning look. Chrissie picked up her fluffy blanket and started to cuddle Faye.

'Get away from your mother. We've got things to do. Go and sort your damn hair out.'

Chrissie went upstairs to find her hairbrush. Her usual distraction when it came to spellings. Her feet thudded on each step, annoyed at having to find the brush herself.

Faye moved towards him, still standing by the worktop, now

eating a banana. Darius wondered what she was going to say. She looked menacing. She crept feline towards him and in a whispered vicious voice said, 'Do you know what? I'd really like to see you with a special need's kid. Someone with Downs or ADHD. I wonder how you would cope.' She jabbed her finger on the wooden worktop to make her point.

'Is that what she has? I did wonder.' Darius smirked. 'I think I'd have strangled her by now if she were my kid. *You* didn't have much intelligence to go with the moron in the first place and get pregnant.'

Faye's face suddenly darkened, yet looked calm. He wondered what would happen next. Her hatred was like the wind outside. He knew it was real but couldn't see it. In one swift action she jabbed him in the neck with a finger.

'Don't you fucking...' He was quick. He grabbed her finger, thrust it back at her chest and walked away.

Meg came down, said a robotic 'good morning,' quietly poured some milk over cereal and sat down next to Tim who was eating in silence.

'You're the most sickly annoying boy in the school you know.' Meg digged. Have you looked at your eczema lately? It's all disgusting and flaky. And if you see me in the corridor at school by the way don't say hello because I don't want my friends to know you're my brother,' she said viciously.

Darius looked at Faye and waited for her to say something. All she managed was a feeble, 'shut up squabbling.' Things were never going to change. Darius had reached rock bottom with it all.

'I know what I would do with your bitch of a sister, Tim,' he said, huffing. Meg and Tim said nothing as they always did. He thought it odd how they never hit back, acting in unison, as some sets of twins did, never challenging him, docile, apathetic creatures. It was unnatural. What had made them so unresponsive he wondered?

32

DARIUS
FEBRUARY 2011

The bitter chill of January 2011 crept into February. The coldest winter since Met Office records began wasn't relenting.

It was Sunday morning. Snow had fallen heavily overnight. He reached over and started to massage her breasts with one hand while gripping his IPhone with the other. He put the phone on the bedside cabinet and reached down to shove a finger into her very slippery vagina and started to kiss her back. She was his temporary comfort.

'I'm your antique. Have my name, my wallet', he whispered, nuzzling into her hair. 'Do you want to go back to the 'bring-and-buy sale'? You're not going to find a better man you know. I'm everything you want. I do it for you, Faye. It's time to give up life as a prole.'

She turned and stared at him. 'Do you know how confusing you sound? After all the things you've been saying lately. I thought you wanted to end it. Now you're doing the sales pitch to the church aisle.'

'Maybe I do want to end it. My life I mean. I'd like to die on top of you, pumping away. It would be the perfect way to go.'

He thrust his torso into her side and resumed fingering her fanny. Soon he was down between her thighs. He always felt as if he were in another world when her legs were muffs around his head and his tongue was inside her, lapping at the stickiness and hearing her whimper. Her fanny was a place of refuge. It was a perfect crimson red lobster, plump and fresh from Harrods, the finest there was. He would miss all this but what alternative was there? He was better on his own.

Soon he was inside her, focusing on climbing the mountain— an insurmountable task, higher and higher, each thrust never reaching the summit. He imagined the summit and reaching that target, his boys arriving at destination ovary. He thought of her swelling belly, hard and heavy under the weight of his baby, her tender, engorged breasts suckling. He wanted that so much. It gave him reason to stay with her, a connection between them, greater than the thread of friendship, a purpose to his life and something good to come out of the mess of everything. Holding onto the vision of her naked, sitting cross legged on the bed feeding their baby turned him on in new ways he had never imagined. His cock grew harder, more determined and when he came, there was a slight pain and then exhaustion took over.

He buried his head in her neck, panting. Her lemon perfume was still fresh and zesty, a fragrance he wouldn't forget.

'I did consider spunking all over your tits, your face - a kind of Creme Anglaise. But I want you up the duff. So I carried on. I'd like a positive pregnancy test or failing that some sticks of wood to make my coffin - for my birthday please.'

'You're cheerful. As ever,' she tutted.

Faye prised herself away from him. Their bodies were clammy and sticky and it felt like a Band Aid had been ripped from his body.

Faye

It was becoming harder to stay calm. But she had to. She didn't want a massive argument, him walking out, leaving her with the rent to pay.

Play the game she told herself. Anger bubbled and boiled inside her. His moods were swinging like a pendulum. She couldn't keep up. Couldn't trust anything he said anymore. He was totally consumed with his own problems in a childlike and vulnerable way.

Darius

There was still no sign of a thaw in sight–– for their relationship or the landscape outside. Silence hung all around. Life had ground to a halt. Darius was determined to get to work. He needed to think, to carry on as normal. He set off with a bag containing his laptop and a few overnight bits in case he couldn't get back that day due to the weather conditions and trudged his way through the thick snow and biting wind to the station.

His team had called in, unable to get to work that day. Alone in the office he couldn't focus. He flipped between different porn sites, called the bank, venting his usual frustrations. Then he put his head on the desk, banged it several times, looked at some more porn, made a coffee, kicked the door a couple of times - just for the hell of it, then had a piss. Another coffee, a futile attempt to write a piece about a doughnut entrepreneur in Memphis.

In his office he looked at the swamp of paper on his desk and couldn't bring himself to sort through it all. Invoices, files, bank statements, junk mail that hadn't been binned, sweet wrappers, orange peelings, dirty mugs. He had never experienced such a crushing feeling of futility, of being trapped on a dead-end street. He got up. Even that was an effort. He stood at the window and watched the lorries come in and go out of the warehouse opposite and watched the men unload the goods.

The four walls around him seemed to be breathing, pressing inward. The patterns on the walls became Virginia Creeper, threatening to choke. Were his thoughts trapping him or was the world trapping him? He returned to the computer, could see the reflections of a white lorry on his screen. There was no way out. No light at the end of the tunnel because the end ultimately meant darkness. All roads, all avenues led to the same thing.

Darius had never known such crippling lethargy. It was starting to get dark outside. He dreaded the night when his nightmares returned. As the hours went by, he became less concerned, giddy, blank, trancelike.

Through the malaise he typed into google the words, 'suicide how to.' Various 'exit' sites sprung to his screen in the gloom of the unlit office. He didn't know what he felt. It wasn't distress or pity, simply a quiet resignation. Ideas were spinning round his head. This wasn't difficult. It was an easy route out. The only route. The more he pondered that the more excited he became. There was so much to read and many choices but lots of risks of it going wrong. All he really wanted to do was go to sleep; a deep and peaceful drug induced sleep and not to wake up the next morning. There was nothing to wake up for. He had no ties to Faye. At times he felt like he was living on another planet and no one understood what he was going through. He felt as if he'd lost himself. Who was he?

Some words caught his attention:

'The will to live is so strong that in all but the most exceptional cases it will prevail until the end. But if you regard your life as special (as it is), if you are the sort of person who likes to be in charge of their own life, then the final segment should be one of your own choosing.' He liked that. It was dignified, respectful and obvious.

He began to imagine what it would be like to be dead. Free from the pain. Free from the hand that entered his mind with increasing frequency like a flashbulb; memories sneaking up unannounced. His mind couldn't process the scrambled past.

He closed his eyes to imagine what death would be like. That total nothingness. But all he could see was being trapped somewhere. Was it a church vestry? Was it a toilet? He could hear the clack of metal on stone. Footsteps. The swish of a robe. And rows and rows of pews going on and on to infinity and the wooden door ahead tiny; too far away to reach. He willed himself to reach the door but when he reached it the mocking face of the priest appeared. It was like a dagger in his heart slowly twisting, with no escape.

He opened his eyes. The screensaver illuminated in the gloomy light of his office. A picture of Sam, the young boy, innocent, smiling, his sexuality not yet fully formed swinging happily in the meadow at Nettlebed. Beautiful flowers, all the colours of the rainbow splashed across the computer screen. But sometimes - in his head - the vision of Sam was replaced by the girl standing outside the toilet in Rhyl. She filled the meadow. He could see her blonde plaited hair on top of her head, the scared look in her eyes. And she was destroying the peace and tranquility of the meadow. Consuming his head space, his computer screen. Staining everything. Why hadn't she raised the alarm?

But he had always known the answer and it had been a simple one. She was just a kid. And then he knew what he had to do. It was easy. It was pain free. One jolt, a quick snap and it would all be over.

He began a fresh search and within minutes had ordered the equipment he needed, carried it to the shopping cart, clicked the purchase button. He was in control. He wasn't being reckless but rational. Part of him was shocked at how calm he was. It seemed so easy and acceptable - judging by the dozens of blogs written about it and books explaining how to carry out the method. Relief swept through him. He wasn't alone. Hundreds were living scared lives planning the same thing. He found this comforting. Resources were being pooled. With all this information he thought, it wasn't going to go wrong.

That evening he slumped down on the sofa bed he kept at the far end of his office suite. He felt light-headed and slightly out of it after several whiskey and sodas at a grotty pub round the corner. With a cushion behind his head, he tried to sleep, but it was cold. Thoughts ran through his head, like wild horses. He suddenly remembered something G.K. Chesterton had once said. *'By killing yourself you insult every flower on earth.'* Why did people have to think so deeply into suicide? It was just a route out of a difficult life. And neither was he 'falling victim to suicide.' It was a life choice - a choice he wanted to take. And in the morning, when the snow had disappeared, he would carry out the plan.

33

Darius
February 2011

He fell into a deep sleep waking at around three with a banging head. A sense of nothingness washed over him. Several texts had pinged in while he'd slept. He scrolled through, but didn't bother to read them properly. They were all from Faye and Sam asking how he was. Then he checked his inbox. Several emails needed his urgent response. He sat up, suddenly feeling charged with energy. This was a good opportunity to make a few calls to Australia, get on top of things, catch up with contacts.

He went through to his office, switched on the computer. Yesterday seemed a long time ago. Had he really ordered rope to kill himself with? It now seemed surreal.

By 9am he had connected with the outside world and written an article for the next issue. He sat back satisfied. Something had lifted from his shoulders.

He returned to the house that evening in Marlow, his head buzzing with ideas. He was exhausted, ready for a good sleep in a proper bed. It had been a busy day. He hadn't given his exit idea another thought.

When he got home, Faye was standing in the kitchen, her face a picture of thunder. He yanked his tie, tossed it to the ground, poured a whiskey and went to his study, slamming the door behind him. He wasn't going to be made to feel like a naughty schoolboy for sleeping in the office overnight. But the look on her face accused him of having an affair. If only people could wear mood indicators on their foreheads, he thought. *I've had enough,* his forehead would read.

···

THE ATMOSPHERE in the house hadn't really improved a couple of evenings later.

The kids were upstairs when he got back. He'd long given up on them coming down to say hello. Faye was cleaning shelves, sorting out bottles of alcohol, throwing some out, dusting others. She gave him a dismissive look and went back to cleaning.

'You really have no idea how stressful life is until you run a business.' Darius dumped his green leather case on the pine table.

'More problems?' She pulled out a chair, sat down.

'Running that place is like steering a ship through a storm. I never know what will happen from one day to the next.'

He took his glasses off and rubbed his eyes.

Faye smiled sympathetically and handed him a glass of brandy, then poured herself one.

'Fancy finishing off this bottle?' She asked.

He looked at the row of bottles sitting on the table. 'There's a cocktail called 5 o clock in the morning. Brandy, rum, gin, vodka. Throw it all in. Grab a glass. I'll make you one.'

He began opening bottles, poured an inch from each, while Faye gave a relaxed laugh. Soon they were light-headed and making up names for all the different combinations they could think of. To hell with his heart condition.

Darius was swigging a bloody Mary. 'I looked at you lot in that poky flat and wanted to rescue you. You were sharing bath water for Christ sake. But the truth is it would have taken me 20 years to sort you all out. But now *I* need rescuing. There's no reason you should saddle yourself with a defective product.'

'It shouldn't be like that. Not if two people truly loved each other, Darius.'

'What is love as Prince Charles once said?' He took another swig. Flopped his head on the table. 'You'll get over it. Out of sight, out of mind,' he mumbled.

'Great. What's it all been about then?'

'God knows Faye. I feel like a case conference. There's a

webcam on ice like a bear documentary. I'm remote. I'm merely an aberration of myself. I don't have a good relationship with your kids. The twins are developing sexual awareness, Chrissie is struggling at school. I don't like the way this house is run. I don't fit in. I gave you lot a good Christmas, now I'll quietly slip away.'

'Why don't you poke your nose round their doors and say hello?'

'No point. Metaphorically they are so shut it's like Fort Knox.'

'You only look at the negative.'

'That's right. Have a dig, Faye.'

They didn't hear Meg come down the stairs and creep up on them. Her eyes were red and Faye stood up with concern. Meg was wearing the same baggy pajama bottoms and cotton top she always wore around the house.

'I don't want to go to school tomorrow. I keep telling you I want to leave, go to a new school but you never listen.'

Her voice took on an irritating whine, rising to a fever pitch as the conversation began. Tears welled. Her long ginger hair hung in rag tails around her oval face. Darius's head thumped. Christ, he didn't need this.

'What's happened now?' Faye asked.

'A really popular boy on Facebook has got it in for me, saying nasty things and I might get beaten up. Oh my God.'

She started stomping round the kitchen, repeating the mantra 'oh my God' as if she was a Muslim walking round the Kaaba in Mecca.

'It'll blow over,' Faye said dismissively.

'90% of the kids at that school are chavs. In a virtual world everything's open to all. It's nasty, pernicious and far too powerful to be left in the hands of immature people. That's what you're up against,' Darius sighed.

'But this boy is the most popular boy in the school. They

will all believe him and side with him against me. Oh my God. I hate everyone.'

She was sobbing now, fighting back her tears, emotions spilling as she tried to control them.

'All I want is to change school and then I'll shut up and be timid and come off Tumbler and Facebook and be invisible. I can leave myself behind.'

'You'll always be up against different people, accused of different things.' Darius thought back to his own school days.

'You've got to learn to cope. Say fuck you. Practice it in front of the mirror. Shout it. Let it roll on your tongue. Don't ever be scared to use the F word. Then turn up at his house or meet him head on in the corridor.'

'They're just teenagers. They'll soon forget'. Faye headed for the kettle.

'They think I'm pathetic. They'll think I'm a complete bitch if I swear at them.'

'You'll be out in a couple of years. You need to toughen up. We all have to. You're bright, good looking. Look at your strengths. Otherwise, you may as well kill yourself,' Darius said.

Faye looked away. There was a momentary silence. 'Can't I just get home taught?'

'No one can disappear. You're just passing through. School's soon over. Then real life begins. Use it, chew it then spit it out.'

'Concentrate on you.' Faye rubbed Meg's back.

'Then they will call me selfish. Oh my God.'

～

THEY WERE IN BED. Darius had his hand on Faye's pubic mound for warmth. 'Three kids is a lot. I don't have the energy. That business with the bullying - it was draining.'

'But you said all the right things. Relax.'

'You're up against a lot.' Darius closed his eyes, then placed his hand on her breast, wondering if he could find the effort to suck her nipple.

'You knew I had kids when you met me. I don't know what you expected.'

'Not this.'

'I don't know what to do. Neither do you.'

'I feel completely disinterested Faye if I'm honest. I don't have the will to do anything.'

'I used to think you had fight inside you, that you were going to make the world a better place for us.'

'Whatever made you think that?' He turned to look at her. Their heads were resting on a pillow. She looked young, innocent.

'You just always gave that impression. I remember you always saying trust your Darius.'

I'm defeated by it all.' He sighed, looked at the ceiling.

'Life. The long, hard struggle of it all. I just want to go to sleep and not wake up. A coma would be nice. Or amnesia.' He paused. 'You know sometimes I imagine you standing at my funeral, crying.'

'You make it sound like an armed struggle, the struggle for black freedom, in South Africa. When did that struggle begin?'

'I don't know.' He turned again, pulled at a lock of her hair. 'Gradually. Suddenly. The exhaustion never goes away.' He kissed her on the forehead.

34

DARIUS

February 2011
 Darius and Faye woke in an embrace, made love. Sometimes achieving an orgasm was so easy, like taking a stroll through the park. At other times it was like carrying a heavy load. The only way he could carry on, remain firm was to imagine her pregnant or cradling a baby. This was a massive turn on which sustained his energy. He flunked back onto the pillow as she swiped tissues from a box nearby, mopping up, then wriggling around to avoid lying on the wet patch before flopping towards him - her arm now slung across his belly. His mind was in turmoil. When he was pounding away inside her, he knew he couldn't leave her. He still loved her. But he had to put himself first. He didn't want to 'dump' her back at the overcrowded, shabby flat on the council estate. But she wasn't his responsibility. That arsehole dad should be doing more to help, he kept reminding himself. He felt like a Robin Reliant towing a caravan.

 All sorts of feelings shot through him. Bitterness, anger, fear, regret, but mostly just a dull pain that seemed to pervade every cell of his body. One of his rules was to ignore the heart, trust the mind and listen to what the gut was saying. Everything came from the gut. But sitting here now it felt as if his heart was divided into all sorts of different compartments, like a haberdasher's.

'That was a lovely meal the kids made last night, and the conversation was lively. Everybody was engaging. You can't say my kids are always aloof and quiet.' Faye's statement was more a question, seeking his reassurance that things had improved. He knew they hadn't. She was in denial. Everything was far from ok. He felt total disconnection from them all.

'Was it?' He responded limply.

'You're always negative. The enchiladas were really tasty, and Meg made a lovely creamy pie. Key lime pie is really special in our family. It kind of brings us all together, a shared love. Rather like having a puppy or a baby.'

'It's you lot and me.' He gave a resigned sigh. 'I once read a quote I liked. Can't remember where. *When the food runs out, the family reunion is over.* It's so true.'

'They were happy to wash-up. You should have washed-up with them. It's all part of it.'

'And I should have played on the Wii at Christmas with them, I can hear you about to tell me for the millionth time.' He sighed.

'You have to join in. Seize the opportunity if it's presented.'

Darius was sitting up, poised to begin the day, when he heard a ringing. Neither moved. 'What's that?' He got up, disorientated.

'I think it's the landline.'

'Where is it?'

'How should I know? It's never rung before.'

'You must know where it is.' He tutted grabbing his towelling robe.

He ran downstairs cursing about the lack of a line in the bedroom.

'I'm sick of this shithole,' he shouted, as Faye padded on behind him. As he passed through the playroom towards the ringing phone, he registered that Chrissie was curled up on the settee in her nighty snuggling her blanket watching CBeebies. Every time he looked at the kid, he found it hard to erase the visions he had in his mind of her conception with the untermensch. He still couldn't work out what had been on Faye's mind. He wouldn't have handled his semen with a turkey baster if he were the last humanoid on the planet.

'Turn that bloody thing off,' he shrieked as he passed. She glared back. It was a glare that stirred something deep within. All at once he was transported back in time. He could see a blurred memory like a watermark on vellum. He could see the girl with the blanket standing outside the toilet in Rhyl waiting for it to be unlocked, waiting for them to come out. Banging, banging on the door. As he headed for the phone a sense of anger took hold as the memory became real in the living child, Chrissie, the girl who years back should have risen the alarm, called for help, saved him from the hands of the priest.

The clock on the study windowsill read 7.20. When he heard Sam's voice, alarm rose within.

'Why are calling on the landline?'

'Your phone was switched off.'

'Shit. Yes.' He sensed something was wrong. He was confused. Sam's words spat out at machine gun speed, escaping from his mouth quicker than his brain could formulate the sentence. In one breath Sam told him he had imagined the police were coming to take him away. Then he jumped on in random fits. His friend had laced his food with hash and he could no longer trust the food in his fridge. Then he said something about hearing Auntie Kathleen singing in his room late one night. Then he went on to explain that on a few occasions he'd been late into the salon a few times and there were people wanting him out.

It was muddling and disjointed. The TV was distracting his thoughts, stopping him focusing. Stress mounted. He couldn't think what to say, what to do, how to help. But at the back of his mind, he sensed that Sam was stoned. This wasn't normal behaviour.

As he puzzled Sam's mental state, wondering whether he was on drugs, the TV swelled in his head. Laughter, children's voices, music and Sam's confused words played a death dance in his head. He threw the phone down and could hear Sam still yabbering on. He flung the door back and flew like a raging bull towards the settee where Chrissie was still curled up, her cheeks pink, damp bed hair matted across her flushed face, thumb in mouth, pulling pieces of fluff from her blanket to stuff up her nose and form a balcony across the rim of her lip. He couldn't process any rational thoughts, for there were none.

He could hear Faye in the kitchen putting crockery away. He fleetingly registered Cameron's voice talking about cuts over the kitchen radio. Every day the list of services planned for cutbacks grew like a shopping list. The smell of fresh toast wafted through.

'Turn that thing off,' he shouted at Chrissie.

She looked down. He wondered, as he always wondered, what sort of a family this was and why they always cowered into silence. She curled her body tighter like a spider in a bath plug. He could see her knickers, tight across her opening. She pulled her legs together as he came closer, her arm tight around them. His eyes bored into her. He could see Shayne in her body outline. Suddenly he flew towards her. How dare the kid ignore him. She looked up now. He didn't like the look on her face – grabbed her arm, yanked it. And in a flash, he saw into her mind and didn't like what he saw. In her eyes he could see pure contempt burrowed through to her soul. Defiance shone from those innocent eyes that had turned evil. It was as if her eyes were communicating words. 'You can't make me, I'm going to ignore you.'

Nobody ignored Darius. Not since the day he'd fled from the priest's grip, knocking him to the cold flagstones in the church, terrified of what would happen next. He'd made sure of that. He couldn't exist, do the things he needed to do without a certain level of order, control and continuity.

'Get up,' he barked. 'Turn that racket off.'

She bent her face lower, like a petal curling in rain. He knew in that second that he hated that kid and everything she represented. She was the miniature incarnation of her father.

Sam would be waiting. He couldn't think, couldn't process. He needed to get back to the phone, find out what was going on. He grabbed her tiny arm, yanked her towards the TV. Still she said nothing. She was a stupid, lifeless rag doll with a sewn on snarl across her face. The image of a rag doll had been etched into his mind for so long – the priest grabbing the little girl's arm, shouting at her for banging on the toilet door.

He took a step nearer to Chrissie. The music from the TV swelled in his head, thudding, consuming his thinking space. He wanted to rip the blanket away, tear it up, burn it. But why had he wanted to? It wasn't the first time he had questioned his anger towards the girl. What was driving his anger? He wasn't sure but he knew, at the back of his mind that it was more than a loathing for the fact that she hadn't raised the alarm. Looking at Chrissie his heart banged in his chest as he tried to push the thought away. Had he enjoyed the experience with the priest? Surely not. But he couldn't deny that a tiny piece of him had felt annoyance that the girl had disturbed them. He desperately now tried to squash that thought. Nobody enjoyed being a victim of child abuse. Why was his mind playing these cruel games?

And then Faye was in the middle, the referee and he was

shouting at the pair of them, screaming for them both to give him some peace, some silence.

'Everybody trashes over my feelings in this place,' he shouted.

He flew back to the study, banging the door behind him but Sam had gone, and he was late for his train and had to get on.

He showered and dressed and came down for breakfast doing his buttons up. Chrissie was asking what breakfast cereal she could have.

'Oh shut up. Sit down or you'll really have something to cry about. Where's your spellings anyway? You don't give a shit about your education.' He walked towards the counter where Faye was pouring cereal. 'Have you stopped talking too? Christ, this places gets worse.'

Faye didn't reply. Her body was rigid at the worktop. He didn't remember her being this quiet. He looked at her face. Her upper lip was quivering again.

'So what did Sam want? What's happened?' she eventually asked in a timid voice.

'He's been late to the salon a few times. There are people that want him out. I didn't really get the whole story. Your little shit here saw to that.'

His words drummed across the kitchen. He looked over at Chrissie, the anger had subsided but was still simmering in the pot. He was aware that if Faye hadn't come in at that moment, he would have flown the child through to the next week, a thought that didn't sit easy. He knew how the course of history could change in seconds.

'What? Chucked out of the salon altogether?'

'You stupid bitch. Stop repeating what I've just said,' he screamed.

They swam in a tense pool of silence for several minutes. He huffed, poured a coffee from the filter jug. She slammed a yogurt pot, with great force onto the worktop next to him. The bottom cracked. Thick pink creamy blobs spurted and squirted, reminding him of a decorating accident with Dulux.

'Don't you ever call me a stupid bitch again. Do you hear me?' Her face was stony.

'Well, you're very slow on the uptake at times,' he stoked.

'You didn't need to shout at her. You could have just closed the study door. She had already turned down the volume.' Faye was close to tears.

'You did nothing to help. Don't blame me. Next time it happens, I might be forced to strangle her.'

Faye swept out of the kitchen, saying nothing, taking Chrissie with her.

What a pathetic woman, Darius thought to himself. He half wanted her to snap. Maybe one day she would.

35

FAYE

February 2011

Dreams and news scrambled in her transitional state of sleep and consciousness. Soldiers and rioters throwing tear gas, hand grenades and petrol bombs. A reporter from Al Jazeera talked of rioting in Tahir Square. The leader of Eqypt, Mubarrak had toppled from power.

'You have no idea how bad it's all going to get. An Arab Spring. And here: cuts and more cuts. Darius offered his daily analysis.

When Faye went down to the kitchen, Chrissie was standing on a chair reaching for cereal on top of the fridge, blanket and fluffy camel pinned under one arm.

Faye grabbed the cereal and whispered into Chrissie's ear. 'Don't forget to say good morning when he comes down.'

'I always do. Mummy, you look scared.' She held Faye's hand.

'Why is your hand shaking?' She was aware that her breaths were short and jagged. Her whole body hurt. Misery seemed to be closing in around her. She hated this way of life – treading carefully around Darius. She glanced at the calendar on the wall. Absent mindedly counted the weeks until they could move back to her flat.

She chiseled into her thumbnail, still studying the calendar as she tracked each thud of his Hush Puppies descending the stairs.

'So, you're finally learning to be civil now I'm about to leave you all.' Darius had his back to her, took a bowl from the Welsh dresser as she dutifully gave him the loudest, politest good morning she could. He took out his IPhone. Faye could see he was scrolling through properties on Rightmove.

She felt trapped in a cauldron of competing emotions, bubbling to the surface, one big toxic concoction and nowhere to escape.

He pushed the bowl away, got up, put his jacket on, complaining about stiff aching shoulders.

Picking up his green leather laptop satchel he said, 'When you're ready then, dear.' Faye bristled. She hated to be called that. And hated her new and main role – that of taxi driver to the station. She sensed he was aware of how she felt.

Seeing the frosted windscreen Faye nipped back in to fill a kettle of tepid water to swish across the screen.

In the car she closed her eyes, flopped her head onto the dashboard and waited for him to get in. The agency were still trying to find her a new flat. *Keep calm*, her inner voice screamed.

Bizarrely though she still loved him. Would miss him. Hers was a conflicting bag of emotions: she feared loneliness but also craved the solitary experience.

In the past 24 hours she had kicked herself for an emotional response, but none had come. What sort of mother would feel blank after a threat to their child's safety? Maybe deep down she saw a broken man full of hot air.

The passenger door clunked open, the woody aroma of his

aftershave filling the car. Tim's friends were gathering on the pavement, waiting to cross.

'What's wrong with *you* then? Living with me given you depression too then? What have you got to look so sullen about? He smirked.

She ignored the missive but inside her head a storm was brewing, a change descending and engulfing. She looked at the boys as she reversed. Their ties were loose, hanging in big gaping knots halfway down their shirts, none of which were tucked in and their hair was unkempt.

'I wish they'd learn to dress properly.' When she spoke it wasn't her, It was a veneer.

'Bunch of scum. They should all be shot. And you want to stay in this area because of the school?'

She refused the spoon of provocation.

'Why did you use a kettle of water on the windscreen?' He digged.

'It's quicker to defrost.'

'What's your problem? I told you to buy some deicer.' His voice had risen.

'It corrodes the wipers.' Her reply was flat and to the point.

'You're talking bollocks again. Listen to yourself. Is this what I'm going to have to put up with? Things are going to have to change. You'll be driving me around for a long time to come. We wasted three minutes doing it *your way.*'

A red mist descended as swift as a storm cloud, a pressure cooker inside her head waiting to explode. In the moments that followed everything changed and was redefined. She inched up into the seat. Goddam it. She deserved so much better. *What am I doing?* her inner voice screamed.

She remembered an Ernest Hemingway quote she'd read somewhere, a long time ago that applied so much to Darius. *Happiness in intelligent people is the rarest thing I know.*

Every possible emotion thumped through her veins,

settling in her stomach, a pool of acid. She was trembling as uncontrollable anger ripped. The floodgates had opened and there was no stopping her. It was as if she were having a fit.

'You miserable, miserable, miserable cunt.' She spat the words, enjoying the flavor, the texture, the explosion. She couldn't remember when she had ever used the 'C' word, but it felt good – forbidden and vulgar. Its power washed through her like a stiff whiskey, and she could sense Darius shrink in his seat beside her.

'I'm sick of *your* problems, *your* misery, *your* nasty behaviour. How dare you? You're not getting away with it. I'm not a push-over. It's all about you. You, you, you. I'm sorry you suffered at the hands of a priest. But that was a long time ago. Get it out of your head. Move on, because it's eating and destroying you and destroying us.' She banged the words out, thumping the steering wheel with each shot. 'You selfish man. You don't give a damn about anyone but yourself.'

She ranted on trembling and shivering as if she were in icy water. She thought she heard him call her a crazy lunatic. Her brain had frozen over. His words weren't registering.

By the time they pulled into the station forecourt she was pulling his collar. The car stalled, jolting forward behind a taxi. She tugged and pushed him. The car was still running. He had morphed into a rag doll. And like throwing a rag doll across a room, this seemed so easy. His glasses flew to the footwell. He crouched to retrieve them covering his head for protection. She carried on tugging and pushing and screaming.

She pushed him out, watching him crumple to the pavement in full view of gawping potential witnesses. His wig was flying across the car park like a rat spinning through the air. She looked in the mirror. Her face was ashen. He was reaching in his pocket for his fags. She was shaking. She lost her grip on the foot-peddles. As she pulled away, she saw him brushing himself down, adjusting his glasses, wig back on head, shell shocked, as if he'd just been mugged in a dark alley. Her heart tugged and in a flash, she felt sorry for him. But she couldn't run after him. That would prove she was in the wrong and he in the right but what had she done? Maybe she was mad, as he had often told her. But part of her felt pleased. Free and liberated like a chick hatched from a shell.

Faye went straight round to talk to a friend. 'I'm not at all surprised,' the friend said. 'He's been seeping away at your confidence for months. You've changed. When you're both calm you need to tell him it's not a healthy relationship for either of you.' And another friend said 'he's a controlling pig. You're best out of it. Let him get a rope to hang himself.'

∼

IT WAS the evening and she waited for him to come home. Kept glancing at the clock. He didn't return.

'I'm not coming back. It's unsafe. You're a bloody lunatic Faye,' he texted.

'I'm sorry. Please come back.' Her emotions were mixed bag of fear, shame, confusion, love and it was ridiculous, but in a practical sense all she cared about was the unpaid rent and a roof over their heads until she could find another flat or house.

'I'll look for a new rental,' he said, resigned to the task ahead.

Everything she had hoped to achieve by her outburst in the car had been fruitless. Yet again he was in the right and he was the victim – a vulnerable man and she was the aggressor. The crazy woman.

Part of her wanted to make it up to him. But inside her head was a drum beating, warning her of all the things that wouldn't improve.

'Come back. We can talk.' She said without really thinking.

She called the rental agency, pleading with them to find her a new flat to rent so they could leave him. She was stuck. She had to bide her time. What if he came back? Better that he did Faye thought. Keep him here, paying the bills.

Darius

After Faye's tirade at the station, he took a taxi back to the house, knowing she had headed out for the day and wouldn't be home. He nipped into the house, collected the parcel that had been delivered the previous day and got into his Mercedes, heading out of town towards Nettlebed. A red mist had descended, his thoughts were spiralling down and out of control. With his hands tightly gripping the steering wheel, foot flooring the accelerator, a camera flashed, a car swerved out the way, but he didn't notice. His eyes were fixed ahead, his mind transported to the meadow, his final resting place, the place of peace where it all would end.

Before he reached Nettlebed he pulled over into a layby, his mind whirling as he wondered how to tie a hangman's noose. He took out his IPhone, then watched a five minute clip on You Tube and began to practice the knot. His blood ran hot and cold, his hands shaking. Did he have the courage to carry it out? His resolve was starting to crack. Tiny doubts were creeping in. But he carried on practicing with the nylon twine, his mind resolved but his stomach backing out. A chill ran through him as his body temperature started to drop, the engine turned off, the car losing heat.

He headed on, as if on auto-pilot, arriving at the house where he knew his ex wouldn't be. She was away, again in Florida. As he parked on the gravel he thought nothing of the silver Fiesta parked next to the garage. It wasn't a car he recognized. He suspected it was a neighbour's car, left there to make the place look lived in. A blanket of pearly mist shrouded the stream behind the cottage and the sky was a milky white. The landscape – full of colour in the summer - was now eerie and ghostlike. He wondered if more snow was on its way. But it wasn't something he needed to worry about. The snow was melting fast, but the earth was hard and crunchy under foot. Amid the snowy grasses the solitary willow stood, gently creaking in the icy breeze. Tendrils of mist drifted above the frozen earth at the foot of its' wide trunk. Sam's wooden swing that he had rigged up so many years ago still hung from the branch, a swing that would never see grandchildren sway to-and-fro.

As he walked towards the tree - carrying a ladder and the rope - tears now streaming down his face, he carried the weight of what had been and what would never be. With one last look around at the view, his sanctuary and retreat, he propped the ladder against the tree and began to climb, reaching the first branch, which held the swing. It was a journey many troubled men before him had taken and many would take long after him. He didn't feel so alone when he thought about the statistics of how many men chose to end their lives. It was almost becoming a chosen path, especially for men following divorce and business collapses. In Frank Sinatra's words he was doing things his way. *This is my way* he muttered as he eased his way onto the branch. With frozen fingers he inched his way slowly along the branch, began to tie a knot around it, breaking off now and then to warm his hands under his breath.

And then he stopped. From nearby, a leaded-light window creaked open. He looked over, heart banging in his chest. From behind the criss-cross of the leaded slats he saw the bare chest of a man and behind him the bare chest of another man–– his son. And then they were screaming. He inched further along, the rope now in place, his fingers throbbing, numb with the cold. And then he wobbled, lost his balance, tried to claw at the bark to regain his position but the next thing he knew he was on the ground, his face whacking the hard earth. Rory and Sam, bare chested, bare footed staring down, alarm coursing their shocked faces.

And then humiliation and anger hit, rising like a phoenix from the ashes as he put his hands on the ground finding his footing, leaning against the tree to compose himself.

'Dad. What the fuck are you doing? Dad, don't.' Sam was screaming and shivering, hysteria rising, his tumbling dark curls lifting like commas in the icy breeze. But there was something written across Rory's face that he didn't like. A smugness seemed to flash across his crow-like eyes. Suddenly he saw him in bed with his son. He could see their naked bodies entwined. He could see Rory entering Sam and he could hear Sam's moans of pain and pleasure. He was back there. In the church. In the vestry. Pinned to the blanket of robes hanging on the walls. The hand was there. Was it the priest's hand or was it just Rory's hand moving towards him to guide him into the house.

And then he couldn't take it anymore. He reached out, grabbed Rory's hair, yanking him towards the earth, his other hand grabbing his cheek and slicing into it with sharp finger nails. Rory's legs buckled. In the mist that swirled around his mind it was the face of the priest, mocking and evil. And then Sam was pulling him away, screaming, telling him he loved Rory.

Now he knew how Christ had felt on the cross. Tiny droplets of red violence pricked to the surface. Blood which could so easily become a river of blood, then a sea of blood, staining yet purifying. This was the pain of revenge. This was the blood of revenge. The colour of violence that screamed across every nation, the droplets that tore families, groups of people apart and all in the name of religion. Four raw gashes cried in anger. Rory was clutching his face, staggering towards the house, leaving a trail of droplets bleeding into the snowy ground.

Like Christ, he had been defiant in the face of the evil priest, triumphant and yet at times he couldn't see that. All he could see was that his soul had been defeated in the face of power, twisted and crushed, never to fully recover.

~

Faye

It was the following evening. Faye heard his key turn in the lock. Her heart thudded as she listened to his footsteps on the wood and the creaky doorknob turn. Blood drained. She sat down, in shock. Heard his footsteps in the hall. Her body was rigid. Fear coursed through her.

'You're back?' She tried not to gasp. She had been on the phone with Sam. Knew what had happened and that Rory had been to the police station to report Darius.

He dropped his bag. Didn't smile. 'I'm not staying.' His words were cold, matter of fact.

'Where will you go?'

'Back to the office.' His face showed no emotion. Faye got up, tried to hug him. Touched his face.

'Stay... please.' They stood in icy silence. After a several minutes he lifted his arm, put it over her shoulder, a limp half action.

'Sorry. I still love you.' She touched his face again.

'You're a crazy bitch. I thought you were going to attack me in the car. Suddenly I could see the bitch and the metal coathanger and I was terrified. You've got quite a temper.'

'Sorry. You were driving me mad.' She tried to placate him with a look of sympathy.

'I don't know where we go from here.' His eyes looked softer. His guard was melting.

'That's the problem.' Faye squeezed his shoulder. For a moment they gazed at each other as if trying to understand what each other was really thinking. In the depths of her stomach, a voice screamed *let him go, let him go.*

'Would we end up killing each other?' He touched her hair, his words disconnected from his actions.

～

For a few days the atmosphere was charged but bizarrely there was a level of normality and even superficial hope. Faye played it cool.

The following evening, he called the kids down. Everybody sat around the pine table in awkward silence, their bodies rooted to their chairs.

'Your mother and I are always arguing. Then there's you lot.'

She wondered when that would come.

He sighed as if describing the burden of tackling a heavily overgrown garden. A ghastly tiredness swept over her. He rubbed his forehead.

'Quite frankly *you* lot don't help.'

Here they were again, back on trampled ground, a place they had been a thousand times before.

Faye counted to five in her head while she tried not to react. Part of her felt strangely disconnected from the scene.

'I came into this wanting to change your lives. I've given you a lot, but I get nothing back and that doesn't make me feel great.' He sounded like a failed missionary in Libya. 'You're never here. You're always in your rooms. As soon as you've eaten you slope off. We have the disappearing routine every evening, then you're off to Shayne and Steve. And woof... your life will be gone. This is like a flat share. The type of life you'll have at university. Everyone tolerates each other but that's as far as it goes. Tolerance isn't enough. And basically...' Darius cradled the mug of coffee in front of him, as if it were his emotional prop. 'I'm not putting up with it anymore. It's not how it should be. It's abnormal. It's not a good quality of family life.' As if he knew what that was.

'What if we move to America?' Tim had been dabbing his running nose with a tissue. His eyes were suddenly bright and electric. He was like a hamster that had suddenly woken.

'That's not going to solve anything. You'd sit in your room there instead.'

'No, we wouldn't. We'd go to Mc Donalds. They're way cooler over there.'

'Or sunbathe in the desert. Please can we move over there?' Meg's eyes were wide. She linked her arm into Faye's and squeezed Faye's hand pleading with her pleases and her whines.

'It's not dangerous in America, Mummy.' Tim said.

'I didn't say it was. Apart from the gun laws.'

'If you're worried about tornadoes - well - per square mile its more dangerous in England.' Tim smiled.

All at once Faye felt sad for Tim's feather-like vulnerability in the face of this huge thing she was attempting to erect – a modern stepfamily. She'd placed the first bricks on the cement, but the bricks were the wrong shape, and the cement wasn't hardening.

'What if we move to Glasgow? I've seen a really cheap house on Rightmove with seven bedrooms. The bank would give you a small mortgage. We could have massive parties and go fishing,' Meg said.

'That's bad for fish.' Tim gave a smile not directed at anyone.

A swift change came over Meg. She got up. Her arms were in mid-air, her voice high pitched. She was an animal on stage at the Lion King.

'I'm very sorry we're not the perfect kids for you, Darius. We do try talking to you, but you go on and on and most teenagers prefer their bedrooms. Why would I want to sit down here all evening and talk to you two. Jesus Christ.'

'Meg! Don't say that,' Faye scolded.

'That's fine. The kid's alive.' Darius put his hands in the air in mock defeat.

'I don't want her swearing like you,' Faye scowled.

'That's about average.' Tim shrugged, a glint in his eye.

Chrissie sat snuggling her blanket, her head on the table.

FAYE

February 2011

It was the evening after Darius had returned home after the attempt on his life and the fracas with Rory. She wondered if and when the police would be visiting to take a statement from him.

Faye watched him undress and toss his socks and underpants to one side, place his folded trousers on the wicker chair. He sang in a Bob Marley voice 'it's time for a urination across the nation' as he peed into the porcelain then took his heart medication.

He devoured an orange in the pool of light from the street outside, tossing the peel across the white floorboards, as he did each night. They were the facade of a couple, their naked bodies inches apart, body odour and dead skin cells mingling under the sheets. Their clothes hung side by side in the wardrobe, their damp bath towels together on the heated bath rail. But they were two bodies lying in limbo. Unspoken though the issue was, they both knew that in a matter of weeks it would be like a bereavement: two people joined together, sharing their lives for a while - about to become strangers once again. The brief time they had spent together would be a blot on the landscape of their lives, yet they would carry the scars of their short time together.

She listened to him sleeping in the midst of the phoney war they had created. The attempt on his life was the elephant in the room and both were carefully side-stepping around it. And that was totally out of character for him for a man who normally played bull in a china shop. But suicide was a conversation stopper not a conversation opener.

Her whispered voice broke the silence. He almost jerked in surprise. 'Have the police been in touch yet about Rory?'

'Not heard anything. Don't expect they are that interested in a minor domestic. Bigger fish to fry,' he replied.

'It was serious what you did to Rory. You can't blame him for reporting you.' She was stirring him.

'It's probably way down their list of priorities I imagine,' Darius said in a cold tone.

'I'll ring in the morning if you like. Find out what's going on,' she suggested and tugged the duvet.

'Don't bother. I wish Rory was dead,' he snapped.

Faye thought her pounding heart would rip through her chest. She curled her body into a foetal position, butterflies dancing the tango in her stomach, scared of what he might do next to Rory.

When daylight flooded through the curtains Darius reached over to touch her breasts. Maybe from habit. She didn't know. He worked his fingers around a nipple. Warmth crept across her thighs seeping deep inside. Part of her wanted to respond but she remained still, refusing to react remembering what lay ahead.

His hand wandered down the side of her body resting on her pubic area.

Soon you'll be at the police station. Having fingerprints taken,

DNA. *How can you ignore what's happening?* Her silent voice screamed. She gritted her teeth. Lay rigid.

'I feel close to you yet distant. We're the scene in Titanic when they're shivering in the icy water. They're over but waiting till death consumes them,' he said.

'How cheerful.'

'We're all waiting to plunge into a David Cameron hell hole.'

He touched her breasts again.

'I'm not in the mood.' She inched away.

'You're slowly turning into my ex. Maybe it's the menopause.'

He cleared his throat. 'Ladies and gentlemen this is your captain speaking. The weather is heavy at London Gatwick. We now begin the descent to menopause. Please stow your tampons, plug in your seat belts. The cabin crew will be coming to collect all tampons, pads, belts, pins, sanitary ware.'

∼

Darius

Darius was at the police station in the interview room. He was looking down on someone else's life as if watching the scene from the ceiling, like an episode of Eastenders. Detached from his body he could see a copper and a man in a wet suede jacket.

I wish I'd killed Rory. His head screamed. *Prison would be an escape.*

The only bad thing he had ever done in his entire life was run a cat over and defend himself from a metal coathanger which could have ripped out both of his eyes. All it had taken under the willow tree was for the release valve that held his patience together to be pulled.

The officer went through some paperwork and explained

that he would be taking a DNA swab and fingerprints later on. Pleasantries filled the void while they waited for the duty solicitor, held up in traffic.

'Do you know what ABH is? Actual Bodily Harm. That's what you are accused of,' the officer said.

He felt his body shrink. Closed his eyes and imagined swinging on a rope in the meadow.

'Does he know I'm here - Rory?' His name was gristle in his mouth.

'Yes, he knows you're making a statement this morning.'

'Fucking poofter' his inner voice screamed. His hands tightened to fists in his pockets.

'Be very careful what you say to the solicitor. Just to warn you. If you tell him you intend to lie, I don't think he is able to represent you.'

The solicitor arrived, dressed in a black suit and looked more like an undertaker. He was flustered, brushed the rain from his jacket complaining about the weather and the traffic. He shook her hand.

They were left alone.

'Did he provoke you?' The solicitor scribbled notes, listened intently as the story came tumbling out.

He hesitated. Darius sensed his calculation. An adjustment. He inhaled. Sat up in his chair. He didn't immediately speak.

'If he didn't provoke you, has he threatened you before? Were you frightened of him?' The solicitor asked rubbing his chin.

'No.' Suddenly he felt that he was losing the fight.

'So he was about to attack you first? You were in an argument? His hand was raised?' The solicitor looked straight at him. Darius frowned. A haze descended.

'Maybe. I don't remember scratching him.' Darius shrugged.

'Maybe you were scared. Acted in self-defense?' The solicitor leaned forward.

'No. If anything he was probably scared of me at that moment.' Darius admitted.

The solicitor sighed again. 'You can admit this. Or deny it. Or state that it was in self-defence.'

The solicitor studied his face for a moment, rubbing his chin as he thought. He stared at the floor.

Then the solicitor sat up, pinning his eyes.

'Oh come on. You lashed out because he provoked you. He had a look on his face. He raised his arm, like this.' The solicitor was feeding him fiction. He smiled, liked the game.

'And *you* thought he was going to strike you. I would say, categorically that you were acting in self-defense.' The solicitor's voice had passion. He was good at his job; good at twisting the facts. He imagined him in court. He wasn't sure if he was playing through all the possible scenarios or trying to redefine what actually happened.

'I'm not telling you to lie. It just depends on how you see the truth,' he added.

Darius was puzzled - more confused than ever.

∽

THE TAPE WAS ON. He glanced at the solicitor, who nodded and half-smiled. Then the penny tinkled and dropped.

The police officer turned to the machine. It was as if Darius had been drowning in a pool of porridge, slowly giving up the fight. But now he was swimming - hard to the surface.

'We were arguing about their gay relationship. His hand was raised and I thought he was going to hit me. I don't remember what next, just of being terrified.'

The officer presented pictures of the wounds. He stifled the shock. Tears began to well.

'Can you explain these cuts?' The officer handed some pictures over for him to see.

'I don't know. How could I have done that? I'd just fallen out of a tree. I was dazed. I was distressed. About to take my life and suddenly he appeared from the house. I wasn't expecting either of them to be there.'

Faced with the pictures he was struggling.

'So you deny doing it?'

'Yes.' But it was one of those yeses that could have easily been a no.

'And if I did do it, I don't remember doing it, it was in self-defense.'

'Thank you.' The machine clunked. The officer removed the tape and allowed him time with the solicitor alone before taking DNA samples. He saw the solicitor's visible relief.

'Well done. That was great. I really don't know how they will charge you now. All we can do is wait.'

Darius didn't feel his optimism though.

Doubts niggled in his mind.

∼

It was Sunday evening when Darius took the call. Relief washed over him.

'Thank God. Thank you.' He told the police officer down the phone.

'What was that about?' Faye asked.

'The CPS have dropped the case. But I've had an official warning so it will be on record unfortunately. That's all down to that fucking cunt. The poofter that's rogering my son.' He snapped.

'Darius just drop it. I wish you could accept the way they are,' Faye replied.

37

Faye
April 2012

Faye thought it ironic that they should be eating their 'last supper' in the Harvest Scullery, the family restaurant they both detested. It had been over a year since they'd parted. The parting had been reasonably amicable, both accepting of the situation and their belief that they would be happier apart. Faye moved back into social housing, the estate in Slough where the mothers lugged their Iceland carrier bags up the steep hill and where most, including herself were reliant on Government hand-outs. But she was happy, and the kids were happy, and she'd started dating again with renewed vigour to find the *right one*.

Darius and Faye had exchanged the odd text over the months, they remained on amicable terms, which Faye imagined was a first for Darius. But they had resisted meeting up ...until now.

The atmosphere was tense between them, like a first date but without any of the hope. They couldn't even joke about the bucket of croutons they both detested and the limp rabbit style salad lined in troughs at the salad bar. But when the chicken breasts arrived, and Darius complained about the size, they soon started laughing when he told the waiter: *it's obviously been a very long time since you saw a breast and I can tell you it's been a long time for me too!*

They fell quiet for a time. She waited for his apology for everything he'd put her through.

'So. Let's just get this over with shall we?' Faye pushed the last of the fruit crumble around the dish. The meal had been disappointing.

'What is it you needed to tell me that couldn't have been said in a text? I haven't heard from you in months. Why now?' When Faye had received his text asking to meet up because he had something important to tell her she imagined he was going to say sorry. She longed to hear those words: a final acknowledgement that he was wrong and shouldn't have treated her or the kids so appallingly.

'I just wanted to share some good news with you.'

'News?' Faye thumped her drink down, flushed with irritation.

'Look, if it's any consolation leaving you wasn't easy.' He rubbed his forehead, finished his cheesecake. She remembered watching him standing on the pavement outside the house as his removal van pulled away, a pained look on his face.

Darius pursed his lips, in that pained way he always did. His eyes were translucent tiny pools of blue.

'It didn't take you long to get a rental sorted. You're quick and decisive when you want to be. Making plans that suit you, Darius. Fail to plan, plan to fail as you always said. Anyway. What's the new place like?' It seemed polite to ask but she didn't want the answer.

'It's just another rental. What can I say? I spend half my time staying over at mum's. I'm juggling work and looking after her. She's a lot slower, getting very muddled and anxious about day-to-day things. Soon she'll need carers. She suddenly became incontinent. It's been very distressing for her. I think her kidneys are failing, due to the heart. Bloody NHS.'

Darius shrugged. The harsh lighting in the restaurant made him look sickly.

He sighed.

'Look Faye. I'm not a great catch anymore. I'm staring down the barrel of old age and it doesn't look great. You were looking for a surrogate parent for your kids. What you got was a dying man to fill the vacancy of those drift away, fade out loser dads and quite frankly if we were getting back together, you'd have to eat your dull kids first.'

She looked down at the crumble. An icy chill shot through her blood.

'I didn't come here to try and get you back. Don't bloody flatter yourself. I just came to hear what you had to say,' she snapped, shock painted across her face.

He steamed on, ignoring her. 'It was like somebody put an old gramophone on but they'd paid their money and the vinyl was scratched. That's basically my life in a nutshell. I feel impudent and useless, chained and doomed and sick and washed out. It was all of it Faye. What were we looking forward to together? We weren't going to have kids. We weren't even going to grow vegetables in the back garden. It was all one delusion. One big lie. My biggest problem is me. You'll have no problem pulling. Until they discover the three kids, fathered by two dads that is. It was never going to work between us.' He sighed.

'If you knew that, why did we bother?'

'Stepfamilies don't work. Everyone warned me. But I had to experience it for myself.'

'Nice. I was your social experiment.' She sniffed, trying to look disinterested.

'People think they can buy into the dream, but the dream doesn't exist. Blended families, stepfamilies whatever you want to call them, they're a complete mess. It's like bringing together the cast of a film knowing the characters are wrong for the set. I was never Mr. Step-Family Man. I was Mr. Steptoe and I had to step away.

We were crash on impact Faye. The plane trundling down the runway. When it reaches V2 it has to be committed to lift. It needs to commit at V1. We didn't reach V1, we couldn't commit.'

The waiter came over and asked if they were finished. 'Oh we're most certainly finished. That I *do* know.'

The waiter returned with the bill.

'How's Sam?' she asked.

'Oh Jesus, Mary and Joseph. He's still snorting cocaine. I'm trying to get him help. You just have no idea how awful it's been. And the little shit blames me. Says it helped him cope with my homophobia.'

'Shit. I suppose that would explain his weird behaviour. You give him a rough time. Being gay should be something to celebrate not condemn. We aren't living in the 50s anymore.' It was another dig.

'You know how hard I find it all. It goes back to my childhood...'

They fell silent, both in reflection. A mirthless atmosphere settled around the table.

'So..?' It was time to find out the news he wanted to share.

'I found Kathleen.' Faye froze incredulous.

'Kathleen. Oh my God. How? What? Where? By the way I never did find the cloth gingerbread man. I must have chucked it out years ago. That will always be a mystery.' Faye wanted to know all the details about Kathleen.

'She sent a letter.'

Faye's eyes filled with tears and without giving it a moment's thought she reached over and clasped both his hands inside hers. A smile began to warm his face and in the moments that followed she witnessed tenderness as his eyes misted over and in the comfortable silence that wove between them, they clasped hands, both painfully aware that this was the dying embers of love and the culmination of a journey to find Kathleen that they had taken together.

'Can I get you a coffee, on the house?' The waiter had arrived to break the spell.

'No. Like I said we're finished.' And with his cutting words she returned to the harsh reality of where they were. Truly finished but with a sense that at least one good thing had been accomplished in their brief time together.

She watched the man disappear into the kitchen, a fresh waft of garlic filling the air.

They stood up briefly facing each other, eyes momentarily locked. Faye wondered if he was going to wrap his arms around her, but he didn't. He frowned, pain, hurt and regret ingrained into his face. And then she turned to go, her eyes filling once more and that was the last she ever saw of him. At least that was what she thought, in that moment. But she wasn't to know that their paths would cross again and in a way she could not have predicted, in unusual circumstances.

38

MARIA

January 2012

DARIUS PLACED a milky cup of tea on a mat next to where his mother was sitting. She tucked a mohair blanket over her knees and in one hand clutched a gilded metal sacred heart, entwined with thorns and flames, surmounted by a cross, as she prepared to watch the TV show - aired across the nation - that would, she hoped bring her Kathleen home.

These days she was careful not to drink too much in the evening, knowing that she might flood the bed. She didn't understand why she'd suddenly developed an incontinence problem at nighttime, but it was getting worse and despite a short stint in hospital the doctors hadn't established a reason that she could accept, merely prescribing more water tablets. She put it down to age for many of the old folk in her retirement complex wore pads at night, but nonetheless she found it a wretched nuisance. It added stress to her life asking Darius to wash the sheets, on top of the other chores she now needed him to do. He had little patience, talking too fast, his sentences punctuated by expletives. She had learned to filter his voice from her head and as time had gone by thankfully, he'd responded to her constant squeals to *just shut up a moment and listen*. She didn't like being rude, but she couldn't think when he went on and on at breakneck speed. Tonight, a comfortable silence sat between them as Darius prepared to watch himself on TV. It wasn't the first time he had been on TV. She recalled an interview on South Today several years back on the rise of the International 50 flavour doughnut emporium.

∼

Darius

Darius sat down with a mug of tea, ready to watch the TV programme. He was becoming worried about his mother. He hadn't seen her in a few days and noticed how hollow her face was, her arms covered in bruises and scratches, caused, he imagined by a low blood platelets. And he suspected she was fast approaching end stage heart failure. The doctors had offered her a biventricular pacemaker but were monitoring her situation for now.

Her brain was also slower. It had taken them an afternoon to fill in a form for a new disability badge. And despite pots of money set aside for retirement she penny pinched at every opportunity. *Jesus*, Darius thought. She refused point blank to employ a carer to come in twice a day but was quite happy for him to run around for her on top of his full-time job and worst of all he had discovered dirty Tena pads drying in rows in the airing cupboard. The place now stank. Never before had his patience been tested to this degree.

The TV documentary – about the Magdalene Laundries -

was aired from Dublin where Darius had gone to be filmed the previous month. While there, he'd spoken to the other people in the show–– survivors and families related to victims and had made enquiries. Sadly, nobody had information about Kathleen. The presenter, the widely acclaimed Paddy O'Doyle was tough and eloquent with a reputation for pinning politicians and getting answers out of people. He'd taken a particular interest in the abuse that had happened in the Magdalene Laundries. If anyone was going to fight for the justice of Magdalene survivors, it was Paddy. And if anyone was going to get answers and reunite family members it was Paddy.

The Missing Person's Bureau hadn't been able to find Kathleen. Darius felt he was chasing round a racing track, covering the same ground, same questions yet no answers had been forthcoming. And the national archives office hadn't thrown up that she had got married. Paddy's show was the last stab at finding his sister. He clasped his hands and despite his loss of faith he said a silent prayer as the programme began. This was a Terminator 3 moment when the past and the future were held in fine balance and things could go either way.

Darius looked at his mother while the adverts were still playing.

'Don't build your hopes up, Mum. Sometimes we just have to let people go.' He smiled sympathetically.

'How can a mother ever let her child go?' she snapped. 'You can decorate her absence with any excuse you like. To me she'll always be a missing part of who I am.'

He studied her tired face for a moment, as it locked with the TV. Kathleen was only missing because something much deeper within her was missing. Maybe it was her inability to connect to the soul of those close to her but her grief over the years had been a dripping tap; drip-by-drip she had died with the loss.

The programme had started. The music stopped and Paddy, in passionate words introduced the programme.

'The notion of slave labour in the western world seems like something you would read about in the history annals. But as recently as the 1990s, women, cast aside by society were sent to institutions in Ireland run by the church. Those institutions were known as the Magdalene Laundries for the hard, unpaid labour those women endured doing industrial laundry. Today there is a movement working to right the wrongs of the past.

In the studio today we will be interviewing some of the survivors and some family members who are trying to find the loved ones they sent away many years ago.

And all the way from Alabama, Texas and California in the studio today we also welcome Ellen Mayer, Ashley Biggs and Rachel Humphreys who were born to Laundry women - those unmarried mothers sent to the laundries by their families to avoid the cloud of shame and disgrace they feared from neighbours and the wider society. Ellen, Ashley and Rachel were all adopted by wealthy Americans.

'Ellen, if you knew your mother was listening today what would you like to say to her?'

'I would say to her I know you loved me and that you had no choice and I'd want her to know that I've had a good life. I was treated well by my adopted parents.'

Maria's eyes were pinned to the TV, her face hard as pottery. She glanced over at Darius.

'What if there's a grandchild in America?' Maria simpered.

'Oh Mum.' Darius shook his head, sighed. 'There probably is but we can only search for Kathleen.'

'Do you think she's spent her life searching for her baby?'

'No. It would be for the child to search for its mother when it reached 18 if it wanted to.'

'And Kathleen has made no attempt to look for me.' Maria threw him a look of despair. Does that mean she doesn't love me Darius? What does it mean? I let her down but for that she's disowned me.' Maria was now out of breath as if she had just ran round the block. Her face was flushed. He was worried. This had been a new turn of events over a couple of weeks. Her struggle for breath was getting markedly worse.

'We hear from Margaret, Brigid and Niamh who describe themselves as the forgotten ones.' The presenter introduced the three survivors.

'Margaret you were sent to a laundry in 1958 because you were pregnant. What would you like to say tonight to people watching the show?'

'The church was a disgrace. We had our freedoms denied, our identities striped away, our humanity denied. I'm still haunted by the past. They destroyed my life. I couldn't adjust to normal life and in my first marriage I couldn't cope. I was ashamed. I had thought of myself as a bad person for so long.'

'Oh God.' Maria clapped her hand to her mouth. Panic had set in.

'And how would Kathleen have been affected? We'll never know.' Tears were pricking her eyes again. 'She was my baby, Darius, and what I did could have affected her emotionally, for the rest of her life. We'll never know.'

The presenter was on to the next survivor.

'And Brigid what would you like to say today?'

'Not a day goes by when I don't think of my child, snatched from me at six months old. The nuns were cruel. All they wanted was to beat the sin from us. They didn't care about taking our babies and handing them over to wealthy families. I cried night-after-night but they didn't listen.'

'The horror stays with you,' Brigid added.

Patrick continued. 'In the Bible Mary Magdalene was of course the fallen woman who repented and became one of the most faithful followers of Jesus. In the 18th century orders of nuns throughout Europe opened houses in her name where they tried to convince prostitutes to leave the streets. By the 20th century the houses in Ireland had a broader vision of taking in unwed mothers and often young women who were simply not wanted by their families. The original intention of saving souls had evolved into a money- making business built on unpaid unwilling labourers in a very strict regime.

'Let us hear from Niamh.' The presenter looked for Niamh in the audience.

'They took my belonging away. Gave me a uniform. A new name.'

'It was like being in prison?' Paddy asked.

'Every window had bars. We weren't allowed to go out.'

The presenter turned to the camera again.

'The claims of abuse only started to surface in the early 1990s. When nuns sold part of their land at one property and a mass graveyard was discovered. The bodies were exhumed and moved to another cemetery.'

'Would you like to hear someone say I'm sorry?' The presenter asked.

Maria began to dab her eyes, silent tears falling.

'I'd like the chance to say sorry to my daughter for sending her there.' Maria said to the TV. It was a simple request, yet it meant everything. It meant sharing in the pain, binding mother and daughter together again, a hole refilled, the wrongs of the past corrected. Sorry was a sacrament, an offering, a gift and yet that gift could not be given. Maria clutched the sacred heart close to her own heart and continued to dab her eyes as she listened to the stories of abuse - from the survivors -unfold. For many years Maria had believed that the only way out of the labyrinth was to pretend it hadn't happened, that she didn't really have a daughter, but the truth had stared her in the face for years and that truth was a deep grief that had never gone away.

'We also meet today in the studio Darius, Lyndsay and

Michelle who all hope to trace their loved ones and to say sorry for sending them away.'

'Darius what is your story?'

'We lived in Liverpool and when my sister, only 14 years old got pregnant my mother couldn't cope. My father died in the Troubles in Belfast and I think she found it hard to cope with my wayward sister. Kathleen was out every night. This was the early days of punk rock and the way she dressed and spoke scared my mum. Getting pregnant was the last straw and our priest arranged for her to be taken to a laundry to have the baby, but this was the mid 70s. We didn't expect her to remain incarcerated in the institution beyond the baby's birth and yet we never heard from her again. My mother would like closure. It's been eating away at her soul for years but one day she woke up and told me that it was her dying wish to find her daughter, Kathleen O'Brien and so if by any small chance Kathleen is watching today please, please get in touch. Mum wants to say sorry. She wants your forgiveness. Only when she has been reunited with her daughter can she die in peace. Please Kathleen, allow her to die in peace.'

'And I ask Margaret, Brigid and Niamh would you like the Irish Government to make an official apology-- a recognition for the serious wrongs?'

'Yes, we need an apology, we need recognition that the state was involved and we need justice, compensation for what has been done to us.'

∽

THE WORD COMPENSATION jarred in Maria's head. It meant many things and came in any number of guises. She closed her eyes tight remembering something she had done a few years ago. One thing was settled in her head at least.

39

DARIUS

June 2012

'Why am I here? When am I going home?' Maria had asked the same question every day since admission to hospital three days before. And again, Darius gave the same answer knowing a while later she'd forget again.

'You could hardly breath. They did tests on your kidneys...'

Darius hoped the Oromol would soon kick in and allow her peaceful sleep. He didn't want to tell her the hard truth: that her creatinin levels were extremely high at 498; her kidneys were barely functioning, and her blood pressure was low at 58/60 and worst of all her heart ejection fractions were only 23 per cent. She'd only get confused and ask *who's telling you this information? What does all that mean and when am I going home?* He knew she wouldn't be going home. This was the end. All he could do was wait. It felt like he was back at Heathrow waiting for a long-haul flight.

'Tidy up around the bed, will you? Otherwise, we're going to get into such a muddle when I go home.' She pushed the bottle of Ribena towards him then began fiddling with notes of paper, a pen, napkin and hairbrush. 'Must keep tidy.' She snapped.

Vascular dementia was slowly stripping away the very essence of her being. He was, in one sense glad that this was just the beginning of the dementia journey and would be thankfully a short journey, for her heart was rapidly failing. She wouldn't be travelling the full journey of dementia travelled by so many; becoming the shell of the former person they once were - almost ghostlike. The ultimate relief from dementia was death.

Part of him envied her reaching that end, the bittersweet release of pain, the letting go, the warmth of nirvana. If only he could close his eyes like her and forget the memories. He longed to close his eyes one final time and not see the wandering hands of the priest upon him.

And yet through his relief and sense of peace and closure her impending death gave came a nagging guilt pricking his conscience. He had found Kathleen, but she didn't want to be found and despite sending Darius a letter, she didn't want to come to the hospital, to say goodbye. She said it was for the best. But she had been selfish. He loathed her for that. All he could do was bring photos of Kathleen, as a small child to show his mother, evoking good memories, recalling smiles and laughter. She remembered it all. Kathleen sitting in the kitchen sink having a bath as a toddler. Kathleen sitting on her Grandpa's knee in the park...

A couple of days later a small team including the heart surgeon and several nurses gathered around her bed to discuss her prospects.

'I'm afraid looking at all the test results we don't think it's a good idea to replace her pacemaker with a bi-ventricular one. The operation would be extremely risky. She'd be in a lot of pain.' Darius didn't want to ask the obvious. *What is the alternative?* He knew the alternative was death even though the doctor wasn't using the word death. He merely alluded to death but left it to him to fill in those missing blanks from the conversation. He knew his mother's brain was now too wooly to fill in those blanks. She would think that the alternative meant going home with different medication. The doctor used the words *make comfortable*. What the fuck did that mean? It reminded him of an old Jewish joke about a Jewish guy knocked down by a car. Helpers put a pillow under his head and asked if he was comfortable.

And they used the word *palliative care* and *rest* instead of the harsh word *death*. In his head the palliative nurse was the nurse of death like a midwife was a nurse of life.

The palliative nurse discussed removing her and her impending death to a *hospice*. One set of people were wiping their hands and another set would begin the end game and after death the bureaucracy of death would crank into motion. Darius saw the disposal of life from earth as an environmental waste problem and the exiting paperwork rather like leaving the country or leaving a job. Forms needed to be filled in. The identity of the deceased erased from earth, her disability badge returned, her pension stopped, the ironmongery shop returned. (The equipment she needed in her flat; the zimmer, the shower stall and so on.) Everyone around the bed knew what the word *hospice* meant but nobody spelt it out. Death was the elephant around the bed, and everyone was carefully side stepping around it.

His mother had slowly crept away, vanishing piece-by-piece. His father's sudden death in the Troubles had come as a bitter blow to her and the loss of Kathleen had proved too much for her. Her loss had come as buses–– one too many. She had carried her grief around, a heavy weight in her pocket. Her daily misery was about her suffering and loss. The suffering and the thinking about the suffering had spread to every vein of her body; she had gradually turned into a tormented soul. Her grief took a cyclical pattern starting with Lent when she focused on prayer every evening and forgiveness, getting worse around the Feast of The Sacred Heart—the anniversary of his death.

After his father's death, the festivities of Christmas had disappeared and in its place came duty and ritual. Instead of offering comforting support to his mother the priest had increased his visits at this sad time but always came holding an old biscuit tin hoping for contributions for repairs to the roof of the church. But at other times he'd been like the pied piper with sweets. Darius had seen right through him.

Moving down to Marlow she had channelled all her energies into her grandson in an attempt to rebuild her life. She had loved looking after him - providing childcare, taking him for walks along the Thames, the park, the duck pond, doing the school run - but her grief remained. The second half of her life had been a tragedy, wasted years of sorrow. All he saw was a dull sorrowful look in her eyes.

When he looked back upon his childhood all he saw was sadness and maybe that was why Kathleen hadn't returned. Even though she must have suffered in the laundry, maybe the break from home made her see that her home was not a place of refuge to return to. He couldn't quite put his finger on what it was. The aura of something in that household that should have been there wasn't. A motley collection of refugees: family members whose houses had been destroyed by the Germans. The Catholic icons dotted around the house: a lamp of the Sacred Heart, a picture of the pope above the fireplace, a crucifix glass globe and small statutes of Mary on every coffee table. It had been a creepy ominous place; a sanctuary to Christ but not a sanctuary where any family could feel at ease and certainly devoid of love.

When he closed his eyes, tried to recapture the atmosphere, the scene from all those years ago, all he could feel was a cold numbness. He remembered sitting in the attic bedroom looking out in the distance to the Royal Liver buildings and the cranes from the Docks, making carts from old tyres pinched from bombsite wastelands. Often, he would be asked to take the pushchair to the coal yard off Low Hill and call into the chippy on the way back.

And most of all when he swivelled back in time he felt a tingling sensation of fear. A fear he had taken home from Rhyl. A fear of being in the bathroom alone with the scary plumbing noises; the hot water tank that made banging noises when the system got too hot, the gurgling when the taps were turned on. Fear in the front room of the wall mounted electric fire that had sparked and arced when it was switched on, reminding him of an electric chair from a US jail. It was hardly the cosy Ovaltine hearth image. He'd longed for the priest to move away so that there would be peace: to escape into a Robin Hood Adventure with a bag of liqourice torpedoes on his lap.

His mother's life had seemed so hard – all drudgery and caring, few pleasures. He could see her frying fish on Fridays at the stove and boiling cauldrons of clothes and the long washing line of steaming clothes in the front room. Their house on Parr Street above a shop had been like a railway terminus before the end of the age of steam.

In the hospice he sat listening to the changing breathing patterns; a rapid, hyperventilating rattle. Then it grew shallow, until it almost fell away and he felt momentary panic. Then it would start up again, like a banger on the London to Brighton struggling to life.

Her hands were now old pieces of steak; huge bruises extending up her arms. Her skin had lost all tone, was dry and flaky, ripples of wrinkles that looked like a low tide on the beach.

∼

HER BEDROOM in the hospice overlooked a pretty courtyard with flowers and plants and a small fishpond. He stood at the window then turned and as he studied her mottled feet bulging from the velvet red slippers her eyes open watching him. He recoiled in shock. Her hazel eyes were pale and translucent, sunken into hollow sockets, the white around her eyes now yellowing fast.

The cloud shaped bruises along her arms had spread with each passing day, staining the skin like blackberry juice. It was a sight he didn't want to endure for much longer.

'Mum.' She attempted a smile. 'Kathleen has written.' He was cautious, unsure of her reaction.

Her smile grew wider. She had no energy to speak. He unfolded the vellum, looked at her again. Her eyes were still open. He began to read.

Dear Mum and Darius,

I saw Darius on the TV and contacted Paddy's show for your address.

When I left home that day in 1974, I made up my mind not to return. Too much had happened. Things I can't tell you about. Don't blame yourself. Although I still love you both and think about you often you are my past. You belong to a different world; a painful world that I can't re visit. Please accept that is the way things are.

My life is reasonably happy. I'm married. We have a son but since the birth I've suffered from terrible bouts of depression. I wake in the night and imagine he's been snatched. I don't like all the night-time sounds. My fear never goes away. Some days I don't get out of bed; I close the curtains and hide under a duvet. Sometimes I envy the dead. But please don't worry about me. Life moves on as it always will...

I had a baby girl in the laundry. You didn't come to visit. I assumed you didn't care. But maybe the nuns didn't tell you.

I love you both, but I missed Dad. I'm sorry.

Love Kathleen.

Darius sat down on an armchair next to her, one arm rested over the bed bars, his emotions in free fall.

Neither spoke. He couldn't think of what to say. The journey was over. Questions hung like a delicate spider's web over the contents of her letter, her life. He wished he could probe for the answers but accepted the journey to find Kathleen had now ended, with his mother's approaching death. Finding out if Father Joseph had raped her didn't now seem to matter as much. It was Robert Walpole, he recalled who had said *let sleeping dogs lie*.

Kathleen had not been a part of their lives for so long. Did it feel like a loss or the closing of a chapter? He wasn't sure.

He got up opened a fresh lemon moistened cotton bud to dab around her dry lips. Caring for the dying was a futile exercise. It was about retaining dignity in dying. But what exactly was dignity? Did she appreciate a pad change? A tiny dab of water on the lips?

He removed the blanket that covered her feet. Looking at it made his eyes well. He folded it, placed it under the bed. He leaned in towards her ear, whispering *sorry* over and over. Was her dying wish complete? He wasn't sure. Then he picked the blanket up again, hugged it to his face, brushed the soft fibres against his cheek, breathing in rose water and old dinner. He closed his eyes, breathed deeper, wheeling back in time; to the sickly smells of the past; milk and talc and vomit, his childhood in the house in Liverpool and the little blonde girl outside the toilet in Rhyl, holding her blanket.

Maria's breathing shallowed and her head turned a fraction towards him. He thought he imagined it. Her eyes flickered. She opened her mouth very slightly. She tried to speak but her heart was slowing. He leaned in as she struggled to whisper.

'Tell Kathleen...' But she couldn't finish her words.

The light in the room was fading. Shadows bounced across the bare walls. A candle burned from a tea light on the windowsill for the blessed Mary. The timeless classic and wonderful upbeat tune by Frankie Valli, *'Can't Take My Eyes Off You'* was gently playing on radio two in the corner of the room, from an old radio in the corner reminding him of his childhood. He remembered skipping into The Baltic Fleet with his dad singing the words. He certainly, at that moment couldn't take his eyes away from his dying mother.

A pungent sweet smell grew each hour that passed, growing heavier, more cloying, signifying her body was slowly shutting down, cells were no longer dividing, the release of toxins - the end in sight. He tried to think of what the smell was like. He sniffed the air, frowned. Was it a mixture of menthol and rubber and roses?

He studied his mother's translucent bruised skin. Microbiology had always intrigued him. Death both repelled and drew him in. He wanted to consume every moment fascinated by the hourly minute -by minute changes. She had lost so much weight and looked much older. Watching her skin was like watching the light fade in the night sky, the subtle colour changes.

He sat down. Tiredness washed over him. Suddenly he felt a cold chill creep swiftly through his body. He looked at the cushion beside him. It was as if there was a presence on the armchair beside him. He could feel it so intensely, so eerily; it was as if Kathleen was sitting next to him, the sister that should have been there to support him through all the hard and painful times.

He leaned in again, stroking strands of grey hair from around her ear and whispered, 'Love you mum.' He brushed the salty tears welling up with the back of his hand.

He lifted up the sheet covering her body and touched her heavily swollen ankles, rock solid feet. Her legs were growing colder, even her arms were starting to chill. The circulation was slowing. Time seemed to be slowing. Soon she would be taken away in a body bag. His heart thudded at the revulsion of the reality of death but also the mystique and beauty of death.

And then the last breath came. Either that or the next breath didn't come. He called for the nurse to take her pulse. And then without warning sobs hit flooding up from his chest, spilling out. A heat of shock and crushing feeling of loss swept his body.

The hospice priest instructed Darius to go home and light a pillar-shaped candle for his mother. Strangely he found himself taking comfort from the rituals of the faith he was born into, the faith that had caused so much anguish over the years.

He returned to the hospice a couple of days later to clear her things. There were very few belongings in the room where she had spent her dying days: a drawer containing neatly ironed nighties and knickers, a hair net, a pot containing her false teeth, a pair of reading glasses, a set of dirty hearing aids and a poetry book. He held up a pair of her large white knickers and thought about how women's bodies were like fruit left too long out of the fridge; their pelvic floors collapsing under the strain of childbirth and life.

He grabbed his mother's pink dressing gown from the bathroom door, her velvet slippers, a bottle of Nina Ricci and slung it all into a black sack taking it to the outside bins. It was all part of the exit process from life.

Sitting at the piano in the hospice reception area he opened the mahogany lid, swept a finger across the keys. He pressed a single key, then another. And began to sing the song of his childhood, *Maggie Maggie Mae* and soon he could hear the tinkle of his father's banjo dancing around his head.

He looked outside. The sky was foreboding, the grass sodden. Splats of rain thudded onto a brick pathway like handfuls of nails. Even the natural world seemed angry. The sky was poised in anticipation. His stomach too felt full of nails, digging, turning, demons that wouldn't leave. He focused on each bubble of water as it hit the ground and one moment imagined they were tiny UFOs; the next they were silvery fish coursing along in ripples.

The sky outside was black and ominous, as if a big confession was waiting to tumble down.

That night he scarcely slept. The exhaustion had drained out of him like anesthetic. It felt as if a great tide had hurled him onto a beach on a deserted island, leaving him to fend for himself.

He had no sense of time, history, or family. They were concepts that no longer existed.

DARIUS

June 2012

The burial took place a week later in a Liverpool cemetery and he arrived with Sam in a taxi from their nearby hotel. Darius asked the taxi driver to wait. They wouldn't be long.

Either side of the road the headstones were densely crammed in, like rows of vegetables. After a short service partly in Latin, heavy on ritual but of no comfort whatsoever the basic coffin containing his mother was carried to the plot and lowered into the precarious hole.

Looking down and throwing a single red rose as the coffin was lowered he knew at that moment that nothing much really mattered in life apart from family and that life really was so short.

They stood in the biting wind and he felt a sense of creeping unease. He found himself thinking about the 3,875 people who had died in Liverpool during the war and how the survivors had dusted themselves down and started again. He wondered how many socialist militants had been buried in the plots and felt a slight pang of guilt that he had become a Tory, abandoning the fighting spirit of the people of Liverpool. He thought about the oppression of his faith and how self-righteous the lot of them had been; their hatred of blacks, Jews, gypsies and Germans. Looking round at the ornate masonry he felt ashamed at the bigot he'd become and the way he condemned his son's sexuality. He'd never accept the way he was, but he could no longer condemn him for who he was and knew that he had to find a way to live with it. Feeling terribly upset and unable to bring himself to talk to his dad after the incident with Rory Sam had written him a long letter instead. It had taken time to digest. But Darius was now half-way to understanding his son better. Sam was right on many fronts.

I could have kept my sexuality a secret from you. But you know the damage that keeping a secret does, don't you dad? He had written.

Accepting my sexuality doesn't mean you have to accept what I do in bed with another man anymore than I want to know what you do with women. It's private. End of.

Being gay is a characteristic like hair colour or eye colour. I can't change how I am. I don't want to change. I can't fight this, I won't fight it. I'm happy with who I am. I want you to be happy for me. I don't want you to feel I'm less of a son. I don't want to be a let down.

The Church has warped so many of your views Dad. It's time you addressed your demons. You've lost Faye. I love you Dad. Don't lose me too.

And he had ended the letter with a passage from the Bible from John 1. 4-18,

There is no fear in love. Perfect love drives out fear.

He had the letter folded in his pocket and as they stood looking into the hole where his mother lay, he reached out and put his shoulder around Sam and gently squeezed his arm. It was going to be hard, but the bottom line was that he wanted their relationship to improve and he knew that he would have to swallow his pride. He looked one last time downward, knowing that as long as he continued to look down, he could not see what was above him. His pride had been his downfall across so many levels.

They walked away to a nearby bench taking in the view over the city. He thought about Kathleen and wondered yet again who the father of her first baby was and what had become of the child.

He thought about the generations of his family who had lived before him and all that they had suffered to create the great city that Liverpool was. Maybe suffering was deep within the blood of each and every one of them, carried from generation to generation.

He thought about his mother's life and how she'd abandoned her daughter. She had acted in the context of the era and the church she had grown up in. But attitudes changed over time. Life moved on. Her ignorance and her circumstances had dictated her actions but the worst thing of all was the lifetime of guilt that she'd carried.

Single parenthood wasn't accepted in the mid 70's and certainly not within the Catholic Church in Liverpool. She couldn't be blamed. She had been a product of her times Darius thought to himself.

Kathleen

Unknown to Darius as he stood at the graveside, a short distance away under the dark umbrella of a cedar tree, her face hidden under a black cape a woman watched the ceremony. Darius wouldn't have recognized her; for life had not been kind and she had changed so much. She turned to go; had business to attend to at the solicitor of Bunn and Fausett. She was glad that Darius had sold the house in Liverpool at its' pinnacle; it had fetched a tidy amount. She smiled to herself.

Money to right the wrongs of the past.

That's what the will had said.

This is the end of 'A Catholic Woman's Dying Wish.' The story continues in 'Every Family Has One.'

AUTHOR'S NOTE

Thank you for purchasing All Things D, part 1: The Catholic Woman's Dying Wish, which I hope you enjoyed. If you did then maybe this will inspire you to read Every Family Has One which reveals what happened to Kathleen. My Book

Also, if you have a moment please would you kindly post a short review on Amazon – reviews are the lifeblood of authors and always appreciated.

Go to the link below to find out about my other books and you can follow me on Amazon to find out about new releases. https://www.amazon.co.uk/Joanna-Warrington/e/B00RH4XPI6/

My best-selling books are 'Every Mother's Fear and 'Every Father's Fear, a two-part drama inspired by the thalidomide scandal: My Book

You can also visit my website at http://joannawarringtonauthor-allthingsd.co.uk

Printed in Great Britain
by Amazon